A GOVERNESS OF PRODIGIOUS SKILL

The Governess Bureau, Book 4

Emily E K Murdoch

ARE YOU SIGNED UP FOR DRAGONBLADE'S BLOG?

You'll get the latest news and information on exclusive giveaways, exclusive excerpts, coming releases, sales, free books, cover reveals and more.

Check out our complete list of authors, too!

No spam, no junk. That's a promise!

Sign Up Here

www.dragonbladepublishing.com

Dearest Reader;

Thank you for your support of a small press. At Dragonblade Publishing, we strive to bring you the highest quality Historical Romance from some of the best authors in the business. Without your support, there is no 'us', so we sincerely hope you adore these stories and find some new favorite authors along the way.

Happy Reading!

CEO, Dragonblade Publishing

Additional Dragonblade books by Author Emily E K Murdoch

The Governess Bureau Series
A Governess of Great Talents (Book 1)
A Governess of Discretion (Book 2)
A Governess of Many Languages (Book 3)
A Governess of Prodigious Skill (Book 4)

Never The Bride Series
Always the Bridesmaid (Book 1)
Always the Chaperone (Book 2)
Always the Courtesan (Book 3)
Always the Best Friend (Book 4)
Always the Wallflower (Book 5)
Always the Bluestocking (Book 6)
Always the Rival (Book 7)
Always the Matchmaker (Book 8)
Always the Widow (Book 9)
Always the Rebel (Book 10)
Always the Mistress (Book 11)
Always the Second Choice (Book 12)

The Lyon's Den Connected World
Always the Lyon Tamer

Pirates of Britannia Series
Always the High Seas

De Wolfe Pack: The Series
Whirlwind with a Wolfe

Welcome to the Governess Bureau

You are most welcome, sir or madam.

When the nobility and gentility of England are at their wits end, they send a discrete note to Miss Vivienne Clarke's Governess Bureau. Only accepting the very best clients, their governesses are coveted by minor royalty, with every governess following three rules:

1. *You must have an impeccable record.*
2. *You must bring a special skill to the table.*
3. *You must never fall in love...*

CHAPTER ONE

March 1, 1813

HELENA BLINKED. PERHAPS if she waited, the words would mean something different. They echoed in her mind, unchanging.

"We're going to have to let you go."

She stared at Mr. Tobias, the stage manager of the Theatre Royal. "You can't do this."

Her words were lost in the noise. The castle background for *As You Like It* was being moved with much shouting and groaning from the stagehands, and she had to shout the second time to ensure she was heard.

"I said, you can't do this! It's not fair!"

It was more than unfair, it was unjust—and totally uncalled for. Helena Patrick was beloved across London, across England, an actress beyond compare. She had been for years. No complaints had been made as far as she was aware. *Let go?*

Mr. Tobias shook his head, his yellowing teeth bared in what he clearly thought was a sympathetic smile. "Hate to do it to you, girl, but that's the long and short of it."

Helena could just about make his words over the pounding

noise in her ears. *Let go? From the Theatre Royal? It wasn't possible. This was some sort of terrible joke.*

"April Fools is the first of April, not March," she shouted over the din coming from the stage as they stood in the wings. "This isn't funny Mr. Tobias."

Mr. Tobias spat on the ground. "I tol' 'em you'd take it like this, Helena, my old girl, but you've got to see it from our perspective. That's how it is in the theater. Sometimes you're up, sometimes you're down."

The pounding in her eyes was continuing, but it was now accompanied by Helena's stomach dropping through the floor. *Down? She had never been down.* Helena Patrick had never given a bad performance in her life!

"The theater is all I've ever known!"

Blast it to hell! Of course the shouting and noise had to stop right then. Everyone in the vicinity turned to stare, and Helena felt her cheeks pink. Well, it was hardly a secret. She *had* been here for years, performed almost every night, brought the house down every time.

And that wasn't enough?

"All I have ever known," she repeated, this time at a more suitable volume as Mr. Tobias smirked. "The only family I have ever known—the only way I can earn money."

For any other woman, perhaps, it would have been a struggle to keep tears at bay. Helena was not that woman. Years of acting, of being able to turn on tears within a moment's notice, had given her the control others lacked.

She was not going to cry. Not here, at any rate, before everyone. Before Mr. Tobias.

He was laughing. "You know, you're not that good, Helena."

Helena bristled. She knew precisely that she was that good. Had they not all read the gossip sheets, the newspapers—had they not noticed she was the person mentioned again and again, and for all the right reasons?

No, this theater needed her. She needed it, but the dependency went both ways.

"You—you cannot just fire me," she said haughtily.

Her manner did not impress the stage manager. "Of course I can. What, did you think anyone can just move in here and decide never to leave?"

Helena swallowed. She was not going to make a fool out of herself—even more than she already had done—but…well, yes.

Of all the places she had lived in her life, it had been here, the Theatre Royal, where she had been the longest. She knew every inch, knew every person like they were family. They *were* family.

She had to stay calm. There was a…a perfectly reasonable compromise they could reach, she was sure. Convincing Mr. Tobias could not be difficult. Everyone wanted something.

Examining him closely, Helena realized there was probably only one way to secure herself here, and the very thought curdled her stomach.

Never before had she used her body to get what she wanted. Others had, of course. It was generally expected that a few of the lower grade actresses took gentleman lovers to supplement their income, but Helena had never been tempted.

She had never needed to be.

Was Mr. Tobias lonely? There was no Mrs. Tobias, as far as she knew. *Was seduction really her only option?*

It would never have occurred to her before. Did desperate times call for desperate measures?

"Don't be daft, girl," said Mr. Tobias, evidently seeing where her thoughts were leading. "You think I'd be where I am now, managing this whole place, if I could be that easily taken in by a bit of skirt?"

Helena flushed.

"Besides, it's not as though you're fresh meat," said the stage manager, looking at her appraisingly. "What are you, four and twenty?"

"Six and twenty," said Helena as haughtily as she could manage.

Blast it all to hell and back. This was not how it was supposed to go. She had never had a plan exactly—what good was planning when God and men ruled the world?

No, it was more of a vague understanding. Older actresses stayed on as long as they could, then they became—well, sort of mothers of the theater. Mending costumes, helping with painting scenery, running lines with the actresses who had succeeded their place.

Helena swallowed, conscious she was saying absolutely nothing.

This was not how she had imagined it at all.

"Look," she said, keeping desperation from her voice as only a professional actress could. *A little wheedling, a dash of understanding, a knowing smile...* "So, this play isn't doing as well as we thought. Perhaps we shouldn't have chosen *As You Like It*—that's all! The audience is tired. We'll do a different one—my Lady Macbeth is—"

"No," said the stage manager in a voice of finality. "It's not the play the people are bored with. It's you."

Helena stared. He was lying. *Why was he saying these hurtful things?*

"I've..." Helena swallowed. For the first time in the conversation, her voice had wavered. *Diction, breathing, pronunciation...* "I have been here for ten years!"

A few stagehands passed by. Surely they would speak for her—but not a single one paused, and they kept their heads down to avoid both her eyes and that of Mr. Tobias.

Traitors.

Guilt washed over Helena. Of course she would have preferred them to speak up, but what were they supposed to do? Stagehands were at the bottom of the pecking order here at the Theatre Royal, at any theater.

They had their own jobs to consider. They had to protect themselves.

Helena had seen for herself how quickly fads and fashions

could change. Popularity came as a spark lit a fire, but it could burn out just as quickly.

"That's your problem. You've been here too long," said Mr. Tobias. "Everyone knows you, Helena. They know Helena Patrick. They know all your tricks, your best performances, your dud ones."

Helena opened her mouth to argue—*dud ones?*—but couldn't get a word in.

"Good, you are—fresh and exciting, you are not."

"Hello, I'm looking for a Mr. Tobias?"

Helena turned. A girl—you could hardly call her a woman, she looked as though she had just been cut from her mother's apron strings—in a scandalously low-cut gown was standing at the doorway between the wing and backstage, looking around in doe-eyed wonder.

Helena turned back to the stage manager with a glare. "I thought you said you couldn't be tempted by a bit of skirt?"

Mr. Tobias leered. "I did, didn't I? I was lying. Just go through there, darlin', I'll be with you in a moment."

The girl simpered and wandered in the direction of the stage manager's finger.

Now Helena was really struggling to keep her temper. *This was outrageous. How dare he?* But, as that irritating voice in her head reminded her, who could do anything about it?

When she focused on the stage manager again, he was licking his lips.

"So predictable."

"Well, you didn't see it coming!" he observed. "There ain't no law against it, so don't you come at me with your moralizing and scandalizing. Who's to say you didn't do much the same thing with old Matthews, him that came a'fore me?"

Panic was filling her lungs, overwhelming her thoughts, so Helena couldn't even refute the outrageous accusation.

She would not be cast aside. Oh, you heard rumors of actresses being abandoned like this, but she had assumed they were bitter mutterings from women who had passed their peak.

Not her. She was better than ever. She was not going to leave.

"Get out," said Mr. Tobias with a sigh. "I've got better things to do today than stand here and argue with you."

He stepped forward, but Helena blocked his path. "But where do you think I'm going to go? I *live here*, Mr. Tobias, as you well know. I have nowhere else to go."

"And that is none of my concern," he said. "You think I care? All I care about is this theater, and you're holding us back, Helena. Just be out in the next hour."

Helena stared. "Next hour?"

This could not be happening. Perhaps she was having a nightmare; that would make sense. A terrifying, terribly realistic nightmare.

"Well, where do you think young Mary is going to live?"

Helena looked over her shoulder and saw the young, pretty girl was back, loitering in the doorway. She simpered as she heard her name.

Dear Lord, save her from men and their irritatingly predictable nature. They only thought with one organ, and it was not their brain.

"Out, in an hour," said Mr. Tobias. "And I wish you luck finding work at any other theater round here. They'll be looking for new and fresh, just like we are. You might try it out in the countryside—if they have theaters there."

Without another word, the stage manager strode across the wing and said something in a low voice. The girl smiled, a pretty blush covering her cheeks.

Helena stared at the pair of them. What else could she do? There did not appear to be any budging the man, not now he had found someone to replace her with.

As if she could carry off Lady Macbeth, Helena thought savagely. *Like she had any comprehension of the depths that Juliet required.*

Helena looked around her. The ropes and pulleys above her, the costumes carefully numbered and folded neatly, ready for their next wear. The box of props that became more and more untidy with each passing day until Mr. Tobias shouted, and an unfortunate stagehand was forced to spend his day off sorting through it.

She could just make out the stage from here. The floorboards were polished expertly, as she imagined the dancing space at Almack's might be. It wasn't just the stage, it was *her* stage. She had trodden those boards countless times, knew her marks, could hold the audience in the palm hand if she chose to.

And it was all over. In just a few minutes, she would walk up the three flights of stairs to where the actresses lived. Her small room, magnificent when she had first arrived having shared a bedchamber with her parents and brother, would be emptied, her small possessions placed in the trunk she had inherited from her grandmother, her one item of value.

And then...

Helena could not imagine what came next. The theater had been everything to her—home, livelihood, friends, and family. Now it was over.

Fool, she told herself, unable to take a step toward her bedchamber, as that would mean accepting her fate. *Why did you believe you would have a home here forever? Why didn't you put a little money by every week for just such a predicament?*

A stagehand wandered past, hesitated, then stopped. "No...no hard feelings, Helena."

She glared. "And what makes you think this won't happen to you one day?"

The man seemed utterly unfazed by her snappish retort. "Well, I'm not the pretty face, am I? I don't need to stay young and beautiful to bring the punters in. I just need to be strong. Look after yourself, Helena."

He sloped away before Helena could respond. He was wrong. One day his arms would weaken, and he would find himself just as abandoned as she was now.

Besides, she was young! Six and twenty was not the youngest, but she was hardly frail and tired, was she?

Helena took a deep breath. She had already lost her composure in her argument with Mr. Tobias. It would benefit her nothing to have a tantrum about it all.

Less than an hour was all it took to collect her belongings. Helena looked into her trunk wistfully. She had never felt the need to treat herself to gowns or fripperies, not with the decadent embroidered masterpieces characters. One night, Cleopatra. The next night, Queen Elizabeth.

What gown within her budget could compare?

The fresh spring air of London hit her face as Helena stepped out of the Theatre Royal for the last time. She took a deep breath and immediately wished she hadn't.

For the uninitiated, London was a place of wonder. The streets were paved with gold, they said; a fortune to be made by any man—or woman—willing to work, so went the tale.

It was rather a shock for those country bumpkins when they arrived. Helena had seen them, wide-eyed and eagerly looking for these fabled streets of gold. They soon learned.

London stank. Spring was warming up, and the parts of London that looked pretty under a sheen of snow were starting to smell again.

Helena wrinkled her nose and tried to force down rising panic in her chest. The street was busy, packed with people rushing from one end to the other. Somewhere to go, something to do.

Neither of which she had.

She had always liked London, despite its rather unsavory nature and smell. There were the boxing rings, the pubs where women like her could drink a small pale ale and chat about nothing and everything, the parks open to all regardless of rank.

Now it appeared rather a frightening place. The streets had always been a means to an end, a route on her journey, not a final destination. And here she was, standing on the pavement, with nowhere to go and nothing to do. No one to protect her. No place to sleep tonight.

She gripped her trunk. *No place to sleep tonight.* That was her primary concern. The streets of London were genteel and polite—well, most of them—during the day, but she had lived here long enough to know it wasn't safe for a woman once the sun set.

With no savings, no friends to protect her, and no idea what to do next, she swallowed and tried to stay calm.

How was she going to live? She had few skills, could do nothing but act. That was hardly going to put a roof over her head and bread on the table.

Everyone seemed to have a purpose, something wrenched from her just moments ago. Mr. Tobias seemed to consider it simple enough to force her to leave the theatre, but he clearly had no idea what terrible position this placed her in.

In the theater, she was somebody. She was Helena Patrick, a famed celebrated actress.

Here, in the middle of London? She was a nobody. No one knew who she was or would be willing to help her. She was alone.

"Miss Patrick? Miss Helena Patrick?"

Startled, Helena turned to see a beautiful woman with dark hair and kind eyes. She had evidently stopped dead, for the gentleman whose arm she held looked suddenly startled.

They were both dressed elegantly, and Helena became conscious of her own looks. Wearing one of her two day gowns, a short Spencer jacket over it. No bonnet, no gloves…

"You *are* Miss Helena Patrick, are you not?" said the lady.

Helena looked wary. "Who wants to know?"

Perhaps she should have been politer. There was no cause to believe the lady had any ill-intent toward her, but the bruising conversation with Mr. Tobias had made her mistrustful.

Besides, this woman was clearly a lady. *What did she want with the likes of her?*

The lady smiled. "I would recognize that face anywhere—yes, Miss Patrick, the famous actress. What an honor to meet you."

Shame flooded Helena's body, heating her face and making her fingers sticky on the handle of her trunk. *Not today.* Any other day and this would have been flattering, but today?

"Oh, please don't be embarrassed to be recognized," said the lady. "You must have this all the time, being such a great actress. I honestly think you are the best in London."

Helena swallowed. *The news would get out eventually, it always did.* Perhaps she would be featured not in the gossip pages but the scandal sheets for the first time.

Old actress forced out of theater.

"This is the actress I was telling you about," the lady was saying to the gentleman Helena presumed was her husband. "The one I was telling the children they should come and watch when they come to London for the wedding."

The gentleman nodded. "Pleasure to make your acquaintance, Miss Patrick."

Helena smiled weakly. *Would this nightmarish day ever end? How was she to extricate herself from this mortifying conversation?*

"Oh, when I saw you as Hermia, I wept, absolute tears," the lady was saying. "I took the children, of course, and so wasn't able to return for another two weeks after saving my wages, but as soon as I could, I purchased another ticket. Oh, the way you performed Cleopatra—it was as though you had stepped off the sands of ancient Egypt and onto that stage. I never thought..."

Helena stared in horror as the lady continued. *How was she able to stem this flow of praise—praise she would have gloried in hearing any other day but today?*

Besides, it didn't make sense. *Wages?* Since when did a lady like her need wages?

"—haven't made it to your current play, of course, with all the wedding preparations—but you are the talk of London, no one will ever best your—"

"My lady," interrupted Helena, finally pushed beyond all endurance. "I-I thank you for your kind words. I know they are well meant and...I thank you."

The lady blinked.

"But I must tell you, I am no longer an actress."

The lady's mouth fell open. "Goodness. My word—since when?"

Helena could not help her sad laugh. "Oh, I would say…about twenty minutes ago?"

The lady's gaze moved from Helena's face to the trunk in her hands. There was a moment of silence—or at least, silence between them. The rest of London roared in the background as hundreds of busy people went from one end of the street to the other.

"Galcrest," said the lady finally. "Go away."

Helena did not understand what she meant until her husband-to-be nodded.

"Right, ho," he said cheerfully before he strode off twenty yards or so and stood leaning against the theater.

Helena stared. She could not help it. *What a strange couple they were.*

"Miss Patrick," said the lady in a low voice, taking a step toward her. "My name is Miss Fletcher. I know I may appear to be a lady, and I will be once I am married—Lady Galcrest, actually—but I was not always so. I worked for a living, and that means I know how difficult, how *precarious* that life is."

Helena nodded. For the first time since she had joined the Theatre Royal, she was holding back tears. After the rudeness of Mr. Tobias, the apathy of the stagehands, it was rather startling to be given sympathy, and by a total stranger, too.

"What will you do?"

Helena shrugged awkwardly. "I…to tell the truth, I have no idea. I do not even have a place to sleep this evening, which I suppose should be my first concern. Please, my lady, you need not trouble yourself."

She glanced at the gentleman, who was whistling quite happily as he waited for them to finish their conversation. *A most strange couple.*

Miss Fletcher was silent, examining Helena closely. Helena wished she had a bonnet. It need not be expensive, but no bonnet in society…she would be noticed, and not for the right reasons.

It appeared Miss Fletcher was considering something carefully. After another few moments, she opened her reticule and pulled out something small and rectangular.

She pressed it into Helena's hand. "This is for you. Go here, and speak with Miss Clarke. Tell her Miss Fletcher sent you."

Helena looked at the card. *The Governess Bureau.*

"You never know," said Miss Fletcher with a wry smile. "You might just find yourself a new career."

The Governess Bureau. It did not sound very promising.

"Governess Bureau," said Helena slowly. "Looking after children all day long?"

It hardly sounded like a pleasant way to spend one's time. Helena had nothing against children. They were rather like dogs, in that way. One was always pleased to see one, but you didn't want to have to take it home and bathe it.

Miss Fletcher was laughing. "They're not all bad. Some of them are quite passable. But as a governess…it's bed and board, small but dependable wages, and protection."

Their eyes met. Helena swallowed. It was not as though she was inundated with offers of employment, and right now, she wasn't entirely sure what she was competent enough to do.

Being a governess. What did one do? Prevent children from injuring themselves? Teach them things like geography and history and all of that nonsense?

"I…I don't have much to offer."

What a fall from grace today was—but her pride would get her precisely nowhere, and if she weren't careful, she would reach the evening standing in just this position, no further forward with her life.

"No experience with children at all," she added in a low voice.

Miss Fletcher shrugged. "Well, I'm not guaranteeing you work, of course. Perhaps you should consider adding this to your list of choices."

Her words were not sharp, exactly. There was no cruelty in them, but there was a pointed remark in there somewhere. *What other choices?*

Helena met her gaze, shame washing over her. "Thank you," she said warmly, injecting her tone with gratitude. "I…well, thank you, Miss Fletcher. You are kind."

Miss Fletcher smiled. "Now the rest is up to you. Galcrest!"

Her future husband grinned. "Are we off?"

"We are indeed," said the lady. "Good luck, Miss Patrick."

Helena looked at the card still in her hand. *The Governess Bureau.* She had heard of it, of course. You couldn't live in London without hearing about it. Miss Clarke had a fearsome reputation, and it was certainly not her first choice of occupation but, as Miss Fletcher had so elegantly hinted, what choice did she have?

"But what if—" she began. Miss Fletcher and her betrothed had gone.

The address on the card was just a few streets away. Taking a deep breath and clutching her trunk tightly, Helena started walking.

When she was ushered into Miss Clarke's office, it was diffi-cult not to be impressed by the grandeur of the place. Helena had dined in castles, danced at stately homes, conversed with lords and kings and dukes—but all on the stage.

This was real. There was no mistaking the luxury here, with the beautiful paintings on the walls, the soft resplendent carpet, the—

"Stop gawking," said a stern voice, "and explain yourself."

Helena focused on the woman seated behind the impressive desk. She was examining the intruder with curious eyes.

"I seek employment," said Helena, moving to stand by the desk.

Miss Clarke raised an eyebrow. "You and half of London. Sit."

Helena obeyed, wondering whether this was not a mistake. She was accustomed to…not exactly being fawned over but certainly to be spoken to with more respect than this.

"Who sent you?"

Helena opened her mouth but realized she had entirely forgotten the woman's name!

Blast everything. "I—she gave me your card."

It was still in her hand, and Helena passed it to the owner of the Governess Bureau in silence. Miss Clarke examined it, turning it over as though there was secret writing on the back.

Finally, she spoke in a quiet voice. "I have three rules, Miss Patrick. You must have an impeccable record. You must bring a special skill to the table. You must never fall in love. Those are the rules of the Governess Bureau, and I insist that every governess abides by them. Can you do that?"

Helena almost laughed. *Fall in love?* She had never been tempted before, and it was unlikely one of these sniveling masters and their sniveling children would ever tempt her.

"I believe so," she said quietly.

Miss Clarke watched as though waiting for something. Eventually, she said, "Well?"

Helena was utterly at sea. "I beg your pardon?"

"The second rule is quite specific," said Miss Clarke sharply. "A special skill. What do you bring?"

Helena's heart twisted. *What did she bring?* As she had said to the lady just outside the Theatre Royal, she was not skilled at anything. All her life, she had been in the theater, though she could not imagine a duke or an earl who would be happy that an actress would be teaching his children.

Think, Helena. Think!

"I-I can memorize things quickly," she said in a rush. "I absorb information very fast, and—"

"Memorization is not a skill," interrupted Miss Clarke with a glare. "Everyone can do that, given enough hard work."

Helena smiled. Now, this, at least, she could do. "Miss Clarke, stop gawking and explain yourself. Miss Patrick, I seek employment. Miss Clarke, you and half of London, sit. Miss Clarke, who sent you? Miss Patrick, I she gave me your card. Miss Clarke, I have three rules, Miss Patrick. You must have an impeccable record. You must bring a special skill to the table. You must never fall in—"

"Ah," interrupted Miss Clarke softly.

It was not really an interruption, more an impressed sigh, but Helena allowed herself to stop. She knew praise when she heard it, even if unspoken.

"You have some talent, then," said the proprietress quietly. "Interestingly enough, I have someone on the books now—the Baron Fernsby—who has three children. They don't need much, just a governess with a few simple talents."

Her cold eyes examined Helena closely. She held her breath. *Was this it?* The beginning of a new life? It was not one she would have chosen, perhaps, but right now, she had very few options.

"I'll take it," she said promptly.

Miss Clarke's eyes glittered. "Not without Governess Bureau training."

Chapter Two

June 14, 1813

OSCAR FERNSBY, DUKE of Kilerth, sighed heavily. "I've said it once, I've said it a thousand times, brother—you don't need a governess."

This conversation was going nowhere. Kilerth knew it wouldn't. *How could it when they were going round in circles as they always did when the topic of governesses came up?*

"And how would you know?" Baron Fernsby snapped. "All that attention you pay my children? All the time you have spent here in my home? All your experience as a father?"

Tempting as it was to Oscar to argue with his younger brother, he managed to hold his tongue. *He should be applauded for his restraint.*

Was it always this way with brothers? Was there always this underlying tension that one's decisions would always be critiqued by the other?

Oscar sighed. Being the head of the family, the damned duke, was no joke. His brother, known only as Fernsby within the family, had never complained—at least, not to him. That was how it was. Eldest born sons carried that burden.

It was too hot to think about arguing. They were fractious

enough since Oscar had arrived at the Old Abbey, and there was nothing to be gained by disputing governesses.

Oscar shifted in his seat. He was sticking most unpleasantly to the upholstery. They had believed the drawing room would protect them from the unusual heat, but the room had still warmed rapidly thanks to the large bay windows overlooking the west side of the garden.

"That's what I thought," said his brother sourly. "No response."

Oscar tried to remind himself of all his brother had suffered these last twelve months. He was not entirely to blame for his irritable temper. The poor man had—no one should have to suffer so.

If only he were back at Riverside Manor. Oscar closed his eyes for a moment to imagine how cool his large drawing room there would be. And the icehouse, far bigger than that on the Old Abbey estate. He could bathe in icy cold water back at his home if he had wanted.

He should never have permitted himself to be coerced into visiting his brother. It was Amelia's fault.

"You have no reason to advise me and barely any authority," continued Fernsby. "None whatsoever."

Oscar actually bit his tongue to prevent himself from retorting. *No authority?* He was the head of this family! The Fernsbys had managed to hold onto the dukedom of Kilerth for nigh on three hundred years! Perhaps he did advise his brother overly much. Perhaps he did poke his nose into the old boy's affairs.

But that was only from kindness, Oscar told himself petulantly. Only because he could see the mistakes Fernsby was about to make, and why not step in and try to prevent disaster?

Fernsby glared darkly, and Oscar met his eyes steadily. The younger man looked away.

Oscar sighed again. Somehow, he had managed to hold his tongue. It was a growing challenge, being cooped up here in the Old Abbey without anything to do.

But there were things worth arguing about, and this wasn't one of them.

Still, he was absolutely sure he was right. How could he be wrong? The three Fernsby children didn't need schooling, or a governess, or any of that rot. They just needed a firm hand, and a father who paid more than cursory attention to them.

Governess, indeed!

"Well, I agree with Fernsby," said Amelia. "A governess is a wonderful idea. Just what his children need."

Oscar did his best not to roll his eyes. What a surprise, their sister agreed with Fernsby. She always did. That was what happened when there was nigh on ten years between you and your two siblings. You ended up the third parent—now the only parent.

Amelia took Fernsby's side whenever possible. It appeared to be a principle of hers, regardless of what the topic of conversation was.

Oscar glared at Amelia but said nothing. It was damned irritating, having an unmarried sister of six and twenty lying about the place. Really, she should be shipped off to London and paraded around the parks and trotted out at Almack's.

That would get rid of her, hopefully to a pleasant enough gentleman who had money to keep her in all the things she wanted and gentility not to be a disgrace to the Fernsby name.

Amelia stared back unflinchingly. Oscar snorted rather than speak his mind. The woman didn't seem to want to marry anyone. *Damned nuisance.*

Not that he could have taken her to London last Season. Not after…well, Fernsby had needed them here. Oscar had only a few months back at Riverside Manor before he returned for this unbearable summer.

"*Thank you, Amelia,*" said Fernsby pointedly. "You would think I would know my own children and what they need."

By Jove, it was too hot to have this sort of conversation, Oscar thought irritably. Forcing himself not to rise to the bait his brother offered him, he looked out of the window.

That was what this visit was all about, wasn't it? Helping Fernsby?

Even if he didn't want to be helped.

Still, it was getting more and more difficult for Oscar not to defend himself. It was not as though he wanted the children to run about ragged, totally wild and uncared for.

But a governess? Another person in this household was not what this family needed. They were having enough difficulty looking after Fernsby as it was.

"If Constance had lived, that would have been different," Amelia continued, evidently not thinking of the import of her words. "As it is…"

Her voice trailed away as her mind caught up with her tongue.

Oscar clenched his hands. *Damn and blast it, Amelia, all you had to do was keep your mouth shut. We had agreed not to speak of her. Whenever we do…*

He glanced at their brother and saw precisely what he had expected. Fernsby's face had become pale, his eyes downcast. His hands were shaking, and he placed them carefully in his lap as though that would prevent his siblings from noticing.

Constance, Baroness Fernsby. Amelia was right. If she had lived, it would be different.

Now they were stuck in mourning, mourning that lingered.

The tension in the room grew, boiling with the heat shimmering before them. Oscar's hands were clenched again. If only he could get away for a few hours and—but no, he had promised himself he wouldn't, not while he was here.

It was down to him to break the silence. "There are almost certainly things I don't know about child-rearing, being a bachelor myself. A governess, to be sure. I suppose that would not be the worst idea in the world."

Amelia shot him a look of outrage, and Oscar smiled. She was so like their mother.

"So," he continued. "When will you look to hire one? I can't imagine a good one is easy to find, not out of London."

He realized as he saw his brother's smug smile he had walked straight into the trap.

"I have already done so," Fernsby said with a superior expression. "You think I was going to wait around until I could convince you that I was permitted to hire my own staff?"

Oscar's mouth fell open, and Amelia sat straighter in the armchair she had been slowly melting into.

"Already done so?" repeated Oscar, absolutely astonished. "Dear God, I hadn't believed it possible! How have you—what sort of references has she given? How on earth have you found one without going to London?"

Unless he had gone to London, Oscar thought wildly. *But—no, Amelia would have informed him if such an achievement had been reached.* He glanced at his sister and saw with a strange sort of relief that she was as confused as him.

"Goodness, that was quick!" she said with some surprise. "It was only a few days ago that you first mentioned this scheme. How did you manage to find one so quickly?"

If Oscar could have wiped the smug smile from his brother's face, he would have.

"It was hardly a challenge," Fernsby said. "I went to the Governess Bureau, of course. 'Tis the absolute best place to find one. They cater to nobility and royalty only."

It was on the tip of Oscar's tongue to point out that Fernsby was gentry, not nobility, but he managed to force it down. *Not helpful, man.*

Besides, he was vaguely aware of the place. *The Governess Bureau*…yes, someone had mentioned it in passing. Or perhaps it was the Gardeners Bureau?

"Well done," he said, though the words cost him. *This was ridiculous. Since when did he begrudge his brother a clever thought?* "That was a good idea."

Fernsby shot him a piercing look as though attempting to

work out whether the eldest born was being sarcastic or not. Oscar smiled briefly to show he was being pleasant, but his brother did not look overly convinced.

Brothers. They had always got along relatively well—at least, with the age gap between them. They had never really clashed until they were both adults.

Amelia, however, did not look comforted by Fernsby's pronouncement. "The Governess Bureau? Miss Vivienne Clarke of London?"

"The very same," said Fernsby impressively.

Amelia was not impressed. "I hate to say this, brother, but I have…well, heard some strange rumors about this Governess Bureau."

It was too hot for Oscar to pay her words much attention. One governess was surely much alike another, weren't they? They turned up, wiped the kids' snotty noses, and tried to force some manners into them, and that was it. How important was their pedigree?

"I only bring it up because…well…"

That got his attention. Amelia was never usually one to hold back her opinions, and she looked mightily discomforted at what she was about to say.

"Governesses," she said in a low voice, as though that would soften the blow. "Marrying their masters."

She looked nervously at Fernsby, and Oscar looked sharply at their brother, too. *Well, that would certainly be an unwelcome development.* They couldn't have a Fernsby married to a governess, of all things!

Fernsby frowned. "You don't flatter me much, Amelia! I'm not likely to be taken in by a servant. Have a little faith in me!"

A carriage came into view, rattling down the long drive, gravel flying up behind it.

"Goodness, they are going in a hurry," said Oscar idly, wondering aloud. "Who on earth could it be? I didn't think we were expecting visitors, were we, Amelia?"

He looked at his sister. She had become the mistress of the Old Abbey since her sister-in-law had died, and she had done a remarkably good job of it, too. It was unlike her to fail to mention anything like this at the breakfast table, and that had been hours ago.

But it was Fernsby and not Amelia who spoke. "Well, if everything has gone to plan, *that* should be the governess."

Oscar's mouth fell open. "What the devil do you mean the gov—"

But his words were utterly overcome by Amelia's shriek. "Governess!"

She rose hastily and rushed to the window, staring out at the carriage that was slowing now as it approached the house.

"Fernsby!" she scolded. "You never told me that she was arriving today!"

"Well, why should I?" shrugged her brother. "This is my house, Amelia, not yours."

The look of fury she blasted at him was enough to make any man wince. Oscar was surprised Fernsby didn't melt.

"It is *indeed* your house," she said firmly. "And *I* am the one who has been running it, along with Mrs. Cantrell, for the last ten months! No bed prepared, no additional food supplies in, no table set for this evening, no laundry preparations—where is she going to sleep? Have you told the children? Have you even told McLoughlin and Mrs. Cantrell?"

Fernsby blinked. "Ah."

Oscar snorted. The damned fool, of course he hadn't.

"Right," his brother said uneasily. "And we need to do all of those things, do we?"

Amelia sighed heavily. "I have no wish to scold you, brother,"—something Oscar rather doubted—"but how do you suppose I can help you run this place if you do not tell me something so important as the household changing?"

A broad grin spread over Oscar's face as he watched them bicker. Yes, this was more like it. These were the sorts of memories he had of the three of them as children—well, at least the two of them as children. Just before he had left home for university, their mother's warnings ringing in his ears, Amelia and Fernsby had sparred just like this.

"—much warning do you really need?" Fernsby was attempting to say. "I mean, it's just one woman—"

"One woman! What do we know of her? What references did she send? Do you know how much laundry one woman creates for a household?"

Oscar shook his head wryly. There was just as much fuss now as when the three of them were about to greet their own first governess—though admittedly, that argument had been over which of them would get rid of her first if his memory served him correctly.

Amelia sighed. Clearly, she could not prevent the governess from coming. "I suppose Mrs. Cantrell will manage, though I can tell you, I'll never hear the end of this."

"Will we?" muttered Oscar and caught Fernsby's eye, who grinned.

"I suppose you will introduce her to us?" said Amelia stiffly, choosing to ignore that particular remark.

Fernsby nodded. "Yes, of course, she'll need to know all of us before she meets the children. I've asked McLoughlin to show her through in here when she arrives."

Amelia nodded. She appeared to have gained equilibrium and was seated once more. "Yes, that sounds right. We can inspect her."

Oscar had to laugh. "Inspect her? Amelia, be reasonable. You're not a postmaster inspecting a parcel—she's a person!"

Amelia shrugged. "She's a servant. As long as she does the job well, without getting in our way, that is all that matters. I believe one can tell a lot about a person on first meeting."

It sounded like hogwash to Oscar, who opened his mouth to ask just what she based this mystical knowledge on, but the door opened, and the butler and a woman walked in.

A very pretty woman.

Well, he'd have to be half-dead not to notice. The woman was dressed in a modest, dark blue gown, which looked tired around the edges, but that was not surprising. It was the way she held herself which was surprising. As though she was an empress, as though all before her should bow and curtsey for the mere honor of being afforded her presence.

And then it was gone in an instant. Oscar didn't understand it; it was as though she had transformed into a completely different person. The haughty and rather imperious woman disappeared, to be replaced by a woman just as pretty wearing the same gown but with downcast eyes and a rather nervous expression.

That, at least, made sense. It was surely unpleasant to walk into a room and immediately know one was inferior to all those present. *Not an experience he had ever endured.*

"Miss Helena Kirkpatrick," intoned the butler.

Fernsby rose from his seat—an unnecessary courtesy, at least in Oscar's mind. *She was just a governess.*

"Miss Kirkpatrick," said his brother with a brief smile. "May I introduce my sister, Lady Amelia Fernsby."

Amelia rose and gave a small curtsey—another unnecessary formality thought Oscar. *Really, would they welcome a new scullery maid in this fashion?*

"And my brother, the Duke of Kilerth," continued Fernsby.

Oscar inclined his head but did not rise. *Well, the woman did not deserve such—*

Their eyes met. A flash of something akin to recognition passed between them, and Oscar felt as though he had been buffeted about by wind, slightly off-balance.

He knew her.

But that was impossible. He had never associated with governesses before; he was no fool. His title precluded him from such social circles, and he had never met the governesses of friends and acquaintances.

It was a mistake. A coincidence of look, perhaps. He could

not know her.

Miss Kirkpatrick lowered her gaze, and the hairs on the back of Oscar's neck settled. No, he did know her, though he couldn't for the life of him place where their paths had crossed.

The governess curtseyed again, her gaze lowering, then rising to meet his again.

It happened again. The moment their gazes met, Oscar felt overwhelmed by senses that did not belong to him—but this time, it was far more than recognition.

Something like heat, though the room was already stuffy enough. Heat and passion and the promise of glory. It was like recognizing someone from one's past before that memory slipping through one's grip.

The moment ended as she turned to his brother. "How pleasant to make your acquaintances."

Oscar blinked. His head was spinning, and he could barely understand what had just occurred. If anything had occurred. He had not moved, and the governess had done nothing but curtsey and look at him.

Was he that overheated that he could see something so wild that wasn't there?

"—and the youngest is but four years of age," Fernsby was saying to the governess, having taken a seat. "They get along tolerably well, as I am sure you have found with other children, but I do worry that…"

Oscar shook his head. Punch drunk was the only comparison to how he felt, as though he had supped one too many glasses of port and had tried standing too quickly.

As though someone had knocked him out, and he'd just come round.

He swallowed. *What on earth was this?* No woman had ever generated this reaction, and though Miss Kirkpatrick was indeed rather pretty, she was hardly a lady to dazzle him so.

Oscar examined her as she listened to his brother prattle on. She wasn't just pretty, now he came to look at her. She was…if she *had* been born a lady, he would have described her as beautiful. Dark eyes, hair that shone in the sunlight, some brown, some golden.

She carried herself well, too. The imperiousness was gone, but there was an elegance he would not have expected from a woman who worked for her living.

Yet, as his gaze scanned every corner and curve of her face, Oscar could not place her. He did not know her. Yet, she seemed so familiar.

This was ridiculous. He needed to concentrate.

"—grateful for the opportunity to care for your children," Miss Kirkpatrick was saying. "I am indeed thankful that you selected me."

"I didn't," said Fernsby cheerfully. Oscar tried his best not to smile. "No, I just told Miss Clarke to send me the best, and here you are."

"Oh," said the governess, her smile fading. "I see."

She was more nervous than she was letting on, Oscar realized. One had to be paying close attention to notice it, but—there it was. That flicker of uncertainty that darkened her eyes, only for a moment.

Fascinating.

"Now, to help you settle in here at the Old Abbey," said Fernsby, "I have created this rulebook for you. It's all very simple, you'll see as you read through it, and if you can follow these rules, then we will get along very nicely. It's what I need, you see. For you to be here."

Oscar blinked. *Wait a minute—a rulebook?*

He glanced at Amelia, who looked just as confused as their brother offered a pamphlet to the governess, who took it, looking perplexed.

Surely this was a trick—a jest. The man wouldn't take the time to sit and write out a list of rules for someone to follow like that, it was ridiculous!

But it appeared Fernsby had not been exaggerating. Now

Oscar looked at it, the pamphlet was actually quite thick. *Why, it must be almost thirty pages—of rules, to live here?*

Though careful to keep his face impassive, Oscar would speak to Amelia about their brother. It was a concerning development. *What rules could he possibly have put in there?*

"Thank you, my lord," the governess was saying quietly, flicking through the pages with an interested look on her face.

Oscar allowed himself to sigh. Well, they wouldn't notice, they were too wrapped up in their governess conversation. *Really, this was going too far.*

"I will memorize it," Miss Kirkpatrick said.

Fernsby laughed. "Well, you can try, I suppose, but I think you will find that it's quite detailed in my requirements. Now, you should meet the children. McLoughlin?"

The butler nodded and left the room silently. Oscar grinned. It was impossible not to like his nephew and nieces, especially after he had been here a few weeks. They were old enough to be their own people now. That was when children started to become interesting.

The door opened again and in trotted the Misses Fernsby and Master Fernsby. Altan looked particularly aggrieved, and Oscar was careful to wipe the smile from his own face. It wouldn't do for the boy to think this wasn't serious.

The children went to their father and turned to look at the governess curiously. She curtseyed. They continued to stare.

Oscar gritted his teeth. It was not his place to discipline the children, but he would certainly do a better job than Fernsby. *At least there was a governess now*, he admitted grudgingly in the privacy of his own mind. It would be her job to give them some manners.

As it was, they were not his children, and he had probably pushed Fernsby far enough today. He kept his mouth shut.

"Good afternoon, children," said Miss Kirkpatrick. "May I say how much I am looking forward to getting to know you all."

The children nodded mutely. Oscar had expected little Sylvia to say something—she was the smallest—but she simply looked up at the governess, wide-eyed. Perhaps she didn't understand. Rowena certainly would; she was eight years of age, more than old enough to know what a governess was.

"Thank you," said Altan stiffly. The eldest at eleven, Oscar supposed he felt the burden of speaking fell to him. *The eldest of three. How well he knew that burden.* "Papa, may we go now?"

"Yes, yes, off you go," said Fernsby distractedly. "And take Miss Kirkpatrick with you. Give her a tour of the house."

Sylvia took a step forward without any fear and took one of the governess's hands in her own. "I'll show you my favorite room, it's the library, there are so many books there you'll never be able to read them all, my Papa says…"

As the child prattled on, Oscar saw the governess relax. Yes, it was just nerves. She would settle in and keep the children off their hands, which could only be applauded. Then life at the Old Abbey would return to normal—or at least, as close to normal as it could.

Miss Kirkpatrick had reached the door when she paused and turned to face the adults still seated. "Thank you, my lord, for your welcome." She caught Oscar's eye. "I am sure I will survive several rounds with the children if needs be."

Oscar's stomach lurched horribly. *She knew. Christ, how could she know?*

But that she did was irrefutable. Why else would she choose that wording? Blast, he should have known that his bare-knuckle boxing in London—under a different name, of course, he was not completely stupid—would come back to haunt him at one point or another.

Miss Kirkpatrick was still smiling, and Oscar's heart was racing, painfully rattling against his ribcage.

She knew. She knew his secret.

Though he had been careful to ensure the family would never know, here she was, able to spill his scandalous secret to them all. *It was a disaster!*

Before he could say a word, however, the governess was gone, and the door closed.

"Well," said Amelia with a sigh. "That wasn't so bad. I think she'll be fine, though your rulebook was a surprise, Fernsby."

Their brother nodded. "I…I knew you wouldn't like it."

There it was again—those nerves that were always just below the surface of Fernsby. Amelia and Oscar exchanged a look. There was no point in pushing him today. He had done so much, and really, he should be praised for thinking of the children enough to secure a governess for them. He so rarely thought of them at all.

"Well, I am going for a walk," said Amelia, rising slowly. "No—not outside," she added hastily, seeing Fernsby's face. "In the long gallery. You old men stay here. The heat will exhaust you."

Oscar nodded. He had no breath for words. Not now, Miss Kirkpatrick had entirely knocked it out of him.

CHAPTER THREE

June 15, 1813

H ELENA TOOK A deep breath and knocked on the door.

For all her preparations, the result was quite an anti-climax. Nothing happened.

She waited, sure a voice would ring out, inviting her inside. After all, she was certain this was the right door—the master's study.

It had been easy to memorize the house's layout when the Fernsby children had shown her around. It was large, larger than any house she had ever stepped into, but no more complex than the Theatre Royal. Helena was certain this was where the baron's study was situated.

"Be there for ten o'clock, and I mean ten o'clock sharp," the butler had told her sternly that morning in the servants' hall as they had eaten breakfast.

Some of the maids had stared, but Helena had learned quickly to look away.

"I will," she had said to McLoughlin.

"Be minded that you will," he said quietly. "The master will be expecting you, and he doesn't like…well. His routine must be kept to."

Helena could well believe that. She had spent the last day or two reading through the rulebook that the baron had presented her with when she had arrived at the Old Abbey. She had never encountered anything like it.

A clock chimed somewhere in the house. Ten o'clock. She was precisely on time, waiting outside the master's study, but there did not appear to be anyone inside. *Should she knock again? Was this some kind of test?*

She couldn't just stand here, waiting like a fool. If the last few months had taught her anything, it was that if she wanted something, she couldn't expect it to be placed into her lap—and if she wanted to keep hold of something, there was always someone ready to take it away.

Just as she raised her hand to knock a second time, a voice came through the heavy wooden door.

"Come in."

Helena found she was not nervous as she opened the door and stepped inside. *Stage fright.* Something she had learned to ignore over the years. She didn't have time to be fearful. As Helena looked around her, she saw a beautiful room elegantly decorated and with all the comforts one would expect in a gentleman's study.

There was a desk, of course. mahogany by the look of it, and covered with a wealth of papers and spent quills, two bottles of ink waiting to replace one that looked almost finished. There was the large grandfather clock. Helena smiled. It was running two minutes slow. Paintings adorned the walls, and the windows looked out onto the blue sky, the leaves of an oak tree in the distance. It was another hot day.

Helena kept her eyes downcast as she stood before her master, seated on the other side of the desk.

That had been her mistake when she had been introduced to the family. Whenever she had been nervous in the past, she had merely looked inside herself, found the lines and character of a person from one of her plays, and put on that character. Queen Mab was never afraid, not in any situation. Lady Macbeth never permitted anyone to doubt her. Ophelia may not have made the right choices, but she made them.

The technique had served her well for years, but she was living a different life now. She had felt the surprise of the baron's brother when she had entered the drawing room and, as any good actress could, adapted.

Still, she had to be careful. As Helena looked around, taking in every detail of the room, she was reminded of the differences in their stations. Governess was probably a social step up from actress, but both positions were miles apart from these titled nobility.

Dukes, barons, Lady Amelia…it was a different world.

"Ah, Miss Kirkpatrick," said the baron with a smile.

Helena curtseyed in silent response. It had been a clever idea of Miss Clarke's to change her name. She had not really considered the potential danger until the owner of the Governess Bureau had pointed it out.

"Miss Helena Patrick is a famed, celebrated actress," Miss Clarke had said stiffly, as though it pained her to give praise. "We cannot have an actress in the Bureau. It simply wouldn't do."

And Helena had stared. "You mean you want me to leave? You've only just—"

"I mean, you need a different name," Miss Clarke had spelled out with a sigh. "Really, I cannot be expected to do all the thinking around here, though I inevitably do. Miss *Patrick*. You'll need a new name."

Choosing a new name had been a challenge. Helena was concerned if she ventured far from her true name, she would forget the subterfuge and forget to respond when spoken to.

That would be rather inconvenient.

They had settled on Kirkpatrick.

"Irish," said Miss Clarke at the time.

Helena had swallowed. There was much anti-Irish sentiment

in London, though she did not hold with it. She had presumed Miss Clarke would be above such petty concerns.

"Is that a problem?" she had asked stiffly.

Miss Clarke had smiled. "Only that you do not have an Irish accent, of course."

It had been on the tip of Helena's tongue to respond in a thick Irish brogue. She had often amused herself with mimicry, part and parcel of being an actress. A stagehand had hailed from County Donal, and they had all spent many a pleasant evening in laughter as she attempted to replicate the rolls and burrs of his voice.

She had decided against teasing Miss Clarke, however. Reply to a different name was difficult enough; she did not have to make the thing ridiculous by forgetting an accent.

"My father was Irish, but I was born and raised in England," she had said smoothly.

Miss Clarke's eyebrow had raised. "Really?"

"No," Helena had said with a wry smile. "But it's believable, isn't it?"

"Kirkpatrick," said the baron, leaning back in his hair.

Helena jumped. She had become so lost in her thoughts, she had forgotten where she was—standing before the baron in his study, waiting for instructions.

Because she was a governess now. Not an actress.

"An Irish name, I think?"

Preparation was important. "Yes, my lord. My father was Irish, but after marrying my mother, he stayed in England. I was born and raised in London."

The baron nodded. How easily people believed a lie. It was all very well, believing whatever one saw on a stage; there was a small part of oneself that knew it was all make-believe.

"And how are you getting on?"

"Very well, thank you, my lord," said Helena, conscious of using the right greetings for each family member. *My lord for the baron, Your Grace for his brother, my lady for their sister...* "I have been made to feel very welcome here by yourself, your family, and your household. I am grateful."

Her master nodded. "Good. I hear nothing ill of you, you'll be pleased to know."

Helena kept her face impassive, though someone without her experience on the stage may have sagged with relief. No one must have guessed her background or made a delicate mention in the ear of her master that she should vacate her position.

This was, after all, her first post as a governess.

"Not without Governess Bureau training."

Training indeed. Yes, she had submitted to the training Miss Clarke said every Bureau governess enjoyed—though Helena would have said endured.

Those silly days with those silly ladies—some of them no older than she had been when she had first entered the theater, not even twenty—sitting in rows listening to Miss Clarke talk about how important it was to recognize when a child's language was delayed, and when they just did not wish to speak.

It had seemed rather silly then. It was real now.

And no matter how much training one received in London, nothing could prepare someone for this. Traveling almost a hundred miles from where you were born; entering a house the size of a theater, half of Bond Street; meeting nobility, expected to hold your own before them; mixing with servants, whose family had cleaned those fireplaces and polished the silver for generations before them…

Helena swallowed. It was no small challenge, and she had only been here a few days.

For the first time, she wished she had paid a little more attention to Miss Clarke. Perhaps she had mentioned something about charming masters who gave out rulebooks as thick as the Common Book of Prayer. She had certainly not expected anything like this.

"And how do you like the children?"

Helena concentrated. *This was no time to get lost in her thoughts.*

"I like them, though I admit...I am not sure I know them well yet."

She was taking a risk here. *Were governesses expected to immediately bond with their charges—perhaps understand them within minutes of meeting them?*

But it appeared not. The baron was nodding. "That is a good answer, Miss Kirkpatrick, I commend you. I admit, I would have been worried if you waxed lyrical over them. A few days is not sufficient time to know a child, nor even an adult. One has to take the time to get to know them. To know their quirks, as I am sure you will learn mine."

Helena nodded, though she did not risk saying more without being invited to speak. It appeared most things were a test with this gentleman, looking for a reason to be unimpressed.

Not dissimilar to the audiences she was accustomed to at the Theatre Royal.

"And was there anything in the rulebook that gave you trouble?" asked the baron. "I suppose you may not have completed reading it yet, but—"

"No, my lord," said Helena. "I understood it all."

Tempting though it was to tell him she had memorized the entire thing, she managed to contain herself. The last thing she needed was to draw attention to herself. No, she had to exist in this house, keep everyone happy enough not to complain, and that would be sufficient.

There were no awards, medals, or prizes for the best governess. There was, however, dismissal for the worst.

"All of it?"

The baron looked rather surprised. Helena hesitated. *She was supposed to read the whole thing, wasn't sure?*

As an actress, it was commonplace to be given a playscript one day and be expected to know one's lines the next. It was not exactly a skill—or perhaps it was. She had memorized much longer parts than the baron's rulebook overnight, but if she were to reveal that, it would almost certainly lead to questions.

Questions she had no wish to answer.

Actresses were *respected*, to a point, in London. They were placed in the same social bracket as opera singers and ballet dancers, as far as Helena could tell. Elegant, beautiful, and admirable in their place. *Inside a theater.*

Outside of a theater…well, they were not unfashionable, nor low in rank, but they were certainly not high. Not to be trusted. Not to be admired.

Not to be given charge of a baron's children.

Keeping her history before she arrived at the Old Abbey a secret was best. It would only harm her reputation if anyone were to know that Miss Helena Kirkpatrick, governess, was the same as Miss Helena Patrick, celebrated actress.

"Yes," said Helena, conscious that the baron had asked her a question and only vaguely aware now what it was. "Yes, everything in there made sense, and I agree with it."

It would have been difficult not to. The majority of the baron's rules were commonplace concerns of any parent, and the rest were…strange was too strong. *Quirky.*

Protecting his son, Altan, was understandable. The boy was the heir to the barony, and as far as Helena could tell, the dukedom as well. She would have to read up on precisely how these things worked but keeping Altan safe was not a rule she needed written down. Keeping any of the children safe was not exactly an unusual request of a governess.

For his daughters, the baron wanted to ensure that they did not speak to anyone beyond the family and servants. Helena could understand that, too. Who knew what dangers lay beyond the Old Abbey? Surely at their young ages, keeping those rules would not be difficult.

The only rules that had made Helena pause were those about going outside the house. Though large, the Old Abbey was in the height of summer, and it was natural that the children would wish to cool off in the shade of the gardens. That, however, was only to be entertained if Helena was there to chaperone them.

The baron was nodding approvingly. "I am glad you understand, Miss Kirkpatrick. I believe my brother and sister were a little concerned."

Helena nodded. She didn't, but it was safer to nod than reveal her ignorance.

"My children are still very young," he said quietly. "After losing their mother…"

His voice, previously strong, trailed off, and his gaze became lost in the middle distance, evidently looking at something she could not see.

There was pain in his eyes. Helena bit her lip and said nothing, waiting to see whether the baron would recall himself and continue the conversation, but it appeared not.

The baroness. No one had spoken of her, and Helena had not been introduced to her when she arrived. Though she had been tempted to ask questions—where was she? Was she visiting family or friends, perhaps, or in London?—she quickly realized it was safer not to.

She had died, then. It was clear the baron had truly loved her, and Helena felt pity wash over her. A love like that, torn apart so young—it was unfair. It was cruel.

The baron cleared his throat. "I know my brother believes Altan is old enough for school, and perhaps he is, but I would prefer to…I think it best to keep him home for the time being. There will be plenty of time for him to study later in life."

Helena nodded. "And the girls are younger."

"True," said their father heavily. "Younger and without a mother. Entertain them, govern them when needed, correct manners if required, keep them in order—but there is no expectation of lessons, Miss Kirkpatrick."

Helena kept her face passive, hiding the relief coursing through her body.

No lessons! Was there a child more jubilant than she on hearing those words?

She had told Miss Clarke on the second day of her governess

training that she did believe herself equipped to give lessons.

"Not *equipped*?" Miss Clarke had said, curling her nose. "Nonsense. Any home who takes a Bureau governess will be fully equipped with books, blackboard, chalk—"

"Not that kind of ill-equipped," Helena had said, cursing her choice of words. "I mean…I never received much of an education myself. How can I be expected to teach others?"

And there had been a sparkle in Miss Clarke's eyes, which could almost be described as merriment. "Well, you will have to learn then, won't you, Miss Kirkpatrick? One chapter ahead of the children at all times, that ought to do it."

Helena had thought the owner of the Governess Bureau out of her wits—but now she understood. Miss Clarke had this position, here with the Baron Fernsby's children, in mind when they had first met. The baron had surely told Miss Clarke that he did not require lessons.

Book learning was not instrumental here, and that was all to the good, for she had little.

"Any questions, Miss Kirkpatrick?"

Helena smiled. "No, thank you, my lord."

The baron nodded. "Well, in that case, off you go and govern."

He waved his hand toward the door. She was evidently dismissed.

Despite the abruptness of his dismissal, Helena was not concerned as she curtseyed, turned on her heel, and left the baron's study. He was a baron, after all. Men with titles—ladies with titles, probably as well, did not have to worry about social niceties to grease the wheel of conversation. The title did all that hard work for them.

From any other man, she would have considered it rude—but from the baron, it was expected. *Wasn't that how one spoke to people when one was obeyed throughout one's home?*

She found the children in the morning room. There did not appear to be a nursery at the Old Abbey; at least, the children had not shown her one on their tour. Sylvia was the youngest, and even she was a little old for a nursery at four years of age.

Helena closed the door behind her and viewed them critically. The two girls were by the window, looking out onto the lawn with rather wistful expressions. The heat of the day had not yet peaked, by which time they would probably retreat from the baking glass.

Altan was sitting at one end of a sofa, reading a book. He did not look up as Helena entered the room, but the two girls turned and smiled.

Helena found herself smiling in return. During the long journey from London to the Old Abbey, she had wondered about these children. Altan, Rowena, and Sylvia. Miss Clarke had given her sparse details, either purposefully or because she too had no information.

In her darkest of moments on the road, when she was tired and hungry, she pictured three horrible children, disobedient and irritating. The children of her imaginings, however, bore little resemblance to the children now before her.

"Well, then," she said as she stepped further into the room. "Let's talk, shall we?"

The two girls obeyed instantly, the elder holding the younger's hand as they moved to a second sofa. Altan, however, did not look up from his book.

When he spoke, it was in a testy voice. "Talk about what?"

Helena seated herself in an armchair before considering how to respond.

Children. There were a few in the theater family—there always were, when actresses made friends with gentlemen for their favors and came back with more than a purse of gold—but they usually ended up working there. Running errands for Mr. Tobias, helping the stagehands, going out into London to procure more face paint for the leading lady…

Her. That used to be her.

The children at the Theatre Royal had looked up to her like a goddess. These three children were staring as though she had erupted out of the ground.

Scrambling for a topic, Helena landed on the most obvious. "Tell me about your family. I have just arrived here, so I don't know you all very well."

"You have met them all," said Rowena seriously. She had her father's chestnut hair, as did almost all the Fernsbys, but her eyes were lighter than his. There was mischief there, just under the surface, but it had been dampened by something. "When we met you."

Helena smiled. "Well, that's good to know, but of course, I don't know anything about you or the rest of the Fernsbys."

"You know Papa," chimed Sylvia. Her legs didn't quite reach the large oriental rug beneath her sofa. "He loves us very much. Auntie Amelia tells us so."

Helena's heart twisted. *That was never a good sign.* Oh, it showed the family was pulling together, and the loss of the baroness must have been a terrible shock to them all, but if it was Lady Amelia needing to tell the children that...

"Auntie Amelia lives with us," Rowena said. "She has done for a while now, ever since..." Her voice trailed away, and Helena was minded to end the silence, but in a moment, Rowena was able to continue. "For a year or so. She is lovely."

Helena nodded. She did not need to be an excellent governess to know this about children; speaking of their deceased mother was not the right decision.

Altan still hadn't looked up. "And our uncle the duke is a rascal."

"Altan!" said Rowena in horror.

Altan grinned and finally looked up from his book. "What? That's what Papa calls him."

Helena did her best not to smile. "I had a brother like that, you know."

"Was he a duke, too?" asked Rowena, looking genuinely curious.

"No, not quite," laughed Helena. "But he was a rascal."

"Do you have a brother and a sister like me?" Sylvia said, clearly determined not to be left out of the conversation.

Helena shook her head. "No, just one brother. He was younger than me by—oh, a few years. He…he went away."

She swallowed. How was it possible that this light conversation, for that was all she had intended it to be, could become so dark so quickly? She had not thought of Frederick for years. He had gone off to France to fight Napoleon, and…

Sylvia nodded thoughtfully. "Our mother went away, too."

"Sylvia, you know she didn't go away," whispered Rowena, pink tinging her cheeks.

"She died," said Altan harshly. "She's not coming back."

Helena swallowed. *Time for another topic.* "So, tell me," she said brightly, "what do you three like to do to amuse yourselves?"

"Amuse ourselves?" said Altan. "We don't."

"We used to," said Rowena y. Her arm was around her sister, and Helena noticed the younger girl had popped her thumb in her mouth. "When Mama was alive, we'd go for walks and watch the dances and go horseback riding…oh, so many things. It was wonderful."

It was clear the baroness's death had had a far greater impact than Helena had imagined.

"And…and now you don't?" she asked.

"I don't remember doing any of that," announced Sylvia, though it was difficult to understand her, thumb still in her mouth.

"You were too little," said Rowena quietly.

Altan sighed. "We don't do anything anymore. We're not even allowed to go riding anymore, Papa says. Not since…not since Mama died."

Helena nodded. It was clear this family, though they had rallied together after the loss of the children's mother, was a little broken.

The baron worried about his children excessively if the rulebook was anything to go by. Now the rules about going outside were starting to make sense. The fear over the boy's safety. The requirement that the girls not venture anywhere, for that was the natural conclusion of the rule that forbade them from speaking to anyone who was not a near relation.

The question was, how was she supposed to entertain the children if she was not permitted to let them do the sorts of things children the world over did?

Helena thought back to the rulebook. The rules on keeping the children inside, on restricting their time outside to one hour a day on the lawn only. In the list of things they were permitted to do, which in hindsight was rather short, she could not recall riding or walking or dancing or anything that Rowena had mentioned.

It was going to be an interesting challenge. Helena could not ride herself—when would she have learned?—and so perhaps it was a blessing in disguise that it was forbidden. No, best to concentrate on the things they could do.

"Well," she said heartily. "What are you reading, Altan?"

The boy opened his mouth—doubtless to come back with some retort which did not include the book's title—but he was prevented from speaking by the door opening.

"Where are you, you blag—ah. Hullo, you three. Miss Kirk-patrick."

Helena rose to curtsey to the newcomer. It was only polite, after all, to curtsey to a duke—even if he was about to swear in the search of presumably his brother.

"Good morning, Your Grace," she began. She had other words to say, a whole sentence that involved inviting him to join them.

Then realization hit her. *Helena had seen him before.* Before their introduction in the drawing room, that was, when she had also been hit with the sensation that their paths had crossed.

Now she remembered where. It was hardly an auspicious place, though, in fairness, the duke had won his bout against his challenger most admirably.

But it was not possible. Dukes did not wander into bare-knuckle boxing rings in rather unsavory parts of London—and they certainly didn't waltz back to spend the summer with their brother in the country!

Except…except this duke did. Helena blinked, and the duke's face did not blur or change. It was the same handsome features she had noticed then, all those months ago. It *had* to be him—the two men were identical, only the man in the ring had been called Michaels, not the Duke of Kilkerth.

Helena swallowed. Any boxing, let alone bare-knuckle boxing, was not an acceptable thing for a duke to be doing in public. No wonder he had taken a different name.

The duke was staring most intently—as though deciding whether to strip her of all her clothes and make her beg for something.

She dropped her gaze immediately.

"Right," said the duke uneasily. "Fine. Good. Yes. Carry on."

The door snapped shut behind him.

"Why was he looking at you like that?" asked Rowena curiously.

Helena swallowed. There was only one reason a man looked at a woman like that, but she was not going to be the one to tell the children about *that* part of life.

"I have no idea," she said airily, and with great effort, sat and pretended that nothing had happened. *And breathe.* She was a professional. Within a moment, she was so convinced that nothing indeed had happened that she said, "What did you say that book was, Altan?"

CHAPTER FOUR

June 20, 1813

THE SIGH FROM Oscar's brother was long, languid, and most irritating. It was perfectly designed, as with most siblings, to generate the most frustration in those around him. Oscar was glad he was taking a sip of tea at that moment. The scalding beverage gave him something to splutter about rather than retort with something unkind.

"I just…I was the one who invited the two of you here, to the Old Abbey, to enjoy yourselves," said Fernsby with another sigh. "And all you can think to do is leave!"

Oscar caught Amelia's eye and immediately took another sip of tea.

Sunlight drifted through the windows of the morning room as a clock chimed half past the hour. Elevenses. Oscar never took elevenses when he was home. It was a strange sort of thing: half meal, half excuse to sit down again.

Sit down? All they did was sit down!

"Leave!" repeated Fernsby, obviously unhappy with the lack of response. "I ask you!"

Amelia placed her teacup back in its saucer but said nothing.

Oscar had to admire her self-control. *She had been here—what, almost a year?* Living with Fernsby for any length of time was a challenge, but with him in this state?

"It's not a surprise you wish to leave me," said his brother with a sigh. "I should have expected it."

Oscar pressed his lips together in a struggle not to rise to the bait. The man was being ridiculous, and if he had not been grieving a wife...but Fernsby had to be given time, Amelia had said.

How much time, she had not been specific about.

How he dearly wished to shake his brother sometimes, but even Oscar knew that would be the wrong approach. One did not get to decide how another grieved.

Besides, he had promised Amelia he would avoid any unnecessary fights, and though he dearly wished to say something about how petulant the man was being, for her sake and the general peace of the house, he would keep his counsel.

At least, he would do his best. His promise was about *unnecessary* fights. He did not promise never to have them.

"You did indeed invite Kilerth for the summer," said Amelia into the awkward silence, evidently unable to leave it any longer. "And a lovely invitation it was, too."

Her glare prompted him into action. "Yes, thank you, Fernsby."

He probably could have put more effort in. Even he could hear the sarcasm within the words.

Fernsby sighed. "Oh, how readily those words trip off your tongue."

Oscar swallowed.

"I admit, I understand why you would want to leave, Amelia," Fernsby continued, glancing morosely at their sister. "You have been cooped up here almost six months."

"Almost a year," corrected Oscar.

Both his siblings glared. *Blazes, you couldn't say anything in this house without running the risk of fury!*

Amelia opened her mouth to say something, then closed it again. Evidently, she wished to say something that she knew would be ill-received.

They both took another sip of tea in silence. It was not his job to pacify Fernsby whenever he got himself into one of these moods. He had spent enough time acting as father when the old duke had died.

Now he came to think, Fernsby had always been the melancholy one of the three. The Fernsby siblings were so different; it had been remarked upon in their youth and continued now as they were adults. They didn't even look that much alike, other than the hair color.

Yes, Fernsby had always been the first to declare disaster, the first to assume defeat—and now he had lost Constance…

Oscar placed his teacup on its saucer. Well, he was not in a position to judge. How could he? Love was not an emotion he had dabbled in over the years, and in many ways, he was the confirmed bachelor his mother had always worried about.

"You'll die alone, Oscar," she would say to him when returning from university, her eyebrow raised as he told stories not of balls but of boxing bouts. "Alone, and wishing you had taken a different path, mark my words."

He had laughed then. He didn't really see the attraction, even now. Love was all very well if it jumped out at you, but he had never gone looking for it, and in a way, he was glad.

Oscar's gaze moved over to his brother. There were lines around his eyes that he had never noticed before. *Had they been there a few years ago, or was this the effect of grief upon the body?*

No, love was not worth pursuing. Not if it could lead to something like this—the misery of finding a person who became your world, then losing them.

Fernsby could always find a way to beat himself about the head if he wanted to, and though he had a genuine cause now, that didn't make it any less frustrating for those who cared about him.

"You must be so bored," his brother was saying. "Bored out of your minds!"

"Of course, we are not bored. How could you say such a thing?" Amelia said quickly. "We're not bored, are we, Kilerth?"

Carefully arranging his face into a smile, Oscar said, "Not at all."

Fernsby put his teacup down on a table so hard, tea seeped over the edge. "I can tell when you're lying, Kilerth. It's so obvious."

And that was when Oscar lost his temper. "Well, what did you expect? We are your guests, we are family, and yet you do not permit riding, shooting, hunting, walks, picnics, visits to the village—you don't let us go *out of doors*, Fernsby! You think that in summer, in heat such as this, we are going to thank you for it?"

The words echoed about the room, a strange medley of elegance and anger. Oscar could feel his blood boiling, his heartbeat pounding in his ears. His fingers were gripping the delicate china so tightly, he was surprised he had not broken it.

Amelia raised a hand to her temple and closed her eyes.

Oscar swallowed. And as was always the way with his damned temper, the spark had flared, the words were out, and now he would quite like to take them back, worse luck.

"See," said Fernsby smugly. "I *knew* you were bored."

Amelia opened her eyes and looked at Oscar warningly. Clearly, they were not to antagonize their brother.

That was why, when he spoke, it was through gritted teeth. "It is boredom of your own making, man. You could undo it. If you are truly concerned about our entertainment here, permit us to take *a step* outside."

It was a reasonable argument to him. Oscar had never wished to upset the man, but there was a perfectly reasonable way for Fernsby to permit his guests to leave boredom behind.

It was so simple—yet the baron hesitated. He licked his lips, evidently unsure of what to say, then murmured, "I know...I know I could, but it's so...it's so dangerous out there."

Oscar saw his brother's hands gripping the arms of his chair as though he would slip off the face of the earth if he did not hold on tight enough.

Blast it all.

Taking a deep, steadying breath, the duke rose from his seat to wander to the window. Anything to change the pace of conversation, which had once again hit this dead end.

A concerning one. Even he, who Amelia had once accused of having no fine feelings whatsoever, was starting to truly worry.

It was the real reason he had agreed to come to the Old Abbey this summer. To be sure, Fernsby had invited him—but he invited him every summer, and he rarely accepted.

Amelia's letter, however, had convinced him. What was that line she had written?

I truly believe if you do not come, he may entomb himself in this very house.

That line was engraved in his mind, and Oscar had given the order to pack at once. It had seemed…well, so over the top. Surely Amelia had been exaggerating the problem. He would stay a week, maybe two, calm her and give her a little respite from the children, and once it was proven that their brother was absolutely fine, he could return home.

That had been a month ago.

He could never have imagined that things had gotten so bad. Fernsby had left that bright summer morning last year to attend his wife's funeral, hosted the grieving that afternoon, and had not taken a step outside his own home since that day.

Not to see his gardens. Not to visit the village, church, or neighbors.

His fear of the outside, Oscar could now see, had entirely overtaken his life and that of the children. And it had to end.

How it would end was a different matter.

"No doctors," Amelia had said the second night after his arrival when they had conversed in hurried whispers in a corridor. "I won't have scandal on this house."

"There will already be whispers if he does not present himself in society soon," Oscar had whispered back. "For all we know, there already are!"

Amelia had won that argument, of course, and Oscar had abided by her wishes. *No doctors.* But without medical advice, how on earth were they supposed to help their brother combat his absolute fear of the outdoors?

"It's the children I feel sorry for," Amelia had said that night, and Oscar had brushed aside her concerns. Now he thought about it, that was a pattern he should try to break, for she was quite right.

As Fernsby hid inside his home, so, too did the children. Forbidden from going outside, restricted from all external activities, they were as petulant and sullen as he was.

"I wonder how the governess is getting on," said Amelia lightly.

Oscar glanced up from his position by the window in the morning room. She was clearly attempting to change the conversation, and it was well done, but Fernsby did not respond. He was looking into the depths of his teacup.

The governess. Yes, she could have been a positive change. Perhaps she would have encouraged Fernsby to permit the children to do—well, anything. But that dratted rulebook!

Amelia was speaking. *He should pay attention, really.*

"—in the gardens," she was saying, looking at their brother kindly. "We'll have the house in view all the time, so if at any point you wish to return—"

"No," said Fernsby shortly. "No, I won't go."

Amelia glanced at Oscar.

"Your gardens are looking mighty fine," he said jovially to lighten the mood.

It did not work.

"I wouldn't know," said Fernsby morosely.

Oscar made sure his sigh was not audible. He was not a patient man; he had known this for years, and as much as he could alter his own character, he had attempted it.

It was not Fernsby's fault that he was bereaved.

"Consider a walk in the garden a compromise," Amelia was saying gently. "Come, brother. Nothing dangerous will occur there, and we can enjoy the cool of the shade."

Oscar watched their brother closely. If he had not, he would not have noticed the flicker of uncertainty, the frustration in his brow, the tightening of his hands on the chair.

Fernsby was genuinely conflicted, Oscar realized. He did wish to go, wished to please them—yet he was powerless to do so.

Oscar swallowed. *How did one help a man so utterly lost?* Even if it was in his power to understand the depths of misery fate had pulled his brother down to, how could he, a man who had never known such loss, help him?

"I wonder whether just sitting in the drawing room with the doors open..." Amelia's voice drifted on as Oscar turned back to the window. She was a good woman. She was more than they deserved, really, and she—

She was a disgrace.

Before his eyes, that governess, Miss Kirkpatrick, was striding across the lawn! Worse, she had all three children following in her wake.

The children. Outdoors.

Oscar's heart was racing, but it was nothing to his stomach which had turned over. This was a disaster—if his brother was to see such a thing...it was the last thing he needed. The children had always followed his rules, no matter how strange, but this wild disobedience—*and from the governess, too!*—was not to be borne.

He glanced swiftly back into the room and saw with relief that his siblings were still conversing. Perhaps Fernsby would not see the offending disobedience.

"Well, I should review some estate accounts," said Fernsby, rising from his chair.

Oscar's breath caught in his lungs. He shifted quickly to cover as much of the window as possible, but as his brother turned to say something to him, it was clear that he saw precisely what Oscar had attempted to keep from him.

"Ah," said Fernsby softly. "The children are outside."

Amelia's gaze met Oscar's immediately, and he saw in her face the same concern inside his heart. *This could swiftly become a disaster—they needed to act quickly.*

She rose at once. "I will have a word with Miss Kirkpatrick and explain—"

"No, no, it is quite alright," interrupted Fernsby, a gentle smile appearing on his face. "I gave her permission."

Oscar's mouth fell open. He had never been particularly good at hiding his emotions, and this was such an unexpected response from their brother.

Amelia seemed in a similar mind. "Per-Permission? What about the rulebook?"

The children and governess were carefully laying a blanket on the ground. They sat, Altan opening up his book and the two girls playing a sort of clapping game.

Oscar watched and felt rather than knew that his two siblings were watching, too. *The next Fernsby generation.* They were so innocent, so untouched by the pain of the world.

"Do you think I haven't noticed?"

Oscar turned at his brother's words.

"Did you really believe I would not realize that I am…that I am ill?" All the petulance had disappeared from his brother's voice. "I suppose I know not what else to call it."

Oscar glanced at Amelia. *Was this the breakthrough they had wished for?*

"I do not wish to go outside," said Fernsby quietly. "It…oh, it frightens me in a way that I do not understand. It feels like death to me to even contemplate taking a step outside my own front door. I am a prisoner here but in a cage of my own making, and though I can feel the nonsense of it, I cannot push past the panic that rises like a fist clenching around my throat…"

His voice trailed away, and Oscar's gaze met Amelia's. Their brother was not so unaware as they had thought, then.

But while they were looking at each other, Fernsby was looking at no one but his own children, his eyes misting.

Oscar swallowed. A picnic basket had appeared now, though, where from, he knew not. The governess was taking out sandwiches and handing them round to each child.

"Constance loved the gardens."

Fernsby looked at peace for the first time since Oscar had returned to the Old Abbey. It was rather disconcerting, but also a relief to know the brother they knew and loved was still in there, somewhere.

Amelia stepped forward and placed a hand on her brother's arm. "Yes, she did."

Fernsby did not look at his sister; his attention was all for his children. "They are half *her*, you know. She loved the outdoors. I...I do not wish them to learn my fears. Better they learn her loves."

For the first time in years, Oscar found there were tears prickling in his eyes.

Christ, he had been a fool. How had he managed to lose sight of the fact that his brother had lost his wife and was utterly at sea without her? He had carried on as best he could, perhaps not in the way that Oscarwould have done—but still. He carried on.

He should have more respect for his brother. Fernsby knew, then, that he had not been acting...as he had before. He wanted what was best for his children, and that was to be admired.

He was a good man. Though they did not always agree—in truth, they rarely agreed—they were brothers.

"You...you made the right decision," Oscar said stiffly.

Amelia nodded. "Of course you did, Fernsby. You're a good father. I suppose the question is, are you comfortable with *us* going outside? We won't rush *you*," she added quickly, seeing the same spark of fear, "and it is no judgment on you. I just...I thought I would ask."

It was well done, thought Oscar. Gentle, without guile nor bribery. Just an honest question, spoken with affection.

Oscar waited for his brother's response, but as it was not immediately forthcoming, he turned back to look at the children. At the governess. *Miss Kirkpatrick.*

There was something about her, though he would only admit to himself. *She was…*

Beautiful was the only word he could think of, which was rather uninspired and did not really do her justice. She was…beautiful. Every curve, every line of her face was beautiful. It captured the eye, refusing to let go, forcing you to examine her and marvel at her beauty.

It was intoxicating. It was infuriating. The fact that it could happen from twenty feet away through a pane of glass, seemingly without her knowledge, was bizarre.

Miss Kirkpatrick was saying something to the children, and Oscar couldn't hear the words from here, but he did not need to. He just wanted to watch her mouth move, see the way those lips curved around those words, wonder what it would be like to kiss them.

Oscar swallowed. No, he would not permit his mind to meander down that particular path. Getting involved with a woman like that—any woman in his brother's house!

No, if he wanted to scratch that particular itch, he could have his fill when he was back in London. He was no prude, seeing no need to restrict himself from pleasure when it presented itself, but that did not mean he could pick and choose between the servants under his nose.

Someone was speaking. He should probably pay attention.

"—said, did I make a mistake in bringing her here?"

Oscar blinked. The gentle look had disappeared from his brother's face.

Well, he wasn't going to pretend he didn't know what his brother was talking about. Hadn't he been the one to explain to his brother precisely what happened between a man and a woman?

"Don't worry," he said quietly. "I won't do anything daft."

Fernsby snorted, all that old bravado back. "I should think not! She's my servant!"

Amelia was looking between the two brothers in complete confusion. "What on earth are you two talking about?"

Oscar was not about to admit to his sister—*his sister!*—who probably did not even know what lovemaking was, precisely, what had been going through his mind, but his instinct to move away from the window only revealed the source of their conversation.

Miss Kirkpatrick was now visible to all three of them.

Amelia sighed. "Really, Kilerth? So predictable. A pretty face."

"All I was doing was looking!" protested Oscar. *Really, he should haven't to defend himself like this.* Had he taken a step toward her? Had he even spoken with her more than the few sentences when they were first introduced?

Fernsby snorted. "I hope that's all you ever do!"

Oscar raised his hands in mock surrender. "Look, I've said I haven't done anything, and I won't. Can we move on?"

Despite himself, his glance moved back to the window and to the blanket, but he was disappointed. Though Altan and the girls were seated quite happily, the boy now reading from his book for his sisters, the governess was gone.

A slither of emotion wrenched at his heart. It was one he did not recognize immediately, and when he did, it was quite a surprise.

Disappointment. He had enjoyed looking at her, whatever he said to his siblings, and though he would never act on such an impulse, he would rather like to continue looking at her.

"Your Grace, my lady, my lord."

Oscar spun around, almost tipping himself over in his own haste. As though she could read his mind, Miss Kirkpatrick was standing in the doorway with a genteel smile on her face.

That smile faltered as she looked at the three siblings. "I-I hope I am not disturbing."

Much to his annoyance, both his siblings immediately looked at Oscar. *Did they have to be so obvious?*

"Of course, you are not interrupting," said Amelia, finding her voice.

She must have nudged their brother, for Fernsby coughed. "Yes. How can I help?"

Miss Kirkpatrick took a few steps into the room, and Oscar tried not to notice just how much closer those steps brought her to him. "Well, actually, it is more about how I might be able to help."

Fernsby blinked. "My word, really?"

"The children are eager to be entertained," said Miss Kirkpatrick quietly. "I know your rules are focused on doing that in a safe way. My question is…what do you think of a play?"

Kilerth tried to take in her words and not focus on her mouth, but it was mightily difficult. *It was so expressive, so red. So perfectly formed.*

"A play?" repeated Amelia.

Fernsby seemed just as confused. "Here?"

Oscar knew he should say something, contribute to the conversation in some way. If only he could find his tongue. The governess's presence was overpowering; he had never known anything like it.

Miss Kirkpatrick nodded. "I have experience in…in putting on plays with children. It would be a way to entertain them inside or on the lawn if it gets too hot. I agree lessons would be too formal, but a play would be a wonderful way to encourage their imaginations, their reading, their sense of literature…"

Amelia glanced at Oscar. *Would their brother be able to accept something that would naturally take the children out of doors so often?*

"That sounds like an excellent idea!" Fernsby seemed genuine in his words. "By Jove, I wish I had thought of that!"

The governess smiled. "So, I—I have your permission?"

Oscar could feel something in the air—some tension, some secret, something the governess was keeping from them. *Did she have an ulterior motive for this play of hers?* Why suggest something like this when the children appeared to be so happy outside on the lawn?

But his brother was waving his hand. "Oh, carry on, Miss Kirkpatrick."

"What a wonderful idea," said Amelia warmly, clearly more comfortable now their brother had accepted. "I think a play is a capital way for the children to play in a structured, safe way."

Structured, safe way. Oscar almost snorted at his sister's words, though the governess looked delighted with the praise. *Structured and safe.* That wasn't what childhood was supposed to be about! It was supposed to be running and jumping and climbing and falling over and picking yourself up again!

At least, that's what he remembered from his own childhood, though admittedly, it was a few decades ago now.

Oscar blinked. *The governess had gone.*

"Where do you think you're going?" said Amelia suspiciously as Oscar moved toward the door.

He grinned. "Nowhere."

"To do what?" Amelia's voice sounded concerned now.

Oscar leaned against the doorframe as he grinned at his sister. "Nothing."

Precisely what had made him do it, he did not know. All Oscar knew was that there was a deep-rooted need to follow the governess, to talk to her if he could. Perhaps then this feeling, this desire or whatever it was, would dissipate.

It did not take long to catch her. Miss Kirkpatrick was walking along the corridor back toward the hall, but she stopped as soon as he reached her.

"Is there anything I can help with?" she said quietly, eyes downcast, all the spark Oscar had seen when she spoke of the play gone. "Are there further instructions from my lord?"

Oscar opened his mouth, but to his utter astonishment, no sound came out.

Fool! He had never had this sort of trouble with the ladies, any ladies. His wit and repartee were dependable. *So why, fixed in the gaze of a servant, did his ability to speak suddenly leave him?*

A smile crept along the corners of Miss Kirkpatrick's mouth. "Cat got your tongue?"

And at that moment, he could speak. "What is your name?"

She evidently had not expected such a question. "Miss Kirkpatrick."

Was that fear in her eyes? Why did she not wish to tell him her full name? "No, I meant your first name."

There was definitely suspicion in her face now. "Why?"

He had definitely seen her before—before he had encountered her here, in the Old Abbey. There was something familiar about how she narrowed her eyes. Where had he met her? Perhaps not even met her, perhaps she had been in the background of some schoolroom—at the Astors perhaps, or the Rochdales.

"I think we met once."

Yes, there was fear in her eyes. She knew it, too; she knew their paths had crossed. Oscar's stomach twisted, though whether from excitement or anticipation or fear, he could not tell.

"You must excuse me," said the governess, not lifting her eyes to his own. "I must return to the children."

She walked away quickly, head bowed and hands clasped before her.

Oscar knew better than to follow her. Now she was gone from his presence, his heart was slowing, and he was already starting to feel like a fool for following her out of the morning room. He was no whippersnapper who became intoxicated by any skirt that wandered by.

So why did he find himself so intrigued by her?

CHAPTER FIVE

July 3, 1813

I T WAS ONLY a slip of the hand, but it was enough for Helena to accidentally scatter the raft of papers off her small bed onto the floor. They fluttered, sliding across the floorboards and becoming mingled just after she had spent the last twenty minutes organizing them.

Helena sighed. She had been looking for a particular one not yet found. She knew it was here; she could recall copying it carefully, her fingers unaccustomed to such lengthy writing.

It had not been necessary at the Theatre Royal for actresses to pen anything.

Ignoring those already fallen to the floor, safe in the knowledge she had already checked through them, Helena's gaze moved to the pile still on her bed.

There was a desk in the bedchamber she had been given. It had been rather a surprise, but then Helena had remembered that she was not expected to give lessons.

"In my mind, you are here not to teach but to govern."

Still, it was far too small. The number of parts in the play she had chosen was extensive, and she needed to lay them all out in a patchwork of voices and movements.

She could almost see the stage before her as her eyes roved over the different parts written out. It had been but a few months since they had performed this at the Theatre Royal, perhaps her fifth time. She knew the entire thing by heart.

It was only after she had spent hours carefully reciting the parts to herself, pen in hand, moving from page to page in her attempt to remember the entire thing, that she remembered the damned play might be in the library of the Old Abbey.

If she had just thought of that, she could have asked for a copy.

No matter. There had been changes to make—it was too much to expect the children to perform a full Shakespearean play. She had adapted it, changed it, added bits from other plays she liked, written a few additional lines herself.

She had written the whole thing out now and duplicated it. Sylvia's reading was not sufficient, but the part Helena had assigned her was small.

Her gaze flickered over the pages, all covered in expressive lines of her handwriting. She was sure she had duplicated the part, which meant there was a second. It was so infuriating. Perhaps it was tucked in behind one of the other pages which had now fallen to the floor?

Helena rose from the bed and dropped onto the floor, her fingers spreading out the pages.

There. She had missed it the first time. With a wide smile, she leaned forward and picked up a set of three pages that had begun the hunt in the first place. Grabbing her pencil from the bed, she wrote carefully in print letters at the top of each page.

Altan.

It was perfect for him. Full of chivalry, long speeches, even a sword fight if she could persuade the baron to allow his son to do something so wild.

As the eldest, it was right Altan had the difficult part. *He would probably demand it,* Helena thought wryly. Though their acquaintance had only been weeks, she already saw a spark of rebellion in him. His father would have his work cut out when the boy neared his majority.

Now, Sylvia...

Helena smiled as she leaned against her bed. She was perhaps the child most eager and least able to join in the play, but that did not mean that she was about to be left out.

No, there would be a place for her. Even if Helena had to create one herself, a hodgepodge of fools and children and non-speaking roles from other plays that she could wrought into something new.

After all, there were only so many lines that a four-year-old could remember.

Helena hauled herself up and sat on her bed again, Altan's role in her hand. Well, this was not what she had expected of the Governess Bureau. She had seen a quite different future. Blackboards and marking and having to shout at children who were not attending.

Helena shivered. She had never been to school, as such, but she had performed the role of a tutor once in one of the history plays. It was not one she had relished: uncomfortable clothing and no smiles.

But here, at the Old Abbey? It was almost an idyll. Playing theater with children who had no choice but to obey her?

While other governesses from the Bureau were surely forcing little ones to learn their Latin verbs by heart and recite the Magna Carta, whatever that was, she was wondering whether adding a great tempest two-thirds the way through this play of hers would be acceptable.

Where would they get the backdrops?

Helena smiled, her fingers brushing the parts before her. It was almost like playing with siblings—younger siblings. Perhaps because Altan reminded her of Frederick so much.

Miss Clarke's parting words echoed in her mind. "You are not there to make friends, to win over any hearts, or, God forbid, fall in love. You are there to do a job. Do not let me down, Miss Pat—Miss Kirkpatrick. From whence I plucked you, I could easily return you."

Helena shivered, though the day was warm and her small bedchamber stifling. *Miss Clarke was quite a fearsome woman.* Though she would be reluctant to admit it, there was a part of her that was afraid of the Bureau owner.

She supposed she should be grateful to Miss Clarke for taking a chance on her—for selecting this particular assignment, where she was expected to do nothing more than babysit and play.

Helena closed her eyes, and the same image appeared that always did whenever she laid herself down to sleep.

The Theatre Royal. It was beautiful. Elegant columns, rich velvet carpet for the punters, and squeaky floorboards for the actors. The smell of greasy stage paint, the spluttering of the candles throwing light onto the stage, the sudden intake of breath from the audience whenever she stepped out in glorious costumes…

Helena opened her eyes. That was her old life, her old habits, her old home.

All that was gone now and thinking back to her past was only likely to cause misery.

It mattered not that her entire adult life had been spent there. That she knew people there far better than her own parents, God rest their souls. Her history was there, and she had believed for a time that her future lay there, too. How wrong she was.

At the Theatre Royal, she was beloved, adored, and here…

Helena looked around the bedchamber. She still did not con-sider it *her* bedchamber, though that would change over time.

Who else had lived between these four walls? *A servant.* A servant just as she was. Well treated, as much as a servant could be, she would be the first to admit, but in London, she had been a duchess, an empress, a temptress, a warrior queen…

It was hard to accept that she could never return to that part of her life. Though she had never planned her future—*who did in the theater?*—she once had a vague idea of being one of the old women who were just as much a part of backstage as the sandbags above them.

Helping the younger generation in and out of their gowns for quick costume changes, hastily mending costumes after a fight scene, ensuring the stage swords were blunt.

The idea that she wouldn't end her days there—it had been unthinkable.

Until four months ago. Now here she was. Living a completely different life, where no one here knew of her old one. Miss Helena Patrick was dead, and from her ashes had arisen a quiet, demure governess eager to ensure no one knew the two women were one and the same.

Helena swallowed. She gained nothing sitting here, moping in her own memories. She had built a life in the theater, and now she would build a life here.

Picking up all the parts lying on the bed and stooping to grab those which had fallen on the floor, Helena forced a smile. If she were Mr. Tobias, the stage manager—and in a strange way, she now was—what would be her next step in putting on a play?

They would need a stage for a start. Without a stage, a play was nothing. Though she had not entirely explored the Old Abbey yet, the children had given her a pretty thorough tour of the place, so she had a number of options.

The library? Too small—and the books would deaden the sound, absolutely useless for projecting one's voice. The drawing room was larger, yet still too small. Once you placed a stage in there, there would be no room for an audience. The dining room was the same. The morning room even smaller. There did not seem to be—

A slow grin crept over Helena's face. *Of course.* She didn't know why it didn't occur to her immediately—the perfect place.

It did not take more than a few minutes to slip on her shoes, gather up all the parts into her arms, and start down the corridor toward the sweeping staircase.

Helena smiled ruefully as she stepped lightly downwards. When she had first arrived, the huge banisters and intricately carved wooden spindles beneath it had amazed her. She had barely been able to believe that such a piece of craftsmanship could be just in someone's home, used every day without fanfare.

Now she had already fallen into that habit. She forced herself to notice the holly and ivy carved with berries and birds plucking them. She truly was living in a spectacular place.

Though she had never actually been inside the room that was her destination, the children had pointed it out to her, and Sylvia's eyes had been wide.

"Absolutely huge, Miss Perkpatrick!" she had said solemnly, her little tongue not quite managing Helena's false name. "I've never been inside, but Papa says it's as big as a cavern!"

Helena was quite sure that Sylvia had no idea what a cavern was, but that did not mean it was not perfect for her stage. Memory serving her perfectly, she strode confidently down the corridors as they wiggled their way across the house and stopped before the double doors.

For some reason, she took a deep breath. It was as though she was about to walk out onto her own private stage. The moment deserved to be savored.

Drawing herself up, Helena opened the doors to the ballroom, and her footsteps echoed impressively, bouncing off the mirrors, chandeliers, the highly polished wood.

She had never actually been in a ballroom, and all her imagination had presented her with was a rather large space in which people could dance, converse, and share gossip as matches were made and hearts were broken.

But here…

"Goodness," she whispered.

Helena wouldn't have been able to explain, had someone asked her, just why she had whispered in that moment. It was like stepping into a church. One had the sensation that where one stood was holy.

This was the real thing; no painted backdrops here. You could feel the depth of the room, sense the space. Sylvia was right—or at least, Baron Fernsby was. It really did feel like a cavern.

There was beautiful gold detailing everywhere she looked as Helena stepped further into the room. The polished floor was almost like a stage, a slight spring to the floorboards that seemed to make her soar across it.

And most importantly, the place was plenty big enough for a stage.

"A play?" Altan had said just a few days ago, that expected look of suspicion covering his face. "What we do with a play?"

"Perform it, of course," said his sister. Rowena had that wonderful talent of always knowing precisely what to say to irritate her elder brother.

Altan scowled. "Of course perform it, but where?"

"Does that mean I could wear a pretty gown?" asked Rowena, entirely ignoring her brother's questions.

"Yes," said Helena at the time. She had attempted to field all three of them at once and had a very poor time. "And—"

"What's a play?" said Sylvia, looking between them all with a confused expression.

Helena took a deep breath. "Well, a play is—"

"It's a game of make believe to impress other people, but no one is watching," snapped Altan.

It had taken a great deal of self-control in that moment for Helena not to snap at the boy, as she might have done her own brother. *Well, really! There was no need for that!*

"Someone should be watching, then," Sylvia had said confidently.

Helena had smiled. Too young to be afraid of her own opinion, the world had not taught her yet to hold her tongue.

Besides, she had given the governess an idea. "How many servants are there in the Old Abbey—on your father's estate?"

In the ballroom, Helena could see there would be plenty of room for the servants to watch the Fernsby children perform their play—if, that is, their Papa would permit such a thing.

Of course, it would have been scandalous to assume that the children perform for anyone but family. *The very idea!* But servants were family, in a manner of speaking. There was nothing to stop servants from watching, applauding, giving the children a sense of purpose.

Giving her the chance to be back on a stage once more.

Helena pushed aside the thought. No, this was not a selfish act. She was doing it for the children. It had nothing to do with her, nothing at all.

She placed the papers on the door to act as a marker. She had come here for a purpose, and there was no point getting lost in memories of the children or the theater.

So, which was the scene that required the most space? Surely the swordfight scene. Yes, they would need to ensure Altan did not injure anyone, or himself, during that scene.

Helena stood beside the papers and took a deep breath. "Right. The sword fight of *Hamlet* required forty paces. One, two, three…"

It was not her fault. There was something so freeing, so wonderful about being on a stage again.

Not that this was a stage, but her feet did not know that. They could sense strong, polished floorboards, ready for a dance, a step, a dramatic twirl.

Helena's counting slowed as her feet started to twist, and she raised her arms above her head as she pirouetted—poorly—across the ballroom.

She was Juliet. She had just met with Romeo, and the star-crossed lovers were in the throes of passion, with no thought for the consequences. She was Hermia, dancing for her love of Demetrius across the petal-strewn path of woods on her way to meet him. She was—

"No, come on, Helena," she said aloud firmly, bringing herself to a stop. "This is ridiculous. You are not a child. *Pace.*"

Returning to the papers, she started to count again. "One,

two, three…"

When she reached eleven, there was a sound. A cough?

Whirling around, Helena saw to her dismay she was not, in fact, without an audience. There stood the Duke of Kilerth, watching with unabashed amusement.

Her heart pounded but for quite a different reason than a few moments ago. Whereas before the joy of movement, the desire to inhabit a different character, a new person, with different passions and adventures than her own had utterly overwhelmed her…

Now Helena saw that she simply had not been careful. *What had she been thinking?*

This was a mansion, a household packed with servants. There was almost nowhere one could be completely alone. One was always watched. Easily found out.

Helena did not only feel the flush soar across her chest, rising up her neck but saw it. In a hundred glass and mirror panels around the ballroom, she saw the blush tinge her cheeks.

Was she permitted here? The children had said nothing of restrictions, but why would they? This was their home—and Sylvia had said, Helena remembered with a sinking heart, that she had never been inside here.

How long had the duke been watching her? Just for the second bout of counting or—and Helena swallowed at the very thought—had he watched her prance about like a fool?

And perhaps most importantly of all…why did she care so much?

"Miss Kirkpatrick," said the duke with a wry smile, still leaning against the doorframe. "What on earth are you doing?"

Helena swallowed. It was a rather discomforting position to be in—but she had done naught wrong. *No rules from the rulebook had been…*

Her mind raced through them, quickly reviewing all she had memorized. No, there was nothing there that had been challenged. She had even asked permission to put on the play with the children in the first place, and the baron had been all for it.

Surely it was the children's father who mattered the most, Helena thought wildly, trying to get her mind in order sufficiently to speak. It didn't matter what the duke thought.

Except it did.

"I am pacing out a stage," she said, somewhat baldly.

The duke stared. "A stage?"

Was it so strange? "I thought you would expect me to do so," Helena said with a neutral expression. She would not allow herself to smile, though she saw the ridiculousness of it. *What was she accused of—counting without permission?* "For the children's play, you see. It is imperative I mark out the maximum size required for the most exuberant scene, and then I can create something that will suit the play and be large enough for the children."

He was still looking as though she were a half-wit, which Helena was appreciating less and less.

Did he have to…do that? Somehow, he was looking not just at her, but…well, through her. As though he could see inside her very soul, inside her heart. As though no secrets could remain secret for long.

As though he knew her.

She was letting her imagination get away with her—an occupational hazard in her line of work.

Her previous line of work, she corrected herself. She wasn't an actress anymore. She was a governess.

"Do you have any further questions, Your Grace?" she said, allowing sharpness and just a hint of boredom to enter her voice. "I haven't hurt anyone or broken anything, so I do not see your concern. This may be the first time I have been resident in a house of this size, but I know how to conduct myself."

The duke did not seem to attend to a single word she said. He stepped forward, his footsteps as heavy as hers had been light, heading straight for her.

Helena fought the instinct to step back. She had never been anywhere like this, around people of such quality, but one of the things she had not needed to be taught was not to get too close to a member of the family.

Particularly a member of the family so tall, with dark chestnut hair, a jacket cut to within an inch of his muscles, and *that* look on his face.

Unable to prevent herself, Helena took a step back.

The duke stopped. He was a few paces away but with enough distance to be respectful, which was all Helena was interested in.

You must never fall in love.

Miss Clarke's words echoed in her mind.

Helena had laughed at the time. *How ridiculous*, she had thought. As though there would be anyone in these stuffy, rich homes to even make her think twice.

But the Duke of Kilerth was not just a man. He was a gentleman, a rogue. Why else would she have seen him fighting, his knuckles bound and bloody, in the center of a ring in London?

He was a strange man, to be sure. The fact he did something very strange to her, of course, was beside the point.

Helena raised her eyebrows slightly and examined him. The duke appeared to be a man who was impossible to ruffle.

"I see," said the duke softly. "So, you were looking for a stage and naturally thought of the ballroom."

"Yes," Helena said more defiantly than she had intended.

He nodded. "A good idea."

"I have been known to have them."

The duke looked sharply at her after that retort. Helena tried to keep her face impassive. She should not have allowed herself to speak so instinctively. As his face shifted into a smile, she returned it, her stomach lurching horribly.

She stopped smiling. This conversation was not a good idea. Being bold was all very well when you were an actress who had to amuse the audience and bring back the punters, but she was a governess here, not a woman on a stage!

Though she was not the only one living a double life. The duke watched her carefully, and Helena found herself looking back without fear. The bare-knuckle boxing under a false name, for a start. *What sort of duke did that?* What sort of man needed the money, or the thrill, or whatever it was that his illicit activities gave him?

"Well, the children are most excited for the play," the Duke of Kilerth said suddenly, gesturing to the paper on the floor. "I hope, Miss Kirkpatrick, that you have plenty of experience in doing this sort of thing."

Helena froze. Of course the whole dammed thing was too good to be true: *he knew.*

Plenty of experience.

She had vowed to herself—and perhaps more importantly, Miss Clarke—that she would not permit the family to know of her history. What good could come of it? The idea of an actress from London teaching their children? The Fernsbys would never countenance it!

She swallowed. The duke was watching her, evidently waiting for her response.

This was not quite a disaster, not yet. The Duke of Kilerth may know a secret about her, but she knew his. The best thing they could do, surely, was mutually agree never to reveal them to anyone else.

Mutual protection, that was it.

Helena almost laughed at the thought. Perhaps not the sort of deal she ever thought she would strike, let alone with a duke, but desperate times called for desperate measures.

"Yes," she said nonchalantly. "It…it would be a shame, I think, if anyone was to find out about the truth of a—a certain person's past. Recent past. In London."

His eyes never left hers, but they flashed as he considered her words. "I agree. That would be…a shame."

"One, however, that we could avoid," said Helena lightly.

She spoke as calmly as she could, though her heart beat frantically. *Delicately…*

"And if a certain someone had a past they wished to keep

hidden," said the duke slowly, still not taking his eyes away, "then I am sure it should remain so. It would not help anyone for *that* sort of news to get out."

Helena nodded. "So…so we are agreed?"

He nodded. "Agreed."

It was all she could do not to make her sigh of relief too obvious. "We are of one mind, Your Grace."

Not entirely, it seemed. With her words, the gentleman stepped forward, swiftly closing the gap between them. "I think I would prefer it if you call me Kilerth. Now that we have an understanding."

Helena hesitated. It was informal, but it was still his title. After their rather strange agreement—he to keep her actress history a secret, she to keep his boxing past a secret—they were, in a strange way, protecting each other.

And she was grateful to him. A duke could likely survive a scandal, whereas she…

"Fine, Kilerth," she said with a nod. "But I am still Miss Kirkpatrick."

CHAPTER SIX

July 6, 1813

O SCAR TOOK A deep breath and attempted to focus not on the situation itself—which was all in hand, he was sure it was—but in slowing the nerves in his stomach.

He gripped the reins, and his horse shook his mane. Oscar looked down. His ankles had dug into his horse's sides just as he had gripped onto the reins.

With a great effort, he relaxed. *It was all going well. Nothing had gone wrong.*

Convincing him had been the most challenging part, and that had been successful. Well, *Amelia* had been successful. Oscar could not claim any credit for speaking so quietly and so reassuringly to their brother over the last few days, never pushing too hard but never allowing the topic to be dropped.

"You just have to try," she had said last night at dinner with that warm smile Oscar had never perfected. "Just try, Fernsby."

And he had. Oscar glanced to his right and saw a sight he had not imagined would be possible two weeks ago.

His brother. Outside the house. On a horse, no less.

True, Fernsby was clutching both his reins and the pommel

of the saddle as though he would slip off the horse if he did not. There was a discomforting pallor to his face, and he had not spoken a word since they had left the house.

But they were here.

Oscar breathed in the warm summer air and tried not to think. They had managed to get Fernsby outside. Outside. It was a miracle.

"I-I can't see the house," said Fernsby suddenly. His voice cracked, full of fear.

Oscar looked at Amelia, riding her own horse to the other side of Fernsby.

Amelia nudged her steed closer to her brother's. "Only because of that large oak tree, see? If you wait one moment…there. There it is. We weren't any further away from it than before."

Fernsby's gaze flickered over to the house, the west side. Oscar watched as his brother's body physically slumped, relief clearly pouring through every muscle.

How was it possible for such an outgoing man to be so overcome? There was clearly something more to it than just fear. Oscar had not understood it from Amelia's letter; it had been an intangible thing, difficult to reconcile with the adventurous and wild Fernsby he knew.

But grief did strange things to a person. Oscar had seen it in his friends when they lost their parents; had, in a strange way, seen it in himself when their parents had passed away.

"Yes, yes, I can see it," said Fernsby quietly. "Good. That's good."

Amelia glanced over at Oscar, who nodded briefly. *They were doing well.* Just getting him to cross the threshold had been impressive. He had been sure his brother would balk once they reached the stables. Yet here they were.

It was all Amelia's idea, of course.

"I truly think a ride around the house would do him good," she had said to Oscar a few days ago.

He had, evidently, looked skeptical at the suggestion.

"Well, it would," Amelia had retorted. "We wouldn't need to go far. He would know he could return to the house at any point if he wanted to—I think it's the perfect balance. I'm going to suggest it."

"Don't," advised Oscar sternly.

She had ignored him. She usually did, and now as they meandered slowly around the west corner past the orangery, Oscar had to admit that it was a good thing, too.

If she had heeded him, Fernsby would still be inside, and they would be trapped in there with him.

They couldn't get any sort of pace, going around the house so slowly it was quicker to walk. Oscar itched to force his horse to a gallop just to feel the wind through his hair and rid himself of this dratted heat—but he was in no position to complain after being cooped up inside since he had arrived at the Old Abbey.

"I think we should go inside," said Fernsby suddenly.

Oscar sighed heavily.

"And what does that mean?" snapped his brother.

"Nothing," said Amelia hastily, peacemaking skills immediately surfacing. "You didn't mean anything, did you, Kilerth?"

Oscar worked hard to smile. "I just sighed, Fernsby. I meant nothing by it."

His brother examined him closely, as though seeking out a reason to begin an argument. Oscar smiled blandly, allowing his horse to rock him slowly back and forth.

He was not going to give his brother an excuse to go inside, not if he could help it.

"I…then…fine," said Fernsby slowly.

Oscar said nothing, allowing his gaze to slip away from his brother naturally.

He was being unfair to his brother, he knew. This was the first time Fernsby had left the house after the funeral. They should be proud; he was proud. It was not an emotion he had much experience in expressing, but still. *He was proud.* The man was dealing with it well.

As they turned a corner, Fernsby moved into Oscar's gaze. His fingers around his reins were white, so tightly were they clenched around it.

Pity seared through Oscar's heart. Deuce, they were very different people, and there would be some who—if they knew— would consider Fernsby a coward.

If anything, his brother was the bravest person he knew.

It was not the sort of bravery that won medals, that others could hail, or why some would raise a statue to him. But it was far above and beyond anything he himself had done.

"And there are the stables, see?"

Oscar started. Lost in his thoughts, Amelia's voice cut through them and brought him back to the present.

Visible relief swept across their brother's face. "Oh, thank God."

His cheeks tinged pink, and his gaze dropped to his hands. Oscar looked at Amelia, and in an instant, their eyes met, understanding passed between them. They'd heard nothing.

"Sorry, old boy, didn't catch that," said Oscar breezily. "What did you say?"

It was just enough time for Fernsby to collect himself. With a cough, he said, "I must thank Ford, the stable hand. This saddle is in good repair. He has done an excellent job on it."

"Indeed," nodded Oscar. "Always nice to have one's work appreciated."

Small steps, that was what it was. They could not expect too much of him. Fernsby had left the house. He had been out here for—*what, almost half an hour?*

It was a miracle. The real test would be whether he felt able to repeat the experience…

"Ah, my lord," said Ford. The stable hand had been brushing down another one of the fine horses in the Fernsby stables but stepped forward to grasp the reins of his master's horse. "Did you have a pleasant ride?"

"Yes," said Fernsby.

Oscar looked over as he dismounted his own horse and saw with disappointment that his brother's gaze was already fixed on the side door. *Safety.*

"We could go for a stroll around the gardens," he said quickly. Amelia looked down from her horse with a warning glare, but Oscar ignored her. "Just a short walk, Fernsby, and I can show you—"

"No." The response was short and absolute. Fernsby jumped down from his horse before either of them could say anything. "No, I need—I want to go inside."

"Well, at least wait for me," said Oscar hastily. Every moment that they could keep him outdoors was better, wasn't it? Was that how they would help him heal?

His brother hesitated by his horse, his voice rather strained as he said, "Very well."

He clearly wished to be off as soon as possible, and though he was tempted to take his time, Oscar relented to the obvious strain his brother was under. Stepping over to their sister, he offered a hand to Amelia for her dismount.

But she did not take it. "I...you know, I might do one more circuit of the house."

That was enough to get Fernsby's attention. "What—alone? Are you sure?"

Amelia looked pleadingly at her elder brother. Oscar bit the inside of his lip as he looked at his two siblings, both desiring completely opposite things.

Fernsby had been through enough today. His fear of the outdoors had been conquered, at least for a short while, and it seemed foolish to push that any further than it needed to be.

Yet Amelia had been a virtual prisoner in the Old Abbey for almost a year. Oscar had underestimated the strain it had put her under: running a house, supporting her brother, managing three children, unable to leave the house at all for any sort of exercise or diversion.

He could see it in her face. *She needed this—some time to herself.*

Oscar sighed. *The things he did for his siblings!* It was as bad as having children—worse, for he would never outgrow these two.

"Look at that," he said suddenly, pointing just further along from the house to the lawn. "There are the children! What are they doing on the lawn without their governess?"

Fernsby turned hastily, his face white. "What—where? Where is Miss Kirkpatrick?"

Without a second glance at his sister nor a word to either of them, the master of the Old Abbey marched off toward the lawn.

Amelia chuckled. "I would never have thought of that. Thank you."

"Just don't be too long," said Oscar in a low voice, eyes watching his brother's progress carefully. "You know I won't be able to keep him distracted forever. You probably have…I don't know, half an hour? Use it well."

His sister nodded and quickly forced her horse into a gallop in the opposite direction. Her dark blue riding habit streamed out behind her. Oscar shook his head. Of the three Fernsby siblings, it was Amelia who had a flair for the dramatic.

"Altan! Rowena! What are you doing!"

Oscar sighed. Perhaps he should have volunteered for the governess position; he appeared to be doing far more babysitting than the woman herself.

"Wait for me, Fernsby," he said in a loud voice, handing the reins of his horse to Ford.

It did not take him long to catch up with his brother. Altan was standing sullenly before his father, and Rowena was beside him though looking anxious rather than discontented.

"Papa, you need to let me—"

"I can't see Sylvia," said Fernsby frantically, a hand on each of his children's shoulders as Oscar came to a halt beside him. "Where is she?"

It was unusual for Sylvia to be absent, and a prickle of fear clutched at Oscar's heart, though he forced it away. *What was he becoming?* Children had to run about and play and hide, didn't they? Otherwise, they wouldn't be children!

Run about and hide…

As Oscar's gaze roved over the lawn and the surrounding bushes, it fell upon a bench with one occupant. *Miss Kirkpatrick.* She had her hands over her eyes and was counting.

"…twelve, thirteen, fourteen…"

She was counting. It flared a memory in his mind of another occasion when the delectable governess had been counting…

"A good idea."

"I have been known to have them."

He smiled, despite himself. Governess she may be, but there was a spark of wit he had not expected from a woman whose job it was to wipe noses and listen to children's prattling.

"I think," Oscar said in a low voice, as Altan attempted to pull away from his father, "they are playing."

Fernsby looked at him wildly. "Playing?"

Oscar nodded. "Hide and seek, if I am not mistaken."

He worked hard not to smile. It was an innocent enough diversion. They had probably played hide and seek when they were children—well, Amelia and Fernsby, at any rate. He had been almost off to university by the time they were old enough to play such things.

It appeared Fernsby did not recall those times either. "But where is Sylvia?"

His voice was full of panic, and Oscar saw Rowena wince as her father's grip tightened.

Perhaps hide and seek, purposefully not knowing where the children were, was not the best idea. Surely the governess knew better than that. Had she not read the rulebook?

"Here I am!"

The four of them turned to see Sylvia appear from a bush.

Fernsby relaxed, releasing his two elder children and rushing toward his youngest, pulling her into his arms. "And you are quite well? You are uninjured?"

"Fernsby," said Oscar quietly. "I think—"

"You are not hurt?" said his brother frantically, kneeling before his youngest daughter and looking over her as though she had been missing for a month.

"Of course, I'm not hurt." Sylvia sounded confused, as well she might. "I was only playing, Papa."

"Fernsby, I think we should—"

But Oscar was prevented from extricating his brother from the situation.

"Miss Kirkpatrick!" roared the master of the house. "Here, now!"

Oscar turned. Any excuse to look at the governess who had so captivated him when they had first been introduced and was now far more of a mystery.

Blackmail was a dirty word, but then it had never been spoken between them, had it?

It didn't need to be. She had something over him, and that was enough. He was sure he would be paying for it later, in gold. Anything to keep his secret from the family.

Besides, it was pleasant to watch the governess stride toward them. She moved with such a sense of purpose. He had noticed that when watching her prance in the ballroom.

It had been…*pleasant*. Oscar was hardly a monk, but he had been without female companionship for a while now. And Miss Kirkpatrick was rather wonderful to look at.

The governess curtseyed as she reached them. "Good afternoon, my lord. Would you like to join us in our game?"

Oscar laughed but quickly stopped himself when his brother glared. *Right, of course. This was no laughing matter. Even if it was.*

"Miss Kirkpatrick," said Fernsby sternly. "I admit myself disappointed in you."

Altan looked between his father and the governess with his typical sullen expression, but the girls stood with wide, confused eyes.

Oscar cleared his throat. "Ah. Fernsby, I wonder if the children should be here for…"

He allowed his voice to tail away delicately. It was unseemly to permit the children to be present as two adults argued, even if it was just the governess.

Just Miss Kirkpatrick with curls of hair escaping her pins and her breasts heaving after her rush over from the bench.

Oh, Lord. Oscar clenched his jaw. *He really had to stop noticing things like that.*

"Disappointed?" Miss Kirkpatrick looked astounded. "My lord, I am confounded."

"Con-Confounded!" Fernsby looked ready to explode, and Oscar jerked his head to the children, telling them to leave before reaching out an arm to placate his brother. "Miss Kirkpatrick, I fail to see why! You have not been following the rules that I clearly laid outin the rulebook you told me not days ago that you understood!"

Thank goodness the children hadn't heard that. The moment Oscar had gestured, they had scampered off to the bench to watch the adults have out their argument.

Oscar glanced at the governess. It was hardly a blistering attack—he was half certain she would have received harsher criticism from previous masters—but from the previously quiet man, it was quite a resounding sign of disapproval.

"I respectfully disagree."

His gaze jerked back to the governess. *She respectfully—how dare she!*

It appeared his brother was of a similar opinion. "You—my word!"

"My lord, you clearly state at the top of page eight in the rulebook that it is required of the children to experience fresh air and exercise, except during circumstances of ill weather which prevent this due to concern of illness," said Miss Kirkpatrick calmly.

Her gaze did not leave her employer, and Oscar's jaw dropped. *What on earth…?*

"In fact," continued the governess doggedly, without any

concern for their finer feelings, "I believe the exact wording is as follows. 'The Fernsby children are to be raised as an English gentlemen and ladies and therefore will need to be brought up with an appreciation for fresh air and exercise. This will require—'"

"What are you talking about?" Oscar had not intended to interrupt, but the whole situation was laughable. Besides, when she spoke like that, so sure of herself, so calm...it did something strange to him. To his stomach. *Perhaps further down.*

"I-I..." spluttered his brother. Fernsby swallowed. "It's the rulebook!"

"It is indeed," said the governess with a smile. "As I said, I understood the rules about going outside. I memorized it, too. For just such an occasion."

Oscar laughed. *How could he help himself?* He had pitied the governess at first, a woman coming here alone, stuck with them. But Miss Kirkpatrick was more than capable of holding her own, and she did so with such elegance, such grace.

"You said that it was important, my lord," the governess was saying softly to his brother. "I wished to respect that and—well, I always memorize important things."

Oscar looked between his brother and the governess. Well, this was a turn up for the books. In all the excitement, all the discussion about rules and regulations and what was permitted and what wasn't...

Fernsby had been outside another ten minutes. Perhaps he should seek further disagreement with the woman, continue the conversation?

"My word," said the baron in wonder. "Goodness."

"Tell me, Miss Kirkpatrick," said Oscar, unable to help himself. Her gaze darted to him, and a wash of self-consciousness swept over him. *Where did that come from?* "How did you decide which parts of the rulebook were important and worthy of such attention?"

He had not intended a teasing air to his question, but how

could he prevent it? She was as witty and as wild as the debutante stepping out for the first time at Almack's.

Miss Kirkpatrick's smile met his own. "Why, I had no such decision, Your Grace. I did not select that section in particular to memorize. I memorized the entire thing."

He laughed. *What nonsense!*

But the governess was not laughing. Oscar's merriment died away on the slow summer breeze that wafted past them.

It appeared Fernsby could not believe her, either. "You must be joking."

"I would never jest about something like that," cut back Miss Kirkpatrick, and now Oscar could see the fire in her eyes.

Yes, this was a matter of pride, though he could not understand why. What did it matter to her whether or not they were impressed? They were impressed, but that was beside the point.

It was only then that Oscar's gaze caught sight of the children sitting on the bench a little way off, waiting for their governess.

Governess. Yes, of course, he must not lose sight of the plain and simple fact that Miss Kirkpatrick was not a young lady with a dowry in the wings and a matrimonial bent on her heart. She was a governess. A servant. She was here to impress, yes, but to keep her position.

It was a sobering thought indeed and one Oscar sorely needed. For a moment there, he thought he was about to…*well. Lose his head.*

"I don't believe you," he said stiffly. "Memorized the whole thing?"

There it was again—that spark in Miss Kirkpatrick's eyes that was not only most becoming but most unbecoming from a servant.

"The Fernsby Rulebook," she said, not taking her eyes from Oscar's own. "Page 1. General etiquette and manners. In due time, my children will entertain at the highest degree as family members of the Duke of Kilerth, and to that end—"

"You wrote this?" said Oscar, turning helplessly to Fernsby as the governess recited.

His brother swallowed. "I did not memorize the damned thing!"

It was impossible not to be impressed now. Oscar turned back to look at the governess, all prickles that she had been disbelieved, and passion for proving herself right.

Where did Miss Kirkpatrick get all this skill from? She was no typical governess unless the profession had undergone significant changes since the time they had been children.

Perhaps this was what one got from a Bureau governess?

"I admit myself impressed," he said, cutting across the determined governess who was still spouting his brother's rubbish. "That is a rare thing for me, Miss Kirkpatrick. Consider yourself honored."

Her gaze met his unflinchingly. "I thank you, Your Grace, but I did not actually intend to impress *you.*"

My word, what a minx. Perhaps she had been sent away from a London family after the Governess Bureau decided society was too public a place for this wild little thing.

She certainly seemed too wild to be a governess.

"I see."

Fernsby's words brought Oscar back to the present. Honestly, she wasn't his servant. She wasn't his anything. That was probably worth remembering.

Glancing at his brother, Oscar was surprised to see he looked perturbed. Surely he wanted the woman to pay attention to the rules, didn't he? Why write the damned thing in the first place if he didn't want her to follow them?

Oscar opened his mouth, but it was his brother who spoke first.

"You…you really don't think hide and seek breaks the rules?"

Miss Kirkpatrick drew herself up. "No, my lord. The rules stipulate the children have time outside, that it is spent on the lawn, always able to see the house. It requires them to play together, a game in which all three can partake, during daylight hours, with no rain or chill in the air. So far, I see no contraventions."

Oscar found Miss Kirkpatrick's speech a rather wonderful excuse to look at her. He supposed most governesses were able to speak this way to their masters, not sternly, but with just enough weight that one felt she had to be obeyed.

But did she have to be…well, so alluring? That day gown was pretty, far more impressive than that of a servant's, and the way her hair was—

"And besides," added the governess in a tone that said plainly that her next few words would settle everything, "fresh air is good for them."

Oscar turned to his brother, who swallowed. The conflict in his heart was plain to see, and though the governess may not understand it, he did. Fernsby's fears lived outside, and yet he knew the children could not be chained down to his terrors. He had to be brave, even in a small way *for them.*

"Right," said Fernsby tightly. "Right. Well, carry on, Miss Kirkpatrick."

Without another word, the master of the house turned and strode as quickly as he could without actually running toward the side door.

Oscar watched him go. Though he would never admit it to anyone, least of all his brother, there was a part of him that wondered whether this governess he had found would not be just as good for him, her master, as she would be the children.

"Miss Kirkpatrick!"

Both she and Oscar turned to look at the children. Sylvia was swinging her legs under the bench, and Altan had risen from it, probably as he had shouted.

"We're bored," he yelled rather unnecessarily. "Can we play hide and seek now?"

"Miss Kirkpatrick," said Oscar quietly. "A word."

She nodded briefly without looking at him. "You start, children. I shall join you shortly—Altan, you seek first."

They obediently started the game, and Miss Kirkpatrick turned to face him. "Yes, Your Grace?"

She was distractingly close, but this time Oscar had a purpose for speaking, and he concentrated on that. It was imperative this was said.

"Please, Miss Kirkpatrick, do not mind my brother."

"I don't," she said, then added with a dry laugh, "that is, obviously I do, he is my master. But I have done my job and done it well. I knew I was acting within the rules he had laid out, and it is good for the children to be like children, even for an hour or so."

It was remarkable to hear some of his own thoughts spoken back to him. "I could not agree more. They used to play a lot when she…"

No, he could not continue. It was not his place to speak about Constance. His sister-in-law was not his responsibility nor his burden.

Though he had not completed his sentence, Miss Kirkpatrick nodded. "Yes, I can see—or feel, perhaps that is more accurate—that a great change has come to this house since the mistress died. It must have been terrible."

Oscar nodded as his eyes watched the children. Rowena was attempting to hide behind a bush, most unsuccessfully. Sylvia had given up finding a good spot and lain under the bench.

"Yes, it was," he said quietly. "A hunting accident."

He could say no more. That week, that awful week…it had gone by in a flash, mere moments, but the repercussions were being felt even to this day.

Miss Kirkpatrick shook her head. "A true tragedy."

"And the children…have you cared for the children of a widower before?"

It was an innocent enough question. It was natural, surely, to be curious about her past.

Miss Kirkpatrick dropped her gaze immediately. "Yes…well, no. I have encountered many, naturally. Widowers are common enough in London."

The vagueness of her answer was so out of keeping with the simplicity of the question that Oscar was rather astonished. He had already opened his mouth to ask a more precise question when their last private conversation surfaced in his memory.

"It...it would be a shame, I think, if anyone was to find out about the truth of a—a certain person's past. Recent past. In London."

Oscar closed his mouth. Miss Kirkpatrick had worded herself very carefully, hadn't she? Very precise, with no mention of names, or specifics, or what precisely would happen if he were ever to get on the wrong side of her.

He was going to have to trust her. The last thing he wished to do was push her beyond her tolerance and discover that the next morning his siblings knew precisely what his last London visit had been for.

*The scandal...*Oscar shivered, despite the warmth of the day. The scandal would make his sister unmarriageable and his brother even more of a laughingstock than he surely would be when the truth of his condition got out.

"Are you quite well, Your Grace?" asked Miss Kirkpatrick sweetly.

Oscar nodded. "I—I am needed back in the house. Excuse me."

Though he did not exactly run back to the house as his brother had done, Oscar chose a rather fast pace, making every effort not to give in to temptation and look back.

CHAPTER SEVEN

July 18, 1813

HELENA COULD NOT remember the last time she had descended this staircase without a smile on her face.

"Good morning, Miss Kirkpatrick," said McLoughlin, the butler, as he passed in the hallway.

"Good morning, Mr. McLoughlin," she replied as he disappeared down a corridor.

She paused at the window overlooking the drive. It was going to be another warm day by the look of it. Not a cloud in the sky, and long shadows drawn on the gravel by the statuesque topiary that lined the path.

The Old Abbey was beautiful, but it was not the only reason her heart sang each morning. This life here, it was…wonderful. Better than she could have dreamed.

The Theatre Royal had been wonderful, too. Helena felt a pang of guilt for being so happy in her new situation. She had clung to that old place so desperately, but that was because she had no idea that such a situation for someone like her could exist.

"Miss Kirkpatrick."

"Mrs. Cantrell," said Helena demurely, dropping into a curtsey. It was always a good idea to pay the housekeeper additional deference, something she had learned in her first week.

Lady Amelia may give the orders, but it was Mrs. Cantrell who ran the place, and Helena had been sure never to forget it.

The housekeeper pulled one of the windowpanes open gently to allow a slight breeze into the hall. "A pleasant day."

"It is indeed," said Helena quietly.

The housekeeper nodded and soon strode away.

Helena breathed in. The scent of wisteria wafted into the hall, a veritable sign of summer. She had asked the children what that beautiful flower was, never having seen such a thing in London.

London. Coated in dirt, cramped, busy, packed with people with no facilities to wash.

Helena's nose wrinkled at the very thought.

Another deep breath and another lungful of wisteria. The gardens were blossoming, releasing their scent in the heat of the day, just ready and waiting for Helena to discover them.

"Ah, Miss Kirkpatrick."

Helena straightened up. She had become lost in the breeze, and Lady Amelia was examining her with a partial smile.

"My lady," she said hastily, dropping into a curtsey.

"The children are on the lawn," said Lady Amelia with a brief smile. "I believe my brother wishes you to accompany them."

Before Helena could acquiesce to her gentle yet pointed request, Lady Amelia placed a bonnet on her head and opened the front door.

"I shall not be long," she said and shut the door behind her.

Helena blinked. *Well, that was something different.* She was not aware of Lady Amelia going for walks in the garden by herself. Based on her interactions with the baron, she was surprised he was comfortable with his sister doing such a thing.

Her heart softened. He was a good man, the baron, though a fearful one. She had seen that when first introduced, and every passing day gave further proof of that.

But despite his fears, he permitted the children to go outside, and now apparently his sister, also. That was some progress—nay, a significant improvement. The duke must have—

Helena forced her thoughts to grind to a halt. Thinking about the duke was not a good idea. It was starting to become far too easy to think about the man who seemed to look right into her soul whenever she was in his presence.

"It...it would be a shame, I think, if anyone was to find out about the truth of a—a certain person's past. Recent past. In London."

She swallowed. It was a rather awkward understanding. So far, the duke had been as good as his word. Even with the increasing provocation of the play's rehearsals for the children, he had not breathed a word of her past to his siblings.

The memory of his dark eyes, that intense expression when he questioned her on the lawn—the glances in the corridors, the moments she had been certain he was about to say something...

Helena clasped her hands, her gaze still along the drive but her eyes seeing nothing.

The Duke of Kilerth. He was a handsome man and a kind one if he was here to help his brother. Yet, he was also a sharp man. An unknowable one for someone like her.

She was so far below him in class, she was surprised he seemed to notice her.

And notice her he did. Helena was no fool; she knew precisely what a gentleman and lady could do together for mutual pleasure. She had heard the moans, the thumps against the wall, the squeaking of the beds in the bedchambers next to hers in the theater.

There was more than one way for an actress to gain her coin.

There had been a few times...well, perhaps more than a few, when she had caught the duke looking at her with just such fire in his eyes.

And then it had died away. He, too, saw the danger.

Helena sighed. The last thing she wished to do was jeopardize whatever happiness she could find here by losing control and saying something foolish before a duke.

The lawn. The children. Going through the front door would be quickest.

Helena closed the front door behind her and felt the immediate wash of heat. As she strode along the path to the west of the house, she saw gardeners moving slowly along the beds, deadheading some flowers and tying back others.

"Miss Kirkpatrick!"

As Helena turned the corner, the sight of all three children met her eyes, and she had to be careful not to laugh. Sylvia was evidently fed up with the heat already, as she had been most days this week. She was lying flat on the lawn, eyes closed, facing the sky, in the small patch of shade afforded them at this time in the morning.

"Are you quite well, Sylvia?" Helena asked as she approached.

Sylvia said with far more gravitas than a child of four should have. "I'm melting."

Helena stifled a laugh.

"You're not melting," said Rowena vaguely. She was seated on the bench in the sunlight but seemed to be ignoring the heat by concentrating on the papers in her hands.

Helena saw they were the part she had chosen for Rowena. A flicker of pride rushed through her. *And Miss Clarke had said she might struggle to keep them entertained!*

"You don't know that I might be melting," came the irritable reply from the youngest Fernsby. "You haven't even looked at me!"

"People don't melt," said Rowena without looking up from her reading.

Sylvia stuck out her bottom lip. "I'm special."

"That you are," said Helena hastily, stepping in before the bickering became a full-blown argument. There was no telling what heat might do to a disagreement. "But I think if you stay in the shade, Sylvia, then you are likely to remain whole and not melty at all."

Sylvia grinned. "All right. Do you think—"

"Miss Kirkpatrick," interrupted Rowena, finally looking up with bright and shining eyes. "Did you write this yourself?" She raised the papers in her hand.

Helena smiled and moved to sit beside her on the bench. "I mean, not exactly."

Rowena waited, and Helena wondered how to explain it.

"Well, there wasn't one perfect play for the three of you," she said slowly, glancing over at Altan, who had so far remained silent. He was standing a little way from the bench, hands in pockets, a heavy scowl across his brow. *He really was his father's son.* "And I know quite a few Shakespearean plays that had elements that were perfect for you, so I simply…mixed them together. Most is *A Midsummer Night's Dream*, but there are parts of *Romeo and Juliet* in there, and *As You Like It*."

Rowena nodded solemnly, as though she had studied the entire corpus of Shakespeare's work and approved of Helena's choices. "I see."

Helena smiled. "Each play would have been performed slightly differently, of course, but…well. I thought you could make it your own."

She bit back what else she had intended to say. It wouldn't do to give the children an idea that she was far more accustomed to putting on plays than…well, anything else. Keeping the secret from the family included the children, too.

"I would love to go to London, to go to the theater," said Rowena wistfully, the pages now in her lap. "I heard my Mama and Papa talking about a Miss Patrick once. She's a great actress, the greatest ever, they said."

Helena's heart did not precisely stop, but it certainly had a few uncomfortable moments. All the hair on the back of her neck stood up, and her mouth was very dry.

"I heard my Mama and Papa talking about a Miss Patrick once. She's a great actress, the greatest ever, they said."

Thank goodness she had chosen a different name! What a scandal it would have been!

"Oh, indeed," she murmured nonchalantly. "And…and your parents themselves thought her very good?"

It was wrong to ask. It was playing to her ego, and she should change the subject entirely.

As it was…

"Yes, indeed, they saw her several times on their visits to London," said Rowena, eyes shining. "They said she became the character, and you almost forgot she was on a stage! She…"

Whether her exuberance came from the warmth of the day, the memories of her parents, or just the opportunity to talk, Helena was unsure. Either way, for the first time since she had arrived at the Old Abbey, Rowena was finally starting to open up.

The fact that it was in praise of her governess, even if the girl did not know it, was beside the point.

Helena felt the warm glow of her charge's praise in her heart. It was wonderful to hear such pleasant things, even more so when the child had no desire to impress. *It was all true.*

"—said they never knew an actress to—"

"All this talk about an actress," interrupted Altan.

Helena looked up as Rowena faltered in her speech.

Altan glared. "What is she to us? I don't want to talk about someone I don't know and will never meet. I'm more worried about me!"

If there hadn't been a thread of genuine concern in his voice, Helena would have dismissed him as simply wishing to draw attention away from his sister. But there was a quaver in his voice she had not heard before, and the sullen look had transformed into one of pain.

"What is it, Altan?" Helena asked gently.

He met her gaze only for a fraction of a second before looking away. "I…well, I have a fight scene in my part. In the play."

"There is, in the second act."

Altan nodded, his cheeks reddening. "Mr. Hough hasn't arrived."

It was such an incomplete explanation of his frustration that

Helena waited for him to continue, but there did not appear to be anymore.

Worse, it appeared this was quite sufficient for his sisters.

"I know," said Rowena in a commiserating tone. "It really is unfair."

Altan nodded, a look of genuine sadness on his face.

Helena looked between the siblings for a moment, then glanced at Sylvia to see whether she could shed some light on the matter. The child appeared to be asleep.

Turning back to the eldest Fernsby child, she said, "And who is Mr. Hough?"

"My fencing tutor," said Altan with a sigh, finally approaching the bench and dropping onto the lawn before them, elbows on his knees and head in his hands. "He's meant to come twice a week, for my lessons, but this is the third week in a row that he hasn't come!"

For any other child, Helena would have found her sympathy somewhat lacking. The idea of having a fencing tutor in the first place was one of luxury, of privilege.

But the Fernsbys were different. Forbidden from exploring their own gardens, riding, visiting the village, even London, the fencing tutor must have been like a lifeline to the world.

"It must be frustrating," said Helena quietly, "but I am sure you are already very good—more than proficient enough for the play."

She had chosen her words carefully and was pleased to see the child perk up. At least, the sullen frown had entirely disappeared, and there was a rather proud look in his eyes.

"I could be excellent," he said, puffing out his chest, which made Helena smile. "But I'll never get better without my tutor. It's so unfair."

"Well, why don't I help you?"

Helena had spoken without thinking, a mistake after being so precise with her choice of words. It had been instinct which had spoken rather than consideration, and to her dismay, she saw the two eldest Fernsbys stare in amazement.

"You?" said Rowena.

"A girl, fencing?" came the voice of Sylvia, who was evidently not asleep.

Helena shrugged. *Well, she was down this path now; she may as well commit.* "Why not?"

She had not realized quite how astonishing this pronouncement would be. Sylvia rose and joined them on the bench, all three children staring in shock.

Ah. Helena tried to compose herself, but only exacerbated her anxiety. Clearly, it was *not* typical amongst the daughters of noble families to learn how to fence.

Well, how was she supposed to know? It was not as though she had ever partaken in a genteel education. In the theater, everyone needed to be able to stage fight. *Half the extras who performed battles in the background were women, for goodness' sake!*

Helena swallowed. "Look, we can work on the basics. I make no promises as to my quality as a fencing tutor, Altan, but I'm better than nothing. Come on."

She spoke those final words as she rose from the bench, steeling herself against the foolish situation she had managed to get herself into. *In for a penny, in for a pound.* If she was a governess from the Bureau with magical talents, or whatever it was, then why not fencing?

Helena pushed away the thought that wondered what Miss Clarke would think of all this. *What Miss Clarke did not know could not hurt her.*

Altan looked as though he was so unimpressed with his governess's pronouncement, he was not going to obey. However, after a relatively stern look from Helena, he rose to his feet.

"Fine," he said. "But only to humor you, Miss Kirkpatrick."

Helena smiled. "That's good enough for me. Right. *En garde.*"

She placed her feet in the *en garde* position, thanking her stars—or more accurately, Mr. Jenkins, who had apparently fenced when at university before joining the theater.

A smile cracked Altan's face, despite himself. "I've never heard a woman say that."

"Well, get used to it!" said Helena, stepping away from the bench to give themselves more room but keeping herself in that initial position. "If you impress me with your footwork, I might let you take a stick and practice with me!"

A look of concentration fell upon Altan's brow, and he matched the governess's steps. He had been challenged, and it appeared that Altan Fernsby was not about to let that lie.

Especially not with his two sisters, now seated on the bench, watching him avidly.

"I want to play," came the predictable response from Sylvia.

Helena opened her mouth but—

"It's not a game, Sylvia!" snapped her brother.

Tears immediately appeared in the corners of Sylvia's eyes. Helena wondered how she did it; it was a remarkable talent, one she would have greatly desired when part of the Theatre Royal.

"Of course you can *practice*, Sylvia, but you must not get in the way of your brother," said Helena calmly. *Just keep her voice calm and light, and the children would follow—wasn't that how it worked?* "There is no harm in practicing."

Both girls rose with squeals of excitement, and Helena caught their brother rolling his eyes—as any brother would.

"But you mustn't interrupt us," Helena added, seeing the potential for conflict immediately. "You can follow us, but this is Altan's lesson."

Altan swelled with pride. Helena wondered when he last received individual attention.

"And—advance!"

She shouted her instruction, and all four of them advanced in a line.

Rowena giggled. "What will Mr. Hough say!"

Helena was far more concerned with what their father might say if he looked out of a window and saw his children being taught to stage fight on the lawn, but there was nothing for it now. They were not hurting anyone, and it was brisk clean exercise.

Precisely what the rulebook required.

"And now we have advanced," she said, "we need to retreat!"

Within a minute, all three Fernsby children were advancing and retreating on the count of four. Sunlight sparkled through the air as dust in the parched lawn became swept up in their movements. Sylvia giggled whole-heartedly and was paying absolutely no attention to her footwork while Altan was concentrating proudly, keeping his head high.

Helena took a deep breath and halted their movements. "Right, Altan, I think you have proven yourself more than adequately. Run inside and retrieve two practice foils."

The look of surprise he gave her was impressive. "I...I thought you were joking! You really think you can teach me?"

"Not your sisters—they need to work on their footwork. But you, Altan? You know what you're doing. Go on."

Altan beamed, revealing a good-natured child underneath all the sullenness and irritability. He scampered off, leaving his sisters moving forward and backward.

"And what are you ladies up to?"

Helena whirled around to see the duke striding across the lawn. *Oh, blast.* After all her efforts to avoid him as much as possible, there he was, just as handsome as ever, with that same sardonic smile as he took in the sight of them.

"I think I would prefer it if you call me Kilerth."

"Ah, Your Grace," said Helena, desperately thinking of what to say. She was doing nothing wrong, she knew that—but that didn't mean she wished for the duke to know what she had been doing. "I—"

"We're learning how to fence!" Sylvia smiled at her uncle, innocence personified.

Helena laughed weakly as the duke smiled at his niece. "Goodness, what a wonderful game for you girls!"

It all could have been saved in that moment. If only Helena

had known how to encourage the duke to go away right then, she could have maintained her calm façade.

There was a clatter behind her, and Helena turned to see Altan running toward them, slightly out of breath with red cheeks—and two foils in his hands.

"Ah," said Helena, unhelpfully. *Why did her mind abandon her now? She had years of plays within her. Couldn't she think of anything more to say than that?*

She turned back to look at Kilerth, who was looking first at her, then at Altan, then at the training foils in his hands.

"Dear God, you're serious!"

Well, there was no going back now. "Well, why not?" Helena said as bravely as she could. Arranging her face in the calmest expression she could manage, she looked at Kilerth. "I am, after all, in charge of the children and their informal education."

Why shouldn't she teach the boy to fence? *Well, stage fight.* And what sort of reason could possibly prevent the girls from partaking, too?

It appeared the duke, however, was not about to forbid the exercise. "Well, this I have to see!" Much to Helena's chagrin, Kilerth strode over to the bench and settled himself upon it. "Carry on!"

He intended to frighten her, Helena could see, but that was where he had greatly underestimated her. Had he berated her, shouted, threatened to report her to her master; those would have all been actions to quell her passion and change her mind.

But giving her an audience?

Helena grinned. "Right girls—you practice your footwork as I showed you while I see how good Altan is with his foils."

She held out a hand to the boy, who wordlessly passed over one of the training foils. He did not look anxious, necessarily, but the attention of his uncle was certainly affecting him far more than it was her. The back of his neck was starting to pink.

Taking a deep breath, Helena whipped the foil through the air in the most impressive of twists and turns. *Precisely what an audience expected.* A stir of satisfaction moved in her stomach as she saw Kilerth's jaw drop.

Perhaps he wouldn't be so quick to underestimate her again.

"Right, Altan," she said, seeing his eyes widen at her movements. "Let me see you advance with your foil."

He obeyed without question, something of a rarity from the boy, and Helena watched him closely. She was no fencing expert, not that she would admit that now with the duke right there watching them, but she had spent enough time with a stage sword in her hand to know talent when she saw it.

"You're good," she said shortly.

Altan glowed. "You think so? Papa never comes to watch my practicing."

It took all Helena's restraint not to look at Kilerth. "Well, I think we should do more practice, so he'll be even more impressed when he does. Here's one your Mr. Hough probably doesn't know."

Audiences had always aahed and cheered whenever Helena had performed this one—a clever little flick of the wrist that was almost certain to disarm your opponent.

At least, she thought hastily as she showed Altan, *a stage opponent.* What it would do to someone carrying a real blade…

"Like this?" Altan screwed up his face as he concentrated.

Helena nodded approvingly. "Just like that. And here, if you wish to take a blow—"

"Take a blow?" The boy glanced at his uncle. "Why would I want to take a blow?"

A little late, Helena recalled the goals of stage fighting and fencing were opposites.

She laughed, thinking quickly. "Well, I was thinking of the play! I would not wish you to hurt anyone."

Altan nodded solemnly. "I understand. Again?"

Though it was a warm day, Helena was able to forget the heat in the excitement of teaching Altan a few things she had been taught. She was not, however, able to ignore the gaze of the

Duke of Kilerth that followed her around the lawn wherever she went.

He said nothing, made no movement when she had darted across the lawn and moved the girls out of harm's way, nor chastised her for teaching what was surely contrary to fencing principles.

No. He just watched her.

Helena swallowed her concerns. Kilerth was not going to reveal her past, not if he did not wish for an equally scandalous revelation.

"Ah, not quite," she said, stepping toward Altan. "It's more like—"

"Here," said Kilerth in his impressive voice. "Let me show you, Altan."

He had already risen from the bench, taking the foil from the boy without hesitation and holding it up before him—directed straight at Helena.

Helena smiled. How like a man to expect her to demure at a challenge—how like a gentleman to think it was a roaring great jest. But surely a duke should know not to play games with governesses.

Heart pounding and acting before she could think, Helena advanced. *"En garde!"*

Eyes wide at the surprise, Kilerth parried her and twisted around, flicking up his foil toward her chest, but Helena was too quick. All those years of training had paid off, and she could see as Kilerth almost stumbled that he had not kept up his fencing.

The foils clashed.

"I see you have unexpected skill," said Kilerth with a smile, his eyes dancing.

Helena returned his smile. "Prodigious skill, actually."

Twisting rapidly and making her skirts fly out with a flourish, she raised her foil again and awaited his next advance.

Applause. The children were watching, entertained by their governess and their uncle's game.

Helena swallowed as she looked into the eyes of the man before her. This was dangerous, she knew it, and she knew precisely why. The heat between them was more than the heat of the day; it was something else. Something deeper.

But she couldn't help herself. Being free to move again, stepping with purpose, flourishing, pandering to an audience…

It was in her blood. If she wasn't much mistaken, in a strange way, it was in the duke's, too.

Kilerth's advance was swift, and he grabbed her by the waist, ducking under her wild swing. "But you forget," he murmured in her ear, "you may know how to fence, but I know how to fight."

Helena looked up into his eyes, her chest rising and falling against his in the exertion of the moment. Sandalwood filled her nose as his heartbeat thumped against her body. His hand was on her waist. *Her waist! She had a duke's hand on her waist!*

It would have made the perfect stage kiss if she had entirely thrown caution to the wind, but thankfully—

"I didn't know you could do that in fencing."

Helena and Kilerth broke apart immediately.

"Well, Altan," said Helena with a dry laugh, ensuring she did not look at the duke. "I admit, neither did I! But then the duke has had more training in fighting than I."

She raised an eyebrow. Surely he would understand. The training he must have undertaken before stepping into that boxing ring in the East End of London must have been extensive.

And he must have worked extensively to hide it from his family.

Kilerth smiled ruefully. "Check and mate, Miss Kirkpatrick. Your point."

Handing the foil back to the boy, the duke walked off without a second glance.

Helena was more interested in trying to catch her breath. The fight, if that was what one could call it, had been brief, but Kilerth had stirred her soul in a way most unexpected.

And never to be repeated. She should never have allowed herself to get into that sort of position in the first place. What would his lordship think if he had spotted his brother sword fighting with his governess? Worse, his governess in the arms of his brother?

"Can you teach me that?"

Helena looked over at the bench. Sylvia had dozed off again, the excitement and the heat clearly exhausting her, but Rowena had bright, excited eyes, and Altan was gazing at his governess with newfound respect.

With a smile, Helena could never say no to a challenge. "Of course."

CHAPTER EIGHT

July 30, 1813

O SCAR TOOK A deep breath and worked hard to keep his voice steady, despite the great temptation to bellow or worse— use his fists.

"What do you mean," he said slowly, "you cannot find them?"

His valet, Rondell, blinked nervously, hands twisting together. "Well, Your Grace, I definitely brought five waistcoats with us because I thought three would be adequate, but one additional one for special occasions, a ball, or something, and then another in case—"

"And you cannot find a single one?" interrupted Oscar. *Really, this was laughable! Where were his clothes?*

They were standing in the dressing room adjoining the second-largest guest chamber—the largest had become Amelia's the moment she had moved into the Old Abbey last year.

Getting dressed should never be so complicated, Oscar thought savagely. At Riverside Manor, all he had to worry about was throwing on a shirt and breeches.

But here, he was in *society.* True, it was only his siblings, but still. Waistcoat and cravat and jacket, at all times. It was enough to make a man scream.

Oscar forced down the rising frustration. Though his temper burned bright, this was not the time to release it. When at home, he could take out his frustrations on the homemade gymnasium or in the local ring. No one questioned him there. One did not question the Duke of Kilerth when one lived on his estate. When in London, there was always a ring that would accept a challenge from the Michaels name, safe in his anonymity.

But here, at Fernsby's…

"I am so sorry, Your Grace," said Rondell looking wretched. "I was absolutely certain there would be one ready for you this morning, but—"

"No, no, it's not your fault, Rondell," Oscar said heavily. Goodness knows his valet was not to blame. "It'll be the laundry here, I suppose. The waistcoats will be down there in a wet, soggy pile. God's sakes, you can never trust the laundry at another man's house."

His valet looked relieved, as well he might, but Oscar had spoken the truth. Though he was vaguely aware of the complexities of the laundry—wetting and scrubbing and mangling and hanging out to dry, then some sort of ironing with starch, and…there was something else…

Still. Complex though the process might be, the damned women down there shouldn't be able to lose five waistcoats.

A bead of sweat trickled down the side of Rondell's forehead, and a strange discomfort slid into Oscar's stomach.

Had he managed to strike such fear into his servants, they became genuinely afraid of him, or worse, his temper? Were his servants anxious around him, waiting to be shouted at?

It was a rather unpleasant thought. Oscar did not think of himself as a bad person.

But the true measure of a man was surely how his inferiors felt about him, not his equals. Oscar's sense of discomfort spread from heart to stomach. He would have to think on this later.

Right now, he needed a waistcoat.

"What's the time?" he said abruptly.

His valet glanced quickly at his pocket watch. "Just past eight o'clock, Your Grace."

Oscar nodded. It was early, but not so early the servants wouldn't be up. He had time before his siblings went downstairs for breakfast to investigate. *Find a damned waistcoat.*

"Don't wait for me," Oscar said to his valet, picking up a shirt and pulling his arms through it hastily. "I can do my own cravat when I return."

Rondell blinked in unflattering surprise. "You—you can?"

Oscar laughed. "I am not totally useless, Rondell! I can tie a semblance of a knot."

The valet nodded. "As you wish, Your Grace."

Throwing open the door to the corridor, Oscar strode down it, breeches and socks on but boots left behind, his fingers absent-mindedly buttoning his shirt. Well, if this is what it took to find a damned waistcoat, then he would do it—but it did feel rather foolish for a duke to go hunting in the laundry for his own clothes.

As he turned a corner, a strange sight appeared before him: Amelia. *Up at this hour?*

Stranger still, Amelia was not leaving her room but rather opening the door to return.

"Amelia," he said by way of greeting.

His sister started, turning with a look of terror that relaxed. "Kilerth. You frightened me."

Oscar stopped and grinned. "What are you doing up so early?"

His smile faded. Her eyes darted down the corridor as though terrified he was not alone, and there was a hunted look on her face.

She slipped into her bedchamber and closed the door to a crack while still peering out. "What?"

Oscar frowned. "I said, what are you doing up so early?"

Only now did his gaze take in the details of his sister's rather disheveled look. Her hair was not pinned back but was flowing over a shawl on her shoulders, and she had her riding boots on—boots that were damp.

"Early walk?"

Amelia smiled nervously. Yes, there was definitely embarrassment on her face, which Oscar could not understand. It was not like her to be up this early, but it was hardly a crime.

"Where have you been?" he asked, dropping his voice.

"I don't—I didn't..." Amelia's voice trailed off as she glanced down the corridor once more. "I didn't want Fernsby to know. I went for a walk in the gardens. A chance to stretch my legs, go beyond the house."

The tension that had been building in Oscar's stomach immediately melted away. There was nothing nefarious in Amelia—he could not imagine her even lying!

"He is getting better," Oscar said quietly. "Thanks to you, I think."

Amelia's smile was wan. "I know he is, but you know how he gets if I go out on my own. The last thing I would wish is to cause a relapse simply because I wished to walk in the arboretum rather than the lawn."

Oscar nodded. *She had a point.* Fernsby's recovery, if they could call it that, for he still did not entirely understand what had been wrong with him, was slow but steady. Any sharp shock would surely put back that growth.

"Good idea," he said quietly. "I might join you one of these days. I feel the need to stretch my legs myself."

"Oh no, you don't have to—I mean," Amelia corrected hastily, a blush tinging her cheeks. "I will be quite safe, and you do not need to chaperone me."

Oscar waved his hand. "Oh, no, 'tis no trouble. I shouldn't just be letting you wander off on your own, anyway, even here. You're my sister. I'll see you at breakfast."

He started back along the corridor as Amelia called after him.

"Where are you going?"

"Off hunting a waistcoat!" Oscar threw back over his shoulder.

It took but a few minutes to wander downstairs and along a servants' corridor to the kitchens. He did not know the way, as such; he had never been in the servants' quarters of his brother's home, but all corridors led back to the warm, steaming kitchen eventually.

Oscar breathed in appreciatively. He would say this about Fernsby—he knew how to choose a cook. Every meal had been delicious, and it appeared the kitchen staff had been up for hours, based on the lines and lines of prepared food on one counter. A man who must be the cook was berating a kitchen maid for the inconsistency of her glaze, and a rather harassed girl was taking dirty mixing bowls through to the scullery at a great pace.

"Your Grace!"

The startled shriek rent through the air as Mrs. Cantrell marched toward him.

"Mrs. Cantrell," said Oscar with a wry smile, nodding.

The housekeeper dropped into a low curtsey. "Your Grace, what on earth are—your valet should have asked you for anything you wanted. We would have been happy to oblige!"

The scullery maid had looked around at Mrs. Cantrell's words, dropping a wooden spoon. This was followed by a round of expletives from the cook as he turned around, which trailed off into a strangled yell as he saw his master's brother standing in his kitchen.

"Y'Grace," he said nervously, bowing low.

Mrs. Cantrell tutted and gestured to the duke. They stepped through the kitchen and into the servants' hall, where a few footmen were finishing their breakfast.

"Oh, settle down," she snapped as they hurriedly attempted to wipe their mouths, put down their cutlery, stand up, and bow all at the same time. "His Grace has not come down here for the likes of you!"

Oscar tried not to smile. She was the queen of her domain, and he should not forget it.

"Mrs. Cantrell," he said in a low voice that was stern but not unkind. "My valet cannot retrieve what he requires, and so I have come here to find it. Where is your laundry?"

The housekeeper blanched, her face pale.

"The laundry," amended Oscar hastily. "*The* laundry, where laundry is done!"

Wordlessly, Mrs. Cantrell pointed to a door.

"Thank you," said the duke, temper rising again as he stepped toward the place that waistcoats went to disappear.

He would be civil, but he would also be firm. This could not be permitted to continue. He would speak to the girl in here, tell her forcefully he expected far better service when—

The door had opened, Oscar had taken a step forward, and in the quiet of the room that smelled of starch and lavender was...

Miss Kirkpatrick. She was seated quietly in a corner on a wide-backed wooden chair, a wicker basket by her feet and a gown in her lap. She had been concentrating on threading a needle with a delicate white thread but looked up politely as he stormed in.

Oscar stared. *Her—here?* It was such an unexpected sight he was utterly lost for words. The pounding pulse of his temper was transformed into something else—something he knew well but certainly should not be feeling for a governess.

"Hello, Kilerth," Miss Kirkpatrick said softly.

Oscar pushed the door shut without looking away from Miss Kirkpatrick. Her hair was woven into a long plait with a red ribbon at the end, and the intimacy of that alone was enough to confuse his mind.

"Arghhhh..." *Blasted hell, could he say nothing more useful than that?* "I just—this is the laundry room. And I—waistcoats. Rondell."

Miss Kirkpatrick looked at him politely as embarrassment shot through Oscar.

Was that all he could manage? He had danced at Almack's, met

Prinny several times, and taken some truly awful hits in the boxing ring. *And he couldn't construct a sentence when faced with a pretty girl?*

"I beg your pardon?" said the governess politely, lowering her hands onto her lap.

Oscar swallowed. *He had to get a grip.* He was a duke. He was not going to permit himself to fall apart just because he wanted to...*well...*

"What are you doing?" *Yes, those were words, and they made a sentence. Good.*

Miss Kirkpatrick, however, looked rather confused. "Why, mending a gown."

She lifted up the gown as though explaining it to a fool. Perhaps that's what he was: a fool. Oscar had never felt so off-kilter in a conversation before, let alone one with a servant.

But Miss Kirkpatrick was more than a servant, wasn't she? She was a governess, and that was more than a servant. And she was...more than a governess, somehow. Eloquent. That moment between them when they had been fencing...

Oscar swallowed. *He had only dreamed about it once. Once had been enough.*

Though his heart pounded, he was not going to be frightened away, not by a governess.

"I can see that," he said gruffly, "but why? I was not aware it was required of governesses to mend—is that Amelia's gown?"

White with silver beading. Very exquisite, very delicate work. *Why on earth—*

"Ah, yes, Lady Amelia's gown," said Mrs. Cantrell.

She had bustled into the room with no sign of embarrassment, though Oscar was absolutely certain she had been listening at the door.

"I know it's not part of Miss Kirkpatrick's duties," rattled on the housekeeper, leaving Oscar no chance to say he did not need the details, "but it is such a delicate piece, the last thing I would wish is for it to become damaged in the attempt at a repair—"

"Yes, fine," said Oscar hastily, trying to stem the flow from Mrs. Cantrell. He was almost sure Miss Kirkpatrick forced down a smile. "What I meant was—"

"And there was no one else who could do it—at least, not that I would *trust* to do it," continued Mrs. Cantrell, showing no regard for the duke. "We were going to send it out, and you know what sort of expense that could be, but then Miss Kirkpatrick said she could do it, and she does seem remarkably talented with a needle and—"

"Yes, fine, thank you, Mrs. Cantrell," Oscar said with an air of finality. "Now go away."

The housekeeper dipped a low curtsey and returned to the servants' hall without another word. The duke shut the door behind her and sighed.

"Do you always speak to people like that?"

Oscar turned to see Miss Kirkpatrick examining him closely. "What do you mean?"

"Well," said the governess. "As though they don't matter."

Opening his mouth, Oscar found that once again, no words came out. He closed it again for fear of looking a fool—though it appeared he had already managed to do that.

A strange prickly sort of feeling was creeping up his spine and into his mind, making a detour to his heart at the same time. It was an emotion he did not recognize. *Guilt.*

Lord, he had not felt that emotion in years. Had he really spoken so rudely?

His mind flashed back to the valet he had so clearly upset just a few minutes ago. Was he a monster as a master? Was he truly that bad?

"I don't think she doesn't matter," he said lamely.

Miss Kirkpatrick raised an eyebrow. "But you don't think she does matter?"

Oscar swallowed. This conversation had entirely got away from him. He had only come here to find a waistcoat, for goodness' sake! Now he was being forced to re-examine the way he thought about…well, servants.

His mind turned to his own housekeeper, Mrs. Rowland. Did he speak to her rudely? She had been with him now for a few years, and he had never received any complaints.

But then who, Oscar thought wryly, *would complain to a duke?*

Miss Kirkpatrick filled the silence. "Yes, this is your sister's gown. Apparently, there is going to be a ball, and she wished to have the beading on the left mended in time for it."

Oscar stared. Each of the words Miss Kirkpatrick had said made sense, and in any other context, the whole sentence would have done as well.

But a ball? Here? At Fernsby's place? Now?

"A-A ball? But there hasn't been a ball since—not for the last—are you *sure*?"

It did not seem possible. Fernsby had been resolutely against balls for the last year, ever since Constance had died. He and Amelia had understood it at first. He was in mourning, the whole family was. But after six months, the expectation had been…

Fernsby was not well. He was not entirely recovered. Was a ball really a good idea?

"You are quite sure," said Oscar, taking a step toward Miss Kirkpatrick, his voice finally level. "You are *very sure* my brother considers this plan of Amelia's acceptable?"

Miss Kirkpatrick smiled. "Well, I was saying to your brother only yesterday that the children are doing very well at getting plenty of fresh air, but they probably needed a little socializing, especially Altan. It will not be long before he is at school, of course."

Oscar stared. The governess was taking liberties left, right, and center. Hadn't Fernsby been terrified about the idea of his children leaving the house and going to school? Had no one told her that topic was completely off-limits?

"And your brother was naturally nervous about sending the children away to visit friends, relations, that sort of thing," continued Miss Kirkpatrick with a wry smile, "and so I gently pointed out, only a suggestion of course, that there was no need to send them away at all. People could come here."

Oscar felt his mouth fall open, but there was nothing he could do to stop it.

It was…it was a brilliant idea. A genius one. Why hadn't he thought of that? Instead of his brother being cooped up in the house, afraid or unwilling to go out, *bring the people here.* A ball was safer than a house party, after all: one evening, plenty of people to entertain each other, give his brother a chance to practice at polite society once more.

It was incredible. She was incredible.

Despite all his efforts the last months and Amelia's for almost a year, Miss Kirkpatrick had achieved more with Fernsby in just a few weeks.

Oscar's gaze moved over her and saw with surprise that her fingers on her left hand were red and sore. The needle, of course.

"You shouldn't be doing that," he said gruffly.

Miss Kirkpatrick looked at the gown. "What do you mean?"

"You…you're hurting your hands," said Oscar quietly. *Why did it matter so much?* That it did, he could not deny. The idea that she was in pain, all for his sister's stupid gown… "That's servants' work."

The moment the words were out of his mouth, Oscar saw his mistake. *Damn and blast it; he was standing here in the servants' quarters!* Who knew how many servants were behind that door listening in, as Mrs. Cantrell had been!

The smile on Miss Kirkpatrick's face was too knowing. "Ah. Someone ought to have told you, Your Grace. I *am* a servant."

When had he stopped thinking of Miss Kirkpatrick as a servant? When he had noticed the curve of her body more than her purpose in this household. When he had seen the spark of her wit, been blackmailed by her about his boxing, pulled her into his arms when fencing…

How could he think of her as a servant after all that?

And now he took the time to look at her this morning, he saw she was wearing another beautiful gown, far unlike the gray, dull fabric he would have expected a governess to afford.

It was strange. Oscar had never seen a servant, or anyone below the rank of a countess, dressing almost as richly as Amelia.

Miss Kirkpatrick met his gaze steadily. She was a complete mystery to him, Oscar realized. What did he know about her, other than she was awfully familiar when they had met?

He had asked about her, of course, just in passing. But no meaningful information had ever passed her lips. Perhaps he should take a slightly different tack.

With the well-practiced art of a rake, Oscar smiled. "Looking after children, fencing, now mending clothes...Miss Kirkpatrick, I do declare that you can do everything."

Rather than be cowed before him, however, Miss Kirkpatrick did the most disobliging thing and smiled. "Yes," she said. "I can."

Heavens alive, what was she doing to him? Oscar had never considered himself a true rakehell, to be sure, though he had experienced his fair share of women over the years. None of them had tempted him to offer anything but his momentary protection, and not a single lady of good breeding had tempted him to offer...well, himself.

Yet, here he was, standing before a *governess* of all people, unable to think of anything to say. Her gaze had dipped to her mending as though he wasn't there. As though he wasn't worth her notice.

Oscar's jaw tightened. Though he could not put his finger on what it was—and he would dearly love to—he could not explain just how Miss Kirkpatrick was able to get under his skin like this. It was most infuriating.

And he knew her...

Or at least, he thought he did. Their paths had definitely crossed before. She had evidently attended one of his boxing bouts, for she knew all about that.

Perhaps Miss Kirkpatrick had become so much a part of the household at the Old Abbey, Oscar thought frantically, *that his memories were merging*. Perhaps he had never seen her before she had arrived here.

"This gown is beautiful," said Miss Kirkpatrick into the silence. Her fingers had returned to work, carefully threading beads onto the silver needle and passing them down the thread. "One of the most beautiful I have seen, I think."

Oscar nodded, unwilling to trust his mouth at this moment. *Miss Kirkpatrick*. She had won over everyone, it seemed. The children liked her; the servants called on her for complex tasks; his brother was won over by her arguments. Even his sister appeared to like her, and they all knew how hard Amelia was to please.

"I suppose they teach you all those skills," Oscar found himself saying. "At the Governess Bureau."

"Oh, no," said Miss Kirkpatrick distractedly as she concentrated on pushing the needle through the fine fabric. "Before the Bureau."

"Really—where?"

Miss Kirkpatrick looked up. "Pardon?"

Oscar smiled. *Finally, he had her on the back foot.* "All your skills, your multitude of talents. It must have taken real dedication, practice. Rehearsals. Where did you learn them?"

Yes, she was definitely flustered now. There was a crease of concern between her eyes, and the governess looked at her work to avoid his gaze.

"Oh, here and there," she said nonchalantly. "You know how it is, Kilerth. Some skills just burst out of you. Some you have to work for. A real fight."

A smile lifted the corners of her lips.

Oscar swallowed. *There it was—the reminder that she held over him a power he simply did not over her.*

His boxing secret must stay with her, it was imperative. Call it a shot across the bow. Whatever it was, Miss Kirkpatrick did not want to hear any more questions.

"Did you come here because a button is loose?"

Oscar jerked his head toward her. "What?"

Only then did he become conscious that he was improperly dressed. Here he was, talking with a woman on her own, and he hadn't even buttoned his shirt right!

Fingers scrabbling to give him some decency, Oscar recalled precisely why he had come here in the first place: to find a waistcoat.

"Waistcoat," he said stupidly. "I need—waistcoat."

"But if you're in no hurry, Kilerth," added Miss Kirkpatrick, causing a smile on Oscar's face as she said his name, "you can always join me."

Though her fingers were still busy at work with Amelia's gown, she nodded at the chair beside her. Oscar swallowed. He had only come for a waistcoat, he tried to remind himself. A waistcoat. That was all.

It did not matter. Oscar found himself seated in the proffered chair, listening to Miss Kirkpatrick. He may contribute to the conversation, but she was doing a marvelous job at it.

"—coming on well, though Sylvia struggles learning any lines," said the governess softly as she pulled at her thread. "I think Altan takes it upon himself to help her, which is all to the good."

Oscar nodded. He could listen to this woman read the prices of fish, and she would still captivate him.

"All in all, I would say progress is good," she said with a smile.

"Good," Oscar said. They were so close, their knees were almost touching. "I suppose it's a good way to keep the children entertained."

Miss Kirkpatrick laughed. "Yes, it's always entertained me rather well."

"You are very good for keeping them entertained," said Oscar honestly. Goodness, how was she drawing this nonsense from him? "The theater is so tiresome."

A shadow passed across her face. "What do you mean?"

Oscar had not meant much by it; just an offhand comment to keep the conversation going. He was rescued from having to explain himself, however, by the entrance of his sister.

"Ah, Miss Kirkpatrick, there you are," said Amelia breezily. She had pinned her hair, and her shoes were clean and unmarked. There was no hint she had been outside whatsoever. "And when do you believe the gown will be ready?"

Miss Kirkpatrick had risen. "Why, it is ready now, my lady—and I really should be going upstairs to care for the children. Your Grace."

With a small curtsey, she passed the gown to Amelia and slipped out of the room.

A leaden weight dropped into Oscar's stomach. *And just like that, she was gone.* It was a crying shame; he had barely noticed how enjoyable the conversation was until it was over.

"Did you really need the dratted thing right this second?" he snapped.

Amelia's eyes widened. "No, I just asked—why, did you wish to speak to her yourself? Goodness, what about?"

Oscar opened his mouth but then closed it again. Miss Kirkpatrick held the truth of his time in London over his head. The last thing he should be doing was spending more time with her. Perhaps it was fortunate that Amelia had come upon them.

"I am looking," he said defensively, "for my waistcoat."

Amelia laughed. "I tried to tell you before you stormed down the corridor earlier. They were brought up with my day gowns accidentally—come on, they're in my room."

CHAPTER NINE

August 4, 1813

IT WAS DIFFICULT not to watch with a critical eye. For the first time, Helena knew what Mr. Tobias had meant when he said that watching a rehearsal was like watching a newborn foal attempt to gallop.

Sylvia sat decidedly. "I'm tired."

Helena suppressed a smile. "I am sure you are."

"And I don't want to keep going," said Sylvia insistently, her voice echoing in the ballroom where they were rehearsing. "I don't have to, do I?"

"How can I practice without her?" demanded Rowena. She had attempted to pin her hair up, as her aunt did, with uncertain results. It looked fine, but whenever she moved or spoke, another few strands of hair escaped. "Miss Kirkpatrick, tell her she has to rehearse with me!"

"You will need to use your imagination," said Helena, holding out a hand to the younger child. "I know you can do it, Rowena. I have been very impressed with your acting."

The middle Fernsby child, ignored by most in the household, drew herself up smartly. It must be difficult not being the heir and not being the baby of the family.

"And you have done very well to learn your lines," she added. "I especially noticed the warmth you had in that last line. Why don't you show me again?"

Sylvia slipped her hand into the governess's as they watched her elder sister on the stage.

Well. Helena had called it a stage when they had come in here to practice when the sun had simply become too hot. It *would* be a stage, certainly, but at the moment, it was just her rather rough markings with chalk.

"Roro!" Her little sister waved as she started her lines.

Helena tried hard not to laugh. It must be distracting, attempting to recite Shakespeare with all the feeling it required while one's sibling was waving vigorously opposite you.

But Rowena kept calm, and it did not detract from her performance.

"Careful," Helena said after a few moments as she watched the girl's feet move. "I think you just slipped off the stage."

Rowena's face flushed, but she continued with her lines, merely moving her feet so they were once again within the fabricated stage.

The ability to continue under criticism or taunts from the audience was a rarity. There was clearly more to Rowena than initially met the eye.

"Is it time for my battle yet?" Altan rushed onto the chalk-marked stage, cheeks flushed, training foil in hand, clearly eager to wave his sword about.

His sister scowled. "You interrupted my best lines!"

"Who cares about your lines?" Altan waved his sword about, his imagination clearly picturing it being twice as heavy and twenty times as sharp. "My fight scene—"

"Miss Kirkpatrick, he's doing it again!"

Helena had never believed she would slot into the role of governess so easily, but in just a few short weeks, she knew what that tone of voice preceded.

"Altan, stop it. Rowena, step away from your brother," she said instantly, dropping Sylvia's hand as she stepped forward. "I'm ending this rehearsal if you cannot behave."

The two children looked stubborn at first, but with a glare from their governess, the boy allowed his sword arm to fall by his side, and the girl took a few steps back.

"All I asked was whether it was time for my battle yet," Altan said petulantly.

*Governesses—real governesses—*thought Helena, *have the patience of saints.* How on earth did they put up with this? How was she going to?

And then, in an instant, without her doing anything, and utterly to her confusion, it was over. Rowena grinned at her brother, and he smiled sheepishly back.

"You did look splendid waving that sword," she said admiringly. "Can I hold it?"

"Of course," said Altan immediately, holding it out.

Helena stood there watching them, utterly lost. She had forgotten this part of being a child. Frederick and she had had their arguments, to be sure, and she was sure they had ended them. How precisely, she had forgotten.

Rowena was waving the blade about. "Like this?"

"Are you two ready to start rehearsing that scene again?" said Helena, stepping forward gingerly. Rowena looked as though she could take out someone's eye with that blade, albeit a training one. "That way, we can practice your big entrance, Altan, and you can do your speech again, Rowena."

"And what am I supposed to do?"

Helena smiled at Sylvia. "You have the most important job. You're our audience."

Helena tried to tuck a curl behind her ear. Even in here, it was starting to become uncomfortably humid. "Let me show you," she said.

It was rather like being back at the Theatre Royal, Helena thought. "Building tension in a scene is rather like baking a cake."

Altan frowned. "How do you bake a cake?"

Helena hesitated. *Perhaps not the best example for the heir of a duke.* "What I mean is, it's like running a race. You don't want to use all your energy at the beginning, or you'll not be able to get to the end."

Rowena seemed to understand. "So, if we become too violent too quickly, the ending won't work?"

Helena nodded. "If you break the tension too early, no one is able to enjoy it properly. You have to remember that your audience is there, waiting for you to tell the story."

The two older Fernsbys nodded. They all glanced at Sylvia. She had fallen asleep.

"Your future audience, that is," amended Helena with a chuckle.

"Now, back to that line you love so much, Rowena, the one with all that alliteration," said Helena, taking a few steps back. "When you are ready."

The children moved to their places obediently, and Helena felt a rush of joy overwhelm her. She had not realized it was possible to feel this alive.

The theater had been her first love—her first and only. Treading the boards had given her fulfilment she had never known before. Being forced from it had felt like death.

Yet here, in the safety and protection of the Old Abbey, she had found something else. Something deeper. A joy that came with this play, these children, that she had not expected.

This much joy, away from a theater…well, she had created her own theater here.

Rowena stepped forward, her face sorrowful and her eyes expressional. "When all love's lost loves linger here in this dull void…"

Helena watched as she completed her speech, and her brother broke onto the scene, their lines mingling beautifully and precisely how she had imagined. It was wonderful. They were incredible. What were the chances that children of a baron would have such talent?

"Goodness," said a voice behind her. "I had no idea the play was so advanced."

"Anny Amelia?" Sylvia opened her eyes. "We're doing a play, you know."

"Yes, I can see that," said Lady Amelia with a knowing smile at the governess.

Helena dropped into a low curtsey. She had not heard the woman come in and did not know yet precisely what the sister of her master thought about her. Did she approve of this play, or was she concerned it was leading her nieces and nephew down a scandalous path?

Lady Amelia clearly had a great influence over her brother, and if Helena wished to remain here under their protection, it was clear that she would need his sister's approbation.

"You have been working hard, Miss Kirkpatrick," said Lady Amelia lightly.

Helena curtseyed again. "I thank you, my lady, but the real credit must go to the children. They are the ones who have been working hard."

Lady Amelia raised an eyebrow. "Indeed. You have them rehearsing on the floor until the stage arrives?"

"We already have a stage!" cried Rowena, full of enthusiasm. "See, Miss Kirkpatrick drew it for us!"

Helena opened her mouth but then decided against it. She was about to try to explain, but Lady Amelia had already taken a few steps forward to examine the "stage."

"Is that chalk?" she said sharply. "Chalk, on the ballroom floor?"

Helena swallowed her irritation. *Did the woman think she went about destroying the home of her master?*

Smiling beneficently, she said, "Indeed it is, my lady. When I spoke to Mrs. Cantrell about the best way to go about marking a stage on the ballroom floor, she suggested chalk and procured some for me herself."

"Ah."

"Mrs. Cantrell assures me it will be easily removed in minutes," Helena added for good measure. "In plenty of time for the ball."

"The ball—yes, not long now!" A smile broke across Lady Amelia's face. It could not be more obvious that she was desperate for the ball to arrive, for the Old Abbey to be full of people again, to converse with a gentleman to whom she was not related. "I don't suppose the play would be ready by then?"

Helena hesitated. Tempting as it was to please her ladyship, if this rehearsal was anything to go by, they were nowhere near ready.

"I would consider it a great personal favor," said Lady Amelia with a look Helena was starting to privately consider "the Fernsby smile."

If only Helena could depend on the children to learn the rest of the play in double time—but it wasn't possible. All she would be doing was putting them in a discomforting position, and the three youngest Fernsbys had suffered enough already this last year. The last thing they needed was to be trotted out before all and sundry to perform a play that was not finished.

She knew what Miss Clarke would say, of course.

"Your employers are there to be obeyed," Miss Clarke had said on Helena's last day of training at the Bureau. "I do not wish to hear you have been obstinate or disobedient, merely because you have not wished to do something. Bureau governesses are obliging."

"But what if you are asked to do something you can't!" A fresh-faced governess whose name Helena had not known spoke up.

Miss Clarke treated them to a rare smile. "Once you say yes, you'll always find a way. Because you have to."

Helena took a deep breath and looked straight into the eyes of Lady Amelia. "No. I am afraid not, my lady. The play will have to be performed after the ball."

She braced herself for an outraged response.

Lady Amelia shrugged. "Ah, well, it is probably better that

way. Now I think about it, we would have struggled to fit your stage in here along with the musicians, the food, drink, and all the guests. And we must have room for dancing, of course."

Helena blinked. This was not what she thought was the natural response from a lady. Where was the tantrum, the demands, the expectation that the world would fall into line?

"But you will perform it after the ball?"

"Y-Yes," said Helena. *Blast, she needed to keep calm.* She was the greatest actress London had ever known; she would control herself. "For the servants, yes. I don't think His Grace would like—his *lordship* would like his children to be paraded before strangers."

She had corrected herself quickly, but surely their sister must have caught her mistake.

Blast! Curse her tongue for allowing thoughts to dictate her speech!

It was only because her mind had drifted to Kilerth—to the duke—so often. If only she had been dull and insolent when he had interrupted her mending her ladyship's dress. Then she would not have caught his attention so.

She needed to stop thinking about Kilerth. *The duke!* She needed to focus on the conversation she has having right now!

Lady Amelia was examining her carefully. "You know, I have never met a governess who…"

Helena held her breath. *Was this it?* Was this going to be the end of her short governess career? Would she be back on the streets of London by this evening, with nowhere to go and no one to turn to?

"…who had such a deep understanding of the theater," continued Lady Amelia. "From where did you get such experience?"

All she had to was stay calm. That's what Helena tried to tell herself as she gazed into the face of a woman who could, by her mere curiosity, unmask her as an actress.

Unless Lady Amelia already knew. Unless it was not a random question as it seemed, and she was giving Helena a chance to confess?

Helena swallowed. Her ladyship was surely guessing—that, or she was genuinely curious. How long did Mrs. Cantrell say the baron's sister had been here, a virtual prisoner of the Old Abbey? *Nine, ten months? A year?*

Out of the corner of her eye, Helena saw a flash. Movement, but not just movement. A flash of sunshine on a blade—the training foil. Altan was waving it about, teasing his sister—who was attempting to grab at the blade with her bare hands.

"Altan, now that's enough," said Helena swiftly, stepping away from Lady Amelia with relief. "You are not babies to be squabbling so! Give that to me."

Altan handed over the training foil with a dark look. "It's my sword."

"It's a training foil, used for practice only by gentlemen who can behave themselves," said Helena severely. She was conscious of Lady Amelia's gaze still on her, but she was not going to allow herself to turn around. *Not yet.* "And you, Miss Fernsby, should know better."

Rowena hung her head. Helena immediately regretted her harshness, but what's done was done. All she could hope was that they would learn from it.

"I do apologize, Lady Amelia," Helena said breezily as she stepped back to her.

The distraction had been excellently timed in two ways. Firstly, Helena had been able to recenter herself and decide precisely how to respond. Secondly, Lady Amelia seemed to have forgotten what they were talking about.

"The rascals," she said fondly, looking at her nephew and eldest niece. "It seems like only yesterday they were born. When Constance…"

Her voice faded into nothingness, and Helena saw a look of pain pass across Lady Amelia's face briefly. Then it was gone.

"The children are very talented," said Helena quietly. "I must admit they have been a pleasure to work with. I believe it will stand Altan in good stead when he goes to school. When will he go to school?"

Unfortunately, the mention of the play seemed to have re-minded Lady Amelia what she had previously asked. "I am sorry, I did not catch where you learned so much about the theater. So, this is your first play?"

Helena swallowed. She was not a liar by nature, never had been. Her mother had snorted when she had said that at the tender age of seventeen.

"Not a liar!" she had jeered. "And there you are, flaunting your wares and lying every night of the week!"

Helena had flushed. "It's not like that—it's a perfectly respectable establishment!"

She had no wish to lie to Lady Amelia now, but she had little choice. Unless…

"This is the first play I have been in charge of, yes," said Helena firmly.

The vagueness would rescue her, she was sure. Lying was not an option, but neither was telling a truth that would lose her the position of governess.

"I find that hard to believe."

Both women turned. Helena's heart stopped.

There he stood. The man who had derailed many a thought since she had last seen him, the man who was, rather disobliging-ly, starting to appear in her dreams. The man she absolutely should not be speaking to.

The Duke of Kilerth strode across the ballroom, boots echo-ing. His jacket was cut tight to his body, showing his strength and the way he looked at her…

Helena could feel her hands trembling and felt incredibly conscious that she was still holding Altan's fencing sword.

A smirk appeared on Kilerth's face, and Helena turned hastily, cheeks warm. She was only able to buy herself a few seconds as she placed the fencing foil carefully at the side of the room before returning to Lady Amelia, and it was not sufficient to calm herself.

Why was it that every time she told herself he wasn't handsome, he appeared again and proved her wrong?

"You are certainly a professional in this matter," said Kilerth with a grin.

Helena glared. *Had he entirely forgotten their agreement?*

"It…it would be a shame, I think, if anyone was to find out about the truth of a—a certain person's past. Recent past. In London."

"I think most governesses, Amelia, are competent enough to put on a bit of Shakespeare," continued the duke carelessly. "Miss Kirkpatrick is just one such governess."

His gaze met hers, and Helena's glare did not dissipate. *What was he playing at?* Why was he teasing her about her actress heritage—or worse, why was he teasing her at all!

They had an agreement. Kilerth surely had just as much to lose as she did, should the truth be revealed. The whole point was that she knew of his secret as a bare-knuckle boxer, and he knew of her secret past as an actress. Why would he risk this?

"Yes, that is true," she found herself saying. "As a Bureau governess, I am well-prepared for many things, including new ways to entertain children."

Kilerth's eyes did not leave hers. "So no matter what happens, you can act, right?"

If he was not careful, Helena thought savagely, *she was going to spill his secret, no matter how handsome and seductive he was…*

Seductive? Where had that thought come from?

The fact was, Kilerth was pushing this when she believed they had an understanding.

Time to fight fire with fire.

"Oh, I don't know about that, Your Grace," Helena said. "But I think you'll always find I can fight my way out of any corner."

The knowing smile disappeared from the duke's face. Those brooding eyes narrowed as though preparing for a fight.

And wasn't that what they were doing, thought Helena wildly. *Wasn't it a war of words rather than fists?* Wasn't it time that they stepped away from each other, agreeing that an impasse had been reached? Why did neither of them seem able to do that?

Someone cleared their throat. To Helena's surprise, she realized Lady Amelia was still there.

"My word," said the duke's sister lightly, looking between them. "It is as though you are speaking a secret code. Is there something I don't know?"

Helena raised an eyebrow. "I think His Grace understands me, don't you?"

Kilerth did not back down, but he did not respond immediately either. At that moment, he appeared to be looking so deeply into Helena's eyes that she was unsure how she was still standing.

There was a power there. Not just of strength, which was evident now she saw the taut muscles straining under his shirt sleeves. No, it was more than that. Power of mind, of will. Here was a man who was sorely tempted by something or do to something, yet he had not permitted himself to do a thing.

What did he want from her, this duke?

If Helena had been in one of her plays at the Theatre Royal, she would have known what he wanted. To make love. To touch her and be touched in return.

She shivered, and Kilerth made a movement which he quickly stopped, but it almost looked like…

Like he was going to reach out to her. As though he wanted to be closer to her, as close as he could get.

"I understand you perfectly," Kilerth said softly, his gaze dropping to his boots. "And on that understanding, I am expected by our brother to play cards in the drawing room. Far be it for me to disappoint him. Good day, Miss Kirkpatrick."

He was gone before she could say another word.

Despite that, her gaze followed him, alighting on the training foil on the floor by the door. Why did they always do that: always fight or spar, which was probably more accurate? Why did the Duke of Kilerth have to pry? Why did he want to know so much about her?

"You have quite an effect on my brother, don't you?"

Helena glanced at Lady Amelia. "I don't—I haven't…"

It was pointless to try to defend herself. What was there to say? She had done nothing wrong, not overstepped any boundary that was proscribed by society.

Not yet. Not even with the great temptation she felt—to be in his arms again, to feel his strength around her, to know with complete certainty that she was where she belonged.

Helena swallowed. She had laughed before she had come here at the idea of falling in love with a gentleman in a house where she was a governess.

That was before she had met him. That was before he had looked at her like that, as though she were a delicacy just out of reach.

"Miss Kirkpatrick, I…I say this out of kindness," said Lady Amelia in a low voice. The children, bored by the antics of the adults, were bickering by the chalked-out stage. "Please, leave him alone. He is a duke, you…you are a governess."

There was probably nothing else that Lady Amelia could have said that would have been so mortifying for Helena to hear. *The very idea!*

"I have not—no expectations are—"

"It is easy for us ladies, I think, to get swept up in our feelings," Lady Amelia said as she cut across her. "To believe we are in love—to think the fairytale will end as we wish it…"

Once again, her voice trailed away, but this time Helena was eager for her to continue. *The fairytale?* Lady Amelia knew a little of love, then, even if she had been locked away in this house with her brother. Who on earth with? The butler?

Lady Amelia swallowed. "Just—just leave him alone."

It appeared to be a Fernsby trait, the sudden rush out of a room when conversation had become tiresome. Lady Amelia was gone before Helena could explain just how little had taken place between her and her brother.

Or was there so little? Helena swallowed and turned back to look at the children. Months, that was how long it had been since she had left the theater, yet each day felt like a lifetime. There was something about living with one's employer—or one's fellow actors and actresses. One became familiar far quicker. It was the proximity, somehow. It accelerated one's intimacy.

Helena smiled ruefully. She felt as though she had known Kilerth most of her life. The snatched conversations she had overheard in the dining room; the hours in the drawing room as the children had spoken to their elders, and she had sat in the corner.

That moment when he had held her in his arms…

She shook her head. This was foolishness, and worse, it was dangerous. At any moment, Kilerth could break the agreement they had and reveal to the whole family just where she had come from before the Governess Bureau.

It was a wonder, really, that a duke was content to have an actress in charge of his heirs, but evidently, Kilerth was not a normal duke.

No, it was the children she should be focused on now. Not good-for-nothing dukes.

"And we'll have no more fighting, thank you," Helena said aloud. "Right, where were we—that scene, from the top?"

CHAPTER TEN

August 8, 1813

OSCAR WAITED. *SURELY it would all be over if he waited?* It had never gone on this long before. If only Amelia were here. She always knew what to do.

"No, you can't force me," whispered Fernsby.

His hands were gripping the arms of his chair so forcefully, Oscar could see the whites of his bones. His eyes were closed, scrunched up tight, and his knees were locked together.

Oscar hesitated. His words were never as eloquent as Amelia's nor as kind. But he had to say something. They couldn't remain like this forever.

"I am not trying to make you leave the house," he said quietly.

Fernsby's eyes shot open. "Leave the house? Why would we—who said I had to—"

"No one," said Oscar hastily, but it was too late.

The very thought had brought even further terror into Fernsby's mind, and his shoulders began to shake, his hands still clutching the armchair.

"Why on earth would we leave the house?" whispered Fernsby, his eyes darting about the drawing room. "The house is safe. It's safe in here and out there—it's dangerous out there, Kilerth! Why do you—"

"Let's stay here."

Fernsby looked at his brother, who had spoken in a slow, calm voice. "Really?"

Oscar nodded. *Dear God, but he was unequipped to deal with this sort of thing. Where was Amelia? She was never around when he needed her.*

That wasn't fair. She had barely left the house until he had come back from Kilerth.

Still, it was in moments like this, when Fernsby got himself into a state and couldn't calm down when Oscar felt the lack of Amelia immensely.

"Really, let's stay here," he said aloud, slowly lowering himself into the armchair opposite his brother. "It's safer here."

Fernsby's hands did not release the armchair, but the shaking stopped. "It's dangerous out there."

"But it's *safe* in here," said Oscar slowly.

His gaze flickered over his brother as they fell into silence, and Oscar bit his lip. There was still so much he did not understand about this change in his brother. He had listened as best he could to Amelia's explanations, but they were just guesses.

Neither of them were doctors. *Were there even doctors for this sort of thing?*

He had never heard of anyone being so afraid that the very idea of stepping over their threshold could leave them in paroxysms of panic. No, he did not understand his brother—but Oscar knew precisely where the fear had come from. *Constance.* If she had not died…

But she had. How did one argue away fear like Fernsby's with logic?

The trouble was, until now, Oscar had avoided speaking of anything so personal as feelings. Gentlemen…well, they *had* them, but they did not discuss them. Oscar could not recall telling anyone how he felt since…

Goodness, it must have been a long time ago. He could not even remember doing it.

Oscar's gaze moved to Fernsby again. His breathing was shallow, his fingers surely in agony gripping the armchair so tightly. This could not continue. Whatever he needed for right now, they would give him.

"Fernsby," Oscar said quietly, and his brother's head jerked up. "What would make you feel safe? Right now?"

Fernsby wet his lips but did not seem able to speak.

Oscar waited and, after a minute or so, prompted, "I am your brother. And I am going to do everything I can for you."

Their eyes met. Oscar remembered when Fernsby had been born. Ten years an only child, then a screaming, scrawny babe had been placed into his arms, and the thing had stopped crying immediately. It had looked up at him with wide, astonished eyes, and Oscar had looked down on the child he knew would one day be his friend, his companion.

The eyes were the same now: wide, astonished. *Vulnerable.*

"I…" Fernsby swallowed. "I want to go to bed."

Oscar nodded. "Well then, that's what we'll do."

His brother had clearly not expected to be given his own way, for when Oscar rose and offered out a hand to help him up, Fernsby just stared.

"Come on," said Oscar quietly. "Let me help you."

He was not sure whether it was the words he spoke, how he said them, the outstretched hand, or if the fact Fernsby was being offered an escape. Slowly, one by one, his brother's fingers released the armchair. He rose slowly, shaking, weak as a kitten.

Oscar reached out an arm and placed it around his baby brother's shoulders. *Why was it that he still saw the man as a child, thirty-odd years later?*

"Right then," he said quietly. "Bed."

They walked slowly; that was, Fernsby walked slowly, and Oscar walked with him, arm still round his shoulders. Mrs.

Cantrell passed them in the corridor to the staircase.

Fernsby lowered his face, a pink tinge splattering across his cheeks.

Oscar tightened his grip around his brother's shoulders. When the housekeeper passed, he muttered fiercely, "You do not have anything to be ashamed of, Fernsby, particularly not before your servants!"

A sort of righteous fire had filled his bones. *A man should not live in his own home and feel such shame; it was an outrage!*

His brother did not respond until they reached his bedchamber. Oscar used his free hand to open the door and had to release his brother to get him through the doorframe.

"I know full well I should be ashamed," murmured Fernsby.

Oscar closed the door behind them. "No, you do not!"

Fernsby dropped onto the end of the bed. "I can't...describing it, I think, is beyond my ability. It's like...like the whole world has collapsed without her. As though this house is the only bit left."

Oscar swallowed and hovered near the door, unsure what to do next. It made sense. At least, he and Amelia had always supposed this whole problem stemmed from Constance.

Yet try though he might, Oscar could not understand. Not when he had never loved anyone like that, not even, in truth, his own siblings.

He was no monster. He would hate to lose them, but he had hated losing their parents, and he had continued on. *Life continued on.* That was what happened when you lost someone you cared about; you had to keep going.

Fernsby dropped his head into his hands.

Oscar hesitated. If only he had some point of reference, someone in his life who meant something so much to him that—

Miss Helena Kirkpatrick flashed through his mind. The heat of her body against his, the sparkling wit that seemed to cross him at every turn, the curve of her body that appeared all over the house, even when he promised himself he was avoiding her—

No. Oscar pushed her from his mind. It was too easy to become distracted by thoughts of Miss Kirkpatrick, and he was attempting to help his brother here.

"Do you feel safer here, Fernsby?"

His brother nodded.

Oscar stepped forward, moving one of the chairs by the bed toward the oriel window. "Look here, a beautiful view of the gardens. You'll be quite safe here in your bedchamber, and you'll be able to see the sun."

He turned to look over at his brother, seated in the shadows on the bed.

Fernsby looked up. "Do…do you think I will be safe there?"

"Yes," said Oscar firmly.

It took a few minutes, but eventually, he coaxed his brother into the chair. Oscar watched carefully, but Fernsby did not grip the arms of the chair as he had done downstairs. He did seem calmer. There was a tension in the eyes that had gone, though he still looked pale.

"The children should still go ahead with their play."

Oscar nodded. "I am sure Miss Kirkpatrick will continue to entertain them."

"And the fencing," said his brother, his eyes unfocused toward the window. "A gentleman should know how to fence. He should still keep going with his lessons."

Thinking privately that he would have a word with the fencing master whenever he deigned to appear at the Old Abbey, Oscar nodded. "I will see to it."

"Can't have the boy learning an ungentlemanly sport like…like boxing," Fernsby said with a wry smile. "Eh?"

Oscar's heart constricted. Boxing. Deemed by his parents as an uncouth entertainment that only fools got themselves into. He had kept it on at university against their wishes and kept the truth of his passion for the sport a secret ever since.

Ungentlemanly sport. *Yes, well, any sport which drew blood was considered ungentlemanly,* Oscar thought bitterly. You had to be there, in the moment, feel the hum of the crowd, know precisely where your fists were going to go, see the movement through the air before it happened.

Dear God, if Fernsby was ever to find out that the Duke of Kilerth and Michaels, the East End boxing champion, were one and the same…

"You can go, Kilerth."

Oscar bit his lip. "I…well, I would rather not leave you."

What he was afraid of, he was not entirely sure, but he had the sense Fernsby was not to be left alone, not to be abandoned.

But his brother appeared to guess what he was thinking and smiled wanly. "Fear not, Kilerth, I will…I will sit here for a bit and read and think. You can be quite sure I am safe."

Oscar looked searchingly into his brother's face. These last few weeks had demonstrated that Fernsby was often happier alone.

Oscar nodded crisply. "Fine. But you ring the bell if you need anything—anything at all—and you can have someone send for me. I won't be far away."

Fernsby smiled. "You're a good brother."

There was something so innocent in his smile, as though he never doubted Oscar would have come to visit. When in truth…well, Oscar never liked leaving Kilerth. He had doubted the importance of the matter when Amelia had written to him.

Guilt washed over him. His brother was fighting a real sickness, whatever it was, and it was clear he was suffering.

"Go on with you," said Fernsby gently.

Oscar laughed. "Yes, sir."

He closed his brother's bedchamber door. *Dear God, this was a challenge.* He did not have unlimited reserves of patience, and though he wished to be kind to his brother, with every passing day, there was an increasing chance that he would lose his temper and say something…

Unforgiveable.

He had to speak to Amelia. *Where was she?* They must discuss what to do next. She had been particularly difficult to find these last few days. Well, he could hardly blame her. Now that he understood how she had been living here, he was not surprised she had taken the opportunity to escape the tension of the house.

Being cooped up with a man who refused to go outside would eventually drive anyone to find refuge in nature.

Oscar shook his head as he descended the staircase. He should not have left after the funeral last year. He should have stayed, noticed Fernsby was starting to act strangely. Instead, he had headed straight to London, beaten the pulp out a few men in the boxing ring, which had purged his grief, and returned to Kilerth, where he was happiest.

Leaving Amelia to bear the burden alone.

He sighed heavily as he reached the bottom step. He should have returned. If only helping was in his nature. He was not the sort of man to speak kindness or even speak softly.

No, his typical recourse was with his fists.

He looked down. The scars from his last fights were healed, only a memory now. They itched to return to the ring to feel the rush of power and glory, to dance through the air so quickly only he could see them...

But this was not the place. There wasn't anyone here he could trust to know about that part of him. Miss Kirkpatrick...even she attempted to hold that knowledge above him.

A strange noise interrupted his thoughts. It was a sound he recognized, but it was so alien to the Old Abbey that it took him a moment to realize what it was.

Laughter.

Laughter, here? It was not forbidden, but Oscar had never seen it. *What on earth could those children be laughing about?*

That it was the children, there was no doubt. The high-pitched giggling appeared to be coming from a room just off the hall: the library. Oscar had spent little time there, books being the sort of thing one *had* rather than one *read*. The door was slightly ajar, and a peal of raucous laughter escaped through it.

He could not help himself. Oscar wandered over to the door, peering through it.

There was Miss Kirkpatrick. His stomach clenched at the sight of her, a fact Oscar tried to ignore. It was because he hadn't touched a woman in months, that was all. Miss Kirkpatrick could be anyone, and he would surely find her desirable.

It didn't help that she was absolutely beautiful, tempting beyond all temptations…

She was seated on the floor with the children around her, and Altan was doubled up, clutching his stomach as he melted into peals of laughter.

"Do it again!" said Rowena.

Oscar's gaze flickered between the children and the governess, who was grinning. She started speaking, but in a strange way totally different from her normal manner.

Within seconds, he knew precisely whose voice it was.

"Oh no, my linens, whatever shall we do!" said Miss Kirkpatrick in Mrs. Cantrell's voice, eliciting much hilarity from the children. "Now, if you scamps could avoid walking on my newly beaten rug, I would thank you most kindly!"

The children were roaring with laughter, even little Sylvia, though Oscar was not entirely sure whether she quite understood the joke.

This was unbelievable. Oscar found his breath tightening in his chest. *How was it possible that a mere governess could—*

"Do McLoughlin!" said Altan eagerly.

Miss Kirkpatrick smiled. The smile then disappeared as she rearranged her face into a stern frown, and Oscar almost gasped aloud.

It was amazing. He did not understand it; it should not be possible, but in that mere movement, she…*became the butler.*

"Now Altan did I or did I not tell you what would happen to naughty boys who sneak into my pantry and eat all my cheese!"

Miss Kirkpatrick spoke in a low voice—*no, that was not quite accurate,* Oscar thought. *She spoke in McLoughlin's voice. It was uncanny.*

Altan tipped over with laughter, unable to contain himself. It was only then, with a rather sickly lurch to his stomach, that Oscar realized why the laughter had felt so strange.

The boy had not laughed since his mother died. Not until now.

Oscar's gaze moved from Altan to his governess, currently mimicking one of the maids by the sounds of what she was saying. She was doing this to make the children laugh, to see them happy. To give them a reason to find joy in the world.

Did she understand just how wonderful that was? How had she seen the need within them, a need that even he, their uncle, had not understood until now?

And perhaps the most prescient question, how was it possible for a mere governess, who admitted nothing about herself and her past, to mimic others so precisely?

He was listening, he told himself, not because he was enjoying himself but because he needed to discover more about Miss Kirkpatrick. But the truth was, he could not drag his eyes away. Intoxicating was not a word he used for women, but it was perfect here.

Every time he tried to pull himself away from the door, he merely got closer.

He had to find Amelia, had to talk to her about what to do about their brother. Yet, he was watching Miss Kirkpatrick imitate a pirate, a naval captain, the king of England...

Oscar knew he shouldn't be here. Miss Kirkpatrick was dangerous—or at the very least, she had the potential to be. She had the potential to reveal the secret he had closely guarded from his family for years. And yet...

Oscar pushed open the door, and the effect on the room was immediate.

The children stopped laughing, Altan turning red and Rowena pale. Miss Kirkpatrick stood hurriedly and curtseyed. He could see the flush of her décolletage and neck.

Her décolletage. He swallowed. *Blast, he shouldn't be looking there.*

He forced himself to smile. *The governess did not know how long he had been standing behind the door, he had to remember that.* He had the upper hand here.

Oscar's stomach dropped. If he had arrived sooner, he might have seen impressions of himself. Fervently glad that he had not, he took a deep breath.

"Children. Out onto the lawn for some fresh air, please, but stay close to the house. You know your father's rules."

The children scrambled to their feet, Altan helping Sylvia, and they swiftly left the room. *Left him alone with Miss Kirkpatrick.*

He was doing this for his brother, Oscar told himself. Fernsby wasn't well enough to deal with the governess, not yet. He wasn't staying because he enjoyed her company.

"If anyone is to be punished," said Miss Kirkpatrick in a clear, confident voice, her eyes not looking away, "then it should be me."

It was such a surprising statement that Oscar was not entirely sure how to respond. Punishment? To the contrary, it had been wonderful to see the children…well, as children.

But he wouldn't tell her that. He had to keep the upper hand or some semblance of it. Miss Kirkpatrick always had the upper hand, no matter what he attempted.

"Walk with me," he said abruptly.

Oscar turned on his heels and started toward the hall. Miss Kirkpatrick obviously had not expected such a pronouncement, and she only just caught up in the hallway.

"I just thought—the children needed a reason to be children," said Miss Kirkpatrick rapidly. "And I have always found that mimicry is an excellent way to—"

"Just—just walk with me," interrupted Oscar. He could see what she was trying to do to justify her actions, to explain what she had done.

But that did not matter. His need for explanations had never been great, not after seeing Altan laugh.

No, he was overwhelmed with quite a different desire now—

a need to speak with her. To talk with her, actually spend more than five minutes that didn't end in a threat of blackmail or a sword fight.

"We cannot talk here," he said distractedly, looking around him. *No need for whispers of scandal to reach either of his siblings.*

"Out here," he said abruptly.

Oscar stepped forward and opened the front door.

Miss Kirkpatrick hesitated. "The children—"

"Will be perfectly fine on the lawn," said Oscar. "Anyway, it's high time they learned how to entertain themselves."

A flicker of amusement shown the governess's eyes. "That is precisely what I think."

She stepped through the front door, and Oscar followed, feeling the rebellion in every muscle. *He should not be doing this. He should leave her alone, yet she drew him to her in a way he did not understand. Did not want to understand.*

"A walk in the gardens, I think," he said briskly. "Come."

He started walking without waiting for her to agree, and she kept to his side but with rather a surprised expression.

It was rather odd. Oscar could not see why a walk in the gardens would be so strange; they were perfectly pleasant, and the heatwave had not yet abated. It would be cooler here.

Only then did he remember. *She was a governess. He was a duke.* They could not be more different, and yet here they were, striding along under the canopy of oaks.

Oscar wanted to speak but found he could not construct the perfect opening. How to begin a conversation with a governess? He knew so little about her, and she had prevented any attempt for him to discover anything more than the fact that she was a governess.

So when the first words tripped from his mouth, they were more instinct than planned. "You are very talented, you know."

Miss Kirkpatrick smiled. "Yes. You were the one who called me a governess of prodigious skill."

Oscar had to smile. "So I did. I have to admit most ladies are more accomplished than me—my sister Amelia certainly is."

He had expected her to disagree, to flatter him, to say that he was a most charming and accomplished individual.

He did not expect her to laugh.

"That is easily explained," Miss Kirkpatrick said. "That is because gentlemen have no need to be accomplished. They marry without them. Marry for them, I suppose."

It was a clever remark. Oscar was impressed. "I have never noticed that."

"I would not expect a duke to have done so," said the governess as they turned a corner into a new part of the garden.

Unsure whether to be offended or delighted that their conversation was so natural, Oscar nodded. "I suppose so—but then, as the head of the family, I am supposed to be the talented one. The skilled one. The one with all the answers."

How had his words become so bitter? Oscar had not expected his feelings to rise so quickly to the surface. There was a safety in Miss Kirkpatrick, along with the danger she stirred in his loins.

She was quiet for a moment. Then, "You are thinking of your brother."

Oscar nodded. Amelia had been the only person he had spoken with about Fernsby; there was no one else he could trust. It was pleasant to have someone else to confide in.

Even if that person was devastatingly beautiful.

"You have a great deal of responsibility, being the head of the family."

Oscar stopped. They were in an enclosed kitchen garden, mint and lavender wafting in the air. The apple trees had lost their blossoms months ago, and fruit peeked out from luscious foliage. They were alone.

He nodded. "Sometimes I...I cannot bear it any longer. As though the weight of it will crush me. As though I will be crushed by it all."

They were words he had never tied down with actual syllables before. They had tied him down, heavy chains of panic and fear he had never permitted to rise.

They rose now. They poured from his mouth as Miss Kirk-patrick stood before him, her gaze open, willing to hear him.

"When our father died—it was so sudden, so unexpected," Oscar said. "It was my responsibility, as the new duke, to take care of our mother, my brother, and sister. They are so much younger than me."

Miss Kirkpatrick nodded. She seemed to understand any interruption would dam the flow of words.

"And here we are, years later, and I am still at it," said Oscar bitterly. "Fernsby...I worry he will never be the same again. I said I was coming here to see how Amelia was doing, but it's the children who—I will have to take care of them, bring them into society, and I don't know what...and Amelia is unmarried!"

"She is young," said Miss Kirkpatrick softly. "What is she, twenty?"

Oscar smiled wryly. "Closer to five and twenty."

"Well, that is not so great an age," she said with a smile. "Close to my own."

"Unmarried, and at five and twenty," Oscar said, hardly knowing what he was saying. "Soon to be unmarriageable if she keeps this up, and yet who would I be to force a marriage on her? I wish her to be happy. That's the problem."

He slipped into silence, but it was a comfortable one. He had never felt more comfortable than with Helena. *Miss Kirkpatrick.*

"Helena, I—apologies, I should call you—"

"Helena is..." she said softly.

Oscar's eyes met her own. "Oscar. Kilerth is so dry, and it's my father's name." *How was she drawing this from him?* "Helena, I am responsible for their happiness. Do you know what it is to be responsible for someone else's happiness? And not just one person, but many?"

Helena's smile was a knowing one. "I have a little, yes, but not compared to you."

A gentle breeze ruffled his cravat and her hair. Oscar was

suddenly very aware of himself. "I should not have…you must think me a fool," he said ruefully.

Helena smiled. "No. Only a very good man."

By God, this was—Oscar could not explain it. Somehow, she had taken all the strain, as though a pressure valve had been released.

"I…I feel so alone sometimes, as though the whole world is separate from me."

"Better than no family at all, I suppose."

Oscar laughed dryly. "You understand then—you are just as alone as I am."

Helena's smile changed. *Was she truly alone? Was that why she understood him so instinctively?*

"More, I think."

They fell into silence. Oscar had always hated silence. Packed full of anticipation, the potential for misunderstanding, frustration, anger.

But not here. The sun baked down, but there was nothing stilted between them. The governess was…

Oscar swallowed. It was remarkable. He could speak to her as he could no one else. Her gaze flashed, a playful smile on his lips.

"I am warm," Helena said quietly. "What weather we are having."

Oscar knew he shouldn't have said it. That knowledge did not stop him. "Come with me."

He had almost reached out for her hand, so instinctive was the movement, but he managed not to. Instead, he strode forward through a garden gate into another part of the garden.

The koi pond. Perfect.

Oscar dropped to the side of the pond and started pulling off his boots. "Come on."

Helena's laugh made his stomach lurch. "What on earth are you—"

"Well, it's hot enough," said Oscar with a grin, looking at her, who looked partly scandalized, partly amused. "Why not cool off?"

Helena stepped forward hesitantly as Oscar pulled off his socks. "And the fish won't mind?"

He glanced down. "Mind?"

Mind? His mind wasn't engaged. It was something else leading him along this nonsense, this romantic foolishness.

Yet, it did not feel foolish. It felt…wonderful.

"Sit with me," said Oscar softly.

Helena hesitated. They were alone, the stillness of the summer heat interrupted only by the buzzing of the bees. No one would watch them. No one to be scandalized.

Oscar smiled as she sat beside him, her shoulder knocking into his own.

"I must be mad to do this," she muttered quietly, fingers picking at the laces on her boots.

"Perhaps," he said, making her laugh. His stomach lurched again. Why was it so good to make her laugh? "But you'll feel cool, which is surely worth the extravagance."

Helena's boots and stockings were off, and they both lowered their feet into the water at the same time.

"Oohh!"

They both exclaimed in delight as their feet hit the freezing water. Helena's hand clutched the stone around the pond—or would have done if Oscar's hand hadn't been there already.

Her hand was warm. Oscar swallowed. He wouldn't look down. That would be a mistake. Maybe this whole thing was a mistake. The desire to fight was ever present in his body …

With Helena. Nothing else mattered.

He looked down. There were their feet, both in the water. As though they were equals. As though this was their garden, and they had days upon days to talk and—

"You were right."

Oscar blinked. "What?"

Helena was smiling. She was so close. When was the last time he had been this close to a woman? A woman like her?

"You were right," Helena repeated. "I do feel cool. Worth the extravagance. Thank you, Oscar."

Perhaps it was the vulnerability she revealed; perhaps it was something else. Whatever it was that made him do it, Oscar did not hesitate. He could not stay away any longer.

Pulling Helena into his arms in a quick movement, Oscar closed the gap between them and crushed his lips on hers. He knew in that instant he had acted badly; the poor woman didn't want random gentleman abusing her trust and scandalizing her honor!

But Helena did not push him away. She did not cry out in disgust or demand that he never touch her again.

She clung to him, returning his kiss with such ardor Oscar barely knew what to do. His lips worshipped hers as she opened, allowing him in deeper, his tongue caressing her own and teasing with pleasure as his hands pulled her closer.

The kiss ended. Oscar blinked, unsure how long it had been since he had reacted so scandalously. He did not release her. He did not want to.

"I...I do apologize," he breathed. "I should not take liberties."

Helena did not look away, nor flush, nor declaim him. "Please do not apologize for something I enjoyed so much."

Something was stirring deep within Oscar, and it was more than lust. It was...it was an emotion he did not know. *He had to stop himself.*

"I-I promised myself I would stay away from you," Helena whispered. "But I don't seem to be able to do that, no matter how hard I try. And neither can you. I can see it."

Oscar did not reply. At least, not with words. He lowered his lips to hers, and this time the kiss was slower yet more passionate. Her hands had moved to his neck, pulling him closer, and knowing she desired him just as he wanted her gave Oscar the excuse to keep her close.

Eventually, the kiss ended.

"This...this has to stay between us."

Helena nodded. *Of course she understood,* Oscar thought ruefully. She had just as much to lose as he did now.

CHAPTER ELEVEN

August 10, 1813

HELENA BREATHED IN the luscious scent of the last of the roses as she sat on the shady lawn. She had never known flowers like it. She had seen roses in London, but only ever through the windows of the wealthy, or in the buttonholes of gentlemen who would admire her on the stage.

Unlike one gentleman she now knew…

A smile crept over her face. She would not be disturbed here, not for at least another hour. Baron Fernsby had called in all three children after luncheon, and Helena knew that meant they would not be permitted to leave the house for the rest of the day.

Quiet, undisturbed, peace. *Bliss.*

She could sit here, in the chair McLoughlin had permitted her to bring out from the dining room, and watch the world go by.

A movement. Helena watched in fascination as a bumblebee flew lazily toward her before settling on the paper on her lap. Its little wings paused for a moment, sunlight glittering through them, then it was off again.

London was always cramped, but she had never known how much she was missing by never being in the countryside. All these insects, birds, flowers…

It was as though she had been invited to the garden of Eden.

Helena's eye moved to her lap, and what was required of her: Miss Clarke's report.

A small wooden writing desk, perfectly designed for a lady, sat on her lap along with three pieces of paper gifted to her by Mrs. Cantrell and the letter that had arrived yesterday.

"A letter—for me?" Helena had not been able to hide her surprise.

The footmen looked at the letter with barely concealed interest as they passed it down. Helena had accepted it from one of the maids with genuine shock.

Who on earth could be writing to her? She had no friends who could write—friends she had hardly had time to miss since she had arrived at the Old Abbey. There had simply been too much to do.

Mr. Tobias would not write, would he? A flicker of hope, then panic, soared through her chest. What if he wanted her back? If she had received such an apology while training at the Governess Bureau, she would have leapt at the chance to return. Now…

But after opening it, Helena saw to her surprise that it was from Miss Clarke.

In the shade of the house, Helena picked up the letter from the writing desk and smiled at it wryly. She had forgotten to send her one-month report.

Of course she had. There had been so much to do, to learn. The play had to be created, the children understood, the vagaries of life in the Old Abbey navigated. Every day rushed by in a daze of excitement, bleeding into each other until Helena did not know what day it was.

Helena unfolded the letter and read it through.

Miss Kirkpatrick.

I expected better—though perhaps I should not have done, actress as you are and not a true governess! Your one-month report was due weeks ago, and I am most disappointed to find you have not had the courtesy to follow my instruction.

If I have not received your report in the next two weeks, mark my words, I shall bring you back from the Fernsbys and ensure you receive a much less pleasant situation—if you receive one at all.

Yours faithfully,
Miss V. Clarke

Helena had to smile. It was full of the proprietress's bluster. She could almost hear the words jumping off the page.

But Miss Clarke did not hold all the cards in this situation. Helena had heard the rumors; half of London had. It was everywhere, in all the salons, in Almack's even.

Governesses from the Bureau kept marrying their masters.

It was an outrage—a scandal. Helena was impressed Miss Clarke had managed to keep so much of the detail under wraps.

The last thing Miss Clarke needed was for the world to know she had hired an *actress*, with absolutely no governessing experience, for her latest client! No, it was much like the rather delicate understanding that she and Oscar—Kilerth had reached when she had first arrived here.

Both she and Miss Clarke stood to lose by the revelation of her past.

Still, Helena was not a cruel woman. The last thing she wanted was for the Governess Bureau to be mired in even more scandal, or worse, be forced to close.

It was not as though she had any warm feelings for her employer. Baron Fernsby was a good man, but not for her. The duke, on the other hand…

Heat blossomed up her neck. Helena knew there was no point attempting to fight the flush; it would only make it worse. Hopefully, if anyone espied her from the house and wondered why she looked so discomforted, they would assume it was from the heat of the day.

But it wasn't. Helena could not stop the memories of that kiss in the kitchen gardens flooding her mind, causing her stomach to twist, her legs to feel weak, her heart to thunder.

And it wasn't just the one kiss. Or a second kiss. Many kisses...

"I...I do apologize. I should not take liberties."

Helena had not asked anything of the duke. She could not imagine what a man like that could offer her. Oscar—Kilerth had made no promises. He may make her feel things she was sure only married ladies were supposed to feel, but that was beside the point.

Helena cleared her throat and looked down once more at the small writing desk that she had borrowed from the drawing room. It would be so much more pleasant, she had thought at the time, to write this report Miss Clarke needed outside.

And she had to do it today. It would be a shame for her report to arrive late in London and increase Miss Clarke's anxiety. Putting down the letter, Helena picked up her pencil and looked at the blank sheet of paper before her. How to begin?

Miss Clarke would definitely wish to have her worries put to rest, but Helena was not entirely sure how to do that. How could she put into words enough comfort to convince the owner of the Governess Bureau that she was caring for the children adequately?

The trouble was, the primary way she was caring for the children was by distracting them from their limited existence with...a play.

A smile danced on her lips. Miss Clarke would probably not wish to hear about that. Putting on a play with rehearsalsand acting and costumes...that was probably too close to her past for comfort.

Well, she had to start somewhere.

Dear Miss Clarke,

Helena looked at the three words she had written. *Blast.* She had expected them to look far more impressive, perhaps cover more of the page. But they were just a small portion of the very top left corner.

"I-I promised myself I would stay away from you. But I don't seem to be able to do that, no matter how hard I try. And neither can you. I can see it."

Helena dropped her pencil. *Oscar Fernsby, Duke of Kilerth.* Why was she permitting him to have such space in her mind? She needed to concentrate. Then she could go back to daydreaming in peace. What if they had not been able to restrain themselves? What if that kissing had continued in the warmth and secrecy of the kitchen gardens?

It was certainly not the thoughts a lady should be having. Not that Helena was a lady. Perhaps that was the problem. If she had been a lady, she would not have permitted a duke to take advantage of her.

An advantage she had wanted to give him.

If she had been a lady, perhaps instead of pulling her into his arms and kissing her senseless, Oscar would have offered for her hand…

Helena coughed and picked up her pencil. Thinking about their kisses was getting her nowhere. She never thought she would feel sorry for a duke, not with all the power and wealth and prestige—but Oscar had managed it.

Perhaps it was the genuine helplessness he so clearly felt about his brother. There was love there, a brotherly love Helena had never seen before. Lady Amelia did a great deal, Helena reminded herself—but now she thought about it, the Fernsby sister was seen less and less around the house these days.

She was undoubtedly taking advantage of the pleasant weather and Oscar's distraction of their brother to take more walks around the grounds of the Old Abbey. Helena could not blame her. It must have been a long winter here, with nothing to do but try to keep up the spirits of a man wracked with grief.

As her thoughts meandered to the baron, Helena's smile

faded. The poor man. Losing one's wife so young.

It was difficult to imagine. After finding that person you wished to spend the rest of your life with, not an easy task—and from the little Lady Amelia and Oscar had spoken of her, Constance appeared to be a love match—to then lose that person…

Her mind flitted to Oscar. There was a man she could spend every day of her life with.

Helena forced the thought away. Governesses did not marry dukes. Governesses did not marry! Dukes married other dukes' daughters or wealthy daughters of earls.

Oscar wanted fun, that was all. It could not be clearer to Helena that he wished for something a little more. And she had let him kiss her, because…

Helena swallowed. No one else could hear her thoughts; it was perfectly acceptable to admit, in the privacy of her own mind, that she was lonely.

Alone. There was no one in the world she could trust. No family, no friends save for the actors and actresses who smiled to your face but spread gossip behind your back.

Even Miss Clarke could not be entirely trusted.

"Do you know what it is to be responsible for someone else's happiness? And not just one person but many?"

And when a lonely woman was isolated in a grand house, far from everything she knew, and a handsome duke wanted to kiss you…

Helena sighed happily. He was handsome. And charming. And vulnerable, with far greater depths than she had expected.

But it was a kiss, nothing more. Well, several kisses. But nothing more than that. Whatever this was between them, it started and ended in that garden. Even if she had wanted it to go further, which she absolutely did not, it would not be possible. How could it?

Oscar would not kiss her again.

"It…it would be a shame, I think, if anyone was to find out about

the truth of a—a certain person's past. Recent past. In London."

A smile appeared on her face again. They had an understanding already, didn't they? He protected her secret; she protected his. It created an unexpected bond between them.

And the *duke*, he knew of her background. He knew she had been an actress, a level of society below a gentlewoman and just above a whore, yet still, he had kissed her.

"This…this has to stay between us."

Helena squirmed in her seat at the memory of his words, of his warm breath on her neck. *Did that mean he intended for there to be more kisses?*

Oh, God, she hoped so.

No, this was getting foolish. She was far too old to be thinking these wild, girlish thoughts. The duke did not consider her with any affection beyond what was generated in his breeches. She was lonely and clung onto him for some human connection.

Meanwhile, there was a report she needed to write. She needed to concentrate. The moment her letter was finished, no matter how pleasant the slightly cooling breeze or the birdsong, she would need to go inside and care for the children.

Particularly Sylvia. While Altan was coming out of his shell, and Rowena seemed perfectly happy now the play was before her, Sylvia was in danger of being overlooked.

Helena twirled her pencil in her fingers, then finally put it down to the page.

Dear Miss Clarke,

Thank you for your letter, and apologies for the lateness of my own. I have learned much over the last weeks and have been distracted by my dedication to my duty. I hope you will forgive me.

The Fernsbys are a wonderful family. Baron Fernsby has given me clear and precise direction, which has enabled me to care for his three children more than adequately. He has spoken praise of my work. I hope this reassures you.

Baron Fernsby's brother and sister are also currently in res-

idence, and I am careful to adhere closely to their expectations. The baron is ~~quiet~~ respectful, and I see little of him.

Helena examined her progress. Yes, there was enough detail in there to keep Miss Clarke happy—and sufficient apologies, too.

There was little more she could write about Baron Fernsby without mentioning his fear of the outside. *The idea of that gossip swirling around London…*

Her jaw tightened. She would not do that to the baron. To any of them. She continued with her letter.

As I believe you were aware, I am not required to give educational instruction as such, merely being expected to care for and entertain the children.

Helena had to laugh at that sentence. *Well, it was all true.* What Miss Clarke did not know about a certain play and a certain stage which had been ordered by the master and was currently being built in the stable yard, would not hurt her.

Probably.

In summary, I believe my time here at the Old Abbey is going well. I have cordial relations with both the housekeeper and the butler, though they tend to leave me to myself, which I prefer. I have, however, been of some use to the housekeeper and laundry mistress with a small amount of mending and sewing for Lady Amelia, of which is my pleasure to assist.

Helena tried to look at that paragraph critically. Would Miss Clarke believe the work of a seamstress to be beneath that of a governess? It was hard to tell. Some of the best seamstresses, who could create the spectacular gowns adorning ladies at Almack's, were surely paid a small fortune for their skills, and Helena believed her work to be just as good.

It often had to be when a gown for an empress had to be worn on stage within five minutes, and half the beading had been ripped off in the previous scene.

There was just so much about service she did not know. The intricacies of privilege and who had priority over the other in the servants' hall had utterly befuddled her when she had first arrived, and still did at times.

Of course, a junior footman would give way to a senior footman; but what about when a junior footman and an undermaid met? Or a senior footman and Lady Amelia's personal lady's maid?

In all her life, she had never expected to spend her days in a big house like this. Teems of servants, corridors that seemed to go on forever, no end of duties to do…

Her home had always been the theater. Though now she came to think about it, there wasn't a huge amount of difference.

Time to complete the dratted letter and get it off into the post.

Helena hesitated. The play had consumed so much of her time here, it felt wrong not to mention it. But was it possible to couch it in such terms that Miss Clarke would approve?

It was not seemly for children to perform in public—at least, beyond the family. That would be the proprietress's only concern with another governess, but for Helena to admit that she had gone straight from the theatre to creating a new theater at her first position…

Was it possible to write it in a clever way? Helena played with the idea of talking about history and literature and culture. Would Miss Clarke find such a description helpful or merely confusing? Would it raise questions that Helena was simply not prepared to answer?

No. It was not worth it. Helena had no wish to risk her position, a position she had gained through complete chance. The last thing she needed was for Miss Clarke to believe she was slipping back into old habits.

> *I am very grateful to you, Miss Clarke, for taking a chance on me. You saw in me something that few others would have, and I am very pleased to be able to demonstrate to you my commitment: not just to the children under my care, but to*

yourself and the Governess Bureau.

Helena examined the words critically, tilting her head. There were few people who would have seen a down on her luck actress and thought she could be molded into a sufficient governess, let alone one suitable to represent the Bureau.

It was Miss Clarke's kindness, and that alone, which had kept her off the streets of London and instead whirled her to a far nicer home than she could have imagined.

I look forward to your next letter.

Yours sincerely,
Miss Helena KirkPatrick

Helena chuckled ruefully. She had written her own name at first, her true name, and had managed to squeeze in the Kirk before it. She would have to be careful not to make that mistake again.

It took but a moment to fold up the letter, which only spanned one page, and address it to Miss Clarke. She did not know the precise address beyond the street the Governess Bureau was situated on, but that was no matter. It was so renowned, Helena had no concern it would not reach its intended recipient.

Picking up the small writing desk along with Miss Clarke's original letter, Helena stepped through the side door. She would need to find McLoughlin; the butler was the only servant with a seal, as far as she knew.

Rather than attempt to find him so heavily laden, Helena slipped into the drawing room. She had only just placed the writing desk back on the bureau when a voice spoke.

"Don't touch that!"

The voice was sharp, anxious, and as Helena turned, she saw Lady Amelia glaring.

Thanking her stars she had been discovered at that precise moment, not earlier, Helena dropped to a curtsey. "I was just—"

"I said, don't touch it," said Lady Amelia sternly.

It was a miracle she had not spotted Helena using it outside. Lady Amelia strode over in a flurry of skirts and moved the writing desk slightly.

"It..." Lady Amelia swallowed. "It was Constance's."

Shame rushed over Helena. *Of course it was; why hadn't she thought of that?* The baron would hardly have used such and delicate writing desk. It hadn't occurred to her.

Helena nodded. "It...it must have been an awful shock for you all. When she died."

Lady Amelia said nothing.

A strange thought struck the governess. If Lady Amelia had lived here the last year, and if it was also true that during that time she had not been permitted to leave the house...

Why, then, she had not spoken to a woman near her age in all that time. No wonder she was so starved of freedom. No wonder she took any opportunity to walk in the gardens alone.

"Yes, it was a terrible shock," said Lady Amelia quietly. "We never thought that...she was so young, so healthy. Until—"

"Amelia?"

The two women turned quickly to the door, which was pushed open by the baron.

Helena's heart thumped wildly. *Had he heard them?* The topic of his wife was not forbidden—at least, not in the rulebook she had been given—but still...

The baron smiled wanly. "What are you two up to?"

"Nothing," said Lady Amelia hastily.

The smile faded at the quickness of her response.

Helena forced herself to smile. A little brightness, a touch of pleading... "It really is so inconsequential. I have a letter to send, and I was just inquiring of your sister whether she would permit McLoughlin to seal it for me."

She raised the letter in her hand as proof of her words.

The baron looked between her and his sister but appeared satisfied. "Of course, 'tis no trouble. Inform McLoughlin that I have given permission. Thank you, Miss Kirkpatrick."

The dismissal was implied, but Helena understood. Curtseying low to them both, she slipped past him and breathed a sigh of relief in the corridor.

After all her gratitude to Miss Clarke for finding her such a position, she had to be careful. She could easily lose it if she were not more guarded.

Chapter Twelve

August 14, 1813

The dark amber liquid burned his throat, but it was welcome. Oscar swallowed and held his glass languidly, leaning against the arm of his chair.

"I have said it before, and I will say it again," he said mildly. "I think it rather wild you are here, Amelia."

Amelia smiled as a summer storm battered against the windows of the billiards room. Candles flickered as the breeze seeped through the edges of the windowpanes, and there was a relief in all inhabitants of the Old Abbey as the blistering heat chilled for at least one evening.

His sister took a sip of her gin and water. "And I think it rather wild that in a household with no other ladies for me to talk to, you would expect me to sit in the drawing room alone!"

Fernsby laughed. "She's got a point, you know."

Oscar rolled his eyes, but it was primarily for effect. He could not remember the last time the three of them had sat there, laughing away the evening with chatter and nonsense.

A long time ago.

"No wonder you're not married," he jested, "if you never

wish to play by society's rules!"

Amelia laughed but was not quick enough to hide the pain flashing in her eyes.

It was only a moment. If Oscar had not been attending to her that very instant, he would have missed it. He regretted his comment immediately. Evidently, Lady Amelia Fernsby was not so happy with her single state as she made out to be.

He had not meant his comment in a cruel way, but it could be taken that way. *He was a fool.* He needed to learn to keep his mouth shut.

"Ignore me. I always do."

The smile on his sister's face was not brave, exactly, but masked a deeper pain. *Blast it all, he needed to pay attention to Amelia.* He would if he could ever find her.

"Well, I suppose I could say the same for you," said Amelia lightly, draining her small glass. "I am not the only one in this family who has never married!"

"Not without opportunity, though," grinned Fernsby.

Oscar glared at his brother. He may have made a slip up with Amelia, but that didn't mean he wanted to revisit all the nonsense he suffered all those years ago. "Anyway—"

"Those poor Mamas!" crowed his brother, an unexpected grin on his face. "Honestly, Amelia, you were too young at the time to really notice, but when Kilerth came out into society, there were more ladies lined up than for anyone else!"

Amelia descended into peals of laughter, and Oscar smiled weakly. "Now, it was not quite like—"

"Some of them were quite pretty though. I am not sure why you did not pursue any of them," interrupted Fernsby with a mocking frown. "None of them quite take your fancy?"

Oscar sighed ruefully. "No, none of the daughters really took my fancy—nor the mothers, however much they may have wished it!"

The three Fernsby siblings collapsed into laughter, Amelia's giggles making her hiccup, which only made her brothers laugh harder.

Oscar chuckled as he took another sip of whisky. *This was what life should be about.* This was what he had imagined when his siblings had started to near adulthood—evenings full of conversation, laughter, and back and forth between equals.

Everything seemed to be going well. This evening's dinner had been delicious, as it always was. He really must get this cook to write down some recipes for his own kitchens back in Kilerth.

The children had behaved themselves, for the most part. Altan was in high dudgeon, having had his toys taken away, but that wouldn't last long. The dudgeon or the punishment.

Even the weather had cooled for their benefit, and though rain was a disappointment, Oscar looked forward to being able to sleep through the night without overheating.

Best of all, Fernsby had, today, agreed to a walk around the house in the gardens—and completed it.

Yes, it had been a good day. Oscar smiled as he watched his brother and sister jest about some of the potential suitors their eldest brother had scorned. This was what he had always thought family would be like.

One could almost forget, in this moment, that he and Amelia were only here because Fernsby was…having difficulties.

"Come on, Kilerth," said Fernsby with a smile. "There must have been someone you took a fancy for, even if it did not end in matrimony. Perhaps a lady without sufficient title—"

"Or wealth," chimed in Amelia. "Not that we need it."

Oscar smiled. "You know, there wasn't a single lady who I met in those first few years of society who ever caught my eye— no, truly! To be sure, there were some beauties and even a few wits, but trying to find the two together in one person!"

Amelia nodded sagely. "Ah, that is the trouble. Finding one person who fits all the qualities one is seeking."

"I still think you could have looked a little further afield," said Fernsby, who was uncharacteristically merry this evening. "I know that you did not find a perfect match, but the mamas were hoping otherwise, and I do not think they would have worried whether it was for themselves or for their daughters!"

"Now come on!" protested Oscar, as Amelia raised an eyebrow suggestively. "I said there was no one who took my fancy!"

"So you say!" said Fernsby triumphantly, his eyes wide. "But there are always plenty of widows who…widows who…"

His voice trailed away, and Oscar's heart contracted. *Damn. They had been doing so well.* The entire evening had been spent in pleasant conversation and at no point had they veered near any topic which could be considered dangerous.

The rain splattered against the windows, the wind roaring around the house.

Somehow, they always managed to come back to Constance. *Even when speaking on a topic wholly unrelated to her,* Oscar thought savagely, *she suddenly reared her head and utterly derailed their conversation.*

Poor Fernsby. He looked pale, his hands now clasped in his lap, his gaze low.

Of course it was impossible to forget her. He did not wish that for his brother; he had no desire to wipe away her memory. Constance was a part of them, a part of their family. They saw her every day, in the smiles of her children. Now she was gone.

"Fernsby," said Amelia gently, for which Oscar was grateful. He did not wish to be the one to break the silence. "You do know…no one is expecting you to find someone else. You need never marry if you do not wish to."

"Yes," agreed Oscar quickly. "Many people decide never to remarry, and that is their right. We would never…you don't have to…"

Curse his tongue! If only he could explain things properly, but he had never been one to spill his feelings. Not until a certain governess had looked at him, sunlight sparkling through her hair and lavender in the air…

"Please do not apologize for something I enjoyed so much."

Oscar's jaw tightened. This was no time to lose concentration. It was Fernsby they should be worried about, not his own foolish desires. Delicious though they were.

His brother was smiling weakly. "Thank you. You are most…I do not…where would I even start, should I wish to do such a thing? It would be a foolish endeavor. Everyone would be compared to her. Everyone would fall short."

Oscar understood. Those feelings were natural and could not be argued away. "I can imagine," he said quietly. "I mean, you knew her for so long."

Amelia nodded. She had placed her glass on the small, spindly table beside her and looked uncharacteristically serious. "Well, we grew up together."

Oscar nodded but said nothing. It was not strictly true, at least not for him. Constance had indeed been a neighbor, and with an earl for a father, she was considered quite the right sort of playmate for the three Fernsbys.

Two of them. He was ten years older than his brother, and Amelia was five years younger than that. A decade separated him and his sister, and Constance was around her age. A mere child, to his eyes at the time.

By the time he was being packed off to Cambridge—much against his wishes—Constance had been but six years old. Not even Rowena's age now.

It had all been such a long time ago…

Fernsby was smiling again. "I remember," he said wistfully, his eyes not seeing the drawing room before him. "I remember when I first realized I loved her. The coming out ball."

Amelia snorted. "I was mighty young for that, really. What was our father thinking!"

"You were seventeen!" said Fernsby. "Perhaps a mite young—I would not want Rowena having her own ball at that age—but you were the baby of the family, and I think Papa was eager to have you out."

There was a wry smile on Amelia's face. "He was not the only one, as I recall. I think Mama was quite insistent."

Oscar chuckled. He could well remember the conversation, though neither of his siblings were party to it. He had been called into their father's study with their mother, and his opinion had been sought about the right time to push Amelia into society.

He could also remember his response. "Have you asked her?"

"And Constance wanted to attend," Amelia was remembering with a smile, "and her parents had almost decided she could not. Her older sister had not yet married the colonel, and so she could not really come out."

"And what a fuss she made!" Fernsby's smile had a hint of sadness. "I had never seen someone make demands so passionately, so violently, yet so sweetly."

Amelia snorted again. "She always had a way with people, did Constance."

"Our father was good enough to include her on the invitation, and I think that settled it for them," said Fernsby. "What I did not know at the time was that on that invitation, he offered me up as her first dance partner."

Oscar could not help but laugh. "And you put up quite a fuss if I remember correctly."

For a moment, he thought he had overstepped; he was not the jesting type, at least not with his brother, and it was a delicate topic.

But Fernsby laughed. "I did! I mean, who could blame me? I had known her for what felt like forever, always tagging along after me, always Mimi's little playmate—"

"Ugh, I hated that nickname!"

"—she was almost like a sister to us, wasn't she?"

Amelia smiled. "She was to me…but things changed for you that night."

Oscar watched his brother closely. *Was all this talk of Constance going to undo the progress they had made with her husband? Would this conversation stall the work achieved?*

"I could never have predicted it," said Fernsby slowly, "but having her in my arms, seeing the way other gentlemen looked at her, feeling her pulse in her wrist…I realized life would never be the same again. And it never was."

Oscar sipped his drink silently. No, that was the truth—and just over ten years later, she would be dead. Now his brother would be forced to spend the rest of his life without the woman he loved.

No matter how many happy memories he possessed, no matter the good times, the agony of losing her could not compare. He had seen it in Fernsby's face that terrible day. That terrible week. The terrible year that had followed.

Fernsby sighed, breaking the silence. "'Tis foolish to look back on the past. It is gone. Over. It cannot be repeated."

"If it brings you joy," Oscar found himself saying, quite to his own surprise, "any joy, then you should grasp it—grasp it with both hands. You grasped her, didn't you?"

Amelia caught his eye and raised her glass, and Oscar immediately rose to refresh her drink, so he was not looking at their brother when he responded.

"Grasped her? Married her within six weeks of that ball! I don't think her parents were particularly impressed."

"Not impressed?" Amelia sounded astonished. "Married to the son of a duke—and not impressed?"

Oscar knew what his brother was going to say, even with his back turned.

"Ah, but not the *heir* to a duke!" Fernsby's voice held no bitterness, to Oscar's relief. They had always had an understanding about the whole thing, and besides, Constance was made for him. He had never seen her that way. "I think the earl had plans for his daughter to marry a certain *someone else*, no matter the age difference."

Oscar had to laugh as he returned and handed Amelia her drink. "That just went to show how little he knew me, then! Me, marry a girl I had held in my arms as a newborn babe? He must have been mad!"

"Such differences have occurred in happy marriages," said

Amelia hastily.

Oscar glanced at her, now concentrating on her drink. "Who do you know with—"

"I am just saying it happens," Amelia said, a flush in her cheeks. "'Tis not impossible."

"There were over four years between Constance and me," said Fernsby. "But I wanted her, and I had the fortune of catching her eye, too."

Oscar nodded. "There you go, then. You saw happiness, and you took it."

The rain had subsided during their talk, still pattering against the windows, but in a gentler tone than before. The worst of the storm was over.

Fernsby had a faraway look on his face. "Whenever I saw her, the day was brighter. Music was more beautiful, food tasted better. She made my stomach lurch in a most uncomfortable way."

Amelia's cheeks were still pink as she said wistfully, "And is that love?"

Oscar glanced at his sister. She was getting older; he had barely noticed. She had just turned four and twenty when they lost Constance, and here she was now, almost six and twenty. Her life was slipping away.

Damn. It was his responsibility to care for her, now their parents were gone. Her marriage was in his hand, in his keeping. And what had he done? What suitors had he sought out? What indication had he given to the *ton* that he was willing to accept suggestions?

A curl of guilt clutched at his heart. *Nothing.*

When all this was over—when Fernsby was back to full health—he would have to start making a move, if it was not too late already.

"Love? I think so," said Fernsby slowly. "I have never felt that for anyone else, at any rate. It's impossible to tell when you don't have anything to compare it to. When the person you love is incomparable to all others."

Oscar's stomach lurched. Hearing his brother speak of Constance so fondly was all very nice, and he had heard it all before—at their wedding, the years after they had married…

But hearing it again now, fresh after his rather passionate encounter with Miss Kirkpatrick—it had a new resonance.

"Whenever I saw her, the day was brighter. Music was more beautiful, food tasted better. She made my stomach lurch in a most uncomfortable way."

He was no expert, but Fernsby's description sounded rather pertinent to his own strange feelings whenever the governess was in the room.

Amelia and Fernsby continued to chatter on, but Oscar was unable to join them. How could he when his mind was reeling from the very suggestion that…

He was not in love. He was not the type of gentleman to fall in love. He knew that! He took pleasure where it was offered, and that was all. Entangling himself with another person, becoming entirely reliant on them—it was not something that had ever tempted him.

The sudden loss of Constance had convinced him of that. To be so vulnerable…

Oscar found he was clenching his hands as though ready to fight. No, he would not permit himself to drop his guard.

"Love? I think so. I have never felt that for anyone else, at any rate. It's impossible to tell when you don't have anything to compare it to. When the person you love is incomparable to all others."

His brother's words were ringing in his ears, and Oscar was unable to forget them. They were so accurate to his own rather confusing feelings towards Helena—*Miss Kirkpatrick*—that he hardly knew what to do.

But it couldn't be love. Love was different; it was what other people felt—other fools.

True, she was a pretty thing: clever, talented, with all the accomplishments and more that a duchess would expect to—

But he can't think like this! Oscar took another sip of whisky as though that would help keep his mind steady and tried his best to push Miss Kirkpatrick from his mind. *He had to ignore her.* A few stolen kisses in a garden did not make a woman perfect for him.

"I-I promised myself I would stay away from you. But I don't seem to be able to do that, no matter how hard I try. And neither can you. I can see it."

"—and of course, once the banns were announced—"

"Was that the same Sunday her papa decided to come to the house and—"

Amelia and Fernsby continued to chatter away, but Oscar could not keep up. He must untangle precisely what he thought—and felt—about Helena. Miss Kirkpatrick. *The governess.*

There was passion there, by God, yes. When he had first kissed her, overwrought with desire, he could never have expected such desire to be returned.

He had kissed plenty of others—nameless faces who drifted through his mind at times, in the darkest of nights, when he felt the most alone and stiff for a woman's touch.

But none compared to Helena. The intensity of her, the taste of her—it had undone him, and he had been unable to let her go, clinging to her as though she was the only woman in the world. *The only woman. Incomparable.*

Oscar swallowed. *This was madness!*

But was it the madness of love? Was it what Fernsby had felt for his wife?

And if it was, what on earth was he going to do about it?

Helena appeared in his mind: elegant, curvaceous in all the right places, with that teasing smile on her lips that he so often saw when she was looking at him.

Oscar drained his glass. He had to ignore this wild, meandering path. She knew his secret, knew about his boxing passion. And for that reason and that reason alone, he should be careful. At any moment, she could undo him.

In more ways than one.

"—shouldn't wait much longer, for you are getting older with every passing day!"

"You think I don't know that?" Amelia's glare was something to behold, and Oscar was pulled from his daydreaming back into the conversation. "This may come as a surprise to you, Fernsby, but I wish to marry for love, too! And if I do not meet anyone I love, then I will simply die an old maid."

Fernsby looked heartbroken. "An old—"

"And why not?" shot back his sister as Oscar watched in amusement. "You assume matrimony is the only way to be truly happy—but I am quite happy with the life I have already, thank you very much!"

Oscar glanced between his siblings and decided this moment was not the right time to rejoin the conversation. *What could he add to it, after all?*

Besides, he still had thoughts of Helena absorbing his mind. It was such a tangle. If she had not known of his boxing, if she had not—well, it wasn't exactly blackmail, was it? She had been very careful about that...

"It...it would be a shame, I think, if anyone was to find out about the truth of a—a certain person's past. Recent past. In London."

How was it possible to have feelings for a woman who would do that to him? How was it possible to have feelings for a woman who was a servant anyway!

Oscar smiled wryly. Perhaps that was the problem. He had met—oh, countless ladies in society with good breeding. They would never dare to even think about blackmailing a duke.

Helena was different. She was no lady, and she clearly saw an opportunity to protect herself—and why not?

And their kisses...they had not felt like kisses between a duke and servant. Like a kiss between equals... between lovers. Between—

"You are awfully quiet, Kilerth."

Oscar started. Fernsby was watching him with great concern.

"Oh, I'm just tired, that is all," he said hastily. "In fact, I think

I am going to retire."

"Goodness, does that mean I will be last to bed?" teased Amelia. "How the tables have turned!"

"Well, I am almost an old man, remember!" Oscar said as he rose. "Good night, you two."

Their murmured goodnights disappeared as he shut the drawing room door behind him. Well, it had been a good evening, mostly. Fernsby did not seem too affected by the conversation of Constance, and perhaps that was part of the recovery, too.

It was important—it would be very important for the children to hear about their mother. The sooner she ceased to become a forbidden topic, the better.

As he climbed the stairs, Oscar could not get Helena out of his mind. He had never inquired as to where her bedchamber was—had never felt the need to know.

His body needed to know, now.

Every inch of him was taut, desire flowing through him at the mere memory of their kisses. If only he could find her and repeat that glorious experience. Perhaps be invited in. See her bedchamber...lie upon her bed and—

Oscar swallowed as he reached the top of the stairs. *No.* That was a line he must not cross. There were some things one simply did not do in someone else's house.

Even if greatly tempted.

A door to his left opened, and out came Miss Helena Kirkpatrick. The moment she saw him, a flush tinged her cheeks. "Oh—hello."

Oscar smiled, his loins stirring at the sight of her. *Tarnation, but she was beautiful.* "Hello."

Hello? Was that all he could manage? Here he was, a duke, educated to within an inch of his life, and all he could manage when speaking to a governess was "hello"?

"I was just—"

"I was only—"

They laughed awkwardly, their mingled voices echoing along

the long corridor.

Oscar's hands itched. *What did one do with one's hands?* How were they meant to hang by one's side? It was as though all reason had left him as soon as Helena had appeared!

He knew what he wanted to do with his hands. He wanted to tangle them into her hair, pull her close, breathe her in, and—

"Two more days," said Helena quietly. "Until the ball."

Oscar nodded mutely. *Dear Lord, he was an imbecile.* He had no hope of getting the woman out of his system if he couldn't even talk to her!

Say something, man!

"Yes, the ball," he said blandly. *Something interesting!* "All the preparations have been made, and half the county invited."

Helena laughed gently. "Yes, so Lady Amelia has informed me. I think she is quite looking forward to it. The children have been invited to to watch. I am excited myself. I have never been to a ball before."

Oscar's mouth fell open. "Never been to a ball? What, never? What about all your other charges, have they never been to balls?"

Only now did he realize just how close she was. He could easily reach out and touch her—taste her. Know her.

"Usually...usually mothers chaperone their children," came the quiet reply.

Ah. Yes, of course. Oscar was a fool to forget. "Well, I hope you enjoy your first ball."

Helena laughed dryly, and Oscar's stomach twisted. "My first ball at six and twenty? Does that make me an old maid?"

"No."

His response had been instant, instinctual. Helena had a smile dancing on her lips.

This time, Oscar could not lie to himself and pretend he did not know why he did it. He wanted to, that was all. He wanted her.

Leaning forward slowly to give her plenty of time to step

back if she wanted, Oscar kissed her. It was a slow kiss this time, unlike the heated frantic kisses they had shared before.

It was…loving. Reverential. Helena pressed herself against him, welcoming the kiss, but made no move to cling to him as she did before.

Which was right, thought Oscar. Whatever this was, and he wasn't entirely sure, there was no point in rushing it. He wanted to savor the pleasure.

"I…I will see you there," Helena managed before stepping away and walking down the corridor.

Oscar hated it. He wanted her close to him. He wanted—

"May I have the first dance?"

Helena turned in surprise. "The first dance?"

Oscar nodded. "Yes."

Whatever had possessed him to ask, he could not tell—only that he must. The idea she could dance with another man, be in another man's arms…

"I…I am not actually invited," she said hesitantly. "I am there only to chaperone the children."

"Consider yourself invited."

CHAPTER THIRTEEN

August 15, 1813

THIS WAS NOT precisely where she had imagined she would be, merely two months after joining the Old Abbey household, but Helena had never been one for planning ahead.

If she had, she wouldn't be loitering just outside the servants' hall, desperately wishing she had thought about this yesterday when no one would have thought anything of her request.

Now it was too late.

Helena peeked around the corner and saw the hustle and bustle of the servants' hall packed with people rushing about in their finest livery, all attempting to do what they could for the ball.

The ball. Helena heartily wished she'd had her senses about her when he had asked…

"Consider yourself invited."

Heat rushed through her, a tingling sensation dancing around the back of her neck. What had he been thinking, offering his hand—and what had she been thinking, accepting it!

It had not escaped Helena's notice that as the only servant invited to the ball—a ball which, by the sound of the carriages pulling up along the drive, had already begun—she had started to gain a few strange looks from her fellow servants.

Well, not exactly fellow servants. Mrs. Cantrell had tried to explain it to her last week.

"The thing is, my dear," said the housekeeper warmly, "there are servants, and there are servants."

Helena had tried to follow that conversation yesterday. Mrs. Cantrell had warmed to her swiftly after she had managed to stop the children from raiding the pantry of the delicate sweetmeats, and they were seated in her private study as they conversed.

"Servants and—servants?"

Mrs. Cantrell had laughed. "I don't wonder you look confused! I felt so myself the first time Mrs. Brown explained it to me—she was the housekeeper when I first joined service."

Helena had nodded. There was a trick to drawing things out of people, she had found, and she had a talent for it. Perhaps it was her theater background—the need to draw out of a character precisely what it wanted to achieve and why.

"It all comes down to writing," the housekeeper had said. "The butler, housekeeper, governess—sometimes even the steward or land agent—are all expected to write their own name."

She had said the words so impressively that Helena had waited for the rest of the explanation and had laughed when it became clear to her that that was all she was to receive.

"What, that is it?" Helena had asked. "Writing your name—that's it?"

The housekeeper had shaken her head. "Where would they learn it? What use would they put it to? It's an uncommon thing to have a free school in a town, Miss Kirkpatrick, as I am sure you know, so most people get by without it."

Perhaps she shouldn't be surprised. It had been thanks to a kind neighbor that she had her letters. Her memory was good, but she balked at the idea of learning a script by ear.

"Reading and writing. I never thought of those skills as particularly valuable."

That was what placed her and Mrs. Cantrell and McLoughlin in the middle. Between servant and served.

A shout brought Helena back to the present.

"Another three carriages!"

The two footmen who had almost sat groaned but rose again.

Helena bit her lip. There was a flurry of activity, everyone with a purpose to ensure the Old Abbey and the Fernsby family were not ashamed by the evening's entertainment.

Food was piled high, ready to be plattered up; huge bowls of punch lay ready mixed, with rows upon rows of wine bottles waiting to be uncorked. There were champagne glasses being inspected by a serious looking McLoughlin, while a nervous footman hovered beside him, and the scullery maid was red in the face from running around obeying everyone's bidding.

Well, there was nothing for it. She couldn't stand here all evening.

Stepping forward and giving a gentle cough to announce her presence, Helena tried to look defiant. *A little Juliet against her nurse, some Hermia...*

"Good evening," she said quietly.

The whole place stopped, with every eye turned toward her.

Helena had always been good at controlling her expression, a requirement, in her line of work. No longer, apparently. Despite the fact she was accustomed to audiences of over two hundred, just twenty people now staring at her was enough to cause a flush to her face.

"Ah, Miss Kirkpatrick," said the housekeeper who bustled over. "I don't know what you lot are gawking at, but there's platters to be taken upstairs!"

The servants' hall came to life once more, heads bowed under the watchful eye of Mrs. Cantrell, who turned back to the governess. "And what is the problem?"

Helena swallowed. "I...I cannot get into my gown properly."

The moment the housekeeper raised her eyebrows, mouth open with shock, Helena realized she had phrased the whole situation badly. *The woman would think—*

"Not like that!" she added hastily.

She knew precisely what Mrs. Cantrell had assumed: that the red silk gown she was wearing loosely could not be tied up because she was with child.

Well, it was a common problem amongst households like this. One of the maids had whispered some astonishing gossip to Helena just a few days ago, stories which Helena hardly believed could be true.

"It's—well, the lacing at the back," said Helena quickly. "My day gowns button at the side but this—see, here." Turning, she peered over her shoulder. "You see? Would you mind?"

Mrs. Cantrell regained her composure. "Goodness, Miss Kirkpatrick, for a moment there, I thought…but I should not have. I know you to be a fine woman, not likely to be…yes, come here into my sitting room. Stand still."

Helena's shoulders relaxed as the housekeeper started to pull at the complex lacing at the back of her gown. It was rather old-fashioned, she knew, but it was the only beautiful gown she'd had time to take from the theater after her rather abrupt send off.

It wasn't stealing, not really. It had been her performance in it as Juliet which had brought in the most money for one play in the whole history of the Theatre Royal.

Her acting had paid for that dress.

"What an honor to be invited to the ball," said Mrs. Cantrell. "I think you are the first from downstairs."

Helena had no idea what to say. *How did one respond to such a remark?*

"I look forward to chaperoning the children," she said as she found her voice, gown growing tighter. "It is hard to believe in six years, Altan will be attending in his own right."

"Chaperoning, eh?" Mrs. Cantrell gave a huge tug, and Helena gasped. "That's not what I heard."

If anyone else had spoken those words, Helena would have twisted around in horror—but Mrs. Cantrell had no malice in her tone. She had thought a theater was bad for gossip, but it turned out that a large house like the Old Abbey was just as bad, if not worse.

Helena swallowed and composed herself before saying lightly, "Well I don't know what you've heard, but I can assure you, it is nonsense."

The housekeeper was silent for a moment. "The rumor is the duke invited you."

There was nothing she could say to that. Helena did not lie, not unless absolutely necessary, and the last thing she wanted to do was confirm a rumor like that.

There was a sniff behind her. Obviously, Mrs. Cantrell did not think much of her silence. "You're all done."

She was about to thank her when the housekeeper dropped into a low curtsey.

Helena blinked. *What on earth…?* She was dressed as a fine lady, and it felt strange without a stage beneath her feet, but surely that did not necessitate such strange manners.

"My lady," murmured Mrs. Cantrell.

Helena stared. *Had the world gone mad? Was the gown sufficiently fine to—*

"Mrs. Cantrell," came a voice behind her.

Ah. That made much more sense.

Helena turned to see Lady Amelia in the doorway of the housekeeper's sitting room, a look of absolute frustration on her face. Was she angry her brother had—

"My lady's maid is indisposed and can no longer help me prepare for the ball," said Lady Amelia, a tinge of panic in her tone. "And I have no one to finish my toilette!"

That was perfectly evident. Lady Amelia had a delicate layer of powder across her face but no rouge on her cheeks, and her hair was pinned but unadorned.

Lady Amelia shouted into the servants' hall above the hubbub. "Can anyone help?"

Helena knew she might regret what she was about to offer,

but there was nothing for it. She could not permit the lady of the house to attend the ball like this.

"I can."

Lady Amelia twisted to stare. "You?"

Helena tried not to be offended by her ladyship's tone. She was, after all, merely a governess in her eyes.

"Right. Come on, then, Miss Kirkpatrick."

There was a glorious swish of her skirts as Helena walked, now her gown was properly fitted. It felt wonderful. Was there anything better than being dressed in the finest of silks, feeling the luxury on your skin, knowing all eyes that looked at you would admire you?

They took the servants' staircase and were within Lady Amelia's bedchamber in moments. Helena tried hard not to look around with too much awe. Never before had she been inside a room like this. Resplendent was the word; not quite opulent, for it would require more gold trimmings for that.

But it was comfortable. Cushions and throws scattered the bed and the chaise lounge at the end. There was a pile of novels by the bed, which Lady Amelia was evidently going through, and beside it a handkerchief. Obviously, the novels did not all have happy endings.

The room's owner dropped onto the stool by her looking glass and pointed to the jars and boxes before her.

"My lady's maid knew precisely what to do with all these ointments and clever things," said Lady Amelia. "I admit I do not. You have experience in such matters?"

Helena could not help smiling as she stepped toward the toilette. There they were, all the lotions and potions she had used time and time again at the Theatre Royal.

It was like being back. She could smell the same smells, taking her backstage in a breath to when getting one's face decorated was rather more like warpaint than a social nicety.

"Miss Kirkpatrick?" Lady Amelia's reflection glared. "Do you know what to do?"

Helena swallowed. She was being useful; that was something Miss Clarke had been very strict about. *It was important to be useful.*

"Yes," she said aloud. "Now, if my lady would be so good as to close her eyes…"

It was not difficult. In a way, it was rather fun; actresses were expected to lather on their own face paint, as Mr. Tobias had called it, and so Helena had never taken her time.

It didn't hurt that Lady Amelia had more much expensive versions of all the things Helena had been expecting. She did not recognize the names on the boxes, but that did not matter. As soon as she opened them, it was clear as day what they were used for.

"And your hair, my lady?" said Helena, placing the final tub down.

Lady Amelia opened her eyes. "My—my word! Look at me!"

"Your hair?" repeated Helena quietly.

The sounds of commotion were rising upstairs, just the loud busyness that occurred when a previously empty house suddenly hosted hundreds. Shouts, laughter, names called out, and the sound of many feet pacing through the hall and toward the ballroom.

"Oh, yes," said Lady Amelia quickly. "Here—this ribbon. It matches my gown."

It did, and it was a tricky thing to weave in and out of her mistress's curls.

"Careful!"

"Sorry, my lady," said Helena quietly, without saying it would be easier to get the pins into Lady Amelia's hair if she didn't move.

She managed to hold her tongue, and she was just about to fold the end of the ribbon behind the rather extravagant bow she had managed to tie when the door opened.

"Amelia, are you ready to—Helena. Miss Kirkpatrick. Hello."

If only that dratted mirror had not been there! Helena did not need to see her cheeks to know that they were pink, but the last thing she wanted was for Lady Amelia to see the same.

"Your sister is almost ready," she said quietly, leaning back slightly, so she was not in the direct view of the mirror. "Does she not look wonderful?"

Oscar was standing rather awkwardly in the doorway. He was dressed to the nines in the most beautifully tailored jacket and breeches Helena had ever seen. The waistcoat peeking through was embroidered all over in silver thread, so he shone when he moved, and there was a rather complex looking cravat nestled under his neck.

A neck that bobbed whenever he looked at her.

Helena tried to concentrate on finishing Lady Amelia's hair. As soon as she was done, she could leave. *That was best.*

"Amelia, you look smashing," said Oscar in some surprise.

Lady Amelia laughed, almost causing Helena to drop a pin. "No need to sound so shocked, Kilerth! Now, Miss Kirkpatrick, are you quite finished?"

Helena straightened up. "I am, my lady."

"Good." Lady Amelia rose and twirled for her brother. "Time to go."

Her brother held out his arm wordlessly, and the two of them left the room.

Helena followed a few feet behind, eyes cast down. A half completed thought—that she wished it could be *her* on the duke's arm as he entered the ballroom, and not his sister—floated through her mind, but Helena pushed it aside. Lady Amelia rightly had that place.

Murmurs rose in the hallway as the three of them descended the staircase.

Helena's breath tightened in her chest, and she concentrated on not slipping down the last few steps. *Had the red gown with the black lace been too much?* It was her best gown—her only gown suitable, really—but it was…startling.

Raising her gaze, Helena saw that half the hall's occupants

were looking at Lady Amelia and the other half…

She dropped her eyes. It was just one evening, then it would be over.

The crowd parted to let the Duke of Kilerth and his sister through but closed before Helena could join them. She had to fight through the crowd of gentlemen shouting for friends, ladies fluttering fans to make snide comments behind them before she reached the ballroom.

A ballroom which was completely different. The last time Helena was here, Rowena had been practicing a rather dramatic death scene, and they had been forced to lay down a mattress onto their chalk-marked stage to prevent harm.

Now the ballroom was opulent. Candles glimmered in every candelabra, chandeliers simply dripping with sparkles. There were tables groaning with food at one end, and alongside those, plinths with punchbowls and glasses set beside them.

The room was packed. Everyone from the county indeed had been invited, as Oscar had said, and there were shouts of greeting, laughter at outrageous outfits, the sneers one at any woman who wore too many feathers, smoke rising from one corner where a group of older gentlemen were lighting their pipes.

Helena swallowed. It was overwhelming. The place had been empty since she had arrived, no visitors, no guests of any kind. She had forgotten there was a real world out there.

All because of the baron. He slipped into her memory like a knife, and Helena looked around hurriedly, desperately seeking him out. Wouldn't he be overwhelmed by such a crowd? Had he really intended there to be such a large invitation list?

Her gaze found him. Seated in a corner in one of the arm-chairs brought through from the drawing room, Baron Fernsby looked nervous, but he was not alone.

There were two chairs beside the baron's, and one of them was filled by a gentleman Helena recognized as the undependable Mr. Hough, the boy's fencing tutor.

Helena's stomach relaxed, and her breathing slowed. The

man may only have come once since her arrival, but he was clearly trusted by the family with Altan's education. It was right that someone sat with the baron. He should not be alone.

"Is it all as you expected?"

Helena smiled before turning to see Oscar standing right behind her. She would know that voice anywhere, but she had to attempt to keep some distance between them. Especially as they were in public. "Far more impressive than I had imagined, actually, Kilerth."

Oscar smiled. "I think I would prefer you to call me Oscar."

He spoke softly. They were so close together. Helena's heart quickened, and she looked around them, nervous to see who else could have caught such a response.

"I-I don't think I should," she managed.

Oscar—for she would never think of him as Kilerth, not now—stepped even closer. "Yet I would like it."

Helena tried to take a step back but was prevented by the ever-increasing crowd.

"Mind yourself!" said a rather uncouth gentleman who was passing.

Though she flushed, Helena was not offended. She had, after all, stepped on his foot—and the interruption seemed to have reminded the duke that they were not alone.

"Fernsby always puts on a good show," he said in a louder voice. "Though I admit, it's nothing to what I would have planned for Riverside Manor."

Helena was forced to step forward to prevent herself from being stampeded by a gaggle of ladies, all of whom appeared to be desperate to see Lady Amelia.

Now she was too close. *Very close.* If she moved an inch, their hands would meet.

Helena quickly clasped hers. *This was getting ridiculous. She must not lose control.*

"Riverside Manor?" she said lightly. "Your home?"

Oscar nodded. "Yes, a much larger place than this Old Abbey.

The ballroom is bigger, too, and I find the musicians I am able to source from—what on earth is so funny?"

Helena had not been able to prevent herself from laughing. "'Tis nothing."

"'Tis something," he said, put out. "What did I say that was so amusing?"

Helena would never have been honest with a duke. But Oscar did not feel like a duke, dressed though he was in fine and splendor. He was just a man. *A man she liked.* And why shouldn't she? She liked lots of people. She liked the baron, though that feeling wasn't tempered with a desire to see what he looked like without his fine jacket…

"It really is nothing," she said with a smile. "It was just…it felt like what children say. My horse is bigger than your horse, and my father is stronger than your father."

"Maybe," Oscar said with a chuckle. "Maybe I was. Maybe I want to impress you."

If only her heart wouldn't beat so loud, it would be possible for Helena to think. The heat of the room was growing, and that tingle on the back of her neck was back.

"Maybe you do," she said lightly. "But maybe I cannot be that easily impressed. You will have to excuse me, Your Grace, I need to see to the children."

With a great effort, Helena turned away and toward the door where the children had entered the ballroom.

Sylvia appeared unable to contain herself. "Miss Perpatrick, look at my gown!"

"Very beautiful," said Helena with a smile. "You three will have to make sure you don't get in the way."

She looked purposefully at Altan as she spoke, who sighed but took his youngest sister's hand. "We won't, Miss Kirkpatrick. We'll stay on the edge of the room and watch—look, there's my fencing tutor—goodness, he's going to dance with Auntie Amelia!"

Helena's head turned. Whether or not Lady Amelia danced

with Mr. Hough was neither here nor there, a pleasant courtesy to thank the man for sitting with her brother, no more.

No, it was the fact that the dancing was about to begin that made her chest tighten. *Had he remembered?* After all the gossip in the servants' hall, was he still going to honor his promise to her?

Yes, there he was. The Duke of Kilerth, her Oscar, was walking toward her.

Helena swallowed. Surely he would not be so foolish as to dance with her in public—and for the first dance!

Oscar stopped before her. "Can I tear you away from your charges?"

"You want to dance with Miss Kirkpatrick?"

Did Rowena have to sound so surprised? "Don't be silly, Rowena, he—"

"Of course I do," said Oscar smoothly with a wink at the children. "If her dancing is anything like her swordplay, she'll be the best dancer here."

His hand was outstretched.

The world seemed to pause in that moment. The choice before her was simple, wasn't it? Take Oscar's hand and be the most important woman in the dance, on a duke's arm, in her borrowed—*well, stolen*—finery.

It was a heady image.

"Miss Kirkpatrick?" Oscar prompted.

Helena looked into his eyes. There was fear there, a fear she did not understand. He had surely never been rejected, never unwanted. He was a duke, for goodness' sake!

The eyes of the entire ballroom—or at least, those around her—were on her.

Helena swallowed, reached out, and took his hand. She didn't have any gloves. There never were gloves in a production at the Theatre Royal, so there weren't any to steal.

He wasn't wearing gloves either. The contact between them, skin to skin, finger to finger, was electric. The tingling at the base of Helena's neck spread across her entire body as though she had come alive for the first time.

"Go and behave, children," said Oscar carelessly before he turned and led Helena to the line of dancers.

Helena did not permit herself to look at him, the man who clasped her hand so tightly, as though he, too, was aware that what they were doing was nigh on madness.

Baron Fernsby was not joining them. He was still seated in his armchair, his face toward the dancers but making no move to mirror them.

"He won't dance."

Oscar had evidently seen where she had been looking.

"He won't?"

The duke shook his head. "He says he won't dance now, and I don't think he will."

She wanted to ask more questions about the baron and his wife and what happened to her, but the musicians struck up, and the first notes of the dance heralded them. Oscar bowed and took his place in the line.

Helena had never danced in public like this before. The dances she knew were those of the theater, and to her relief, the music for the first dance was one of the few she knew.

Still, she was rusty. As she stepped forward with the other ladies, she saw Lady Amelia beside her, the fencing tutor opposite. It was a real kindness to show to the man.

The dance shifted, and Oscar stepped toward her to link hands. Their hands touched, and Helena tried once again not to notice the intensity of that moment. Side by side, they started to promenade down the line.

"I have been thinking about this all day."

Oscar's voice was so low, Helena barely caught it, but there was no mistaking him.

She had to stay calm. She must not read into this any more than she already was. "Yes, the ball has been quite exciting."

"That's not what I meant," said Oscar quietly. "And you know it."

They separated, the music compelling them to release hands and return to their lines, to Helena's relief. *What was happening— and what on earth would happen next?* She had but a few moments to compose herself when they stepped forward and clasped hands once more.

"I...I have very warm feelings for you, Helena."

No, this was too much. How could he say such things to her, and in public?

Helena pulled her hands from his grip and almost walked straight into Lady Amelia beside her. Muttering apologies to those she pushed past, Helena broke away from the dance and headed blindly toward the closest door she could find—to the nearest escape.

The hallway was mercifully quiet, calm, and cool.

If only there weren't footsteps behind her.

She turned to see Oscar slam the door behind him in his haste. "Helena, I—I am sorry, I should never have—"

Helena took three strides forward and kissed him full on the mouth. All that frustration, all that fear, all the desire she felt, and the need to be close to him overwhelmed her, and the only way she could think to release the tension building in her was to show him.

Oscar's arms quickly wrapped around her, and the force of his passion made Helena take a few steps back. His tongue teased her lips, and she immediately opened for him, welcoming him in, welcoming the shivers of pleasure he created.

"Helena," he murmured into her mouth, evidently unable to stop. "Oh, Helena..."

She had tangled her hands around his neck in an attempt to bring him closer, and as he took another step forward, she fell.

The terrible rushing sensation did not come. Oscar had caught her, held her close in his arms—but she was not to stay there.

Unbeknownst to Helena, they had reached the staircase. She was only made aware of the fact as Oscar lowered her gently onto the bottom steps and covered his body with his own.

Oh, it was glorious and terrible and wonderful! It was scandalous—they were kissing right out in the open, his strong chest covering hers, pressed up against her breasts, Oscar's hand pulling her leg around him, and Helena let him.

She would let him do anything.

Her body was on fire for him, ripples of heat flowing wherever his fingers rested, if even for a moment.

This was what she wanted. Helena had not known it until it had happened, but this was like she had fallen into a dream—someone else's dream!

"Damn, Helena…" murmured the duke as he kissed her neck.

Helena could barely see, her senses were so overwhelmed, but one thought managed to make itself heard.

This was someone else's life. Accustomed as she was to inhabiting the lives of others on the stage, this wasn't the stage—this was real life. Another young lady should be kissing the duke, not her!

Another few minutes passed in intoxicating kisses, and finally she had the strength to push him away.

"No," she panted, and Oscar straightened as she pushed herself upright. "No, w-we can't make a habit out of this."

"Why?" said the duke, eyes bright, his cravat half untied and his hair mussed. "I want to."

Helena opened her mouth, but no sound came out. *How could she respond to that—how could she articulate just how wrong this was, when everything about Oscar felt so right?*

The sound of footsteps.

"Have you cooled from the heat of the dance, Miss Kirkpatrick?" Oscar said loudly as a footman entered the hall.

Helena glared. *The dratted man knew quite well she was warmer now than she ever had been in her life!* "Yes, thank you, Your Grace."

"Then let me escort you back to the dance," he said, holding out his hand.

There was a sparkle in his eyes Helena knew was for her. *He wanted her.* She had wanted him in that moment, and it was good fortune alone that had prevented them from being caught by the footman. *No, she had to take back some control.*

"Thank you, but I think I will do no more dancing," she said politely, leaving Oscar's hand unclaimed. "I wish you luck with your next partner."

Helena had only just managed to step into the ballroom when she was immediately accosted by the duke's sister.

"Miss Kirkpatrick!" Lady Amelia rushed toward her. "I said to Mr. Hough myself just before we danced, it was far too hot in here—are you quite well?"

"I overheated a little," said Helena automatically.

"Yes, 'tis so easy to become overly warm," said Lady Amelia sagely. The fencing tutor had joined her and nodded in agreement. "I think we may have to wait to put on the play until we are sure the children won't be affected."

"The play?" said Mr. Hough.

"Oh, yes," Oscar said impressively. "Hel—Miss Kirkpatrick is putting together a rather wonderful play with the children. I am quite certain it will be incredible."

"That would explain young Master Fernsby's new interest in fencing," said Mr. Hough with a dry laugh.

Lady Amelia and her brother laughed.

"Oh, I think that particular scene is charming," said Oscar breezily. "I must say Miss Kirkpatrick has taken real pains with the children. I was particularly impressed by…"

Discomfort crept up Helena's spine as she was forced to stand there and listen to Oscar, who had moments ago been pulling her leg closer around him, pressed up against the staircase.

For a moment, she could suspend her disbelief and imagine that she was a part of this world. *Of his world.*

"And you are a friend of the family?"

Helena blushed at the question from the fencing tutor. Of course, she had not been introduced!

"Something like that," said Oscar.

Lady Amelia looked with surprise at her brother. "Miss Kirkpatrick is our governess. We thought it would be nice for children to see the ball. After all, it is their first—where are the children, Miss Kirkpatrick?"

Helena dipped into a curtsey. *Here it was, her perfect excuse to escape.* "I will go and look for them, my lady, Your Grace, sir."

As she left and started hunting out the Fernsby children in the crowd, Helena tried to remind herself of two things. Firstly, that Oscar Fernsby was the Duke of Kilerth, and secondly, that she was a governess—or more accurately, an actress masquerading as a governess. Those two had no future together.

CHAPTER FOURTEEN

August 18, 1813

NO MATTER HOW long he looked at it, the ceiling above Oscar did not seem inclined to change. It was most irritating. He needed some sort of entertainment, though what could possibly interest him at one in the morning, he did not know.

He lay there on his back, hands clenched. It was all Helena's fault.

"No, w-we can't make a habit out of this."

He'd been a gentleman, as best he could since she had uttered those words. He hadn't sought her out in the house, though he had been sorely tempted. When he had accidentally come across her, he had not lingered longer than was expected. He had even, when asked by Amelia how the play was going, resisted using her question as an excuse to ask Helena.

He was almost a saint.

Yet despite all that, one person appeared in his mind, lying beneath him on the stairs, lips pink with the passion of his kisses, eyelids fluttering as she accepted his touch…

His nails bit into his palms. *Helena.* It had been three long days since that moment on the staircase. Three days of agony.

Three days of holding back.

She was avoiding him. He knew it. The Old Abbey was not large enough to accidentally not see someone for that time. She was purposefully ensuring they did not meet.

Oscar sighed heavily.

What was wrong with him? Never before had a woman so consumed him, had taken all his ability to think and simply thrown it away.

Obsessed, he thought darkly. That was the only word that could describe him, and it was the first time he had ever used it for himself.

Obsessed. Unable to think of anything or anyone other than her.

"Kilerth? Kilerth, can you hear me?"

It had been the constant refrain from both his siblings since the ball. No matter the topic of conversation, after a few minutes, Oscar's eyes glazed over, and he was lost once more in thoughts of Helena. *Daydreams of Helena. Lustful hopes of Helena.*

Oscar groaned and rolled over onto his side. This was ridiculous, and what was worse, he knew precisely what he could do to rid himself of such feelings if he had been at home. Or in London. Anywhere but here.

His mind flickered to the gymnasium he had constructed in the older part of the stables, back at Riverside Manor in Kilerth. It was set up to his specifications and helped relieve his frustration more times than he could count.

Everyone at Riverside Manor knew not to disturb him in there. All his servants politely refused to see what was in there, and he had never once been concerned that the truth would get out. But here…

Oscar sighed. He had no doubt his brother's servants were good sorts, but they were not his servants. He could not pour his tension into his boxing, and instead, it grew within him, desperate to pour out in fighting or lovemaking. Either would be a relief right now.

No, this was foolish. He needed to sleep.

If only it were that simple. Closing his eyes, Oscar was unsurprised to see images flicker past his mind, all with a common theme. *Helena.*

Helena, playing with the children, getting Altan to laugh for the first time in months.

Helena, helping his sister with her hair, as though she were one of the family.

Helena, at the ball, quiet but clearly the prettiest woman there.

Helena, dancing with him.

Helena, squirming with pleasure beneath him on the stairs...

Oscar's eyes snapped open. *Damn.*

If he was in any way capable of being rational, he would leave her alone. What good could come of pursuing a woman like that? A governess, for goodness' sake! What on earth would a woman like her and a duke have in common?

It didn't matter how hard he tried to convince himself. Her company—it was the finest he had ever known. She was so interesting. Where had she learned to fence like that?

Every time Oscar was certain he understood her, there was another revelation. Something in him knew her on a deeper level than his consciousness. She didn't understand it any more than he did.

No other lady shone as brightly as Helena did. No one made his spirit soar when they were together. *No one kissed as she did.*

Oscar sat up abruptly. No, this was ridiculous. He was not going to get any sleep like this, his mind racing over and over the same things, tied in knots over Helena.

Perhaps bedding her would rid Helena from his system. Perhaps it was the forbiddenness of it all, the forbidden fruit, that made her so tantalizing. Though he had been tempted many times, he had never attempted to find the governess's bedchamber.

If only he was home. If he had been in Kilerththe warm summer evenings would lend themselves to horse riding or slow walks along the Long Border.

He couldn't do that here. If a servant noticed him saddling up a horse or, God forbid, Fernsby did, he would never hear the end of it.

The last thing he wanted was to cause his brother concern, especially after the ball had gone so well. Even Amelia had remarked upon it; how kind old Hough had been to sit with him, how Fernsby had enjoyed his company and seeing friends and neighbors…

There was even talk, though Oscar could hardly believe it, of going to *visit* some of those neighbors. He would believe it when he saw it, but that wasn't the point. The point was, Fernsby was talking about it.

Perhaps Helena could accompany them. Perhaps they could walk in a new garden, find new ways to kiss, to please each other to—

Oscar swallowed. There were two things he desperately wished to do, both of which would be frowned upon. He was not ready—not yet—to attempt one. So that meant the other.

It took him but a few minutes to slip on breeches, socks, and a shirt. There was no point finding a waistcoat, even if he could, nor a jacket. He wouldn't need them.

The door creaked, but Oscar was not concerned. No one would be up at this hour, not even servants. His socks were soft on the carpet. No one would suspect.

It felt strange, creeping down the corridors in the gloom of night. Thank goodness he had been here months now; he knew the way without needing a candle.

Was his idea foolish or brilliant? It was hard to tell.

If it worked, he would be blessed with a few hours of sleep, and that would make all the difference. Fernsby was much easier to appease when both of them had a decent amount of kip the night before.

Only five minutes later, Oscar had slipped into the stables. If he remembered correctly…yes, there it was—an empty pen. A few strands of straw still lined the floor but most was untouched flagstones. *Perfect.*

Oscar closed the door behind him, hoping his presence wouldn't alarm the sleeping horses, and took a deep breath. *This was it—his chance to finally relax.*

Stretching up on his tiptoes, he reached as high as he could, then slowly folded himself in half, reaching down to the floor. Oscar repeated this a few times, feeling his back stretch out, feeling the muscles loosening.

Then he stood straight and twisted at the waist, first left, then right. Yes, it was all coming back to him. His body knew what to do, even if his mind was overwhelmed. His muscles slotted into place and picked up his warming routine.

Four different stretches later, Oscar was ready. His heart was racing pre-emptively, knowing full well what he was about to do. Lifting off the back of his feet, he bounced on his toes and suddenly lunged forward, punching the invisible person that stood before him.

An upper cut to the jaw.

Darting about as though the invisible man had attempted to cuff his ear, Oscar bobbed and weaved, his breath rising and his heart pattering, before he lunged once more.

One, two. Right then left, leading with his dominant hand.

It was glorious. It was precisely what he had missed all these months. As Oscar moved around the stall, feet silent on the cobblestones and no hint of his presence save for his heavy breathing, he poured himself into the movement, losing himself in the dance of the fight—albeit a pretend one.

Lungs working hard, the effort raised his spirits immediately. He should have thought of this before. Why, he could have come down here every evening.

It felt glorious. As Oscar ducked from his imaginary opponent, he felt life course through his veins once more. It was a special kind of relief, boxing. True, it did not have the satisfaction of feeling his knuckles make contact with skin, but it was close enough.

How long he was there, Oscar did not know. It was impossible to tell. By the time he came to a slow stop, beads of sweat had collected on his forehead, and he was out of breath.

Oscar leaned against the stall and smiled. He was losing his form. When he was back in London, he would have to train harder—whenever that would be.

He had promised Amelia he would stay three months. *Three months?* That time had been and gone, and he was still here, locked up in the Old Abbey.

Helena kept him here. Oscar shook his head. He was not going to admit that to himself, let alone anyone else. *Time to return to the house before the damned governess could seep back into his mind again.*

As he gently closed the side door, Oscar paused to listen. If he had disturbed someone on his way out, they could still be awake. The last thing he needed was to try to explain why he was wandering about the place in his socks and breeches.

Silence. Hopefully he would continue to be just as fortunate in the future when he could slip to the stables and fight an imaginary man.

However, silence was not to accompany him all the way to his bedchamber. To the contrary, as he stepped down the corridor toward the staircase, a noise arrested his ears, and he paused immediately, listening. Was it a servant, finishing late for the night? One of the children, unable to sleep and wandering about?

No. No, it sounded like…Helena. But not Helena.

Oscar shook his head as though ridding water from his ears. Was his mind truly so fixated on the woman that he could not even tell whether she was speaking?

The sound seemed to be coming from the ballroom. Tiptoeing over, Oscar saw light pooling out from under the door. Taking a deep breath and unsure whether he should return to his bed, he opened the door.

Light. Candles, several of them, all at the other end of the ballroom. The rest of the room was in darkness, including where he was. Within the dazzling light of the candles, Helena.

She was moving elegantly, striding around and speaking softly, though her words carried across the empty ballroom. She appeared to be—rehearsing?

Oscar shook his head. He had never encountered a governess who was so dedicated to her charges. *Was she truly working on the play at this hour?*

Within a moment, he knew he was wrong. His mouth fell open.

Helena was rehearsing, but it was unlike anything the children had created. As he stood in the shadows, entirely unnoticed, Helena delivered a performance worthy of an actress on a London stage.

"Soft, soft the night that secrets hide when misery of truth decides to creep," she said, her face an agony of misery. "And though the herald of the sun doth rise, none here can welcome truly without sighs."

Oscar closed his mouth hastily. She had not seen him, her eyes dazzled by the candles, and she continued. What sounded like Shakespeare poured from her mouth, yet it was not the words themselves that amazed him.

Ye gods, she was wonderful. Helena was another character: her movements, her mannerisms, the exquisite pain on her face, and the tremble of her voice…

None of the actresses Oscar had seen perform in London, and he attended the theater fairly regularly when in town, had ever come close to this.

And Helena was a mere governess!

How he could ever have thought her just a servant when she first arrived. Had she not given him ample opportunities to recognize her brilliance? Her skills, numerous and extensive, should have been enough, but no, it was not until now that he saw her for what she truly was.

Marvelous. Talented. Beautiful.

"Oh, leave me not alone to my dark thoughts," she murmured to an invisible person on the pretend stage. "When death alone can bring me to my fate…"

Oscar swallowed. *She was…magnificent. There was no other word for it.*

When he had jested, what felt like eons ago, that she had prodigious skill, he had no idea just how true those words were. What else was there to discover about this woman?

Oscar's heart was thundering again just as violently as it had been when he had been darting around the punches of his invisible opponent. *Helena Kirkpatrick.* How was he ever to look at another woman and not compare the two?

He tried to step closer, his desire drawing him inexorably closer, but there was a squeak. A floorboard. *Damn.*

Helena stopped immediately. She straightened, all vestiges of the character falling away, and the glare she shot into the darkness was precise.

"Who's there?" Her voice was not nervous nor upset. It was more…*curious.*

Oscar swallowed. This was not what he had planned for the early hours of the morning, but it appeared fate had different ideas.

"I-I am sorry," he said, hating the quiver in his voice. *What was wrong with him?* "I did not intend to interrupt."

Helena's features softened, and Oscar's heart leapt traitorously.

"Oh," she said softly. "Well. In that case, come forward."

"I did not—if you would rather practice alone, I can—"

"Nonsense, don't be daft," came the decided reply from the governess. "I was just about to start the soliloquy, and it feels odd to finish the scene without it. Are you happy to accommodate me?"

Accommodate her? Slightly unsure what he was agreeing to, Oscar nodded. Then realizing she could probably not see him, he said, "Of course."

Helena smiled, but the smile did not last long. Instead, she rearranged her features into a somber, longing look. She knelt on the floor, and after a moment's silence, began her speech.

Once she finished, silence echoed around the ballroom. Oscar found his breath caught in his throat.

What wonder was this? He had heard Juliet's speech before; read the dratted thing; even seen it performed a few times. But this rendition had utterly moved him. Emotions he had never felt before roared through his veins. *How was it possible for mere words to elicit this?*

Helena cleared her throat. "End scene. Oscar, you are the perfect audience."

Oscar laughed dryly, stepping into the glare of the candle-light. For a moment, Helena had been adorned in silks and diamonds, so powerful was her performance.

"I hope the children are this good."

Helena laughed. "I think they will be better, and they will act with more heart than I do."

"Does this mean your heart is otherwise engaged?" Oscar had not thought, and the words had simply poured from him.

Helena hesitated before responding in a quiet voice. "I...I don't think it's a good idea if I answer that question."

Oscar's heart was thundering in his chest. Could she not hear it? Surely the whole world could! "Perhaps not. Come, join me in the drawing room. We can talk for a while."

Anything to spend more time with her. Anything to draw out this strange night, where imaginary boxing and imaginary stages ruled hearts and minds.

Helena did not jump at his suggestion. "What have you been doing at such an hour?"

She already knew too much about his boxing. "We all have our secrets."

That, at least, made her smile. "The drawing room it is, then."

Oscar dropped into an armchair by a window, curtains now

drawn, and indicated that Helena should join him. She curled up like a cat instead, sitting on the floor by the window, but not before she had pulled it open.

"I like to see the stars," she said by way of explanation. "You never see the stars in London."

Oscar looked at her, her face turned upward to the heavens. Something painful stirred in his stomach. "You never fail to astonish me," he said softly.

Helena chuckled. "I will be disappointed when I do."

"Not possible."

"No one is truly unique," she pointed out. "There must be a hundred women like me."

"Perhaps a few as beautiful. One or two as talented. Maybe a handful as kindhearted. But all of that combined into one?"

Even in the gloom of the room, he could see a blush painting her cheeks. He had embarrassed her. Was that a good thing?

"Honestly, I...I have never met anyone like you."

Helena avoided his gaze. "You must have done. You, a duke. You have moved in circles far wider than I ever have, encountered a great number of people."

"And yet..." Oscar allowed his voice to trail away to indicate just how unusual she was. And she was. *If only he could make her see that.*

"Well, every woman is different, I suppose," said Helena, finally dragging her gaze away from the window and smiling. "Look at myself and Lady Amelia. We are very different."

Oscar had to laugh at that. "My word, yes. I think there's probably only room in the world for one Amelia. And Constance, she was different again."

He probably should not have spoken about her, but Helena...she was a part of this household. A part of his life. Though Oscar had no idea how she was going to fit into his life, he was now certain that she would be, one way or another, a permanent fixture.

He could not keep hiding Constance. They couldn't.

"I..." Helena swallowed. "I do not know much about her. Constance, I mean."

Oscar hesitated. "She... is not spoken of. It is not forbidden, Fernsby doesn't have the capacity to consider that. It wouldn't hurt you to know, I suppose. You care for the children."

She waited. *Blast.* If he had thought about this, he could have prepared something, a short, concise speech. As it was...

"Constance was the daughter of our neighbors in Kilerth," Oscar said with a sigh. "A few years younger than Fernsby, close to Amelia. They grew up with her. All of a sudden Fernsby saw her for the woman she was, and they were married."

He swallowed. *All this talk of matrimony, it was strange between them.*

"Two children arrived in relatively quick succession, and then Sylvia, and then just three years later...the accident."

Oscar's jaw tightened. It was painful, even now. He always thought it would be easier, yet time seemed unable to heal that wound.

"A hunting accident," he said, his voice a little harsh. "None of us thought much about it, she only scratched her arm and injured her wrist. Rest, that was what the doctor said. Rest and recuperation, and she'd be up in a few days. Ha."

His laugh was mirthless.

"But she wasn't."

"The wound...it became infected. The next day she was in bed with a fever. The day after, she did not know her husband. The next day she was dead."

Oscar found he was gripping the arms of his chair and forced himself to release it. *Dear God, that it could all be over so quickly.* He had thought there had been a mistake when the message came— that terrible letter.

"And when she was alive?"

Oscar blinked. Helena looked somber, but her gaze was still curious. "Alive?"

She nodded. "When Constance—when the baroness was

alive. What was she like?"

It was a strange question. "Honestly, when I think about her, I think of the accident."

"That's sad," said Helena softly. "It sounds like, from the little I have heard from the other servants…well, that she lived a joyful life. A love match, three children she adored. It is sad indeed that because of her loss, none of the happy memories are remembered."

Oscar stared. *He had never considered that.* "You continue to impress me with your insight, Helena."

She laughed softly. "Oh, I don't know about that. When one is not part of the family, it is easier to look at things."

The words were on the tip of his tongue to say that he wished she was part of the family. That she would be with them, with him, forever.

Oscar managed to restrain himself. He was feeling sentimental, speaking of Constance. That was all. He needed to get a grip not of the chair but himself.

"So that's why your brother does not wish to leave the house?"

Oscar nodded. "I worry about him, but the best doctors have said it is grief keeping him here, nothing else. We have to support him best we can until he recovers. *If* he recovers."

He had never spoken of his fear that Fernsby would remain as he was, not to anyone—especially not Amelia. She needed hope, not reality.

"You care for him very well. You are…you are a good brother."

Why did her words matter so much to him? "I do what I can."

"You do it well, and other than your sister, you do it alone," said Helena quietly. "I…well, I think often about our conversation in the kitchen garden."

A tingling sensation spread up his spine at her words. *So did he, but perhaps for very different reasons.*

"You said that you bore great responsibility for them—your

family—and that you did it alone," Helena murmured. "I...I wish you didn't have to. Do it alone, I mean."

Oscar swallowed, and they fell into silence—a silence layered with the words they could not say.

If only she was someone different: a lady, a daughter of a friend of the family. How different things could have been.

"I always feel better with you," he whispered.

Helena's eyes met his. "Oscar, you mustn't speak to me like that."

Oscar met her gaze. "Why not?"

"You know precisely why not," she said softly. There was no frustration in her voice, but there was deep emotion. Emotion he didn't understand.

"I don't want to deny what I feel." Oscar could barely believe he was saying this. "What I think we feel."

There wasn't a word for it.

She rose and stepped to him, settling herself on his lap and lifting his chin.

Oscar welcomed the kiss. There was passion there, true, but this was different from any other kiss they had shared. This time, it was as though their souls had connected. The desire to be held, to be understood, not to be alone in the world...it overtook him. The feel of her on his lap, the reassuring weight of her, the way her hair fell around him as she kissed him...

He lost himself in her. He *wanted* to lose himself in her. She was everything, everything he wanted. *Everything he could not have.*

Helena raised her head and smiled wryly. "Look at the two of us here, without any finery. I could almost believe we were equals."

Her voice was rueful, and Oscar looked with something akin to desire but deeper filling his heart. "We are equals."

She laughed softly at that. "My skills may outnumber yours, but your rank—"

"It's just the two of us." Oscar's eyes raked over her face, taking in every detail, desperate to prolong this moment. "When it's just us, just you and me, I don't want to think about rank. I don't want to think about what separates us, what divides us. I want to think about the connection we feel, the desire we share."

He raised his mouth to be kissed again, and she obliged, her hands around his neck and his cupping her buttocks. This was glorious; this was all he wanted.

When the kiss finally broke apart, Helena was smiling. "I don't know what this is."

"Neither do I," admitted Oscar. "I don't think it needs a label. We can discuss that next time."

Helena raised an eyebrow. "Oh, so there'll be a next time?"

"There shouldn't be," Oscar said, pulling her closer for another kiss. "But there will be."

CHAPTER FIFTEEN

August 21, 1813

Helena smiled and took a step back. "There, that should do it!"

The footman who had helped joined her to look critically at what they had spent the entire day working on. "Does it?"

Helena chuckled. "Well, I wasn't expecting the Royal Opera House."

"The what?"

She looked at the footman, Johns. Never left the county, she had heard him once say in the servants' hall. Never had any desire to, he had said. What was there out there that home couldn't offer?

"Never mind," Helena said quietly. "The point is, the stage is complete."

Her gaze drifted back to the stage they had built in the ballroom. Well, as close to a stage as one was likely to get without damaging the floor, which was something Lady Amelia was insistent about.

"I will not have my brother's ballroom floor ruined, even if it is for the children," Helena had overheard Lady Amelia say to

Oscar. "What stage do they need, anyway?"

Helena smiled. It was not high, perhaps three feet from the ground. The careful wooden slats had been nailed down expertly under her critical eye.

"It's just a load of boarding!" protested the stable hand assigned to help her. "Why go to all that bother just for—"

Helena had stared him down. "It's a stage for the baron's children, and we don't want any accidents, do we? No splinters in fingers or nails in toes?"

He had given in with good grace, eventually, but there had been some muttering Helena had chosen not to listen to as he trudged back to the stables.

But here it was. Relief rushed through her. A theater for the children. It was finally finished.

"Looks good, that," said Johns. "Is that what you wanted?"

Helena hesitated. It was never going to be like the theater she loved, she had reminded herself as the pieces had come together that afternoon. But it was hers. Theirs. The children's. In a way, it was better than she had imagined. More intimate. More for the imagination to do.

"It's perfect," she said quietly. "Thank you."

The footman beamed. "All in a day's work, Miss."

Helena remembered, a little too late, that Mrs. Cantrell had warned her about the footmen. Apparently, many of them had…well. *Gained expectations.*

"Expectations!" Helena had said in horror just the day before. "My dear Mrs. Cantrell, I have never—"

"Oh, I don't blame you, not in the slightest," the housekeeper had said good-naturedly. "It was always going to happen, a new woman in the servants' hall. Just you mind yourself. You don't want any of them getting ideas."

Johns grinned beside her. "You want me to help you up onto it?"

"No," said Helena decidedly. "No, you can leave me to—"

"Miss Kirkpatrick, it looks wonderful!" Altan was standing in the doorway of the ballroom, staring in wonder at the construction completed in just one day. "The stage!" He rushed forward, and Helena put out a hand to warn him to be careful—but it was unnecessary.

As though suddenly conscious of both himself and those around him, the boy slowed to a saunter and looked at the stage as though he was inspecting a pig at the fair.

Helena smiled. It was a strange sort of time, eleven years old, especially for a boy. Not really a child like his youngest sister, but nowhere near an adult, Altan was starting to become conscious of all the ways he would be different in a few years. When he was a man.

At the same time, there was no getting around the fact that he looked intensely excited.

"And it is going to be big enough?" he asked Helena with a gleam in his eyes. "For my big fight scene?"

"And my dramatic death scene," chimed in Rowena, who was walking slowly across the ballroom with her sister's hand in hers. "You can't forget that!"

"Each of you will have plenty of room to perform your scenes beautifully," said Helena, forestalling any argument. "I would like you to take your sister—hello, Sylvia—and walk across the stage. Slowly, Altan! It will take you time to get used to it."

She watched as the two elder siblings pulled up Sylvia and started slowly to walk around the stage. Their confidence grew with every step, she could see.

Helena's heart warmed. All three children had spoken of their excitement for the play, and Rowena and Altan had worked hard on their speeches.

If Altan had not been born the son of a baron, the heir to that title—not to mention the current heir of his uncle's—he would have made a good actor.

No. She shook her head as though to dislodge the thought. *No, that was foolishness.* The baron only accepted this whole endeavor because he saw it as a game, a way to entertain his brood. She could not imagine how her master would react if she even mentioned that Altan might do well on the stage.

Oscar might understand, though. After all, he knew of her past and had permitted her to create a play for the children. He was not so narrowminded as his family, nor other dukes and titled gentlemen who would consider it an outrage for her to even be here.

Oscar. Helena smiled, her heart warming at the very thought of him. Somehow, her thoughts always meandered back to the duke.

Which was foolish. Though they enjoyed their kisses together, sweet moments of heat that awakened something within her, she did not fully understand. He did not care for her. Oh, he liked her, certainly. The Duke of Kilerth enjoyed her company and found her pleasing to look at, which she supposed she should be grateful for.

But anything more than that?

No. A duke and a governess do not have happy endings. Theirs was the tragic sort of story, and she would be best to ensure her heart did not become entangled.

Helena sighed. If it hadn't already.

"Look, Miss Perkpaptrick!"

At least there was always Sylvia to put a smile on her face. Helena grinned as she stepped forward to the stage, as Sylvia raised her hands in triumph.

"I'm on the stage!"

"That you are, Sylvia," said Helena warmly. "How does it feel?"

The little girl looked cautiously over the edge. "High."

Helena stifled a laugh. "Yes, I suppose it is."

"No, it isn't!" objected Altan at once, as though disagreeing with his sisters was the only acceptable reaction. He wobbled as he came too close to the edge.

Rowena giggled but ceased doing so as soon as Helena gave her a look.

Siblings. There was something unique about siblings, about being raised in the same home. You didn't always get on as children, yet as soon as one was threatened, the whole lot would come against the threat.

It had always been that way with her brother. She could see it now, with the younger Fernsbys—and with the older generation. What was sibling loyalty if it was not the duke and Lady Amelia abandoning their own lives and coming to live here with their brother?

"Right," she said aloud. *Time to get moving.* "We have replaced our chalk stage with a real one, but we will still have use for the chalk. Where is it?"

"It's here, Miss." Johns rushed toward her with a sycophantic smile.

Helena hesitated, then took it from his hand. "Thank you."

He grinned inanely, saying nothing, doing nothing, and only when Rowena's giggles erupted around the ballroom did Helena do anything.

Really, this was ridiculous. She had never given him any sign she was interested!

"Don't you have something to do for McLoughlin?" she asked innocently.

The footman sighed. "I suppose the old man does need me, but—"

"Then please," said Helena brightly. "Do not let me detain you."

Perhaps it was her aloof voice, or her words—or maybe it was the snort of laughter that erupted from Altan.

Whatever it was, the footman finally got the message. Flushing a horrible puce, he slunk out of the ballroom, leaving the governess alone with her charges.

"Now," said Helena. "Now we have the chalk, we can start to mark the stage so you can see important points in the scenes and where you need to be."

"But won't the audience see?"

It was a good question from Rowena, and Helena shook her head as she clambered onto the stage. "No, not from this height."

Then she hesitated. *Well.* That had been true at the Theatre Royal, but here? The stage was so much lower, the audience so much closer.

"Anyway," she added hastily, "once you are rehearsed sufficiently, we can clean the markings away. Your body will know the steps by then."

A smile crept over her face. It was the same advice her very first stage manager had given her, and now she came to think about it, Miss Clarke had said almost the same thing.

"You're a woman of the world," the owner of the Governess Bureau had barked. "You'll know what to do."

Now it came to actually living in a master's house and caring for his children; however, Helena was not entirely sure that was accurate. Every day she was here, there seemed to be another scenario that brought her closer and closer to…Oscar. The Duke of Kilerth.

Helena swallowed. Even when he wasn't here, he distracted her thoughts. What was happening to her?

Love, a part of her whispered.

She pushed away the thought immediately. *Love?* Love occurred between equals, between two people who could entirely trust each other.

She and Oscar didn't trust each other. Not really.

When they had first met, they had recognized the threat the other posed. True, there had been some conversations that made her think…

No! She had to concentrate. She was a governess, not a duchess!

"So, the question is," she said aloud, "which scene do you want to rehearse first?"

"The wedding!"

"The fight scene!"

"My scene!"

Helena smiled. "Well, that shouldn't be a problem! We'll do

all three of them—no, Altan, before you say anything, we will not perform them at the same time. That's only for when I want the stage destroyed. Let's start with Sylvia's scene. I'm not in that one, so I can watch and admire you from here."

With disappointed looks from both Altan and Rowena, the three children rearranged themselves around the stage for the one scene in which Sylvia played a significant role.

"A touch further back, Altan," said Helena, watching them critically. "And to the right, Rowena, you must remember that there will be a stage curtain there."

"When?" asked the girl with shining eyes.

Helena knew better than to make promises she could not keep. "Soon," she said firmly. "Now, when you are all ready?"

The three Fernsbys looked at her expectantly. A rush of excitement flowed through Helena's body. There was something very special about the theater. Even when a few stable hands and a footman make you one, it was special. It captured all that was beautiful and wonderful about the world.

"And begin."

She had spoken softly so as not to disturb their concentration. *Despite the fact that they argue all the time, they do act well together,* Helena thought.

The play was good. It was almost all Shakespeare, and the few changes she had made tied the whole thing together well in her mind. But it didn't matter how good the thing looked in her mind. It was how the play looked, felt, sounded on the stage that truly mattered. It was not the stage itself but the actors who made it great.

And Altan, Rowena, and Sylvia were really something, even Helena would admit it. Even Sylvia. Almost.

"And then I'm done!" she said happily, sitting immediately on the stage.

Altan rolled his eyes. "You can't just sit. Rowena has four more lines!"

Helena saw the growing frustration in the girl's eyes. "And

Rowena will finish them just as soon as Sylvia stands up. Come on, poppet. Up you get."

She had learned quickly that there was nothing the youngest Fernsby disliked more than being treated as the youngest, so she kept her voice calm and bright.

Sylvia nodded and stood up, rather in the way a baby did when it was learning to walk, push off on both hands before finding her balance.

Rowena finished her scene, and Helena applauded. "That was truly excellent!" she said warmly. She could not have been prouder of them if they were her own. "I must say, all three of you are getting very good. You spoke very clearly. Sylvia, well done, and your finale was exquisite, Rowena."

Both of the girls beamed, but their brother had a rather sullen look on his face.

Helena stifled a smile. "And of course, Altan did an excellent job, too, though I rather think you were saving your talents for your fight scene."

Altan grinned. "Maybe."

"You'll be here for our performance, won't you?" Rowena said eagerly, sitting on the edge of the stage, feet dangling.

Helena nodded. "Of course I will! I'm in about a third of the scenes, aren't I?"

"So you're going to stay with us forever?"

Sylvia's words were innocently spoken, but in the way of small children, they had been almost shouted. Her voice echoed around the ballroom.

Stay with us forever...stay with us...forever.

Helena hesitated. Forever. Forever was a very long time.

When she had been an actress, what felt like a thousand years ago now, she had never planned one day to the next. She didn't have to. Food was provided, her bed was always there, and whatever new script was offered her was swiftly memorized. The evenings were for performing, the days were for recovering.

That was her life. She had never expected it to change. There had been no plan.

Even now, with her governess duties on behalf of the Bureau, Helena realized she never looked further than a day ahead. *The future?*

Imagining herself anywhere other than the Theatre Royal had been utter madness until five months ago, and now…

Now she was here, at the Old Abbey. Could she be anywhere else? Could she picture caring for other children, actual teaching perhaps, being forced to leave the Fernsbys?

Helena swallowed. *Forever.*

In a small part of her heart, well-guarded and often ignored, she knew she wanted whatever future she was dealt to be with him.

Oscar.

But that was impossible. She was not fool enough to think that he would in any way lower himself to her level! A governess of no family, no wealth, and a myriad of secrets in her past—and a duke?

No, it simply could not be. It never would. Helena forced the thought away as it scalded her mind. *Marry the duke?* It was ridiculous. Preposterous.

True, Oscar would have to marry eventually. The thought pained Helena, a sharp slice of agony slipping through her heart and into her stomach. Oscar would find a woman, younger than her, better connected than her, with a dowry and a title of her own, and he would marry her.

"You will stay, won't you, Miss Kirkpatrick?" said Rowena quietly.

All three children were staring, but Helena found she could not speak.

How could she? Her mind was lost in thoughts of him, of the man who had touched her in a way she had never been touched before.

Stage kisses were sweaty moments that were all for show and did nothing to her.

Not like Oscar's kisses. When he had kissed her in the kitchen garden, passionate, eager—or when he had kissed her on the stairs at the ball, a wild, untamed sort of kiss—or their kisses wrapped up on that chair in the drawing room …

Helena coughed. The important thing was that despite every temptation, she had not…*well*. Overstepped the most important line. That was the crucial thing. Despite what many of her fellow actresses may have assumed, she still had her innocence.

She forced a smile on her face. "I have no plans to leave if that makes you feel better!"

It did not make her feel much better. Rowena nodded, but Altan's forehead furrowed.

"That doesn't really answer the question, though," he said slowly. "Does it?"

Helena did not permit her smile to break. If she could get through the great ending scene of *Titus Andronicus* with a sprained ankle, she could do this. "Well, it's not really up to me whether I stay, is it? It's up to your father."

"Oh." For some reason, the boy's face relaxed immediately. "You'll be here forever then, Miss Kirkpatrick. Papa won't ever find another governess. He never leaves the house, and we can never leave either. We'll be together forever."

For the first time, Helena could see a shadow of the future adult in Altan's face. Yes, there was still petulance there, and clearly, some frustration that he wasn't able to go into town, or to school, or do what he assumed other boys were doing.

But there was understanding there, too. A hint of resignation. A slither of pain.

Helena walked toward the stage. This was a delicate situation, and it was her responsibility to get this right.

"Your father prefers you all to stay here for now," she said softly. "That might change, or it might not. As long as he is happy for me to be here, then I will happily look after you."

She thought she had done rather well; it would have been easy to overplay it, to lean into the emotion, but she had decided not to.

It didn't seem to have mattered.

"Not me, though," said Altan instantly. "I can look after myself."

"And so can I," said his elder sister, not to be outdone.

Helena looked at the smallest Fernsby, who stuck out her bottom lip in consternation.

"I'm small enough to need looking after," she said decidedly.

They all laughed.

"We'll never get this play ready if we don't keep rehearsing," said Helena brightly. "Rowena, shall we do your scene next?"

The children nodded and quickly moved into their positions. Well, the two elder Fernsbys did. Sylvia was not in this one, and after Helena helped her down from the stage, she sat on the ballroom floor to watch them.

Helena was in this scene. As she took her place a few feet behind Rowena, she felt that familiar thrill move up her spine.

Yet, it was different. As the scene started and Rowena began her lines, Helena took care not to interrupt the child.

At the Theatre Royal, it was like waking from a deep sleep every time she stepped onto the boards. The rest of her life paled into insignificance, and she became that character for a few hours, losing herself entirely.

That didn't happen here. Something was missing. The joy that being on a stage used to give her was no longer there.

Perhaps it was because there was no audience. Sylvia did not count; she might have done if she had been able to stay awake, but as always, she had fallen asleep, the heat of the day overwhelming her.

As Rowena launched into her soliloquy, Helena's attention was caught not by the sleeping child but by the duke.

Oscar. He had been passing the open ballroom door into the corridor, and he stopped, leaned against the doorframe, and smiled.

Helena's stomach lurched.

That wasn't a good sign. Oscar was not just handsome, not just a duke, though neither of those facts hindered her affection. He was kind. Helena had never known a man as kind as he was. To be sure, she had not met many men. Kindness was a weakness in the cutthroat world of the theater.

Oscar's gaze met hers, and his smile widened. Helena's stomach turned again. *What did he want? What did she want? If only she could—*

Giggling. There was giggling.

Helena blinked and realized all three Fernsby children were laughing at her.

"What?" she said distractedly.

Altan was shaking his head. "Miss Kirkpatrick, you missed your cue! I've never seen you miss a line before!"

Helena laughed awkwardly. "Ah, I was only testing you! You see children, we will have to practice prompts for each other, for each scene. Something to start on tomorrow, I think…now where were we?"

She looked up. Oscar had gone.

"You say…"

The scene continued, but this time Helena was unable to pour herself into the role. She knew now what had happened, why acting felt different.

It was him. *Oscar.* She had fallen in love with him.

It was what the third rule of the Governess Bureau had told her not to do—but it was too late. There was no way she could change her feelings now. Oscar filled her heart as no one ever had before, seeping into every vein, her love for him pulsing inside her.

Not that she would ever be able to do anything about it. Helena knew with absolute certainty that she would have to push those feelings down.

Dukes did not marry governesses, even prodigiously skilled ones.

Chapter Sixteen

August 22, 1813

"WELL," SIGHED FERNSBY, "I think I will go up."

They had finished their game of billiards almost an hour ago, as the sun had faded and the butler had lit candles, and had been talking about…well, nothing.

Oscar smiled wanly. *Talking about nothing.* It was a special skill of the English, as far as he could make out. On his Grant Tour—admittedly a years ago—he had experienced the most intensive conversations with the French, the Italians, even some of the Germans.

But the English?

The conversation could go on for several hours, and you would always come away thinking that they were perfectly pleasant…but with no idea what they said.

"Yes, I will probably go up myself," said Oscar, lifting his glass, "when I've finished my drink."

The evening drew in quickly tonight. The days were shortening. Though the heat continued, there had been a slight chill in the breeze passing the Old Abbey today.

His brother nodded. He looked pensive. Amelia had not let

up at the dinner table about the neighbor's invitation, given so generously after the ball. No response had yet been given.

It was only Amelia who was making such a song and dance out of it.

"Days!" she had said impressively over the sticky toffee pudding. "Days, and yet we have still given no answer!"

"We will answer," Oscar had said as calmly as he could, with a glance at their brother, "when we are ready."

Oscar sighed. *It would have to be answered.* The neighbors would not wait forever. If they did not respond soon—more, if they did not respond in the *positive* soon—questions would be asked. Rumors would abound. Scandal would only be a whisper away.

"We need to give him more time," he had muttered to Amelia after dinner.

She had glared as only a sister could. "How much time? How much longer will we be forced to keep this a secret?"

It was an impossible question. Amelia should know…where was Amelia?

Oscar started as Fernsby rose. *Where was their sister?* He hadn't seen her most of the day, she had joined them for dinner and said she would join them in the billiards room momentarily, as a spectator of course, and then…

She had never arrived. Oscar frowned. *Amelia was starting to become…he didn't like the word flighty, but what else was there?*

Fernsby stretched. "Where did Amelia end up, do you know?"

Oscar stiffened in his chair. *Hell.* Not more reasons for him to be anxious. His brother had come so far, had walked in the gardens for five minutes today, unprompted.

"I imagine she's doing women's things," he said vaguely. "Embroidery. Playing the piano. That sort of thing."

Fernsby sighed. "Ah, you are probably right. Constance used to…well, do all sorts of things. Flower arranging. Things I didn't even realize were things."

Oscar nodded mutely. *Better to keep his mouth shut.*

"You never know," mused his brother, "she might be watching the children practice this play of theirs. I mean, not this late. But earlier."

"Perhaps," said Oscar.

It was a noncommittal response, but the topic verged too close to Helena.

"You know, that governess was a godsend."

Oscar swallowed. His brother was in the mood to talk, which was fine, except for his chosen topic. *Miss Helena Kirkpatrick.* The woman utterly dazzled him without trying. Perhaps that was part of the attraction. *How was he to keep his face calm and serene?*

"An absolute godsend," repeated Fernsby.

Oscar cleared his throat before replying. "Yes, I suppose she is. Weren't you going to bed, old man?"

If only his brother would go upstairs and stop speaking of Helena—but Fernsby showed no sign of following through on his earlier statement. He was still seated in the peeling leather armchair, beaten into softness over decades, his gaze drifting off into the distance.

"Yes, a godsend," he mused. "Miss Kirkpatrick knows precisely what the children need, far more than I. Entertainment, a little hard work, not too much schooling."

Oscar nodded, his jaw tight. Perhaps he wasn't actually needed to contribute to this conversation. Perhaps he could get through it merely by agreeing. *That was enough, surely?*

"She's very talented—well, I knew she would be, coming from the Bureau," said Fernsby with a sigh. "But even I did not think…very skilled."

A rather discomforting thought flittered through Oscar's mind. *It wasn't possible was it that…after their joke before Helena arrived, there was no danger that Fernsby could—*

"But the boy will need to go to school at some point," Oscar said sharply.

He had said the wrong thing. In his attempt to move the

conversation on, an innocent remark had strayed into territory that made Fernsby blanche.

"School?" His brother stared as though he had suggested sacrificing his son to the Egyptian gods. "School?"

Oscar bit his lip. *Well, the words were out, and he could not take them back.*

"School, indeed!" Fernsby's eyes were wide. "School? No, no, Altan can learn perfectly well from here. Here, at the Old Abbey. Where he's safe."

"I didn't mean—"

"If need be, we can get him a tutor when he is older," said Fernsby, looking truly alarmed. "Altan doesn't have to leave—none of them do. They have all they need here."

It was on the tip of Oscar's tongue to ask his younger brother whether he ever planned to permit his children to leave him. How was Rowena to find a husband if she never left the house? Was Sylvia never to see anyone other than those she was related to?

Look at Amelia. She had spent a good year here, delaying her chances of matrimony. *Was he willing to condemn two more female Fernsbys to that fate?*

Oscar managed to clench his jaw together to prevent the questions from slipping through. What good would they do?

"Quite, as you say," he said. "It's late. I misspoke. You are right, of course."

Fernsby's wild expression faded. "Good. Yes. Fine. A tutor, that would be sufficient."

"I am sure a tutor would be quite acceptable," said Oscar in a placating tone. "Now. You were going up."

"What?"

Oscar pointed upward. "To bed. You were going to bed."

His brother. A painful thud settled in Oscar's stomach. *Where was the brother he knew so well? Could he ever find him again, or was he lost forever?*

"Yes, yes, I was," said Fernsby quietly, rising once more. "Yes.

Sleep well, Kilerth."

The door closed with a snap, and Oscar sighed heavily, drooping in his chair.

Every conversation a minefield. No wonder Amelia was starting to avoid them.

Still, it was impossible to deny Fernsby was improving. Slowly. Not every day was an achievement, but over the weeks, slowly and slowly, he was starting to emerge.

"You don't know that," Amelia had said in a whisper last week when they had managed to grab a few minutes just the two of them. "He may never get better."

Oscar had sighed. "Perhaps he won't. But we have to believe he will."

He drained his glass in the billiard room and stared mindlessly at the table. *Perhaps he won't.* The question then would be, how could they make him happy? And what were they going to do about the children?

The door creaked open again. Oscar snapped, "I said we would get a tutor, Fernsby. There is no need to worry about it."

A slightly amused, slightly concerned voice replied. "Goodness, should I be worried?"

Oscar turned and saw Helena leaning against the doorframe, smiling.

Blast.

He rose to his feet. "I didn't—I didn't mean…instead of school, not instead of you!"

Why did he sound so pathetic? Why was he so desperate for this woman to think well of him? It was as though she had become the center of his world. If they were not in balance, he was entirely off-kilter. As though he could not do without her.

Helena was laughing. "Don't worry. I thought it must be something like that. I just hope I will be permitted to stay here once the tutor arrives. To look after the girls, of course."

She had stepped into the room as she spoke, and Oscar tried not to watch the way she walked. Elegantly, calmly. With purpose. With a sway of her hips that did something uncomforta-ble to his breeches.

"I would never want you to leave—that is, I am sure my brother would keep you on."

In silence, the unspoken words between them rose up.

As long as they could be together.

It was nonsense. Madness. Oscar knew he could not stay at the Old Abbey forever. He would have to return to Kilerth—he had never wanted to leave there in the first place!

Except that now…

If he wished to hunt, he could not do so here; there was no parkland at the Old Abbey. He would return to Kilerth, a place he had always found comfortable. A home that would feel empty without her. Helena.

Fernsby could come with him.

It was a wild thought, a desperate one, but Oscar clung to it. Fernsby and Amelia and all the brood could come to Kilerth. Wouldn't it be natural that their governess came, too?

Oscar smiled. "Sit with me."

Though she had walked confidently enough into the room, Helena looked astonished at the invitation. "But…this is the billiards room, Oscar. 'Tis hardly a place for a woman."

"Oh, I don't know about that," said Oscar nonchalantly. "Amelia comes in here all the time—at least, she used to."

When was the last time she had been in here? It had been weeks. Maybe a month.

Still, the governess hesitated. "I don't know whether this is a good idea."

Oscar grinned. "I can't think why you would think that. The last time you and I sat and had a discussion, I think it ended rather well."

"Oh, so there'll be a next time?"

"There shouldn't be. But there will be."

Those kisses, dark and delectable, secret and so warm…

Helena's smile was too knowing. "That was what I was afraid

of."

He could not help but laugh. "Well, if I promise not to touch you, will you sit?"

Her teasing smile was almost too much. How could he hold to such a promise when even now he wanted to pull her into his arms to show her precisely what his fingers could do?

Helena had laughed at his remark and seated herself in the armchair opposite his own.

Oscar's manhood stirred, and he immediately tried to think of cold, calming thoughts. *A cold bath. He would control himself.*

They sat in silence for a while. Oscar had always hated silence, had always sought to fill it with something, but this was different. It was a surprise, to find silence could be just as meaningful as conversation. She was more beautiful each time he looked at her.

"It's odd," he said eventually. "I never thought silence could be so comfortable."

Helena smiled. "I find with true friends, words aren't always necessary."

"Is that what we are then?" Oscar said quietly. "Friends?"

She did not answer immediately. Her gaze flickered around the room, taking in the luscious green baize, the unmistakable signs of wealth and men, the cigar ends, and the empty bottle of port.

Friends. All his friends were gentlemen. A lady friend?

How were they supposed to define this—friends who kissed? Friends who wished to make passionate love to each other?

Oscar swallowed. *Best he left that particular remark unsaid.*

Lovers? No, it was not possible. She was a servant under his brother's roof; that would be scandalous. A mistress? Tempting, very tempting. Oscar could feel his hands itching to take hold of her, to show her just how desirable she was. Acquaintances? They had shared far too much to be acquaintances. That was a line they had crossed long, long ago.

Undefinable. That was what they were. If they attempted to define it, the delicate thing between them would be broken.

Helena chuckled quietly. "You know, I thought my life was on quite a different path. I thought I would stay on that path forever, but circumstances changed, and I am here. I would never before have considered it possible for a man and a woman to be friends, but I think I have proven to myself how little I know. So yes. Friends."

Oscar leaned forward. The debate around friendship was now no longer as interesting as that vague hint she had given about her past. *Where had she come from?*

"You were a governess," he said. "So how did your path change?"

Helena's smile danced upon her lips, but they did not move to speak.

"Tell me," Oscar urged softly. "I want to know you better, Helena. You know all about me."

She had to laugh at that. "No, I don't!"

"Well, all there is worth knowing," he said with a grin. "I'm a duke, I will be a duke until I die, and that's an end to it. But you…how long were you a governess before you came here?"

His question did not seem too probing, but Helena examined him carefully before responding. "There was certainly some teaching to what I did, along with a great deal of pretending, which I think governessing mainly is," she said with a dry laugh. "Children have so many questions, and you always have to be the one with the answers. But you know what I did before, Oscar. We don't need to talk about it."

Oscar nodded. *Yes,* he supposed hearing about the other families she had cared for in other homes did not really interest him. It was she who fascinated him, not who she had met.

"'Tis strange how life's journey can take you down a path you didn't ever think of," he said quietly. "I certainly never thought I would spend a summer here at my brother's place, yet if I hadn't agreed to do so, and you weren't a governess, and he hadn't wanted one—we would never have met."

It was a rather sobering thought. *So many coincidences.*

"And that," said Helena just as quietly, "would have been very sad indeed."

Oscar swallowed. He shouldn't permit it to get too personal. That would be a mistake.

A mistake he was about to make again.

"Do you think so?" he asked. "Would you regret never having known me?"

There was too much pleading in his voice to be comfortable, but Oscar could not help it. He needed her. He didn't know why, only that he did.

Helena balanced the world around him. He had never even noticed that it was unbalanced until she had stridden in, spoken wittily at every turn, and fought him in a duel.

Her eyes blazed. She was holding something back, he knew it, but Oscar could not blame her. Was not everyone holding something back? Was there not always a part of one's life, of one's history that one tried to hide from the world?

"It…it would be a shame, I think, if anyone was to find out about the truth of a—a certain person's past. Recent past. In London."

Oscar's smile flickered. Perhaps it was not possible for them to be completely honest with each other, not at the moment. Not with her delicate blackmail hovering over his head.

Maybe there was too much to keep them apart. *His secrets, her rank…*

"Some of your steps have been remarkably different on this path of yours, of course."

Oscar stared blankly. She had spoken with a smile as though telling a joke.

Helena laughed at his uncomprehending face. "I was referring to…to the sport you partake in. In London. The one we agreed not to speak about."

"Yet we are speaking about it now?" teased Oscar. Deuce, she was good not to spell it out. It would be easier if they never did.

"Well, I don't see why not," Helena grinned. "I have to say, it took me a few days to put together the Duke of Kilerth and 'Michaels.' I was astonished. How did it all start?"

Her curiosity was palpable. Oscar felt an unexpected rush of pleasure at her interest. People spoke to him because he was a duke; he was nobility, therefore worth speaking to.

No one really *listened* to him. They saw no need. They expected him to trot out the same dull topics that every duke did. So he did. How else would they leave him alone?

Helena? She was different. She was genuinely interested in him, not the title.

"It's a sport taught to all boys at school, then at university one can partake in gentlemen's bouts," he said as nonchalantly as he could.

Helena leaned forward, her eyes bright. "And?"

Oscar almost smiled. He had never yet met a man, let alone a woman, who was this interested in boxing—but then, he had rarely spoken of it with anyone before.

"And...I found I could not leave it behind," he said quietly. "When I am in that moment, the rest of the world fades away. I know precisely what I am doing and why. Every part of me is alive, on fire, and I can see almost three seconds ahead—to where I need to be."

He stopped, embarrassment halting his tongue. He was speaking like a fool, and he knew it, but then he had never had this to share before. And it was all true. Boxing, feeling the strength in yourself, testing yourself against another...there was nothing like it.

"Alive is not something I thought I would feel," Oscar admitted. "Dukes hunt, they might fence, they sometimes play a little billiards or sit and smoke a cigar...but boxing?"

Blazes. He had not intended to say it aloud.

"There's something about it," he added hastily. "I never have that feeling elsewhere."

Helena had not looked away during the entirety of his speech. "You don't feel alive any other time?"

"Being a duke is not all it's cracked up to be, Helena. Sometimes I wonder…well. If I left it all behind. Would I be happier as a fighter in London than as a landowner in Kilerth?"

There were only two candles lit in the billiard room, and as they slowly burned down, Oscar did not notice. Time flowed as it never had before. Helena asked questions, posed interesting dilemmas, made intelligent remarks. Oscar was unraveling before her, pouring out his hopes, those dreams he had vowed never to reveal to a soul. But he did to her.

Oscar finally admitted what he had tried not to say since she had entered the room. "The truth is, Helena, that you…you give me the same sensation. The same buzz, the same feeling of being alive."

It was clearly not the praise he had intended. Helena blinked and leaned back.

He laughed dryly. "It's a compliment, I promise you."

"I'm not so sure," Helena said with a quizzical expression. "Are you saying that being around me, in my presence, is like being hit in the face?"

Oscar chuckled. "In the best possible way, I assure you."

"And with that," Helena said ruefully, "I should probably go up to bed."

She rose from her seat, and Oscar mirrored her. "There isn't anything I can say to make you stay?"

She did not reply immediately but started to walk toward the door. "No, there's nothing you can say."

He did not think about it. It was more an absolute certainty that he had to move, had to show her with his body what he could not express through words.

Helena gasped as he grabbed her waist, turned her round, and pinned her against the door.

"And nothing I can do?"

Helena had wide eyes full of desire but a mouth that knew it was wrong. "We—we have to stop this. Oscar, I don't know what this is."

Oscar lowered his mouth and kissed her neck, feeling her quiver beneath him. "I know what I want it to be."

Helena's moan was enough to push him over the edge. Pressing his body against hers and groaning at the soft curves he melted into, Oscar lost control for a moment. His kisses grew wilder, more torrid, desperately seeking her mouth, which she gave him eagerly.

He returned to her neck and whispered between kisses. "You can't deny this, what you feel, what we feel for each other."

She gasped, squirming under him with the pleasure he was giving. "I-I'm not denying what I feel but—oh!"

Oscar's manhood was stiff, desperate to be released from his breeches, and he moved a hand to her breast.

"But I can't…oh, I can't deny the distance between us!"

Oscar took a step back and stared at Helena, who was flushed but defiant.

"I am a governess. You are a duke," she breathed, her eyes not leaving his. "No matter how much I wish it was not so…"

Her words brought Oscar to his senses. He took another step away and raised his hands in surrender for good measure.

"I-I know," he said, his breath ragged. "And I can't make you promises."

"I don't need you to," said Helena quickly. Her hair had almost entirely fallen from its pins, curling down toward her breasts. Oscar groaned. "But this only ends one way, so I need you to think whether you…you want this or not. Whether you want me. Because I need to know."

Oscar hesitated. He knew deep within himself that he wanted Helena, as his mistress or lover or whatever one wanted to call it.

It could not go further than that. Helena knew that, she was no fool.

I need you to think whether you…you want this or not. Whether you want me. Because I need to know.

"Yes," he said, looking into her eyes. "Yes, I want you."

It appeared she had not expected a response so soon. "I…I

want you, too, but I can't. I can't risk it. Not here."

It was difficult for Oscar to follow the conversation, his body so stiff and full of desire, his mind full of lust. Full of something more, something he did not understand.

"At the end of autumn, come back with me. Back to Riverside Manor. Be my mistress there." He spoke honestly, finally able to express what he wanted.

Helena swallowed. Oscar tried not to watch her throat move, tried not to see how her breasts were rising and falling with the shortness of her breath.

"That's a long time."

"You're telling me," he said bitterly.

That, at least, made her smile. "I will…I will think about it."

She had slipped through the door before Oscar could say any more. The passion, the fire, was still within him. It had to be let out. *If it couldn't be lovemaking…*

Another trip to the stables and his invisible opponent it was.

CHAPTER SEVENTEEN

August 23, 1813

SOMETHING WASN'T QUITE right. Helena's stomach murmured, desperate for sustenance, but it wasn't getting any. That didn't make sense because she was at the dining table with the children.

Helena blinked. Her fork, piled high with roast chicken and carrots, was hovering just below her chin.

She'd missed again.

Forcing herself to concentrate and hoping beyond hope the children had not noticed, Helena took a bite of food. Her stomach ceased its loudest complaints. It wouldn't be so unhappy if she'd had luncheon. Why hadn't she? Helena could barely remember; the day had passed in a haze of confusion and irritably.

Oscar's parting words to her echoed in her mind, distracting her from everything.

"At the end of autumn, come back with me. Back to Riverside Manor. Be my mistress there."

Helena cleared her throat and concentrated on another mouthful of vegetables.

Her mouth tingled where Oscar had kissed so vigorously only the evening before. When he had made his offer to her. When he had asked her to be his mistress.

"Be my mistress there."

"You seem distracted, Miss Kirkpatrick."

Helena blinked. Altan had a curious expression.

"I beg your pardon?"

The boy frowned. "There you go again, that's what I mean! You haven't been listening to a single thing I have said, have you?"

Cursing dukes and their ability to make her life difficult, Helena shook her head. "I am sorry, Altan, I am afraid I wasn't."

He did not look offended. "You keep missing your mouth."

Helena raised a self-conscious hand to her lips. "I know."

"You've hardly eaten a thing," said Rowena, curiosity in her voice. "I thought that as Papa wanted us to dine with you that you'd be...I don't know, teaching us manners, or something like that. But you're not. You're just sitting there."

She needed to take back control of this conversation. "I am teaching you manners by living them, Rowena."

Well, it would have been a good response—if it hadn't been for Sylvia.

"But Miss Perpatrick," she said, giggling, "you've got food all over your face!"

Helena's cheeks burned. Raising her napkin to her face as the children roared with laughter, she saw to her embarrassment that she had indeed managed to get food on her face.

That damned Oscar. It was his fault, though she could not admit that to anyone.

She needed to concentrate. Allowing herself to fall into daydreams about a certain duke and the wonderful life she could lead as his mistress, locked away in a manor in Kilerth...

Those were precisely the sort of thoughts she should be avoiding.

The children were her focus—should be her focus. They hadn't been for some weeks now. With each day that Oscar became more precious, the children slipped down her list of priorities.

She needed to think about the children and the play. It would be autumn soon, and—

"At the end of autumn, come back with me. Back to Riverside Manor. Be my mistress there."

Helena tightened her grip on her napkin. *She was not going to be overwhelmed.*

"Well done, children," she said aloud, her voice as light as she could make it. "I was testing you! You spotted the exact things I was testing you on."

It was fortunate, perhaps, that the children were no older. Altan certainly would not have been taken in by such a terribly transparent ploy if he had been older.

As it was, he puffed out his chest. "I knew it!"

Helena smiled. *Safe, then, for another meal.*

She forced herself to focus for five or six mouthfuls as the children started to discuss—or more accurately, argue—about their favorite parts of the play.

"When I swoon and fall to the—"

"Try doing that with a sword in your hand!"

Helena did not interrupt. Learning to argue properly—present arguments, listen to the opposing point of view, accept that you may be wrong about some elements of your debate—was an important skill.

Miss Clarke may not consider it so, but Helena did.

Besides, it gave her the time to think about—*not Oscar.* Helena breathed out slowly. *How long had that been, five minutes? Perhaps less?*

She needed to consider his offer. If he had even meant it. It was impossible to know with a duke. He could have felt it in the moment, his body desperate for hers, but now in the cold light of day, perhaps he would no longer consider her.

This evening, once the children were in bed, when the household was quiet, she could slip into her room, and no one would need her, and she could focus entirely on untangling just what she felt for this man…

Helena bit her lip. *Late in the evening, when she was most isolated from the world…*

That was when she truly wanted him. That was when she wondered what it would be like not just to be in Oscar's arms but in his bed…

Helena placed her fork down. She couldn't eat another bite. Food simply wasn't sufficient to distract her from these wild thoughts about Oscar, a man who had managed to get under her skin.

She had never been tempted by any man, not even wealthy men who frequented the theatre. There had always been another actress desperate for a little more coin who would happily accept their attentions, their affections, their kisses…

Not her. No man had ever impinged on her heart.

Until now. Until him.

"Don't you think, Miss Kirkpatrick?"

And the trouble was, thought Helena, *there was a myriad of reasons why she should love him—or at least, care for him.* If one ignored his title, his wealth, his impressive good looks that appeared to have been chiseled by the very hand of God…

He was so kind. So considerate of others. Witty when he wanted to be. There was strength beyond his arms and hands when he boxed. Strength of character. Strength of mind.

And when he kissed her, Oscar made her feel—

"Miss Kirkpatrick? I said, have you ever performed in our play before, with others?"

Helena blinked. All three Fernsby children had cleared their plates, a rarity in itself, and now they were looking at her with genuine interest.

What had he said? Ah, yes. Now how was she supposed to answer that question?

A hundred productions of Shakespeare rushed through Helena's memory. The play she had given the children was rather a hodge podge of them, so it was a difficult thing to say.

But she would not lie. "Yes, I have performed in the play before—bits of it, not all. Would you all like dessert?"

Helena had hoped her vague answer would end that particular line of questioning, but it was not to be.

"What were the children like?" asked Rowena curiously.

Helena frowned slightly. "Children?"

The girl nodded. "That you performed the play with."

Ah. Naturally, they assumed she had performed it with other children as a governess.

She was not going to lie. She was certainly not going to tell the truth either, but this left her in a rather unfortunate predicament. How was she supposed to explain?

"It was a while ago," Helena said vaguely. That at least was true. The last performance she had given of *A Midsummer Night's Dream* was nigh on five years ago. "I can't remember."

It was the wrong response. All three children looked downcast as Rowena sighed.

"Does that mean," said Sylvia slowly, "you won't remember us?"

Helena smiled. "Of course not! It's different, although…I am afraid I cannot explain how. Now, dessert?"

Altan shook his head. "We don't want dessert."

Based on his sisters' expressions, he was very much wrong on that score, but as the eldest, his word appeared sufficient to quell any complaints.

Helena hesitated. She did not like this. Subterfuge, despite being a part of being an actress, had never sat well. It was different on a stage; the entire audience knew you were pretending and could allow themselves to get swept up in the story.

This was different. This was lying.

But you agreed to this, that treacherous little voice at the back of her mind whispered. *You knew this would happen. Miss Clarke warned you it would be difficult, didn't she?*

"You, Miss Kirkpatrick, will have the most difficult task," Miss *Clarke had said grimly as the other trainee governess left the room. "You*

will not only have to present yourself in your best light, but you will also have to hide the truth of who you are in the darkest corners of yourself. Miss Patrick, the actress, must never be seen."

Helena's stomach curled. *What would Miss Clarke think if she saw her now, with a stage constructed in the ballroom and the children asking about her past performances?*

"Well, if you do not wish for dessert, it's off to bed with you," she said firmly. The sooner these children were out of her hair and not asking difficult questions, the better.

The three Fernsbys slipped from their chairs, but not without protest.

"I want to keep practicing my fencing," said Altan, "but Mr. Hough hasn't been back for weeks!"

Helena sighed. The boy's complaint was valid; she had not seen the fencing master since the ball, and that had been weeks ago. *Why was he so negligent in his teaching?* She had hoped the baron would speak to him about it, but...

"You can practice your footwork in your bedchamber," Helena said decidedly, making a mental note to speak to the baron about the fencing tutor. "Now up you go, all of you!"

They scrambled away, pushing as they all tried to get through the morning room door at once, laughing as they rushed upstairs.

Laughter. There hadn't been any laughter in this house when she had first arrived. It had been one of the first things she had noticed. Now there was laughter almost every day. The house was coming alive through the children.

Who would have thought that working with children could be so...rewarding? Helena had never known satisfaction like it. True, there was more adoration in a crowded theater when the curtain finally went down, and the applause rang in your ears...

But for how long? Five minutes at the most? Then it was scraping off the face paint and carefully laundering your costume, and the whole thing would have to be done again tomorrow—and to an audience who was yet to be convinced. Every night.

How different to build a rapport. To see the efforts of today continue into tomorrow.

Helena rose from the table and pulled at the bell by the fireplace.

Within a minute, a footman stepped into the room. "Yes, Miss?"

"The children are finished," said Helena quietly. "I am going upstairs."

The footman nodded and started clearing the table as Helena left.

She lost a few hours in reading. It was a guilty pleasure, but no one had said she could not take books from the library, and she had been inspired by Lady Amelia's pile of novels.

When at the Theatre Royal, there had been no time for novels, no time to read anything that wasn't a script. Now she could lose herself in the adventures of others, but Helena found her mind wandering as the sun went down, and she carefully lit her candle. Though the books were marvelous, none compared to her own adventures.

None had brooding dukes with hidden secrets, desperately kissing her against a door...

Helena put her book down. *This was ridiculous.* The more she tried to read, to ignore her own life and lose herself in another's, the more Oscar's face kept appearing in her mind.

"Yes, I want you."

Even with all the imagination in the world, she could never have imagined a gentleman so wonderful as Oscar. He was everything she wanted. Everything she needed.

"Come back with me. Back to Riverside Manor. Be my mistress there."

Helena sighed heavily into the silence. If she was honest, she regretted not accepting his offer. He wanted her. He had offered her what he could, which was far more than she had expected, and she...

Well, she had not turned him down exactly.

"I will...I will think about it."

Helena's heart twisted at the mere memory. She had been afraid. She had been unsure, though why she should not trust him, she did not know. Oscar's overtures were sincere. She had seen the honesty in his face. No one was that good an actor.

The idea of making love to him, of him touching every part of her…Helena shivered. It was wonderful. It was scandalous. She would be in trouble if they were ever caught.

But who would he tell? Oscar had—as far as she knew—kept her actress past a secret. He would have been perfectly within his right to tell his brother of the governess's secret past. If she didn't have the same power over him.

Helena smiled wistfully. *It would be nice not to be lonely.*

He was a duke, she a governess!

It was forbidden—in polite society, by the Governess Bureau…perhaps that was why a forbidden lover was so enticing. The less sense it made, the more she wanted him.

Helena rose to move around her bedchamber. As she passed her door, the memory of being pushed up against a door and kissed so wildly by Oscar flashed into her mind.

Her whole body shivered. *If that was what it felt like merely to be kissed passionately by a man as skilled as Oscar, what would it be like to…*

Helena was an unusual actress. Unlike many others in her line of work, she had not permitted gentleman followers. It hadn't been worth the risk.

"Absolutely not," she had said sternly to the stage manager. "No, I have told you, do not permit a single man up here for me, Mr. Tobias. I won't have it!"

Helena had watched other actresses who had believed themselves impervious to love, taking lovers for the coin they left behind or the prestige of their name…

All had been left heartbroken.

Helena sat heavily. *What did she want? Ignore the world: what was in her heart?*

The answer was felt throughout her entire body. *She wanted him.* She wanted Oscar, wanted him to touch her, show her ways of experiencing pleasure she had only guessed at.

Consequences? They could use whatever precautions the other actresses had used. One night surely could not make such a difference. *One night.* One night where society's rules were left at the door, and all they had were each other.

Helena could feel her heart racing. *Was this a decision?* Was she truly about to offer herself to a duke, a man who knew her secret and would have even more power over her once she gave herself to him?

Could she lose everything, all her stability, her new reputation as a governess, everything she'd worked for?

Oscar's face swam into her mind. That smile, that knowing look. That abandon he threw to the wind when he was with her.

She wanted him. Damn the cost.

Helena shivered. His desire was intoxicating. After years of control, ensuring she matched the expectations of her audience, it was finally time to do something for herself.

Before she knew it, she was standing by her bedchamber door. The hinges made no sound. It was late, the corridor painted in darkness, but there was movement.

Helena held her breath. *What was Lady Amelia doing?*

Fully dressed and evidently hoping not to be noticed, Lady Amelia crept out of her own bedchamber and down the corridor. Within a moment, Helena was alone again.

She did not dare move. Her ladyship could have been retrieving a book from the library and would be back soon. But after several minutes of waiting in anticipatory silence, it did not appear that the lady of the house was returning.

Trying to keep her breath silent, Helena left her bedchamber and started to walk softly down the corridor in the opposite direction. Altan had pointed out his uncle's bedchamber on her tour when she had first arrived. Helena found herself outside it far too quickly for her liking; before she could change her mind, her hand was on the door handle.

It was cold. Her fingers curled around it.

The door opened with a slight creak, but Helena had stepped inside and closed it before it made much noise. A huge bed was in the center of the room, four-postered, curtains opened, with a solitary figure within it.

Helena slowly let out the tension in her lungs. A small part of her, one she had despised, had worried that all his protestations of affection—or what a duke could come close to—had been repeated to others. Maids.

But Oscar was alone. He was asleep. He was also, from what Helena could see, naked.

Her cheeks burned as she crept closer. At the very least, he was shirtless, his chest uncovered by the blankets on this warm night.

What must it be like to be curled up with a man in his bed? The thought soared through Helena's mind, and for the first time, she gave herself permission to wonder. To be held by someone in that most intimate of spaces.

Slowly, moving inch by inch, Helena allowed herself to sit on the side of the bed.

Nothing happened. Oscar was still fast asleep, lying on his back, looking entirely peaceful and a few years younger than when awake.

Helena reached out and gently placed her hand on his arm.

Nothing happened.

She had to stop herself from laughing. It was a rather ridiculous situation. If Mr. Tobias had attempted to put it in a play, no one would have believed it!

"Oscar," Helena whispered, his first name tasting forbidden on her lips. "Wake up."

The duke blearily opened his eyes but made no movement. "Helena?"

A thrill rushed through her. No matter what happened this evening, it was worth it just to hear him speak her name.

"Helena."

In one swift movement, Oscar pulled her into his arms and kissed her passionately.

Helena could barely breathe. Her eyes closed as the intensity of the kiss—warm, passionate, from a man naked and in his bed!—overwhelmed her.

The feeling of his chest against her was...overwhelming. Intoxicating. Perfect.

It was over in a moment. Oscar pulled away and said, "Helena!"

"Shush!" she said quickly. "Someone will hear you!"

Oscar stared. He looked...astonished. "Dear God, I thought I dreamt you!" he said, making Helena wonder what kind of dreams he'd had about her. "What are you doing here?"

Helena should have prepared an answer. *As it was...*

"Well, I thought..." she said a little shyly. "I've considered. I thought you'd like to know my answer."

Oscar blinked. "What?"

Helena chuckled. "Your offer. I've come to accept."

Now his gaze sharpened. "Accept me?"

"You sound surprised," she said quietly. She was still seated on the edge of the bed, and the distance between them was insupportable.

"I...I never thought I would be good enough for a woman like you."

There was such vulnerability in his voice, such honesty, that Helena acted on instinct. Closing the gap between them by clambering properly on the bed, she kissed him—a kiss which was evidently welcome. She found herself tangled in his arms.

"Why wait until the autumn," Oscar whispered. "I want you now."

Helena knew there was only one answer she could give. "Yes, now."

His hands held her close, her fingers in his hair, and Helena gave herself up to the pleasure.

And pleasure there was. This was clearly not Oscar's first

time with a woman, not if the speed and delicacy of his hands were anything to go by. Within minutes, she had been stripped naked, every removal of a garment accompanied by delicate and passionate kisses, some as light as butterfly wings, some so intense Helena was sure they would leave marks.

Oscar had affection in his eyes. "You are so beautiful, Helena."

"You have to say that."

That made him laugh. "You think I tell every woman that?"

"Every woman in your bed," Helena countered with a wry smile.

There was clearly little he could say to argue with that. "Well, I only invite beautiful women to my bed."

He dipped his head while his hands removed the thin pantaloons he had been wearing, and Helena gasped as he slipped between her legs.

There was so much of him: so much heat, so much power, so much—

Her hand grazed against something that was definitely not a leg. "Oh!"

Oscar broke the kiss. "You aren't afraid?"

Helena did not have to think. "No. Not with you, Oscar. I trust you."

He groaned. "Damn—give me a moment."

He disappeared, leaving Helena feeling rather alone. Oscar had left the bed and was rifling through drawers on the other side of the room.

"Where the devil is—here we go!"

He had returned before she could ask. Helena watched in fascination as Oscar drew something out of an envelope, then proceeded to roll it carefully down his...well. *Him.*

"I want to give you more," he said darkly as he concentrated, "want to give you everything—but not this."

Helena smiled. Well, she had been under no illusion that Oscar had dallied with women before, and here was the proof. He knew what he was doing.

"Ready?"

Helena nodded. Ready was not a word she would have used: terrified, excited, desperate, wanting more but not knowing what would fill this glowing ache between her—

"Oh!"

Oscar crushed her lips with a kiss the moment he entered her, muffling her surprise.

And it was surprise, not pain. Every woman in London had heard the horror stories of wedding nights or first encounters: the pain, the agony, the blood.

She could feel herself stretching, but the sensation was not unpleasant, far from it.

"First," panted Oscar, nestled between her legs and seeming to be restraining himself, "pleasure."

Helena stroked his face. "Goodness, what have we been doing this whole time?"

"Oh, just a taste of what's to come."

He lowered his head to kiss her and moved gently against her at the same time—but that was not what made Helena moan in his mouth. No, it was his hand. It was lightly stroking the place where he had entered her.

It was unbelievable, impossible. Somehow Oscar knew precisely what she wanted, what she needed, and Helena returned his ardor passionately as her body warmed, glowed, tingled, growing and growing in pleasure until suddenly—her whole body was on fire.

Ecstasy rained down from the heavens, and her legs shook as her body crested over a wave she had not known was within her.

Helena's eyelashes fluttered open. "Oscar…"

Oscar looked pained. "Hell, that was incredible. Watching you—I could do that all day."

All day. The thought was intoxicating. "I might have to hold you to that."

He chuckled quietly. "Ready for more?"

It was different this time and the third. Oscar's hands were in her hair, caressing her as his mouth continued to pleasure her tongue, but the rest of him…

He moved faster now, his manhood gaining a new rhythm—a rhythm Helena's body seemed to know. She arched against him, desperate for more, to repeat the ecstasy she was already craving again.

"So close," she panted, unbale to help herself. "So…so close, Oscar, please…"

Oscar groaned and moved a hand to her breast, capturing her nipple. Sparks of pleasure erupted from her, and Helena gripped the sheets in uncontrolled pleasure as she came again.

"Oh, Oscar!"

Perhaps it was his name that pushed him over the edge—perhaps he just couldn't take anymore.

Whatever it was, Oscar thrust into her as he cried out her name, then collapsed into her arms.

Helena held him close, warm, panting, and entirely hers. Yes, she had lost her innocence, but she had surely gained something else. Something far more valuable.

Oscar's heart.

CHAPTER EIGHTEEN

August 27, 1813

O SCAR SCREWED UP his eyes against the sun. No matter what time he went to bed the night before, or how late he stayed up making love to Helena, hearing her voice crack as the pleasure washed over her—the damned sun kept rising at the same early hour.

He blinked. It was so bright because the curtains were not drawn. Light flooded through the oriel windows, searing and sparkling, onto the naked woman beside him.

A smile washed over Oscar. *Helena Kirkpatrick.*

They had never agreed that their first time exploring each other's bodies would be the only time. That was why, the following evening, when Oscar had ascended the staircase and found her in his bed, he had not questioned it.

Nor the night after that.

Last night, she hadn't been there, and Oscar had found himself strangely disappointed.

No promises. That was the unspoken rule between them. No further offers, no agreements. But he had crept into bed with his heart downcast and his arms aching for her.

The clock hadn't chimed eleven when the door opened, and Helena had crept in.

"I thought you desired a rest," he had said wryly, reaching out in the darkness.

Helena had slipped into his arms. "Perhaps. But I still want you."

They had fallen asleep together, wrapped in each other's arms. Now Oscar had woken, he could see Helena had not moved far. She was naked—they had made rapid, passionate, sleepy love in the early hours of the morning—her hair softly drifting down her back.

Oscar smiled. *Helena Kirkpatrick. The governess.* Whenever his mind attempted to ask him what he was thinking, how this could possibly work, his heart forced it aside.

It would work. Something would work, though he did not know precisely what. But a life without Helena…it did not bear thinking about. He would not even consider it.

His valet was usually good, coming into the dressing room ahead of Oscar surfacing into the waking world, ensuring his outfit for that day was prepared and ready.

That was all very well…unless there was a woman in his bed.

"Not necessary?" Rondell had blinked only yesterday.

"That is not what I said," Oscar had said hastily. The last thing he needed was his valet to be offended. "From now on, please only come to attend on me once I have rung the bell."

The valet had glanced at the dressing room, then back to his master. "I will not have time to prepare—"

"I know, and no fault will be found with you," was the response Oscar had given. "I feel the need for longer slumber, that is all. I wouldn't wish you to inadvertently awaken me."

Rondell had nodded. At last, a reasonable answer. "I quite understand, Your Grace."

So now Oscar lay here, Helena beside him e, with no concerns that his valet may accidentally stumble upon their secret: the duke was bedding the governess.

And what a bedding it had been last night...

"Yes, Helena!" *Oscar had been unable to stop himself when their embrace had become more intimate in the early hours. Wasn't that the correct response when a woman suddenly mounted you and rode you to pleasure?*

He stretched, feeling the exertion in his bones. He wasn't as young as he used to be, and four nights in a row...that was impressive, even for him. Perhaps they should take it easy tonight. Sleep apart.

His gaze flickered to Helena. Dear God, he was in real trouble.

Oscar had never known anyone like her. Everything about Helena pulled him in. Nothing about her repulsed him or betrayed a lack of sense or elegance or wit. He was drunk on her. Utterly besotted, like a fool of twenty when he first encountered a woman.

He did not know how to rid himself of his intoxication for her, and the worst—or perhaps best—thing was he didn't want to.

Maybe that was what was so frightening. Not only feeling this intensity, an emotion he had dared not name for fear of realizing it would utterly undo him—no, it was the fact that he could not comprehend a future now in which Helena was not a feature.

His bed. His day. His dinners. His life.

Oscar glanced at Helena. *She always slept longer than he.* He didn't know how she did it. No matter the noise, or the sun, Helena would sleep right through until luncheon.

If only she could. If only they could stay here, hidden away from the household, their closeness known only to them. The days at the Old Abbey were starting to become unbearable.

Oh, not because of Fernsby. He was getting along quite well, considering. Amelia was no trouble—even less now he barely saw the woman, so obsessed with the gardens as she was.

No, it was because the moment they stepped through these doors, Helena and he were forced to pretend that they were nothing to each other but common acquaintances.

Acquaintances! Oscar had to smile. The woman possessed him entirely, and he had to pass her in the corridor and pretend he didn't know what she looked like without those layers.

Days and nights. That was what he wanted to share: everything.

Everything. Oscar shuddered, his smile falling from his face. He had to be careful. That sounded rather like...well. Some sort of...marriage vows.

His gaze flickered to Helena, then to the wall, where he could not be tempted to rake the subtle curves visible under the sheet.

Helena could not be his wife. She didn't want to be! No woman who expected to be a duke's wife would have permitted him to kiss her where he had kissed Helena.

A smile crept back over Oscar's face. *Damn.*

But what did that make her? Mistress? He had asked her to come with him to Riverside Manor, and though she had accepted, no details had ever been discussed with them. No comprehension of how she would leave his brother's employ and join him.

A bit of skirt. That was what he had called his previous con-quests. A woman for the evening, the weekend if he was lucky. No expectations. No future.

Not like Helena. His heart contracted as he watched her sleeping, breathing slowly.

He was lying to himself. That much he knew. *The question was, how much?*

As though she could hear the intensity of his thoughts, Hele-na stirred. She moaned slightly, as one did when realizing day had arrived a little earlier than one may have liked, and screwed up her eyes before gently opening them.

The first time she had awoken beside him, Helena had leapt up with a start and almost fallen out of the bed, so great had been her surprise to find herself there.

By now, they were becoming far more practiced in the art of the morning.

"Hullo," Oscar said softly. "Tea?"

Helena nodded, closing her eyes again. "Hmm."

Oscar tried not to laugh as he pulled the bellpull; three times, the agreed number for tea to be brought to his dressing room and left there. While Mrs. Cantrell had remarked how unusual it was for him to change his habits, Oscar had merely smiled.

Helena was nothing in the morning without her tea.

By the time it had arrived, and Helena had almost drained her first cup, she seemed able to speak. "Good morning."

"Ah, you have joined the land of the living, then?"

Helena threw a pillow. Oscar tried to catch it, but as he was lying on his front and looking at her, propped against the rest of the pillows, he was unable to prevent it from whacking him in the face.

"And let that be a lesson to you," she said with some severity. "No woman should have to suffer anyone, let alone a gentleman's nonsense before she has drunk her tea."

Oscar snorted. "I shall bear that in mind. Did you sleep well?"

Helena nodded. "Very well, though you left the curtains open."

"Not that you seemed to notice."

She smiled. "I am accustomed to sleeping through noise and light. 'Tis a skill, one has to learn it when absolutely exhausted, as I was at…at the time."

It was on the tip of Oscar's tongue to ask just how many children she had been looking after then when she had found herself so exhausted, but he held himself back. If there was one thing he knew about Helena—and he considered himself quite an expert—it was that she did not like dwelling on the past. Always looking forward, that was his Helena.

His Helena. That was a dangerous way to start thinking.

"Well, I hope you had sufficient rest to care for my rambunctious nieces and nephew," Oscar said cheerfully. "I have the exhausting task today of—what was it? Oh, nothing."

Helena groaned. Oscar laughed; this was one of the aspects about their…connection, for want of a better word, that he liked.

So many ladies had been offended when he had tried to jest with them in the past. So few ladies understood a joke anymore. Amelia was the worst.

But Helena? She took it all in stride.

"I'm not sure whether I can suffer through another rehearsal of that play today, and coming from me, that is saying something!"

She placed her empty teacup down, and Oscar pulled her into his arms. She fit perfectly. No adjustments to be made to ensure they were comfortable.

As though they were made for each other.

Oscar pushed aside the thought. "Maybe this will help you prepare for the day."

He had not intended such tenderness in his voice. Helena just drew it out of him.

She sighed and pulled his arms tighter around her. "Just the medicine I need."

Oscar closed his eyes. All he needed was this. All he wanted was this. He could feel her heartbeat gently moving under her skin. It was all he could to do keep the hug as chaste as possible, when every inch of him cried out to know her better once again—to discover a new part of her that he didn't yet know.

"We really shouldn't be making a habit of this," he breathed.

"No, w-we can't make a habit out of this."

He knew it. She knew it.

There was only one way this situation was going to end, and that was in tears.

Oscar's jaw tightened. No matter how often he told himself they would be this happy at Riverside Manor, he was no child. He knew what happened with mistresses. How many times had he seen it, over and over again with the nobility and gentry of England?

It was wonderful, pleasurable, joyful—and then it was over.

A point in his temple throbbed, and Oscar forced himself to unclench his jaw. He was not a youngling, and Helena was more than old enough to know that whatever future they had, it would not be forever.

"Why not?"

Oscar blinked. "I beg your pardon?"

There was a gentle movement as Helena chuckled. "You said that we shouldn't be making a habit of this, and I said, why not? I rather like it."

There was something so scandalous about the way she spoke—as though society didn't exist, as though they could hide and never face the world.

Oscar held her closer. "Well, I admit, I am happier. The last few days…Helena, they've been wonderful."

Did she know how utterly at her mercy he was?

"Even my brother has noticed."

"Oh dear, what did he say?"

"Only that I looked more content here at the Old Abbey than he had expected. I did not wish to lie," Oscar admitted, "but perhaps a half-truth slipped out."

"Which was?"

"That I was greatly enjoying my time here," said Oscar quietly. "That I had no wish to leave."

They sat in silence for a moment. Then—

"I am glad you are happy," Helena said softly. "You happier is precisely what I want."

They slipped into a comfortable silence. Words were not always necessary between them. Oscar allowed his senses to be overwhelmed by the heat of her, the weight of her body in his arms. The way her breathing quickly matched his. The way there was nothing better in the world than being right here.

You're getting old, Oscar thought wryly. Enjoying intimacy and silence almost as much as lovemaking? He needed to be put out to pasture.

It was mornings like this that shone a glimpse of understanding into matrimony. Was this what his brother and Constance shared? That sense of belonging to another person?

"I should be going," said Helena ruefully. "I need to slip to my own bedchamber, get dressed there. For all I know, one of the children has already knocked for me."

She moved so quickly, slipping out of his embrace, that Oscar was not able to stop her, though he very much wished to. He didn't try too hard, however. Not when he had such a marvelous view.

"I love your body," he said quietly.

Helena turned. Sunlight ringed her like a halo. "You do?"

Oscar nodded and bit his lip. "If you didn't have to leave—"

"Then I wouldn't be leaving," quipped Helena, pulling her slightly threadbare dressing gown around her. "You know that."

She had already reached the door before Oscar could say anything. Looking back, she smiled. "Have a lovely day."

Oscar returned her smile, wishing desperately she was not going. "You, too. I'm sure I'll see you. I make sure I do."

And she was gone.

Oscar fell heavily back onto his pillows. *Well, damn. He was in for it now.*

He had never had it this badly, whatever it was. Desire. Lust. Longing.

He needed to be careful.

"You bed for lust, you marry for logic," the previous duke had *warned him, a steely glint in his eyes. "I never wish to be disappointed with my boys."*

Oscar's smile flickered. *Lust. Logic.* He felt plenty of lust for Helena. There was absolutely no logic; they were two people who absolutely should not be together.

But perhaps there was something else between them, something that defied both lust and logic. Another word beginning with l, that he would not name even to himself.

Oscar lay there, lost in his thoughts, ensuring sufficient time had passed for Helena to present herself downstairs. Then he rang the bell.

"You rang?"

Oscar jumped. *Rondell must have been just outside his bedchamber!* "I did, and I commend you in your gift of flight," he said, sitting upright.

The valet looked pleased. "I have noticed it is typically around a quarter past nine that you wish for my services, Your Grace, so have taken necessary actions for your convenience."

Realizing he would need to ensure Helena was always out of his bedchamber by nine o'clock every morning—Oscar nodded. "Very considerate of you."

There it was again—that strange pride that flashed across Rondell's face. *Was he truly such a brute of a master that any sort of praise given could have such an effect?*

"I think a red waistcoat for today," said the valet briskly, striding over to the dressing room and throwing open the doors. "And a matching cravat, of course."

Feeling rather like a child being attired for a special occasion, Oscar submitted to being dressed. It was all over within twenty minutes, and he was humming a tune when he entered the breakfast room.

Which was, in hindsight, a mistake.

"My word," said Fernsby, looking up from that morning's paper. "I don't think I have heard such an out-of-tune hum in all my life."

Oscar could not help but laugh. "Well, I don't know what to say. You were always the musical one."

His brother snorted. "If you mean I could just about carry a tune, then yes!"

Oscar was too busy loading a plate from the sideboard to respond. All this lovemaking was really building up an appetite. His humming continued. Helena had put him in a good mood—a mood his brother had now noticed. *Damn.*

When Oscar turned to the table, his brother was watching him carefully. He did not comment until Oscar had sat down.

"You are different."

Oscar looked at his food rather than catch Fernsby's eye and made a conscious effort to stop humming.

This was silly. He was over five and thirty, he should control his moods better than this. Or at least hide them when he so greatly desired not to be watched by his siblings!

Thinking of siblings…

"Has Amelia already eaten?"

"What?" said Fernsby distractedly. "Amelia?"

"Yes, I wondered whether she had eaten and already gone into the garden. The weather is so fine," said Oscar blandly as he poured himself a cup of tea.

That was it. Trivial matters. Any topic of conversation, in short, beside himself. The last thing he needed was for either his brother or his sister to realize that something had happened. Something wonderful. Something he himself still not did not quite understand.

"Come on, something has happened," said Fernsby, unfortunately reading his mind. "Out with it."

There was something infuriating about siblings, Oscar decided y as he started to cut his bacon and potatoes. There were no boundaries with the blighters. They felt able to ask a man anything, absolutely anything, and expect an answer. *It was criminal!*

"Kilerth!"

"What?" said Oscar distractedly.

Fernsby glared. "Don't lie to me, man."

Oscar swallowed. He did not want to lie. No part of his life had ever been hidden, save his boxing, and it was not as though either Fernsby or Amelia had *asked* whether he had taken up bare-knuckle boxing in the rings of East End London.

A small twinge of discomfort bubbled in Oscar's stomach. How could he answer?

"Well, of course, you boys started without me. Why am I surprised?"

Oscar turned to look gratefully at his sister, who had just elegantly entered. "Amelia!"

Amelia met his gaze with surprise as she sat opposite him. "My word, you sound as though you haven't seen me in a thousand years."

And his sister looked as though she hadn't slept for a thousand nights, Oscar realized. There were bags under her eyes, and she looked pale—far paler than a lady of leisure, anyway.

Had he underestimated the strain she was under? Was Amelia making herself ill through attempting to care for Fernsby?

"And how are you, Amelia?"

Amelia glared. Oscar grinned back and, for good measure, glanced at Fernsby, who was hiding a smile. Their sister had never been a morning person.

"Amelia, don't you think Kilerth is different?"

Amelia seemed far more interested in the tea she was pouring than anything else, her tired eyes unfocused.

Oscar was about to take his first mouthful of breakfast but most uncharacteristically asked his sister a personal question. "Did you sleep well, Amelia?"

The tea spilled. A dark brown stain swept along the white linen, and Amelia placed the teapot down with a thunk on the table, her cheeks stained pink.

"Perfectly well," she said, looking just past Oscar's shoulder. "Thank you."

"Have you received any good news recently?" asked Fernsby, clearly uninterested in their sister's sleep or lack thereof. "News from London? From Kilerth, from Riverside Manor?"

Oscar took a large mouthful of potatoes to avoid answering. This was the last thing he needed, his brother getting fixated on him and his welfare. If only Amelia saw enough sense not to get involved.

Amelia didn't. She was quiet, Oscar realized. Far quieter than he had expected, but today he was glad. The inquisition was already far too intense.

It did not appear that Fernsby was going to let up. "Look, something is different, and don't try to pretend it isn't. You haven't…you didn't meet someone, did you? At the ball?"

At that precise moment, the door opened, and Helena stepped in.

Oscar choked, swallowing his food too hastily and pouring scalding tea down his throat. *Blast, what terrible timing!*

"Ah, Miss Kirkpatrick," said Fernsby pleasantly, gesturing that she should come further into the room. "We were just quizzing my brother."

Oscar could not help it. He looked up, and his gaze met hers.

"Indeed?" Helena said airily, as though they had barely spoken to each other. "What about?"

Oscar tried not to smile. *She was magnificent. Only a true actress could have done better.*

His brother shrugged. "You know, I am not sure. Something has made him happy, and it's such an unusual state that I am trying to find out why. He won't tell me."

Their eyes met again. Oscar knew he should look away, knew it was a mistake to be so unguarded before his siblings…

It appeared Helena was rather enjoying this. "Goodness, my lord, it must be a great secret if he is unwilling to tell you."

"*Thank you*, Miss Kirkpatrick," said Oscar in his most conversation-ending tone. "Did you need—"

"That's what I thought!" interjected Fernsby with an uncharacteristic grin. "Just what I thought, a great secret! What do you think, Amelia?"

"What?"

Oscar glanced at their sister. She really did look tired and had missed the entire conversation. At least there were small mercies to be found.

Taking the opportunity presented, Oscar changed the topic. "How are the children getting along with the rehearsals for your play, Miss Kirkpatrick?"

He allowed himself to smile. That was permissible, almost polite, to smile at someone you were speaking to. Someone you cared about. Someone who, just an hour ago, had been lying in your arms, skin to skin, feeling the sensation of affection between you...

"Miss Kirkpatrick?"

It was Fernsby who had spoken, and his words broke whatever spell it was between Oscar and Helena.

She blinked. "I beg your pardon?"

"The play, Miss Kirkpatrick, the play that—what is wrong with everyone today?"

Oscar tried not to grin. There was a funny side to this, even he could admit it. There was something delicious and forbidden about his mistress being employed by his brother.

"Ah yes, the play," said Helena, determinedly not looking at Oscar. "Yes, the children are working very hard. I think it will be excellent—a real knockout!"

Only during the last few syllables did she meet Oscar's gaze.

A prickle of discomfort heated across his chest.

"A real knock out."

Since their intimacy in the bedchamber, they had not discussed her promise not to tell the family about his boxing. *Was there a chance...*

No. No, he knew Helena. She would never use that knowledge against him now, not after what they had shared. She was not a blackmailer, not in the truest sense.

Or was she? Oscar failed to follow the conversation between Helena and his brother as they nattered on about the children.

Would Helena ever choose to blackmail him? Was there a chance she was only opening herself to him, allowing him to make love to her, so she could find out more, ensure she had all the details— so that if needed, she had far more material to blackmail him?

Oscar's heart raced. He had certainly told her far more about himself than he had ever told anyone before.

His Helena wouldn't do that.

"—speak to Mrs. Cantrell to select a date for the performance," she was saying to his brother. "I would hate to choose one which would interfere with everyone's duties."

"Capital," Fernsby said.

Oscar swallowed. It was highly tempting to invite Helena to join them at breakfast; there was an empty seat opposite his brother, after all, and a woman needed to eat.

"Miss Kirkpatrick", he began, "why don't you—"

"Don't let us detain you, Miss Kirkpatrick. I am sure you have plenty to do," said Fernsby firmly. "All governesses do, I'll be bound."

Oscar closed his mouth. It was a rather unpleasant reminder of the divide between them, but it was a reminder. Though it could not be plainer that Helena would have enjoyed their company, she instead left the breakfast room, closing the door quietly behind her.

"That's that," said Fernsby happily. He really was happier than Oscar had seen him in months. "You really do look awful, you know, Amelia."

Amelia burst into tears. Without saying a word, she leapt from the table, teacup spilling more tea across the already stained table, and disappeared into the hall. Her frantic footsteps upstairs echoed around the house.

Fernsby blinked, then stared at Oscar. "What was all that about?"

Chapter Nineteen

September 1, 1813

I T WAS TOO hot. How was it still this warm in September? Helena could not remember the end of summer being this stifling., moved in the trees. No breeze lowered the temperature or reduced the warmth upon her skin.

Helena was at least seated in the shade, thank goodness, but the weight of her gown was making her uncomfortable. It was the lightest muslin gown she owned, yet still, it felt constricting around her.

Too hot. That was what she had said that morning to the children when they had asked excitedly whether they were to rehearse the play again today.

"Not today, children," she had said quietly. "I think it will be too hot to—"

"We can rehearse outside!" Altan had said eagerly. Helena noticed his fencing foil already in his hand, which did not bode well. "The shade will keep us cool, Miss Kirkpatrick!"

The shade absolutely had not kept them cool. Helena watched Rowena and her brother attempt to get through a scene without any mistakes—something that was a challenge at the best of times, for it was the most complex scene.

The trouble was, of course, that in the heat, the children became entirely unreasonable.

"No, that's not the line!"

"I know what it is, I—"

"Then say it correctly!"

"Peace," said Helena quietly. The two children glared, but she returned their gazes steadily. "Continue if you must, though I still advise that you sit in the shade and—"

"It has to be perfect!" It was Rowena who was so insistent. Her face was pink, wisps of curls sticking to her face. "We can't perform for all the servants and it not be perfect!"

Helena bit her lip. She should have seen this coming. It was too much for the children to understand perfection was not required, nor what their audience would expect.

They were children, for heaven's sake! More, they were the children of the house. Servants were hardly going to boo the children off the stage—not if they wished to retain the good favor of their employer.

But that hadn't occurred to the children. They were absolutely insistent that the play had to be perfect, which meant rehearsals, even in the baking heat of the day.

"I am sure a breeze will come soon," said Altan, looking at the cloudless sky. "Any moment now. We'll be too cold!"

Helena fixed him with a look, but it did nothing. He looked back defiantly.

"We want to practice," said Sylvia.

Helena looked down. Sylvia had not wanted to sit on a chair; she preferred the lawn and was seated beside Helena.

Altan took her moment of distraction and started his lines again. "And if I intrude, I do so only to gaze upon the beauty of..."

She leaned back in her seat and watched the scene progress. She did not interrupt when Altan fluffed his lines. She said nothing when Rowena was on entirely the wrong side of the stage, making the great movement of Altan's fencing foil far too dangerous.

There was no point. They knew their lines, their movements across the stage. If the temperature was not so high, they would be delivering this perfectly.

But she had pointed this out…*five times? Maybe six, now?*

"No, I know it was wrong, but don't stop me!"

Helena sighed quietly at Rowena's words. She sounded frantic, if not close to tears.

This was the difficult thing with children—perhaps the most difficult. They became absolutely determined they were correct, despite all increasing evidence to the contrary.

This was not what Miss Clarke had prepared her for. Well, not specifically. She had mentioned "the pressure point."

"I don't like the sound of that," Helena had said at the time, eliciting titters from the other governesses in training.

Miss Clarke had affixed her with a glare that would have melted a mountain. "You shouldn't. As I was saying, before Miss Kirkpatrick so kindly interrupted, was there will be a pressure point. There always is with children, no matter the age or temperament of the child."

Her cold eyes had swept across the room. Foreboding washed over Helena.

"It could happen in your first week or the third year, but there'll be a point that becomes a battle of wills, and you must win. You must win, you understand me? Without winning the pressure point, you are nothing as a governess."

Helena tried not to smile. *Was she truly a governess?* Yes, the Bureau had sent her, but what was she doing here? Playing theater with the children by day and making love to a duke by night.

Not exactly what Miss Clarke had in mind.

Taking a deep breath, Helena knew she had to do something. She may not know much about being a governess, but she knew a great deal about being an actress.

"Stop."

She rose to her feet at the same time, giving her words more gravitas, and the scene before her came to a halt. Rowena looked ready to cry, and Altan was red in the face, though through heat or embarrassment, Helena was not sure.

"You don't have to stop us," he said breathily, "we know what we're doing wrong!"

"Don't shout at Miss Kirkpatrick," said Rowena, her face screwing up. "She's our governess. We should listen to her!"

"I don't want to—"

"Don't shout at all!" This came from their younger sister.

Time to take action.

"Now, I am not going to shout, and no one else is going to shout, either," she said gently to the smallest Fernsby before glaring at the two older siblings. "Isn't that right?"

Altan and Rowena murmured dissatisfied agreement.

"Now, I have an idea which may be to everyone's advantage," said Helena quietly, keeping her voice level. *Calm, that was what was needed. Calm with a little encouragement...* "I can see how hard you are all working, and I am very impressed. Come sit in the shade with your sister. Now, Altan."

The three Fernsby children sat in a row and looked at her.

Helena swallowed. It was the only thing she could think of. *It couldn't hurt, could it?*

"If you sit quietly in the shade here, then I will..." *It was just an idea.* "I will show you what I mean, Altan, when I say you need to hold back emotion. Is that acceptable?"

She could see the defiance in his eyes, the desperation to say it was not acceptable, that he knew what he was doing, that he didn't need a governess to tell him what to do, that he was not a child!

Adulthood beckoned, Helena thought. Just a few more years and he would be on the cusp of it. God help them all.

"Fine," Altan said sullenly.

Helena inclined her head graciously, as though he had granted her a huge favor, and stepped towards the "stage" they had marked out with their scripts. It was about the same size as that built in the ballroom, and with no wind to ruffle the pages, it remained intact.

She positioned herself just to the left of center stage. If she closed her eyes, she could still see the Theatre Royal and its audience looking back at her when she had performed this role four years ago.

Four years? Had it really been that long?

The image was still clear in her mind. There was no doubt that she knew the words, the emotional depth needed in this scene.

Helena opened her eyes. She had loved that part then, and she loved it now. Though there was lawn instead of floorboards under her feet, she could feel the power of the play rising into her body, filling her with sparkling light, the light needed to shine the way for this part.

"And if I intrude, I do so only to gaze upon the beauty of…"

The air electrified. Everything in her poured into the part: the pleading, the desperation to be accepted, the knowledge this moment could be over in an instant, but it would last in the memory for an eternity.

The words soared into Helena's mind as though they were her own thoughts. She moved around the stage as though she was a man possessed, and that spark that always flowed through her when performing returned once more.

Yet, it was not the same. It felt strange, and not merely because she was performing on a lawn for three children rather than on the sacred boards of the Theatre Royal for hundreds.

No, there was something missing. Someone.

Oscar.

Though she was doing her best to spend her days looking at him dispassionately—or not at all—a part of her wished that he was here to see her. Perhaps that was what had fueled her in London. Rather than the love of the art itself, it was desperation for an audience.

Now she wished for the audience of the only gentleman she

would love.

Love.

The word had not been spoken between them, but did it need to? Not when a meeting of minds had been entangled together in the rush of intimacy and lovemaking, as they had.

Her mind meandered as she worked through the lines of the scene, and before Helena knew it, she was speaking the very last ones.

"—leave you now, know that it is with a heavy heart that will not be complete before I am with you again."

She held the position, arms aloft, pleading, desperate, and dropped her hands to her sides and looked at Altan. "There. Do you see what I mean now?"

Altan was staring, mouth open. Something must have distracted him, which forced a prickle of irritation in Helena's heart, but no matter. The other two must have watched.

But as her eyes moved along the line of Fernsbys, she saw that all three of them were staring as though she had just stripped off naked and danced away. Sylvia was blinking a few times as though unsure of what she had just seen.

"I said," repeated Helena, her tone more forceful, "do you see what I mean now?"

Sylvia looked at her sister with a wondrous expression on her face, then turned back to Helena. Her mouth was open, too.

It was disconcerting for Helena. *What was wrong? Had they truly thought her so boring that they hadn't taken in what she had done?*

"What are you looking at?" she said.

Altan broke the silence. "You were an actress, weren't you, Miss Kirkpatrick."

He did not ask a question; it was a statement, pure and simple.

Heat flushed Helena's face, though she hoped the children would simply think it was the heat. "I don't know what you mean."

"Yes, you do," said Rowena quietly. "It isn't possible to do that without being an actress. You were, weren't you?"

This was a disaster. Helena tried to think quickly—a challenge with the heat and the intensity of the children's gazes. She did not want to lie. She had never been a liar and wasn't about to start now.

But no one else had directly asked her these questions. She and Oscar had an agreement not to spill each other's secrets, and the baron and his sister had never even thought to ask.

The baron. Helena's stomach contracted. Baron Fernsby would never want an actress anywhere near his children. Helena knew what gentlemen thought of the profession: pretty to look at when in town, but probably accepting a new man into her bed every evening.

An assumption that was true for some, but not for her. Would they believe her?

Helena almost laughed aloud. *How would she convince him when she was accepting the baron's brother's attentions!*

This was ridiculous. The children knew nothing, and they were just guessing. They could not be sure. No one could. All she had to do was act calm.

Helena pushed aside her nerves with an airy expression. "Oh, nonsense."

"It is not nonsense!" said Altan as she sat before them.

"I really have no idea what you are talking about," said Helena breezily. All she had to do was keep calm and show that she was not anxious. "You do get some wild ideas in your head! Now, let's discuss the scene. What was it that I did differently to—"

"You can lie all you want," said Rowena sullenly. "We know it's the truth."

Her words cut far deeper than the girl probably expected. Helena tried to keep her face impassive, to hide the hurt the child's words cut into her heart.

She was not a liar. She never had been.

"Not a liar! And there you are, flaunting your wares and lying every night of the week!"

She swallowed. Her mouth was dry. She was not going to permit the pain of the past to color her future—and she was not going to lie. There were some remarkable things one could do with the truth if handled delicately.

"Now, children, I think you are getting a little fanciful thanks to our play," she said quietly. "You can't possibly think that you know something about me from before I came here. All you have done is see me perform a scene in a play that we have been rehearsing for weeks."

Helena was almost sure that with some children, she would have got away with it.

Altan was shaking his head. "No, you can sword fight! What governess can do that?"

Helena crossed her legs rather than reply. *Blast.* There was a fluttering panic growing in her chest, and she must not allow it to overtake her.

"And you can do all the funny voices," said Sylvia slowly. "Do actresses do that?"

"They do," said Rowena solemnly before Helena could answer. "Auntie Amelia told me that you mended her gown for the ball, and you did her hair for her."

"I am a servant," said Helena firmly. *If only she could convince them—where were her acting skills now?* "Of course I can mend a gown! Really, Rowena!"

But the girl did not look away. "Yes, I suppose a servant would know how to do that. But I think you learned to do them for costumes, not for ladies."

Helena opened her mouth but then closed it again. She should have had a plan, before she had been sent to the Fernsbys, about what she would do if someone suspected her past.

Her true past.

Then she would at least have some sort of idea how to parry these accusations.

If only Oscar were here, she thought wistfully. Then he would have seen her perform, and he would have been able to distract the children. He would not wish her truth to come out any more than she did.

She looked at the children. Each of them looked at her calmly, less pink now that they had been sat in the shade. There was no way around this. Not if she wanted to tell the truth.

She took a deep breath. "If I had been an actress before...would that change things?"

"Change what?" asked Altan.

Helena swallowed. "You wouldn't...you wouldn't tell your father, would you?"

Sylvia beamed. "Do you want us to?"

"No!" said Helena hastily. "I mean...I would never wish for you to lie to your father, of course. But...but I don't think he should hear this particular piece of information."

There. It was said. For better or worse, she had said it.

Altan's eyes were wide as he spoke in a quiet voice. "So...so it's true then?"

Helena hesitated. A blackbird sang gloriously in the oak tree behind her, filling the stifling air with its sweet song.

"It...it would be a shame, I think, if anyone was to find out about the truth of a—a certain person's past. Recent past. In London."

"Yes," she said quietly, "but you have to keep this between us four. I mean that."

"We will," said Sylvia solemnly. "We promise. What's an actress?"

Helena couldn't help but laugh.

"But this is so exciting!" Rowena's eyes were bright. "Our governess was a famous actress!"

"I wasn't famous," interrupted Helena hastily. *No details.* "Remember, this stays between us, you understand? It is very important—Sylvia, do you understand? You are only to talk about this between the four of us, do you promise?"

She fixed the smallest Fernsby with a serious look. The girl nodded.

"We promise," said Altan, and his sisters echoed him.

The fluttering panic in her chest started to disappear.

Well. The world had not ended, and she would have to trust that either the children would keep to their word or that if they did spill the secret, that their father or aunt wouldn't believe them.

Who would? It was a fanciful idea. She didn't know why Miss Clarke had allowed it.

"Now," she said decidedly. "Why don't you go into the kitchens and ask for some ice to suck? I'm sure Cook wouldn't mind, and it is very hot."

Altan nodded, and Rowena said as she rose, "Would you like some, too?"

Helena was tempted, but right now, she needed peace. She needed to be alone. "No, thank you, Rowena. Run along now."

And run they did, the allure of ice too tempting.

Helena waited until they were inside, then allowed herself to fall back onto the lawn. The cool of the grass was a relief. She closed her eyes.

Well. This was certainly not the situation she had envisaged for her first position as governess. Oscar, and now all three children, knew her secret.

Oscar had said nothing to his brother about her past, even before they had...got to know each other better. *She loved him.* She knew he would not betray her, not now they had shared so much.

It was the children she had to worry about. They were young, and Helena was already starting to regret confirming their suspicions.

She was living in a house luxurious to most Londoners' standards. She had wages. She didn't have to give lessons. She liked the children. She liked their father. She liked their aunt. She loved their uncle.

Everything was right with the world. What could possibly go wrong?

CHAPTER TWENTY

September 3, 1813

T HIS WAS PERHAPS the most brilliant idea he had ever had.

Oscar sighed happily and luxuriated in the armchair in the morning room. He should have thought of this weeks ago when this blasted hot weather descended and melted them.

The morning room was positioned to get the morning sunshine, and so now, in the afternoon, it was mercifully cool. At least cooler than the rest of the house. Oscar had spotted his siblings seated in the drawing room, Fernsby with his jacket off and Amelia listlessly fanning herself, and ensured they hadn't spotted him passing.

Though social decorum dictated that the morning room was only habituated during the morning hours, such rules could not have been created for an English summer such as this. No one would be so cruel!

At least here he was unlikely to be forced to speak the nonsense of "polite conversation." It had been Amelia's idea, of course.

"We need to get him accustomed to polite conversation," she had said rather sternly. *"It won't be long before he is returning to society, and he is entirely unpracticed!"*

Oscar had rolled his eyes. "He has been a gentleman his entire life, Amelia."

"And you wouldn't know it to speak with him," she had cut back. "Why, when speaking to—I just think we should make more effort, that is all!"

It was Amelia's crusade, and Oscar had left her to it. If she wanted to force the poor man to practice his small talk—the most boring conversation imaginable—that was up to her.

Besides, they were seated in the stifling drawing room. *The windows faced due west, for crying out loud! It was entirely intolerable!* No, the morning room was far more suitable for a gentleman desperate to keep cool in the heat.

Oscar allowed his gaze to drift lazily to the window. There she was. Amelia. As she walked across the lawn toward the path that led to the kitchen gardens, she looked furtively back at the house, clearly concerned she might be spotted.

The little minx! After all her lectures about spending more time with Fernsby, about getting his conversational skills up to par, she was sneaking out of the house to avoid him!

Well, he could hardly blame her. Wasn't he hiding from their brother—and the heat—right at this moment? It would hardly be fair of him to criticize her for such an escape; he should rather applaud her for it.

What about the kitchen gardens was so fascinating anyway? Oscar pushed aside the memory of Helena in his arms in just such a location. For a woman like Amelia, to whom gardening had never been that fascinating, he couldn't understand it.

Perhaps it was just an excuse to escape their brother. Clearly, she could not tell Fernsby that she was leaving the house to go outside; he was in one of his lower moods at the moment.

It wouldn't do for Fernsby to become more anxious, but that didn't mean she couldn't tell *him*. Oscar would understand.

Well, they wouldn't be able to keep this up for long. Oscar was already getting itchy feet thinking about the hunting season. It was fast approaching, though their brother was showing no signs of interest.

"Hunting?" Fernsby had said, his expression pale a couple of days ago when Oscar had thoughtlessly mentioned the word at luncheon. "Here?"

"No, of course not, absolutely not," Amelia had chimed in quickly. "Now, who precisely would you like to watch the children's play, Fernsby? Household staff naturally, but what about gardeners? Stable hands? Tenant farmers?"

It had been a swift change of conversation, one Oscar was grateful for—though he couldn't help wondering, as he sat in the morning room and watched Amelia disappear behind the red brick wall, precisely what would happen if they gave Fernsby a sharp shock.

Would that help more than the mollycoddling they gave Fernsby at the moment?

Would it shock him into action?

"I think you should be kinder to him," Helena had said a couple of nights ago, holding him in her arms after a highly intoxicating exploration of each other. "He has been through a terrible loss. The idea of losing someone you love…"

She was too good, really. Too kind. Too caring. *Too good for him.*

He had known it the moment he saw her teaching the boy to fence—or at least her approximation of it. He certainly wouldn't have bothered, even with Mr. Hough's continued absences. It hadn't even occurred to him.

But it had to Helena. She had seen the pain in the boy, and she had fixed it. She was an angel—at least until she stepped into his bedchamber.

He had never thought about a future with a woman. After Fernsby and Constance had popped out an heir, it hadn't mattered much. The line would continue, the name would go on.

Marriage? Unnecessary.

Now, he was starting to wonder. Not marriage. But a woman. A specific woman.

What their future could look like, he was not entirely sure. It was the only unspoken topic between them. He didn't know his own mind. His heart, his loins, were doing the thinking.

In a way, it didn't matter. The future would come, and they could deal with it then. In the here and now, he was enjoying himself far too much to worry about it.

"I never thought I'd meet anyone like you," Helena had whispered once as he sunk himself into her, the joining they so desperately wished for making them cry out in pleasure. "Oscar…"

Oscar swallowed. He had said nothing in reply at the time, too lost in the movement that would bring them both to a climax. Those words had stayed with him. *Helena…she completed him in a way he did not understand.*

There was no denying the powerful attraction between them, and unlike with some of his other paramours, there was a deep-rooted understanding of what each person needed.

When she didn't get what she wanted, Helena did not stay silent. Oscar shivered. *She asked.* It was intoxicating.

But beyond the sensual connection, there was something more. Something Oscar had never expected. A…the only way he could think to describe it was an emotional connection.

As though drawn to him by his very thoughts, Oscar looked up as the door opened, and Helena stepped into the morning room.

"What on earth are you doing here?" said Helena with an eyebrow raised. "Don't you know this is the morning room?"

Oscar chuckled. "I should have known a governess would have been more interested in keeping to propriety than actually staying cool."

She shut the door behind her. "I hadn't realized it was so much colder in here."

"I am actually quite intelligent, you know," teased Oscar. "Few would believe it. I have to hide my extensive wit, or I would be inundated with ladies."

"I am sure you would. I should never have doubted you. Do

you mind if I join you?"

"Not at all," said Oscar, indicating the seat opposite him.

It was safe, after all. He couldn't imagine Fernsby would come in here. Amelia had gone traipsing around the garden again, and the children were obviously elsewhere, or Helena would not have been here.

"They are in the ballroom," she said as she settled in an armchair, demonstrating once again that rather disconcerting knack of guessing what he was thinking. "Rowena is determined to have her part in the second act absolutely perfect, and as I am barely in that part, I didn't think it worth staying. Besides, they need to practice arguing."

Oscar frowned. "Practice arguing?"

Helena looked rather knowing. "You never argued with your siblings?"

"Certainly not," lied Oscar with a mischievous grin.

"Well, then, that certainly explains a lot," teased Helena. "I think it's important for children to learn to argue. Get accustomed to being right some of the time, being wrong the rest of the time, and always making up with the person on the opposite side."

Oscar shook his head. *She truly was a remarkable woman. How had she never married? How had no one spotted her for the beauty she was, inside and out?*

"I missed you last night," he said softly.

Helena looked rather pleased. "You cannot endure one night without me?"

"I don't want to," Oscar said honestly.

There was a flash of delight in her eyes, clearly enjoying this power over him.

Oscar could not deny it. There was little Helena could ask of him that he would not do. She had this pull on him, a power he did not understand.

"I would have thought you'd appreciate a whole night to actually sleep," Helena said lightly, mischief dancing in her eyes.

"Get your strength back up."

Oscar laughed. "Goodness, what do you have in mind requiring all my strength?"

He had plenty of things. Delectable things. Things with blindfolds and feathers, and…

He swallowed. *Best not to get ahead of himself.* The last thing he needed was to get hard sitting right here when it was impossible to take Helena upstairs and make passionate love to her.

But why not? The rest of the family was occupied…

"I know what you are thinking, Your Grace, and the answer is no!"

"No?" Oscar said in mock confusion. "You don't know what I was going to suggest!"

"I know perfectly well," said Helena. "And it may be easy for a gentleman to get in and out of his breeches, but you know full well that a lady's gown is a complex thing! I'd never be dressed again in time in case the children needed me!"

Oscar's mind was thinking about something entirely different. "You wouldn't have to get out of your gown. I could just take you on the bed, skirts up, mouth crushed under mine…"

Why did his heart skip a beat when Helena looked at him like that, cheeks flushed but defiantly not looking away? *God, he had never talked to anyone like this. Had never found anyone who made him want to.*

"You are incorrigible," she laughed softly.

"I love your laugh."

Helena laughed again. "I love the way you make me laugh."

"I love…" Oscar swallowed as his voice trailed off, and it was he who broke the connection between them by looking away.

His stomach had contracted most painfully as he had spoken those two words; two words that were leading nowhere, for what could he say?

He saw Helena's face was pink.

Oscar swallowed the words he had been going to say—at least, the ones which had danced around his heart and had desperately pushed forth to be spoken.

Declaring his love for Helena Kirkpatrick would…complicate matters. It was a complication neither of them needed.

Whatever it was they had right now, it was working. It shouldn't work, based on all probability, but it did. The delicate balance they had found was not worth risking, even if it meant saying the words he knew she wanted to hear.

Oscar coughed. Even if he did love her, and this wasn't a mere passing fancy—which he would never know, never having been in love before—he could never speak those words. It would create a debt Oscar was not entirely sure he could pay.

Coughing again, Oscar leaned back in his chair. "Fine, if you won't accompany me upstairs, there is nothing left for me but dull, polite conversation. How is the play going?"

"You know, I am starting to wish I had never suggested it," said Helena dryly. "The work that goes into such a thing—I think I had known, but there is something quite different between seeing someone else do it and doing it yourself? A millstone around my neck."

"I can't imagine trying to get those blighters to behave for more than five minutes—no, that's not fair. Maybe an hour. A play sounds rather more difficult, if you ask me."

"They are doing remarkably well, considering," countered Helena, slipping off her shoes with a sigh. "It's just…I suppose it brings back memories which are hard to reconcile."

Oscar had assumed she would continue, but apparently, there was no more to be said. Helena's gaze drifted past him to the window, and she seemed in no mood to give any details.

It was this silence that piqued Oscar's curiosity. *Well, who could blame him?*

Helena had never been one for sharing much about her past. All he really knew about her, other than being a governess, of course, was that she had a brother. By the tone of her voice, Oscar would guess that they were either not close or he had died. She had not received letters from anyone during her time here, except from that Miss Clarke of hers.

It was odd. In a short amount of time, they had shared so much. There was no one in the world who knew him as she did. Not just the boxing, though that was part of it. No, she had seen him, truly seen him as no one else had. She had not judged him or chastised him for his choice to box in London under a different name. She'd spotted the burden of responsibility.

It was frustrating, in a way, that she was not as open with him as he was with her. After all, she knew the greatest secret he had ever kept from his family, and—

That reminded him. He had intended every evening this week to raise this, yet for some reason, whenever Helena entered his bedchamber and dropped her robe to reveal her naked body, the thought had somehow been pushed right from his mind.

"Sometimes," Oscar said, "the best things you ever do are a struggle."

Helena nodded. "Is that what you think when you're about to go into a fight?"

Oscar glanced about the room. They were entirely alone, the windows closed, so if Amelia returned from her walk, she would not overhear this.

"Look," he said quietly, "I was actually going to raise this with you before, but I have been sidetracked with…well…"

Helena beamed. "I had no idea I was so distracting."

"You don't know the half of it," Oscar breathed, then said in a murmur, "Look, I know we started off on a strange footing—you blackmailing me about my boxing—but I would like to agree to put that aside. Now we have another understanding, it would supersede the first."

There. That should do it. There was no need to be blunt about it, thought Oscar. It was a strange way to start with a woman he was now bedding, but strange things did happen.

Evidently, however, he had been too delicate. Helena was staring in confusion.

"Oscar," she said quietly. "What on earth are you talking

about? Is this some sort of strange joke that I don't understand?"

"What do you think? Do you think we can put it behind us? I really think we can pretend it never happened."

"What do I think?" repeated Helena. The look of confusion had not disappeared, and the room was warmer than Oscar remembered. "I'm thinking, what are you talking about?"

It was unlike Helena to play games. He must be too vague. It was months ago, after all, and she'd undoubtedly done it to ensure his cooperation when she had first entered the house. Helena was not a blackmailer by nature.

It felt strange talking about this during the day. Talking about his boxing at all. What if Fernsby grew bored without their sister and started looking for him? *Best to be quick.*

"Our first conversation in the ballroom," Oscar said in a low voice. "The blackmail."

Helena's jaw dropped. "I-I…you…I would never blackmail you!"

Oscar laughed nervously. He wanted this conversation over as soon as possible. "Well yes, I admit, I suppose that's a little harsh, but you did say—"

"Why on earth would I blackmail you?" Helena interrupted, brow creased in a frown.

Oscar's laugh evaporated as a hot rush of concern flooded his heart. "You are serious."

This didn't make sense. Why was she pretending the conversation hadn't happened?

Helena was staring with just as much confusion as Oscar felt. They had that conversation; he had not imagined it. *Why was she acting as though she did not recall it?*

"I don't understand the joke," she said quietly, slowly as though he had not comprehended her words. "You will have to explain it to me."

Oscar frowned, his heart pattering uncomfortably in his chest. "I was about to say the same thing. This isn't funny, Helena. You did what you had to do to protect yourself, I know, but the blackmail has to end. Now."

"You're right, this isn't very funny," said Helena quietly. Her face was pale, her hands clasped in her lap. "Please, Oscar, I don't want to continue this jest of yours."

"You cannot be serious!"

"Me—blackmail you?" Helena said, her voice rising in her confusion, then dropping self-consciously as she continued, "After all we have shared, after how vulnerable I have been with you, you are the one with more to potentially blackmail me!"

How dare she even think that? "What?"

"And as for me blackmailing you," said Helena with a bitter laugh, "I have no idea what you're talking about."

The room was continuing to grow in temperature, and Oscar wished he could remove his cravat. His neck was too hot, the cravat too tight.

Why was she being so coy about this? He stared at Helena, who looked back solemnly. *This didn't make sense.* Did she want to keep this hanging over him, keep this power?

Why? Hadn't he proven himself to her, hadn't they shared enough to trust him?

"I remember the wording quite clearly," he said coldly. "You were very careful not to name me, and I thank you for that, but your meaning was perfectly clear."

Despite his rational explanation, which Oscar thought was impressive considering the irritation now burning through his veins, Helena just blinked. She seemed to be waiting to see whether he was serious, and when Oscar remained silent, she frowned.

"I am not sure whether you were dreaming or I was, but I would certainly never—you are a duke, the brother of my employer! You think I would begin my time here by doing such a thing?"

"This is wild!" exploded Oscar, then forced himself to speak quietly as he continued, "I cannot believe you are denying this!"

"I don't even know what *this* is!"

Oscar ran his hands through his hair and thought back to that moment. He had been distracted at the time, to be sure, by the graceful and rather alluring movements of the governess, but he was master enough to understand the blackmail when it had happened.

"You said," he recalled, looking right into Helena's eyes as he spoke. "You said it would be a shame if anyone found out about the truth of a person's past in London."

A strange sort of confused understanding flashed across Helena's face. "But that—that was a mutual agreement! I meant it as a mutual understanding, to protect both of us!"

Oscar tugged at his cravat, pulling it loose. "Mutual understanding—protect us both?"

It didn't make sense. She was babbling. Maybe it was the heat?

"Yes, of course," said Helena, her eyes wide. "You think I would—blackmail? Oscar, no! You wouldn't want your family to know about your boxing, and I didn't want them to know about my past either!"

Oscar could only stare. *Past? What past? What did she mean, past?* How was he supposed to know anything about her past? He had never met her until she walked into the drawing room!

But an uncomfortable memory pressed at his mind. He had felt then, hadn't he, that he had met her before? That Helena was not entirely unknown to him. He hadn't been able to place her, hadn't bothered when she had made the allusion to his boxing. A face in the crowd, that's all she had been.

But now?

Helena smiled. "I am glad we understand each other. I would hate to—"

"Past?" Oscar interrupted. *He could not let it go now, he had to know.* "What do you mean, your past? What about your past?"

The smile vanished from Helena's face. "You...I beg your pardon?"

It was taking all his efforts, but Oscar was attempting to remember the exact wording of that conversation in the ballroom.

He would never claim to have the best memory in the world, but that particular conversation had been burned into his mind when he had believed—had *known* himself to be blackmailed.

"This is all a misunderstanding," said Helena quietly. "We'll untangle this—we will, Oscar, then you'll understand I meant no harm."

"No harm?" Oscar snapped. It was not just the temperature of the room that was rising. His blood boiled. *What had Helena been hiding?* "We clearly had different understandings of the conversation, so perhaps it's time you explained things!"

"I don't know what else to say!" Helena said helplessly. She looked genuinely confused, but Oscar pushed aside that thought. *She was hiding something, he knew it.* "I recognized you from boxing, and I thought you recognized me—so I thought, if we wanted to agree not to talk about those pasts, then—"

"Pasts, pasts, you keep talking about the past, but I don't know what you are talking about, Helena!" said Oscar with frustration. *This had all started out as a lovely conversation about how much he cared about her, though he had not said the words aloud...* "You recognized me, that I can understand, and I—I thought I had seen you before, but I could not place you. How do I know you? Where have we met?"

His heart was racing as though he was standing over a precipice and about to fall.

Oscar knew that whatever she said now, some part of the trust between them had broken. *Not blackmail? No one could misunderstand that, surely!*

Helena's laughter grated on Oscar's already fractious nerves. "You...you thought I was blackmailing you! Goodness, it's a wonder you have ever trusted me."

Oscar's jaw tightened. "I'm not sure I do anymore."

His mind was reeling, unable to take in new information. *So...so she wasn't blackmailing him?* But then why had she spoken in such a way, made it appear that...

"What?" Helena looked afraid, her face pale despite the temperature of the room.

Oscar swallowed. "Well, I thought you were…blackmail made the most sense at the time, you cannot blame me for—you weren't clear!"

"I thought you were grateful," said Helena, her voice icy. "That was what you said not five minutes ago. That you were grateful I was not more specific. Was that a lie?"

"That's not the point!"

Oscar tried to breathe slowly, to bring his increasing strain under control. They were arguing; they had never argued. He didn't really understand what they were arguing about.

"Look—"

"How could I have been so stupid?" Oscar interrupted in a low, dark voice. It was foolish of him to lash out at the woman he cared about, but did he really know her? *What was this past he did not know?* "You knew more about me than I did about you—and I never questioned that, never demanded you tell me more, even though you quite clearly had the upper hand over me!"

"Upper hand? You're the duke. You're the one who offered—"

"You took advantage of me!"

Helena looked genuinely shocked, pained, even, by his words, but Oscar forced himself to ignore that. She had been in control since she had stepped into this house. *It was time to take back some control.*

"I—*I* took advantage *of you?*" echoed Helena, her face astonished. "Everything we have shared, it has all been of your own free will! I thought you knew I was an actress!"

The words reverberated around the room as Oscar felt his heart stop momentarily, then frantically return to beating.

Actress.

Actress? It didn't make sense. She was a governess. They had hired her from the Bureau—the very best, Fernsby had said.

"An actress?" Oscar had only been able to breathe the words.

Helena dropped her gaze. "Yes, I thought…I thought you knew. I…I believed we both had secrets we wished to keep—"

"And I can see now why you wanted to!"

Oscar could hardly breathe. It was too warm in this room, too hot. He needed to get out of here, now Helena's betrayal was complete. Now she had wounded him in every way. *Now she had revealed herself as a liar, and a thief of their money, and—an actress!*

"I cannot believe it of you," he said quietly. "An actress—'tis scandalous, that you would come here and pretend to be a governess!"

"I am a governess! At least, I have been trained by the Bureau!"

But Oscar could easily sweep that aside, did so with a wave of his hand. The fury kept at bay over that blackmail nonsense was roaring through his lungs into every word he spoke.

"You lied to my brother. You lied to me. You lied to the children—you've been lying to us the moment you stepped into this house!"

"No!"

"*It…it would be a shame, I think, if anyone was to find out about the truth of a—a certain person's past. Recent past. In London.*"

Yes, he could see his mistake now, not that he would admit it to Helena. To Miss Kirkpatrick, for she could not remain Helena, not now. And to think mere moments ago he had been considering revealing his affections…

But he didn't know her. "An actress. Of course, you can be anyone you want to be. You put on the role of governess, then decided the role of mistress would get you even more protection."

"It wasn't like that!" Helena looked truly distraught.

Oscar pushed aside his qualms. *She was an actress. It was all pretending. She could look like anything she wanted.*

An actress, here. As though the Fernsby family wasn't staving off enough scandal! And they had let the children alone with her!

Worse, he had been alone with her. He had bedded her, as countless other men had done so before. Oscar did not know what was worse; the fact that he had been so easily taken in, or that he had almost…almost believed that he loved—

"This changes everything," Oscar said, rising to his feet.

Helena mirrored him. "No, it doesn't!"

"How can you say that?" Oscar thundered. There was no point in keeping his voice down now; it wouldn't matter if the whole house heard. She wouldn't be here tomorrow to face the consequences. "Lies upon lies. Was any of it real?"

"How can you ask me that?" Tears glistened in her eyes. "You think I would falsify my feelings for you?"

"You're an actress," he spat. "How can I believe anything you say, anything we shared? Good God, I shared—I told you—no one has ever got under my skin!"

His ears were roaring with the thundering of his pulse. Betrayal? The word was not sufficient. Shame poured through his bones as he tried to think back over the months. *Had he compromised himself—that was, even more than he obviously had?*

"I would never—Oscar, you have to believe—"

"It's the Duke of Kilerth to you," Oscar said curtly. "I can't believe I ever trusted you. I want you to leave."

Helena's eyes were full of tears—*tears*, Oscar thought bitterly, *she had no doubt been able to fabricate for years.* "Yes, maybe…maybe it would be better if I leave you to calm down, and we can talk later."

She had taken two steps toward the door before Oscar spoke again. "No. Leave this house."

Helena had tears flowing down her face. "What did you say?"

Oscar steeled himself to say the words he knew he had to speak. It would never do to give her any thought that this could be continued. It had to end, now.

He had compromised himself enough. If she decided to retaliate by revealing his secret to the family, well…so be it.

He had weakened himself by keeping the damned secret in the first place. He had hammered the final nail in the coffin when he had asked Helena—Miss Kirkpatrick—to keep that secret.

Well, he wouldn't be making that mistake again.

"You are not welcome here," Oscar said with quiet fury. Not in his bed, not in his heart, not anywhere near him. "Pack. Go back to the Bureau."

Helena was staring as though she had never seen him before. "This is not your house."

Oscar laughed mirthlessly. He would need at least an hour in the stables punching the air to rid this from his system. "Perhaps not, but this is my family. Leave first thing tomorrow. I never want to see your face again."

CHAPTER TWENTY-ONE

Later that evening…

T HE TRUNK SLAMMED onto her bed. How she would carry it downstairs, packed with all her worldly possessions, she did not know.

She'd have to ask a footman to help her. Not Johns. Not one who would ask questions.

Helena blinked through the tears that she refused to let fall. *She wasn't going to cry.* She was entirely mistress of herself. Crying was weak and for amateurs. She was a professional.

She was not going to permit herself to cry over Oscar Fernsby, Duke of Kilerth.

That was what he wanted. To see her suffer, to know that she had been mortally injured by his words, by his distrust. By his harsh disbelief.

"I can't believe I ever trusted you. I want you to leave."

Helena felt a tear about to fall and quickly brushed it aside. She would not permit it. How had her life become this?

She would not dwell on it. If she truly wished to keep her tears at bay, she would not think about him. She would not remember the coldness of Oscar's eyes, the harsh way he had spoken, the way he had ordered her to leave without so much as a kiss...

Helena strode to a drawer and wrenched out her gowns, stuffing them into her trunk with absolutely no care. *What did it matter?* No one worth caring about was going to see her wear them. She was going to London in disgrace. She may need to sell them anyway.

In a way, they were already not hers.

Though tears still threatened to fall, Helena found it was fury making her eyes water, as well as sorrow. This was ridiculous! What had she done to deserve such treatment?

Nothing. She had done nothing wrong, save attempt to keep her past to herself which any woman—anyone should be permitted to do.

Secrets, secrets. There were far too many secrets in this house. The baron was kept secret from the world; Lady Amelia crept off for secret solitude... Even the loss of Constance was treated like a secret: never spoken of but whispered about by servants in corners and muttered by neighbors at the ball.

And what had she done? Helena forced her house slippers into the trunk with such force, she felt the bottom of the trunk creak. *She had tried to keep her own secret.*

What was wrong with that? *Nothing!* She had the right to keep her past to herself, and it was outrageous that Oscar—that the duke should be offended by it.

"Yes, I thought...I thought you knew. I...I believed we both had secrets we wished to keep—"

"And I can see now why you wanted to!"

Helena sat heavily on her bed next to the trunk, which wobbled dangerously and almost fell to the floor. If only she had allowed herself a moment of calm after her argument with Oscar. If only she hadn't taken it upon herself to make absolutely sure he would regret it.

Her footsteps had rang out on the corridor's parquet floor after that conversation, and Oscar's words still ringing in her ears.

"You are not welcome here. Pack. Go back to the Bureau."

And that was precisely what she intended to do. She would make him regret it. He would calm down and wish he had not spoken to her in that manner—regret shouting at her, at calling her a liar—but it would be too late.

She would make sure it was too late.

That was why, mere minutes after being ordered from the house by the duke, Helena had rushed into the billiards room and glared menacingly at the baron.

"Dear Lord," said Baron Fernsby, dropping his cue onto the billiards table. "Has something—something has happened. The children, are they quite well?"

His immediate concern had given Helena a moment's pause, but she pushed on ahead. Her blood was boiling, Ophelia's madness seeping into her bones.

"I am leaving," she had said firmly. "For London. I require your carriage."

The baron had merely blinked. "London? For how long?"

"Forever," Helena had said recklessly. There was nothing for her here, why not burn the bridge? Why not show Oscar how much it hurt to get what he said he wanted. "I resign."

Her master had looked astonished. "B-But—Miss Kirkpatrick, you can't!"

"I can," she had said mercilessly, ignoring the stabbing pain of regret already piercing her heart. "I apologize, my lord, but the Bureau will send a replacement as soon as one suitable is found. The carriage?"

There was sharpness in her voice, something that compelled the baron to acquiesce.

"Yes, yes, the carriage," he had said vaguely. "When do you—"

"First thing in the morning would suit," Helena had said, averting her gaze. It was too painful to look at him. The disappointment in his eyes was nothing to the similarity of his jaw to a man who had hurt her most grievously. "Six o'clock."

The baron had nodded. "Right. Well. Is there anything I can say to—"

"No." Helena had to be resolute. It would be tempting to be encour-

aged to stay by her master, but it did not matter. The person who really mattered was Oscar. His word was law in this family, and Helena knew she could not remain one hour longer than necessary.

She had to get out. She had to leave the Old Abbey, leave the Fernsbys, leave Oscar.

Forever.

"Was...is it anything I or the children have done?" The baron's words had made her look up. "I know I am a difficult master, but the children adore you, and—"

"No." Helena had felt pained at his discomfort, but there was no possibility of explanation.

"If you want to go into town—just because I don't, that doesn't mean you cannot."

And she had swallowed down all her kind words because she could not permit herself to become even more entangled with this family than she already was.

The baron had coughed into the silence. "I...I know my family considers me a bit of a tyrant, but I have no wish to do so. I don't want to be like this."

His last few words had been spoken in a whisper, and Helena had been overwhelmed with compassion. She had stepped across the room, reached out and touched his arm, and told the master of the Old Abbey precisely what he needed to hear.

"You are doing an excellent job at caring for your children, and my leaving is not a reflection of that."

She had not waited for an answer. Dropping her hand, Helena had stridden to the door and was only stopped by the most piteous words from her old master.

"But I'll never find a governess who can care for them like you."

Helena had hesitated then, one hand on the door, her mind already on the journey back to London, but her heart...her heart was here. If only she could stay. If only the Fernsbys could be her family, of sorts.

"I can't believe I ever trusted you. I want you to leave."

And Helena's heart had hardened. Oscar's anger would never permit her to stay. "I have to go."

Helena dropped her head into her hands as she sat by her trunk on the bed. That had been five hours ago. She had spent the intervening time in her bedchamber, wondering why night had taken so long to arrive. *Why was the agony of departure to be so delayed?*

She had kept tears back then—she was an actress; she could control her expression, and she had managed to keep herself calm until she was alone.

Now she could cry. Now Helena's tears could pour down her face because the pain inside had to get out somehow, even if she did not understand why her heart ached so much.

Because she loved him. Even through his bitterness, his cruelty, she loved him.

London felt like a strange and distant world after months here at the Old Abbey, but this time tomorrow, she would be there. Precisely where she would stay, she had no idea. She had her wages from the Bureau, but they would not last forever.

Miss Clarke was not likely to accept her back into her fold, not after losing her position at her first situation in less than a year.

No, the Bureau would not be able to withstand the scandal— and that was supposing Oscar kept her secret. There was no knowing what he might do. Miss Clarke might decide it easier to just pretend Miss Kirkpatrick did not exist.

Helena smiled wryly, lifting her head from her hands and seeing that they were damp. *Miss Kirkpatrick had never existed. She had been a role, the perfect role for her.*

The Governess Bureau was a lost cause. Was returning to London even a good idea? Helena's thoughts scattered wildly, but she tried to bring some semblance of order to them.

Where else could she go? Brighton? Bath? York? Somewhere with a theatre that might be looking for actresses?

Helena bit her lip. She was alone, friendless, without advice. She had never left London before coming here. Bath and York were days and days away.

She was in precisely the same situation she had found herself in months ago when Mr. Tobias had unceremoniously thrown her out of the Theatre Royal.

No, it was worse. Now she knew what love was. She knew the intensity of intimacy, the desperation of longing. She knew what it was to care for a man, and to be cared for in return—and she knew what it was for that love to be torn out of her heart and cast down, deemed unworthy merely because of her background, which she had been so sure he knew.

Helena brushed the last few tears from her cheeks. However much he had hurt her, she could not stop loving him. Unfair that might be, but it was the truth. She had never lied. She had always been as open as she could be, and yet it was Oscar who believed her to be a liar.

"It…it would be a shame, I think, if anyone was to find out about the truth of a—a certain person's past. Recent past. In London."

Well, none of this miserable thinking was getting her anywhere. As much sleep as possible, that was what she needed, and she needed to pack her trunk before she lost herself in slumber. Then she could awake with the dawn, dress, and leave the Old Abbey forever.

Helena rose and started opening the final drawers of her belongings, carrying the sorry items over to the trunk. It wasn't even half full.

"I cannot believe it of you. An actress—'tis scandalous, that you would come here and pretend to be a governess!"

Helena dropped her small, handheld looking glass into the trunk and pushed it down with such force that it broke. Small slithers of silver poured across her trunk.

Seven years of bad luck. Well, she was a superstitious person, all stage people were.

"You're not the one who has done anything wrong," she told herself, trying to pick out the broken bits of looking glass from her gown. "You're not the one who decided to hate someone just because they were an actress before you met them."

Helena swallowed. Oscar had never struck her as a prejudiced person, but once he knew of her past, her true past, he was quick to reject her. He did not know her at all.

Helena finished removing the broken glass from her trunk. She had to be ready. The last thing she wanted was to run late tomorrow morning and run into the children.

The children. She hadn't told them.

Well, someone would. Their father, hopefully, for if their uncle took it upon himself, then it was likely they would hate her.

It took another twenty minutes to place her final belongings inside the trunk. The only things unpacked were her nightclothes and traveling outfit, ready for tomorrow.

Helena snapped the lid shut and, with a grunt, slid it to the floor beside her bed. *There. It was done.* The clocks had struck ten o'clock a few minutes ago. Within eight or so hours, she would be leaving.

There had been silence in her bedchamber other than her sniffing and heaving of the trunk, but now Helena straightened up, she heard a different noise. A strange one. A strangely familiar one.

It was coming from just outside her room.

Helena crept over to her door and opened it a crack. There was Lady Amelia's room, the door opening—and there was Lady Amelia, struggling to lift a trunk much as Helena had.

Helena swallowed. *This was her chance to ensure the third of the Fernsby siblings knew she was leaving. Perfectly timed.*

Brushing away the last tear, she opened the door. "You are leaving, too."

Helena had not considered her words particularly inflammatory, but Lady Amelia jumped, turned with boiling red cheeks, and snapped, "What?"

It was such an overreaction Helena hardly knew what to say. She pointed at the trunk. "You are leaving. Aren't you?"

Only then did Helena take in the full expression on her ladyship's face. A little fear, a bundle of nerves, and a crease on her forehead that told Helena she did not wish to be caught.

Lady Amelia's gaze flickered down the corridor. "I have to

go."

It did not make sense. Where was Lady Amelia going at this late hour—and with a trunk? Surely the baron would have mentioned if his sister was leaving; he could have suggested Helena leave with her. Half the number of coaches, double the protection. They could have acted as each other's chaperones. Which meant…

Her brother did not know.

It didn't make sense to Helena, but she had a woman's instinct. "Inside. Now."

Her voice was low but the tone insistent, and Lady Amelia immediately obeyed, which was rather a surprise.

Lady Amelia had rather less trouble with her trunk than Helena, carrying it into the room and placing it on the bed.

"I had not known you were leaving, too," she said quietly, keeping her eyes downcast.

Helena examined her closely. There was something wrong here, something out of balance. *Lady Amelia, leaving? To go where?* Had she given up on encouraging her brother to leave the house? Had she simply had too much, living here for over a year?

"Yes, I am leaving," Helena said quietly. "Your brother has asked me to go."

"I can't believe I ever trusted you. I want you to leave."

Lady Amelia looked up. "Goodness, really? I thought he was happy with you. I have never seen a man so pleased."

Helena blinked back tears. *She was not going to cry.* "Well, he isn't anymore. He has asked me to leave, and so that is what I am doing. The question is, where are you going?"

It was only now in the privacy of her bedchamber that Helena took in Lady Amelia's apparel. She was wrapped in a traveling cloak. She had carried in her trunk with ease. It was not possible that she had sufficient gowns, shoes, gloves, and bonnets packed in there.

Helena looked into the nervous face of the lady of the house.

Lady Amelia bit her lip. "You cannot tell anyone."

"Well, you haven't told me anything," Helena pointed out quietly.

Lady Amelia laughed. "True, but I imagine you have guessed. You are, after all, a woman, yourself. Intuition?"

Helena nodded faintly and gently sat on the bed. "Who is he?"

A warm smile, untamed and brilliant, spread across Lady Amelia's face. It was an expression Helena recognized; at least, she knew how it felt to smile that smile. It had inhabited her own face for a few weeks. A few short, heady weeks.

Perhaps only a woman in love could recognize another.

"He's wonderful," said Lady Amelia warmly. "Just the best of men—kind, charming, gentle. Clever. I love him, Miss Kirkpatrick, and I-I won't allow anyone to talk me out of it."

Helena nodded, trying to gather her thoughts. *This was a delicate situation.*

After taking a deep breath, she said. "I see. I suppose I should have guessed as much. You would not risk your reputation for a man you did not love."

Lady Amelia's cheeks flushed as she looked away. "I'm not risking anything. I am going to marry him."

"So, you are eloping?"

Lady Amelia glanced at the door. It was closed. "Yes, but please, speak softly."

Helena could not help but smile. It was what she would have expected of a woman like Lady Amelia. It was so romantic, so wonderful to be swept up in the story—for it was like a story. Like one of those novels she had spotted beside Lady Amelia's bed.

She probably read of a similar tale, or, Helena thought ruefully, *saw it in a play.*

Still, there was a difference between art and real life. Perhaps it was time Lady Amelia was reminded of this.

"Eloping," Helena repeated softly. "I see. Where are you going?"

"Gretna Green," said Lady Amelia promptly.

Helena nodded. *Well, of course.* Half the couples in London looking to elope said they were aiming for Gretna Green. The number who made it that far…that was a different matter.

"And how will you get there?"

Lady Amelia looked as though she was asking stupid questions. "Carriage, of course."

"With one set of horses?" prodded Helena gently. "All the way? I am not an expert, my lady, and I have never before journeyed so far. But one set of horses, all the way to London? All the way to Scotland?"

Lady Amelia's determined look flickered. "Well…no. That would be foolish."

She said no more. Helena watched her carefully as the decided and absolutely certain expression on her ladyship's face slowly faded.

So, she had not thought further ahead than the first moment of escape. She could not blame her. When had Helena ever planned further than the day after tomorrow?

"I am not teasing you, my lady, nor do I wish to censure you for your plan," Helena said quietly. "I am just wondering…whether you have had sufficient time to think about this."

"I love him," said Lady Amelia defiantly.

"And I do not doubt that," Helena said. "I am just not sure whether you have had enough time to plan."

Lady Amelia strode toward the window, tossing her head impetuously as though that would remove all obstacles from her path. The curtains were closed to the night sky, and after a moment, she turned back to face Helena, that same look of defiance on her face.

"Mr. Hough wants to marry me, and I wish to marry him. Isn't that enough?"

Helena thought immediately of Oscar.

"Isn't that enough?"

Not always. Despite the connection they had, the affection

they had for each, the desire they had to be together…it wasn't enough.

She had thought Oscar loved her for a moment. For a few days at most. But whatever he felt for her clearly had not been love. Prejudice was always stronger.

Helena sighed. "Not always."

It was her turn to be closely examined. Lady Amelia frowned. "You look like you know what you're talking about."

Of all the people to bare her soul to, Oscar's sister was not one of them. "Perhaps. I do not pretend to understand all you feel, but I do know this. Your brothers love you."

Lady Amelia looked away.

"They care about you," Helena persisted. "They would want what's best for you. They would probably wish to host your wedding."

Lady Amelia snorted. "Kilerth is such—"

"Ignore him," interrupted Helena. "I am."

She was surprised by the bitterness in her voice. There was pain there; pain which had not yet mellowed to sorrow. The pain had not yet entirely seeped through her heart.

"The baron," she said, forcing herself not to think of their brother. "Baron Fernsby. He cares about you, his little sister. Surely he would want to meet the man you love, get to know him, approve the match."

Only as Lady Amelia laughed dryly did Helena's memory attempt to remind her of a name that had already been mentioned. *Mr. Hough…*

"You think?" said Lady Amelia. "Approve the match—to his son's fencing master?"

Helena attempted to keep her face neutral, but evidently, she had done a poor job—perhaps the first time since joining the Theatre Royal.

Lady Amelia laughed bitterly. "Yes, that is what I thought."

"Unequal marriages are often made," said Helena, though she was not entirely sure she would be able to give any examples if pushed.

Lady Amelia and Mr. Hough. Only now did Helena realize the significance of their dance at the ball. One of the few times they could be togetherin public. No one would question the kindness of a duke's daughter when dancing with a servant to the family.

That must be where Lady Amelia was always disappearing off to! She wasn't walking in the gardens—or if she was, she was not doing so alone.

"Yes, unequal marriages are made," said Lady Amelia, a harshness to her voice Helena had not heard before. "Through elopements."

Helena sighed. "Look, I am not a lady, so I cannot tell what pressures you are under. But ask yourself this. Do you want to spend the rest of your life under a cloud, separate from your family, with discord between you simply because you didn't talk about it?"

There must have been something persuasive in her voice, for Lady Amelia opened her mouth, hesitated, then closed it. She could not refute the veracity of Helena's words.

Helena pressed home her advantage. "I am not a fortune teller, Lady Amelia. I cannot predict the future nor offer you any guarantees. If you speak to them and they do not approve, you could still elope. But you haven't given them the chance to accept him, and you."

Where these words were coming from, Helena could not be sure. Perhaps she was pulling from a play so deep in her memory that the lines had become hers now.

"If you give them a chance, you might be surprised. You could get everything you want. You could marry Mr. Hough and be given away by your brother. By both of them."

Lady Amelia blinked. "I...I never considered that."

Helena smiled. "Sometimes, all it takes is an outside perspective."

Her ladyship's gaze flickered as her eyes darted back and

forth, and Helena held her breath.

"Fine." Lady Amelia did not sound aggrieved, exactly, but there was a hint of finality in her voice. "I-I'll talk to them. Tomorrow. After I've slept on it."

"Won't your Mr. Hough be surprised if you don't turn up tonight?"

A flush tinged Lady Amelia's cheeks. "He...well. He didn't know of my plans. I intended to surprise him."

Helena had to laugh. "You know, I like you, Lady Amelia."

The words had slipped out before she could stop them, and Helena placed her hands over her mouth. *To say such a thing to a woman of Lady Amelia's standing!*

Lady Amelia laughed. "And I like you, too, Miss Kirkpatrick. You have done me a service. Thank you."

She picked up her trunk and, without another word, slipped out of Helena's room.

Though sorely tempted, she did not open the door again to check Lady Amelia had been true to her word and returned to her bedchamber. Helena had done all she could for the Fernsby family. At some point, they would have to figure it out on their own.

If only her own problems were that easily fixed.

Helena glanced at her trunk. Why was she still helping Oscar after he had been so cruel to her? It would have served him right to wake up tomorrow not only to her absence but to the absence and scandal of his sister.

No, that was not who she was. Though Oscar may not believe it, she had morals, and Helena was not going to stoop below them to prove a point.

By the time the sun came up, she would be gone. She would never see the baron, Lady Amelia, the children, or Oscar again. Just as he wanted.

✦

CHAPTER TWENTY-TWO

September 6, 1813

T HE KNIFE SUDDENLY darted down, spearing the flesh. There was no opportunity of escape. Oscar smiled grimly. He pulled back the knife and thrust it forward again, feeling the tension in his shoulders dissipate as the blade found its mark.

"What did that roast chicken ever do to you?"

Oscar looked up with a scowl at his brother. "What?"

Fernsby raised an eyebrow. "Doesn't matter. I'll leave you to it."

Luncheon was a family affair. It always was, ever since they had been children. In a few years, Altan would be old enough to join them, and he, too, would be introduced to the forced formality and the stilted conversation they all endured.

Oscar stabbed his chicken again. *Well, that was not entirely fair.* He did actually enjoy most of the conversations with his siblings. Just not today.

Today, he wanted to be alone. He wanted to feel the misery of his situation in peace. He wanted to punch something very hard, repeatedly, until all the rage and anger and pain searing his veins, clogging them with ire, could be released.

Had he ever been this angry? Even when that scoundrel had attempted to pull a pocketknife on him, their last bout in the East End of London. Righteous anger had fueled him then, winning him the match.

This was different. A fury he could do absolutely nothing about.

He stabbed at the chicken one final time for good measure, then brought it to his lips.

"Lies upon lies. Was any of it real?"

"How can you ask me that? You think I would falsify my feelings for you?"

The mouthful turned sour as Oscar chewed and swallowed. *Why couldn't he get Helena—Miss Kirkpatrick's words from his mind?* He appeared to have memorized everything she said to him in the morning room when her deception had been revealed.

"Why on earth would I blackmail you?"

Oscar snorted. *A likely story.* The more ridiculous her lies were, the angrier he became.

He saw Fernsby and Amelia exchange a glance. *How often had Fernsby been in a bad mood, or Amelia raged about a friend who had slighted her?* They owed him this. To wallow in his own misery, even if he had to come to the luncheon table and socialize for a short hour.

How could he have been so stupid? How could he not have noticed?

The play. The rehearsals. Of course an actress would wish to do such things! The only thing she knew how to do—*other than lie,* Oscar thought viciously—was put on a play.

It was all a game to her.

Time and time again, he had seen evidence that Miss Helena Kirkpatrick was an actress, but he had been blinded. Blinded by her beauty. *Blinded by his lust.*

She had taken advantage of that. *Oh, how she must have laughed,* Oscar thought bitterly as he stared at his plate, unable to stomach any more. Even when he'd stumbled upon her mimicking other members of the house, he had not thought to ask more about it.

The construction of the stage, the mending of Amelia's gown…

Oscar tried to focus on the conversation going on between his siblings.

"—last of them, I'm afraid," Amelia was saying with a sigh. "Cook told me as much. Too late for more tomatoes, apparently, so we will have to start using the preserves if we…"

Oscar's attention faded out. *Tomatoes.* As though that was the summit of their problems.

No, their biggest problem as a family was that he, the head of it, was an absolute imbecile. He'd had an actress in the house, an *actress* known for their low morals and loose skirts, and he had not noticed.

Well. He had noticed for all the wrong reasons.

An image of Helena naked beneath him, eyelashes fluttering, crying out his name, flashed across his mind.

Oscar's jaw tightened. He had been entirely taken in. He had wanted to be. It was pleasant to think he had such an effect on a woman like Helena—Miss Kirkpatrick.

It had been pleasant to pursue her and even more pleasant to win her. To woo her.

A rather unpleasant thought dropped into his mind. She was an actress, wasn't she? She could have been pretending. Every special moment, every connection could be a lie.

Perhaps she didn't even like him at all, Oscar thought savagely, the thoughts only hurting himself. *She hardly put up a fight to stay, did she?*

"I can't believe I ever trusted you. I want you to leave."

She could have argued back. She could have tried to reason with him. Oscar had half hoped at the time that she would. Yet Helena had slammed the door behind her, and that was it. The last he saw of her. That he ever would see.

His stomach clenched painfully, and the meager amount of chicken he had been able to eat shifted uncomfortably. Nausea rose in his throat. Oscar placed his fork down.

It all felt so meaningless. Food. Luncheon. Family. How could he enjoy such things when he had allowed himself to bare his soul to a woman he truly cared about, something that had never happened before—only to discover that it was all a huge joke to her?

She must have congratulated herself, Oscar thought bitterly. *She took us all in her stride, and we fell for her lies hook, line, and sinker.*

His waistcoat was too tight, his cravat strangling. Thoughts of Helena overwhelmed him, the nausea rising. A spike of heat flushed across his brow as a thought occurred to him.

Was it possible…he had taken precautions, of course, he was no fool…but no one precaution was perfect. Was there even the slimmest chance that Helena was pregnant?

"—so the villagers tell me," said Fernsby cheerfully. "You may find we can purchase tomatoes from them if the summer heat has provided the perfect situation for…"

Helena, pregnant. It was a heady thought.

An illegitimate Fernsby. Well, it wouldn't be the first time, but it had been a few generations since a Fernsby man had been so careless. *Careless, that was the word for it.* He had carelessly allowed Helena into his heart, then his bed, and now she could have gallivanted off into the world with his child in her belly.

The thought made his heart patter painfully. *Perhaps that had been her plan all along,* Oscar thought savagely. Seduce the master—or him, of higher standing—to fall for a baby, then demand an annuity for the rest of her life.

It happened. People pretended not to notice if the father was of a high enough standing, but many a gentleman had received awkward looks in society for just such a situation.

It made sense. Helena—Miss Kirkpatrick—must have had a plan.

Oscar swallowed. *He hadn't.* He had found her intoxicating from the first moment he met her. All thought was banished in her presence. She was beautiful. So clever, so witty—so talented.

She was prodigiously skilled, and now she was gone.

A flash of regret soared through his heart, but Oscar pushed it away. He could not think like that. He could not allow Helena's beauty, her charm—*her acting*, he told himself firmly—to cloud his judgment.

He mustn't linger on how she laughed, throwing her head back and losing herself in the joy. Nor the way she had looked at him, awe and desire and affection mingled.

It was all a façade. She was the one who lied to him, who had pulled the wool over his eyes, over all their eyes. He was the one who had been led on.

"And gone so quickly, too," said Fernsby.

Oscar's attention snapped to the table. He knew precisely what this was about.

"Here one day, gone the next," his brother said. "Very quickly. Remarkable."

Amelia nodded as Oscar felt his stomach tighten. He felt the focus of their gazes on him but looked down at his plate rather than face them. Most of his food was still there. He hadn't eaten breakfast at all.

What was the point? Food had lost its flavor. He'd eat dinner, he told himself firmly. He would eat then. By evening, all thoughts—all nonsense of Helena would be gone.

Miss Kirkpatrick. *If that was her real name.*

"Leaving us in the lurch, rather," continued Fernsby, his eyes still on his brother. "Most unfair, I call it. Unprofessional. I mean, what will the children do now?"

Amelia joined in. "The children—oh, the poor dears. They are very upset, you know. They seem to believe that it is impossible for them to perform the play without her."

This was intolerable. Oscar picked up his fork for something to do and stabbed a potato coated in a new white sauce Cook had been experimenting with. The last two iterations had been barely digestible.

Not perform the play, indeed! Little did they know! His family lived in ignorance, and that was precisely how he wished to leave them, though the temptation to reveal the truth grew.

Oscar swallowed the potato. It wasn't half bad.

The play. *The play! Acting was the only thing Helena did,* he thought angrily. They were better off without her.

Fernsby sighed. "She was so talented—I believe I was fortunate to get her. The Governess Bureau only offers the best, naturally, but she was the best of the best."

Amelia nodded. Oscar said nothing.

"The way she was able to help us all—so talented," said Fernsby with another heavy sigh. "I mean to say! She basically wrote that play, helped create the stage, the difference in the children…and she even did a little mimicry, I believe."

"And mending my gown, and my hair and face for the ball," added Amelia in a low voice. "And didn't she teach the boy some fencing, Kilerth?"

Oscar nodded. All the signs had been there. She may as well have been wearing a sign that said "I was an actress!" for all the hints she gave them, time and time again.

And they, fools that they were, were simply too idiotic to notice.

It was embarrassing, really. Here they were, educated people from one of the best families in England, and they couldn't even notice an actress when she dropped into their midst!

Oscar pushed another potato around his plate and tried not to think about it. Impossible, as the conversation about Helena continued on around him.

"Replacement? No, I don't think it possible to find a true replacement," Fernsby was saying. "The children will find problems with any governess we try now…"

Oscar glared at a carrot. What could he have done to prevent this all from falling apart? Could he have realized earlier—why hadn't he seen the signs when they were so clear?

The stage, the play, the acting, the costume, the face paint…

He placed his fork down again and raised a hand to his temple. He was starting to get a headache—no wonder, after being forced to deal with yet another disaster befalling this family.

Once again, he was doing it alone.

"I should not have…you must think me a fool."

"No. Only a very good man."

Oscar's jaw tightened. Helena had seemed so…so understanding. Part of the act, too. He couldn't trust anything she had said or did. Why had he not realized she was a bad egg the moment she had blackmailed him! Surely any reasonable man would have thrown a woman like that out of the house!

His fingers massaged the most painful point in his temple. He had been bewitched. *Hoodwinked.* Entirely taken in by a woman, practiced at wrapping men around her little finger.

"Well, I suppose I shall just have to find another governess, though it will be difficult," said Fernsby with a wry smile. "I wish she hadn't gone."

Amelia stared. "Well, I admit I am surprised to hear that. If you didn't want her to go, then why did you fire her?"

Oscar shifted in his seat. *Ah.* He probably should have found time this morning to speak with Fernsby about this. He hadn't. As soon as he had that conversation, he would have to answer some rather awkward questions.

That was why Fernsby looked so confused. "Fire her? *Fire* Miss Kirkpatrick? I wouldn't fire her, she's the best servant in the place—oh, no offense, McLoughlin."

The butler did not move from the side of the room. "No offense taken, my lord."

"I don't understand," said Amelia slowly. Oscar felt his heart rate quicken. "I spoke to Miss Kirkpatrick when she was packing, and she said my brother had told her to leave."

"What?" Fernsby looked astonished. "There must be a misunderstanding. I would never say that."

It took them a moment. Oscar found himself wishing, cowardly, that they would not put it together at all, but they were, after all, his siblings.

Slowly, they turned to him. His cheeks flushed. *Damn.*

"One day," Oscar said darkly, "you'll thank me for it."

But not, apparently, today. Amelia looked absolutely outraged, and Fernsby cleared his throat a few times before saying, "Blast, man, what on earth have you done?"

"What needed to be done," Oscar said stoically.

Amelia laughed dryly. "You take it upon yourself to dismiss your brother's servant?"

"Don't talk about what you don't understand," snapped Oscar. *This was getting out of hand. He had to end this conversation while he still could.* "These potatoes are—"

"And how can we understand," interrupted his brother, "if you don't tell us?"

Heat blossomed up Oscar's body, his stomach still nauseous, the pain in his temple growing. Deuce. *Helena was still getting him into trouble even with her gone!*

He had been a fool to ever trust her. At least he had done the right thing, eventually. Removing her from this household, from this family…the damage was limited.

Limited to himself.

"I am not very impressed with you," said Fernsby irritably. "Miss Kirkpatrick was a good governess, never heard a word against her from the children, the servants—and now the play can't go ahead!"

Oscar worked hard not to snort. *That damned play!* "It can go ahead without her."

"The children need someone to take care of them!"

Oscar waved a hand. "We have Amelia for that."

It was the wrong thing to say.

"Oh, really?" said Amelia, temper flaring. "You may not have noticed, Kilerth, but I am not just a servant who will do your will. I have my own plans, you know!"

"I didn't mean—"

"You really went beyond your jurisdiction here," said Fernsby, not allowing Oscar to apologize to their sister.

Oscar tried to take a deep, calming breath. It did nothing to prevent his temper rising. He should have spent the morning explaining things to Fernsby—as much as he could—and then punching the air in the stables, just to get some of the anger out.

Fernsby was shaking his head. "I never would have expected this of you!"

Oscar stayed silent. It seemed to be the safest thing to do at present.

"I don't understand," Amelia said slowly. "There's more to this, something you're not telling us. Out with it."

She wouldn't be happy until he said something, Oscar knew. "None of your concern."

This made Fernsby laugh. "Surely it's my concern!"

Oscar glared at his lone potato. He had never been less hungry in his life.

The momentary distraction almost centered him, gave him time to focus—but then Fernsby was speaking again, and this time the anger and bitterness had left him, leaving only sadness. "I…I know I have been difficult—"

"No," said Oscar quickly. He was not going to permit his brother to relapse back, to lose all the progress he had made, just over a silly governess. *Over Helena. The woman he*—"No, you haven't."

He glanced at Amelia. Anxiety was dancing in her eyes.

"No, it's all right. I know I have," said Fernsby simply. "Not without reason. I've lost the woman who completed me, who made the world feel right. The loss of her tilted my world on edge, and I still…I haven't got my balance back yet."

The anxiety had disappeared in his sister's gaze, now replaced with tears.

Oscar could not speak.

"I've lost the woman who completed me, who made the world feel right."

How was it possible that his brother could describe so perfectly how he felt now that Helena had gone from his life?

Was it possible that he had truly cared? That his desire was not purely for her body, but her wit, her kindness? Damn, he had known that long before he had realized she was an actress. He had known how dangerously close he was to truly caring for her.

Hadn't he almost said as much?

"I love your laugh."

"I love the way you make me laugh."

"I love…"

An actress. A liar. A blackmailer. Was it possible that only one of those accusations was true? What if he had lost—no. He could not think that way.

Time to put an end to this. "The children will learn to live without her."

"Well, I won't."

The two Fernsby brothers stared at Amelia, who looked back at them defiantly.

A cold ice grip encircled Oscar's heart. *What on earth had Helena been telling her? More lies about herself? More blackmail, perhaps?*

Amelia's cheeks were flushed. "I…I have a confession of my own."

"Are you quite well?" asked Fernsby.

Oscar barked a laugh. "I am not sure we can cope with more than one scandal in this family."

He had spoken hastily.

Fernsby turned to him with a pale expression. "Scandal— what scandal? Why did you ask Miss Kirkpatrick to leave? What do you know about my household that I don't?"

Tarnation. "It was a figure of speech. Come on, Amelia, what's going on?"

He assumed she would admit she had been taking walks in the garden, or Helena had lent her a gown, something frivolous. What else could a lady of Amelia's standing be hiding?

It was only as Oscar examined her that he noticed the lines of stress around her eyes. The trembling fingers held tightly together in her lap.

Tension gripped his shoulders. *What hadn't he noticed? What else had he been unable to protect his family from?*

Amelia took a deep breath. "You have to promise not to be angry."

"We can't promise that," said Oscar immediately.

Fernsby glared. "Well, fortunately for Amelia, *you* don't get a vote. This is my house." He looked at their sister, his eyes kind, his voice low. "Of course we won't."

Fingers still twisting in her lap, Amelia nodded and took another deep breath. "Miss Kirkpatrick…Miss Kirkpatrick told me that my brother had told her to leave when…when I was about to leave, too."

Oscar frowned. *Leave. Leave and do what? Leave and go where?*

His brother echoed his thoughts. "Leave? To go where?"

Amelia seemed to steel herself to say something terrible. Then she said it. "To elope."

Oscar stood up so quickly, his chair fell to the floor.

"Elope?" repeated Fernsby in confusion.

"Where is he?" said Oscar, his voice full of fury. This was his fault; he had become so infatuated with Helena he had failed to notice his own sister's ruin. "Where is the blaggard?"

"Nothing has happened!" Amelia said quickly.

"I should think not!" Oscar roared. He could barely hear his sister over the pounding in his ears, his hands clenched to fists, his feet ready to take him wherever this cad was hiding. "But I'll still be calling him out!"

Was this Helena's influence? Had she introduced his sister to some charlatan, perhaps, encouraged the foolish ideas his sister had clearly believed?

Oscar's blood was boiling, fury fueling him. *Helena.* She had brought nothing but disaster onto this family. Would they never be rid of her?

"Sit down, you fool," said Amelia sternly. "I said I intended to elope, I never actually… I'm here, aren't I?"

Oscar unclenched his hands as McLoughlin righted his chair. "Yes. Yes, you are."

His breathing was starting to return to normal, but he wasn't done with her yet. Amelia had to be made to understand just how nonsensical this was.

He sat slowly. "So, you decided to stay, to abandon him. Good."

"No," said Amelia simply. "I love him."

The words silenced the room. Oscar stared. *Love him. His sister, love someone?*

"That will be all, McLoughlin," he croaked.

The servant closed the door quietly, and the three Fernsby siblings were left alone.

"I have known him for years," Amelia said softly. "Years and years. It has crept on so gradually, I...I hardly know how it began. It's like Fernsby and Constance. He was always there, just someone in the background of my life, and then... everything else was background."

Oscar swallowed. It was almost beautiful. If he was going to allow such nonsense.

"You really care about him," said Fernsby quietly.

Oscar watched his sister become animated as she spoke of her affection for this man, this fool who hadn't even the courtesy to ask him for his sister's hand. *Love. A strange thing.*

"I love him with all my heart," Amelia was saying to Fernsby, her eyes bright. "Whenever I am with him—"

Oscar could not help but interrupt. "Yet he has said nothing to us. An honorable gentleman would—"

"I told Miss Kirkpatrick you would be like this," Amelia said coldly. "She is the reason I didn't elope last night. Miss Kirkpatrick talked me out of it. She thought you would be understanding. I told her she was wrong."

"But who is it?" asked Fernsby eagerly. "Someone we know?"

Oscar could not concentrate on the discussion of the identity of Amelia's lover.

Helena. Helena had persuaded his sister not to elope. Helena had prevented a true scandal from hitting the Fernsby family, the Kilerth name. Now, why on earth would she do that?

"Helena?" Oscar said, momentarily forgetting himself as he interrupted Fernsby's questions. "Miss Kirkpatrick, I mean. She said that?"

Amelia's glare had lost none of its coldness. "She said that my brothers love me. That they care about me, would want what's best for me, and would want to host my wedding."

They care about me and want what's best for me. They would want to host my wedding.

Oscar leaned back in his chair, hardly able to understand what had just happened.

Helena. An actress. Someone who pretended for a living. But when he thought about it, what had she done since she had arrived at the Old Abbey?

Encouraged his brother to allow his children to play outside. Supported his brother when he ventured outside. Made the children laugh. Helped the servants. Created a reason for the children to get up every morning. Enabled Amelia to have some time to herself. Encouraged his brother to host a ball, to get back to some semblance of society.

Listened to Oscar, moan about his family. Comforted him. Kissed him. Bared as much of her soul as she could to him.

Prevented his sister from making a mockery of herself and bringing scandal onto the family.

And what had he done?

"I can't believe I ever trusted you. I want you to leave."

Oscar closed his eyes. If he ignored her past, as surely a gentleman would, all he saw was goodness. He was the one that should leave. Helena had been nothing but good to him, sweet goodness, and he had forced her to leave in disgrace.

He had lost her.

"So, who is it?" Fernsby persisted.

Oscar opened his eyes.

Amelia's cheeks were pink. "Mr. Brian Hough."

Oscar caught his brother's eye, and they both, uncharacteristically, remained silent for a moment. They knew Amelia. Once she had decided on something, there was very little they would be able to do to stop her.

Oscar took a deep breath. "Your dowry would make him a gentleman."

Amelia smiled. "In your eyes, perhaps. In the eyes of the world. He is already a gentleman in my heart."

"So you are asking permission?" said Fernsby slowly. "Permission to marry him?"

"Yes, I suppose I am," said Amelia brightly. "But fair warning, I will marry him either way."

Oscar smiled wryly. There was the Amelia he knew. "I guessed that. Well, if we are fortunate…perhaps there'll be two weddings in this family before too long."

CHAPTER TWENTY-THREE

September 10, 1813

HELENA TOOK A deep breath. If she concentrated on the flow of her breathing, then she wouldn't be able to hear the catty remarks behind her.

"I thought they got rid of her?"

"Shush, she'll hear you!"

"Oh, what does it matter if she does? She won't be here for long, will she?"

Helena did not look round. She didn't need to. She knew those voices from anywhere. Two of the actresses she had known for the longest period during her time at the Theatre Royal.

That was her first time at the theater.

"—don't understand what Mr. Tobias was thinking when—"

"I said shush!"

Besides, Helena did not want to turn around. What was there to be gained from meeting the eyes of someone speaking to you like that? Nothing. She let out her breath slowly.

There was no point getting entangled in an argument. Not when she was mere moments away from stepping onto the Theatre Royal's stage, after months away.

It had been a long week since she had convinced Mr. Tobias to take her back on.

"I don't like it," the stage manager had spat. "Where have you been? No one's been able to find hide nor hair of you since you left."

Helena had worked hard to keep her face impassive. She had known they would need her. They shouldn't have been so quick to get rid of her, should they?

"Little girly didn't work out?" she had said sweetly.

Mr. Tobias had uttered a rude word—or at least, Helena had assumed it was rude. It was one she hadn't heard before, and it was accompanied by a great deal of gesturing.

"Fine. Fine!" he said eventually. "Same pay. Same expectations. Same—"

"Everything," Helena had interrupted, striding past him. "Nothing ever changes here."

And nothing had. It was bizarre, now Helena came to think, the rushing of stagehands pouring past her as she tried to concentrate on thinking Juliet, of being Juliet.

Nothing had changed. It were as though she had stepped just outside the theater for five minutes. The heat had gone. A few stagehands were new. Other than that, it was the same Theatre Royal. The theater that needed her, it turned out, just as much as she had needed it.

Helena was back where she belonged: with the rag tags of the world, those who saw real meaning in what they created every day on that stage. Her stage.

With quivering hands, Helena smoothed down the folds of her gown—her favorite costume, the gown for Juliet—and took another deep breath. She was almost ready. Before long, she would be out there on the stage, and the audience would gasp, applaud...

Helena swallowed. *Then what?* Another evening of performing for the masses of London, another night spent trying to sleep on an uncomfortable bed, then the whole thing would begin again tomorrow.

You are Juliet, she reminded herself. *You don't worry about such things. You have a palatial mansion. The most important thing you need to worry about is Juliet. Not whether...*

She almost managed to stop herself, but not quite. Not whether the children were rehearsing this as well. Not whether the lines she would be saying tonight had also been muttered by voices younger than hers on a stage constructed by stable hands in a ballroom.

Helena's jaw tightened. She mustn't think about it. She mustn't be distracted.

She mustn't think about the Fernsbys.

"Isn't there another role I can play tonight?" Helena had asked the stage manager desperately hours ago. "Anyone—I'll do Nurse, you said once I was old enough to play Nurse!"

Mr. Tobias had stared. "You, volunteering to play an old maid? What got into you when you were away?"

Helena had not been able to answer. How could she explain the journey she had been on? The people she had met? *One gentleman in particular...*

"Fine," she had said with bad grace. "I'll be Juliet. Much good may it do you."

She was wearing the soft red silk gown now, the ridiculous Italian bonnet in her hair. Mr. Tobias was not the only one curious about where she had been. Everyone had asked Helena, either directly or subtlety, but she had given them the same answer.

"I was away," Helena said each time, "and now I'm back."

Where to start? Even if she had wanted them to tell, her story was so tied up with the Governess Bureau, Helena didn't see how she would ever be able to share that information.

Not after the lecture she had received from Miss Clarke. It had been...an encounter.

"*—blatantly flaunted yourself—*"

"*That's not what happened, I—*"

"Returned to me in disgrace!"

"I have received no complaints from the baron!"

Helena had stood resolute opposite Miss Clarke in the Governess Bureau, the desk separating them—and a good thing, too, Helena had thought privately. Miss Clarke looked fit to burst, ready to throw herself across the desk and physically shake her.

"You," Miss Clarke had said threateningly, narrowing her eyes and pointing a quivering finger, "you have almost ruined the reputation of the Governess Bureau!"

"I didn't say anything to the baron!" Helena had protested. "He doesn't know a thing about me or where I came from!"

Miss Clarke had waved aside her words. "I don't care about the baron. It's the duke!"

Helena's blood had run cold. How did Miss Clarke know? Had Oscar written to her? The best way to complain about having an actress in his brother's house would have been to write directly to the proprietress of the Governess Bureau.

Miss Clarke's brow had furrowed. "I should have known when I didn't receive your report something was wrong. I should have visited you myself!"

Helena had said nothing, though she had felt rather prickled. She had done all she could to keep her background a secret! Well. Until she told Oscar.

"Well, it doesn't matter," she had said coldly to Miss Clarke. "I'm leaving."

The owner of the Bureau had gone pale at that remark. "To get married?"

Her response had been so quick, so nonsensical, Helena had laughed. "Married! Goodness, no. If only he...I mean, I'll find my own way in life. I shouldn't have tried to use the Governess Bureau to get me out of a scrape. I should have done that myself."

There had been a rather strange expression on Miss Clarke's face, something akin to irritation, but also respect. "Well, at least you have the decency to apologize."

It was rather galling, but Helena had not replied. Nothing could be improved.

"Just do not mention this to anyone—you were never here, you were

never a part of the Bureau."

Helena had been forced to swallow her pride. It was hardly her fault she had been sent back by the Fernsbys—by Oscar. It meant nothing to the Bureau, surely. It was all Oscar's fault. All her fault.

How had she been so stupid to assume they had a truly mutual understanding that first week at the Old Abbey? She had been so sure Oscar had recognized her, that their agreement was to protect them both.

How wrong she was. All it did was protect him, whereas she...she had been forced to return to London in disgrace with nothing for all her efforts but a broken heart.

Miss Clarke had sighed heavily into the silence. "I'm sorry, I simply cannot waste any more time on you, Miss Kirk—Miss Patrick. I have a bigger problem to deal with—a governess who has lost her memory."

It was impossible not to be intrigued by that statement. "Truly?"

"Not that it is any of your concern," Miss Clarke had said sharply. "You are no longer a part of the Bureau. Good day, Miss Patrick."

Helena had not been able to get that governess out of her mind since that conversation. *Losing one's memory.* It was a frightening idea. True, her memories with Oscar were painful. They bled into her dreams, awakening her in tears at the thought of never seeing him again…

But better to have those memories, surely? Better to know what one has lost. Better to learn from one's mistakes.

"Watch it, woman, you can't just stand there!"

Helena took a step forward to regain her balance, bringing her back into the present. A stagehand she did not recognize had pushed past her carrying a large box of props and had not seen fit to take a step to the left to avoid her.

"Two minutes to curtain up!"

The whisper was passed along the stagehands like a gentle breeze through willow.

Helena took a deep breath and tried to calm the fluttering in her chest. This is what she had wanted: to remain at the Theatre Royal. The idea of leaving had felt like death when she had been forcibly ejected from it.

Now she was back. She should feel triumphant. She should be

thanking her stars that she had been accepted back into the fold. *Yet…*

Helena's stomach turned as quiet fell backstage. She needed a plan. She couldn't just swan back into her old life and be here forever. If this year had taught her anything, it was that everyone was expendable. Even a governess that a duke had taken to his bed.

Two minutes. One minute. Just a few more seconds until she stepped away from being Helena and became Juliet.

Helena's stomach lurched. A woman in love. It was almost pitiable, really, that this was the role she was being forced to play on her first night back on the stage.

Love. It had felt so wonderful for a while but had flown by so quickly. Before she had known she loved Oscar, he was forcing her to leave him.

No, Helena told herself. *You mustn't think of him.* That would only bring her pain. Tears she had shed, and she would undoubtedly shed more. But not tonight. Tonight she was Juliet, and she was about to declaim like the actress she was. She needed to concentrate.

The light around her was dimming. Stagehands were putting out all candles, leaving only the stage lights to guide her feet as she stepped forward, right onto the edge of the wings.

This was it. Helena closed her eyes, composed herself, and Juliet opened them.

Juliet did not appear on stage until the third scene, so Helena tucked herself into the wing. Her heart was pounding, not a mere flutter but a full thump.

This was it. What she'd missed, though the nausea in her stomach was different.

Listening carefully, Helena could just about make out the sounds of the stage. She was ready. Just a few moments more, and she would be out there with them.

Helena's heart skipped a beat, the irregular rhythm causing her to catch her breath. She wouldn't be overwhelmed. The joy she knew so well was stirring within her, but it was coupled with sadness.

This was not where she wanted to be.

It was where she belonged, that was true. It was her life.

But she wanted to be at the Old Abbey. With Oscar. With the man who made her feel more alive, more free than anything ever had.

Oscar. His face swam into her mind, and Helena forced it aside. She could not think of him now. She could not think of anything except Romeo. She was his Juliet.

"God forbid! Where's this girl? What, Juliet?"

All fear melted away as she took a step forward, striding into herself, into Juliet.

"How now, who calls," she said smoothly to the glaring actor opposite her.

This was it; this was living. This was the exhilaration she knew and craved; this was where she belonged. Not with him.

Only then did Helena make the mistake of looking out into the audience. One face stuck out to her, claiming her attention, demanding she saw it.

Oscar.

It couldn't be. She was seeing things; it was only because she had been thinking about him moments before stepping out onto the stage.

Helena blinked and stumbled over her next line. "And stint thou, too, I pray thee, Nurse, say I."

"Peace," said Nurse, showing only a fraction of frustration in her eyes. "I have done. God mark thee to his grace! Thou was the prettiest babe…"

She glared as they turned from the audience to step across the stage.

Helena barely noticed. *How could she, when she was seeing things?* Oscar could not be here. Her mind was playing tricks on her.

As the scene continued, she glanced into the audience again.

There he was. *Oscar.* It was him. She had not imagined him.

Every inch of her body was crackling with nerves, with the certain knowledge that everything was about to fall apart.

What was he doing here? Oscar, here, at the Theatre Royal? Was it a mere coincidence? Why had he left his brother? Left the Old Abbey?

Helena swallowed, trying to follow the scene, to deliver her lines. But Oscar's physical presence in the theater was distracting.

What was this—a chance to gloat? To prove to her that he was the audience and paying customer, whereas she had to entertain him for her living?

"It is an honor that I dream not of," Helena managed.

It was fortunate indeed there was little complexity in this scene. She chanced a glance over at him again. Yes, he was still there—and he had not taken his eyes off her. He was staring as though he could not believe his eyes. As though she had betrayed him all over again.

And the wash of emotions Helena had tried so hard to keep at bay overwhelmed her. The pain of losing him, of being considered worthless, so beneath him she couldn't even be permitted to stay in his company…

To lose the gentleman she never thought she would have. To lose the man she loved.

Helena's mind clouded, her senses losing connection to what was around her. Words became muffled, the stage before her blurred.

Because she was crying. *She was crying.*

Without saying a word, Helena rushed off the stage. Shocked murmurs echoed around the audience, but that did not slow her. Nothing could prevent her from escaping Oscar.

"Helena—Juliet!" Mr. Tobias shouted, his voice furious. "This is your last warning, girl. You'll be off if you don't—come back here!"

Helena didn't stop. She couldn't. Her legs were doing the thinking, and they wanted to be as far away from Oscar, from everyone, as possible. Barely knowing where she was going, she knew one thing. She had to get out.

Falling into the door, Helena wrenched it open and took in deep lungfuls of fresh air—or what passed for fresh air in London. She had made it to the alleyway.

She was free. Leaning against the wall, Helena slumped, her eyes closed.

"You never told me you were that good."

Helena's eyes snapped open. Oscar was standing before her. Impossible; no one could have run after her that quickly, and he had been part of the audience. How had he—

"What are you—how did you get here?" she asked.

Why couldn't he just leave her alone? Did he have to punish her just for who she was?

Oscar was watching her carefully. "I told one of your people I was a doctor, and he pointed me to where he thought you'd gone."

Helena was still trying to get her breath back, so she did not dignify that with a response.

Blast, he was so clever. Oscar Fernsby, Duke of Kilerth. After stomping on her heart so thoroughly just over a week ago, why did he have to punish her further?

She swallowed. *She would be mistress of herself. Juliet wouldn't permit herself to be pushed around like this.* "Well, *Dr.* Fernsby, you can see I am quite all right. Please go away."

She should be congratulated, Helena thought, *for such restraint.* There were a great number of curse words she wished to say, but she had managed to hold them back for now.

Oscar took a step closer to her. "I can't do that."

This made no sense—he was the one who demanded that she leave! Her mind could not settle, could not understand why he was here. In her theater.

"Fine," Helena said testily. "I'll go."

She managed two steps before Oscar stopped her. "I can't let you do that either."

A flicker of irritation soared through her. "Oscar, this doesn't make—you were the one who sent me away!"

"I know," he said quietly.

"You were the one who thought I wasn't good enough for your family," said Helena, warming to her theme. *It felt good to say this. It felt good to shout.*

"I know."

"You were the one who felt betrayed and lied to," Helena said, her voice strong because she would not let it break. "But you were not the only one betrayed that day."

"I know," said Oscar. "And I was wrong."

"And you…" Helena hesitated. She had not expected that.

Now she looked properly, she could see Oscar looked…miserable. There were tired lines around his eyes; his shoulders were slumped. All the strength and vigor of the man had gone.

He was a changed man. *What on earth had happened?*

"I don't understand," Helena said helplessly, looking deep into his eyes. "What do you want from me, Oscar?"

Oscar said nothing. He just looked at her. He didn't need to speak.

Helena laughed bitterly. "Why are you…I can't keep up with you, Oscar! You made yourself perfectly clear. You don't want anything to do with me and my kind!"

She spat out the last two words into the silent alleyway. Oscar just stood there, taking her fury, taking her bitterness. Why? Why was he here? Why was a duke accepting the fury of an actress?

Oscar took a step toward her. "I shouldn't have shouted at you."

How could she shout at him now, even when she wanted to? Even when it hurt so much that he had not trusted her?

"I thought you knew," she whispered. Her heart was still skipping beats, all because of him. *He had such a hold on her, couldn't he see that?* "About me. About who I am. What I did—do. I thought you knew."

"I didn't," said Oscar quietly, "but that's still no reason to assume the worst of you."

"You wouldn't be the only one!"

"But I should have been different." Oscar was looking at her closely, as though attempting to memorize her face. As though this would be the last time they would see each other.

Perhaps that was it, Helena thought dully. He felt guilty about the argument, and now he'd come to apologize. Soon he'd be on his merry way and—

"I should have known better. I know you as no one else does."

Helena swallowed. Oscar spoke in the voice of a lover.

It was nonsense. It was her own foolish desire confusing things. So no matter how much she wished to step forward, throw herself into his arms, kiss him, and demand that he never leave her again—she couldn't.

She wouldn't. Not after the way he had spoken to her.

"You are not welcome here. Pack. Go back to the Bureau."

"I was wrong—"

"You were," said Helena coldly. "More wrong than you can know."

Oscar laughed dryly, his gaze dropping. "I suppose I deserve that."

"No." As Helena spoke, Oscar looked up, clearly confident he had won her over. "No, you deserve more. Oscar, I opened myself up to you, made myself vulnerable, gave you everything, then as soon as you discovered *one thing* you didn't like about me, you didn't just push me away, you *sent* me away."

There was pain in his eyes now.

Good, Helena could not help thinking. *Perhaps if you knew a little what it felt like to be small, and insignificant, and unable to protect yourself, you wouldn't be so quick to—*

"I deserve every word of that."

Helena blinked. *Had those words really come out of Oscar's mouth?*

What was happening? She had been so sure he would dissemble, pretend he had not spoken out of turn, pretend she was the one she should be apologizing to him.

There was no wavering in Oscar's gaze.

"What are you doing here?"

"You are the one with prodigious skill. Why do you think?"

"I don't know," she said helplessly. "You'll have to tell me, Oscar. After sharing so much with you, after baring my soul, you discarded me. What do you want?"

"Damnit, Helena, I want you!" Oscar said, his voice thick with emotion. "I want you to be my wife."

Helena stared. Here they were, a duke and an actress, or governess, or whatever she was, standing in a moldy old alleyway and the outrage of a theater muttering in the distance.

"I want you to be my wife."

He could not be serious. Oscar was teasing, lying, trying to trick her into something.

"You don't mean that," Helena whispered.

Oscar took another step closer. He was too close now, too close for her to think.

"I know I don't deserve you," he said, a crack in his voice, "and I know there must be no more secrets—but I made such a mistake. I'll never forgive myself for—I am sorry, Helena. Don't get me started on how badly my brother and sister think I've treated you or how much the children miss you."

This wasn't real. Perhaps she was dreaming. *Dukes did not propose to governesses.* They certainly didn't propose to actresses!

But the words Miss Clarke had said were ringing in her mind.

"Well, it doesn't matter. I'm leaving."

"To get married?"

"I don't want you to propose just because your brother thinks badly of you."

Oscar laughed, Helena's stomach contracted painfully at the sight of his smile. "It was my sister actually—by the way, I have a wedding invitation for you. Her and what's his name. Hough."

He offered a piece of paper. Helena took it automatically and looked down. Lady Amelia's name was engraved on it, along with a Mr. Brian Hough.

She could not help but smile. "You gave her your permission. What persuaded you?"

"You."

Helena looked into the eyes of the man she loved, her fingers trembling.

"Oh, you didn't say anything to me about her," said Oscar quietly. "But you made me realize love isn't bound by class or profession. Love is... God's teeth, this would be easier to talk about if I didn't feel...feel so... She loves him. He loves her. Why shouldn't they marry?"

Helena swallowed. She wasn't entirely sure who Oscar was talking about anymore.

Before she was able to say a word, the Duke of Kilerth was getting down on one knee.

"Oscar, no—"

"I know this is madness," said Oscar quietly. "But I don't care. Too swift, too wild. I don't care. I want you more than I want the approbation of the world. Marry me."

Helena stared. Her heart had stopped beating. "You're not serious."

"You can do whatever you want when we're married," Oscar said, his eyes looking up beseechingly. "Keep acting, don't act, whatever you want. As long as you're my wife. I'll do whatever I can to make you happy, though I cannot profess to be skilled at it."

Helena tried to say no. She tried to say how wrong this was, how different they were. How he was a duke, and she an actress masquerading as a governess. How they were bound together by affection, but affection alone simply could not keep them happy.

Helena opened her mouth. Then she closed it.

"Please, Helena," whispered Oscar, his eyes not leaving hers. "Please believe me. Please accept me. I'm begging you."

It was either entirely true or the stage had missed a master.

All her fears disappeared as the one syllable she knew they both needed to hear slipped through her lips. "Yes."

Helena was crushed in Oscar's arms instantly. All the relief, the passion, the fear they had lost from each other was unleashed on both sides, their mouths trying to show what their words could not.

Then the kiss ended, though Helena remained in Oscar's arms. He smiled. "End of act one?"

Helena laughed, happy tears falling from her eyes. "The beginning of act two."

CHAPTER TWENTY-FOUR

October 20, 1813

THE ROLLING HILLS had changed. Oscar had not noticed immediately, for the other passenger in the carriage had more than taken his attention for the last few hours.

But now he glanced out of the window, he could see it. *Kilerth.* They had crossed the border without noticing, but now he saw his mountains and lakes, and knew precisely where they were.

"Home," he whispered.

"Home?" Helena moved across to the window eagerly. "We're already there?"

"Almost," said Oscar with a laugh. "Goodness, I had not realized you were so desperate to arrive."

Light blazed in her eyes. "If you didn't go on about it so much, I wouldn't be excited! Is it really as beautiful as you said?"

Oscar moved back from the window with only a hint of reluctance. "See for yourself."

Helena leaned forward, eyes wide open and a smile dancing on her lips.

His wife. Oscar could hardly decide what was more beautiful, the scenery outside or the woman by his side.

Both were dazzling. Helena had never ceased surprising him the moment they had eloped, the very week he had proposed. No family. No friends. No one to distract them from each other. It had been the perfect wedding.

Now here they were, journeying to his dukedom, which he hoped she would love just as much as he did.

Helena made little sounds of wonder, and Oscar almost laughed.

Home. It had been months.

"You're like a puppy."

Oscar blinked. Helena had turned away from the window and was now laughing.

"What do you mean, a puppy?" he asked.

"Like a puppy," repeated his teasing wife. "Looking for its owner. Did you really miss this place?"

Oscar's smile was paired by the flickering joyful rhythm of his heart. "Well, I wouldn't describe myself as a puppy, but I have been away from Riverside Manor for a long time."

Helena seemed to know what he wanted, even without him saying it. Moving into his arms, she kissed his cheek. "You know, I can't remember ever having a home like that."

She spoke so nonchalantly as the carriage rattled along the road, as though what she said was insignificant. Oscar tightened his grip around her, his hands on her waist.

No home? No true home, a place where one could return whenever needed? A place of solace, of peace, of joy, where one was always safe? The place where one's father and grandfather had also returned for the same reasons?

It made little sense to Oscar. There were many things, it appeared, that he was accustomed to that were mightily unusual to the world at large.

He was learning. He had a good governess to teach him.

"'Tis strange to think we are so different," Oscar said honestly. "Strange to think of not having a home like mine. There is still much you have to teach me."

Helena snorted. "Perhaps, but don't you expect me to act the role of governess too often! That was a very short part of my career, and I have no wish to return to it!"

Oscar chuckled but was distracted from replying as they turned a corner to reveal—

"Is that a castle?" Helena said. "Goodness, imagine who lives there!"

Oscar cleared his throat. "Actually…we do."

It took her a moment to take in his words. "No we don't."

He couldn't have planned it better if he had tried. "I promise you. That's Riverside Manor."

"But…but you called it a manor!" Helena spluttered, eyes darting between her husband and the castle they were rapidly approaching. "You never said—it wasn't a—a castle!"

Oscar shrugged. "I didn't say it *wasn't* a castle."

The carriage rattled around a corner and tipped them together. Oscar put out his hands against the carriage wall to prevent him from crushing Helena. Her eyes were blazing.

Their lips met in a sweet and possessive kiss. He pulled her into him, clutching her desperately. It had been…what, eight hours or so since they had made love?

Too long.

By the time Oscar released his wife, the carriage was approaching their home.

"I've missed the view," Helena said wistfully, trying to put her hair back into her pins.

"You'll have plenty of occasions to leave and come back," said Oscar quietly. "Look."

They were entering through the gatehouse, rolling past the castle walls.

"I think," murmured Helena, "you could fit my entire street into this courtyard."

"We probably have a few times," Oscar said cheerfully. "Times of war, and all that. Riverside Manor has been here a long time."

Helena was not impressed by his title or wealth—she loved him for who he was, which made him unsure whether he was worthy of her.

It was nice to be kept on his toes.

"Do you think it will get easier?" he murmured. "The two of us coming from such different backgrounds, different worlds?"

Helena did not hesitate. "Of course it will. And if it doesn't, I can act like it does."

Kissing her head, Oscar wondered why he had hesitated in going to the Theatre Royal. To think, if he had given into his fears, his doubts, he would not be seated here with his wife.

Of course, Miss Clarke had been rather reluctant to give him any details about Helena. She had not been...happy to see him, though he was sure she would never say it in those words.

His sudden arrival—the sudden arrival of a duke, no less—had been rather unexpected for the proprietress of the Governess Bureau.

"I am here," Oscar had announced boldly in the waiting room of the Bureau, "to find the governess of my brother so that I may marry her."

He had been quickly ushered into Miss Clarke's office at those words, a dark look in her eyes.

"I have traveled here, without sleep, to find Miss Kirkpatrick," he had said as Miss Clarke babbled about gossip and scandal and other such nonsense. "And I am not going away without a fight."

Ah yes, all that talk of scandal...

"Miss Clarke," he had said in a quieter voice. "I would hate for the news to get out that you permitted an actress to masquerade as a governess."

The woman had opened her mouth and closed it again with nothing coming out.

Oscar had pressed home his advantage. "I have no wish for scandal, Miss Clarke. Both of us can get what we want here. If I find Miss Kirkpatrick, I go away. No talk of actresses or marriage would ever occur. No one would ever know."

He had watched Miss Clarke look nervously at the door, at the waiting room where governesses sat with bated breath to hear what was going to happen next.

Scandal was quite the ruination for something like the Governess Bureau.

Miss Clarke had swallowed. "Just how quickly will you leave if I tell you?"

"I am already gone," Oscar had said.

"The Theatre Royal."

He had not paused for thanks. He had already reached the door and was about to wrench it open when seven words made him hesitate.

"And it's Miss Patrick. Her real name."

"What I don't understand," said Helena, bringing Oscar back to the present as the carriage jostled them up the drive, "is how you found me. You came straight to the theater when you arrived in London—what are the chances! Can you believe it?"

"Absolutely not," said Oscar cheerfully. "But it's not the finding you that surprises me, but the courage to attend. I almost...well. I suppose I could have gone the next night."

His wife had that discerning eye Oscar was discovering was far wiser than he had ever imagined. "You were afraid."

It was not a question, so he saw no reason to confirm nor deny it.

A smile broke across Helena's face. "You were too in love with me!"

Oscar laughed. "That's probably true. Here we are."

The carriage slowly came to a halt. Oscar sighed. The knot of tension lodged in his stomach since the moment he had left Riverside Manor all those months ago had finally loosened.

He was home.

There had been a hole in his heart, and Helena completed him. Oscar had never paid much attention to that sort of mushy romantic nonsense. When Fernsby had attempted to tell him, in the early years of his and Constance's marriage, Oscar had waved him away. *Now...*

"What's wrong?" he asked softly.

There was a strange look on Helena's face. If he didn't know her any better, he would say that she was...nervous?

She smiled briefly. "We were married so quickly...no family, no fanfare...I suppose your servants will think I am a temptress."

"You are!" His laughter, however, did not assuage her nerves.

Worse, Helena frowned. "That is not particularly helpful."

Oscar stopped laughing and instead took her hand. It was trembling. "I am sorry. I should not jest."

"No, you should not," said Helena.

It was one of the things Oscar was still learning about her. Though she could act bold, brash, confident, there was a gentleness she often hid. Not from him, not anymore. He had to remind himself that the bold speaking Helena he knew was just one facet of her. There was still much more to discover, more to love.

"As soon as they start to see the prodigious skills you bring," he said softly, "they'll understand why I had to marry you immediately."

"I still think the special license was unnecessary."

"And Amelia will never forgive me for it," said Oscar ruefully. "But I wasn't going to wait. I had to make you my wife. Had to make sure you couldn't change your mind."

His wife's cheeks flushed, and Oscar's heart lurched. *Would that ever stop happening?* He had not known he needed her until forced to confront the terrible fate of not having her.

The door to the carriage opened, and Helena sprang back. Oscar ensured he did not smile. It would take him a little while, too, to become accustomed to the fact that they did not need to hide their affection for each other.

"Thank you," said Oscar carelessly to his driver as he stepped out of the carriage. He turned to offer his hand to Helena. "Your Grace?"

She grinned wryly as she stepped onto the cobblestones, which made Oscar want to laugh. He'd teased her mercilessly about her new title, something she was not accustomed to.

Helena looked up at the castle in silence. Oscar's heart rate quickened. It was important, perhaps too important to him, that she liked his home. He wanted to impress her. *Had he ever felt like this before? Had he ever brought anyone like her to his home?*

"It's…it's majestic," she breathed.

"Truly? You like it?"

"How could anyone not love it?" Helena said, her eyes raking over the battlements, the spiraling tower at the west end, the gargoyles that lined the roof. "And it's all yours?"

He nodded.

Helena descended into peals of laughter. "This is…this is wild indeed! I knew you were a duke, Oscar, but you live in a castle!"

Her laughter made Oscar's whole body tingle. *He could not wait much longer…*

"Well, one doesn't like to brag about it," he said with a grin.

"You know, I once fell through a castle."

There was a teasing look on her face that Oscar should have paid attention to as they walked toward the front door. It opened, servants pouring out to form a line to greet their master and new mistress.

"Dear lord, what on earth do you mean?"

Now it was Helena's turn to laugh. "Scenery, you dolt!"

Oscar chuckled and saw his butler's eyebrows raise.

Helena noticed it, too. She saw the intrigued looks from all the household servants waiting to greet her. There were more than a few suspicious faces there.

Her smile faltered.

Oscar took her arm in his. "My love, welcome home to Riverside Manor. My household welcomes you."

It was perhaps a little formal, but it did the trick. All his servants bowed or curtseyed, and a few of the murmurs from the back were silenced.

"This," Oscar said impressively as they reached the front of the lines, "is Mrs. Morley. My housekeeper and general tyrant."

"Now, Your Grace, don't say such things," said Mrs. Morley, her face flushed.

So, it was not only Helena who was nervous.

"Mrs. Morley," said Helena, inclining her head graciously. "I hope you will be of assistance to me as I find my way around Riverside Manor. I am sure I can rely on you."

There was something rather splendid about her, Oscar thought to himself as Helena made her way down the line, speaking to everyone, no matter their rank. She had been given the part of a duchess, and had modulated her voice, tone, and approach to suit the role.

She was the Duchess of Kilerth.

But to anyone who had known her in her past life, they would not recognize the woman standing before them in a delicately embroidered gown and soft fur pelisse, her bonnet edged not with ribbon but with gold thread.

Oscar swallowed. He was so proud of her. This could not have been easy, this first meeting, and she was approaching it with aplomb.

"Let me show you the great hall," he said as they reached the end of the line of servants. "Leave us be, thank you all."

The newly wedded couple strode into the hall as the servants melted away.

Helena's mouth was open again. "And I thought your brother's house was impressive…but this…"

"Yes," said Oscar wryly. "Fernsby has never forgiven me, really."

"I hope we will have him here one day."

A cloud moved across Oscar's face. *His brother, back here again?* It was a wonderful thought. A hopeless dream for now. "I can make no promises on that score. I simply don't know when he will be well enough to travel this far."

His brother. He would probably never cease worrying about that man, and though Oscar had married and had returned to their family seat, he could not leave his concerns behind.

A squeeze of his arm. Oscar saw Helena smiling softly.

"He's my family now, too, so we can worry about him together. You don't have to carry the burden alone anymore.

Besides, one of these days, I must fulfill my promise to the children and let them finish the play."

A rush of love seeped through every inch of his body. *How had he ever managed without her? What would he do, God forbid, if he were ever to lose her?*

"It feels strange," said Helena, stepping around the hall, looking up at the vaulted ceiling with the shield bosses of all the families the Fernsbys had ever married. "Being this far from the Theatre Royal. For a large part of my life, it was my home."

Oscar nodded. He was born here, where every Fernsby had been born for generations. He had known this was his home for…well, forever. He could not remember a time when he did not know it.

"Right," said Helena decidedly, turning back to him. "I want the tour—and mind, I will be marking you against the little Fernsbys' tour of the Old Abbey, so it had better be good!"

"The morning room," he said as they walked through it and into, "the drawing room—well, the Blue Drawing Room. The Oriental Drawing Room is the other side of the house, for winter. Then you have the sitting room, the parlor, the library—through there is the billiards room, and the smoking room adjoins it. My study there, your study down there—"

"You will have to give me a map!"

Oscar chuckled. "You will soon get used to it."

As they progressed through the house, his excitement rose—but he couldn't show it. He mustn't let her see how his anticipation was growing for one part of the house in particular.

The instructions he had sent to Mrs. Morley had been very specific, but he had not yet had the chance to see whether they had been followed.

Surely they had been. They would not dare risk his ire.

"What is it?"

Oscar came to a stop in the northwest corridor. "What?"

Helena had her hands on her hips. "Out with it."

"Out with what?"

"Don't even try to pretend, Oscar Fernsby. I know when you

have a secret!" Helena said in a mock-serious tone.

Oscar's heart skipped a beat. *It was an occupational hazard when married to this woman.* "How on earth do you know that?"

There was a teasing glint in her eyes. "I always know—out with it, we said no secrets!"

He hesitated. He had actually intended to check on the progress of the work before he revealed it to Helena, but she was right. *No secrets.* That had not been part of their wedding vows, but it may as well have been.

"It…well, it may not be finished," Oscar said as they changed direction.

"Why, do you have building works? I didn't hear anything."

Oscar took a deep breath and stopped by double doors. "This was the ballroom."

"Was?"

He opened the doors. Beyond was…

A theater. A stage, high and wide, with special areas created for the stage candles. Seats; rows upon rows of seats. Plush red velvet. Ready for a performance.

Helena gasped and grabbed Oscar's arm. "You…you have a theatre in your house?"

"No," said Oscar, delighting in the mingled expression of shock and joy on her face. "I made one."

Helena took a hesitant step forward, evidently still astonished, then another. "It's…it's a theater. In your house."

Pure joy flooded through Oscar's body. When was the last time he had ever done something like this for someone? Had he ever done something like this for someone? He could not recall ever making someone so happy as this—well, other than giving Amelia permission to marry that fencing master of hers.

He barely knew what to do with himself.

"Do you like it?"

"Like it?" Helena repeated in a whisper. Her eyes were raking over the curtains on each side of the stage. "You did this…for me?"

"Of course I did. I love you."

She turned to him, stepping forward and kissing him passionately. Oscar clutched at her as though this was the last kiss they would ever share.

One day it would be. He would never want to look back and think he missed an opportunity to kiss his beautiful wife.

"Wait a moment," Helena said, pulling away and raising an eyebrow. "When you say you did it—"

"Well, I got other people to do it. Same thing, when you're a duke."

She laughed. "I can't believe you gave up your ballroom for me! Where are we going to host our friends and neighbors now?"

There was a slightly incredulous tone to her voice.

Oscar shrugged. "I suppose we'll have to use the other ballroom."

"The other—the other ballroom?"

He nodded. Helena collapsed into peals of laughter.

"You really are too much," she said, pulling away and rushing toward the stage. "Oscar Fernsby, I love you!"

"Of course you do," Oscar said lightly as he joined her on the stage. "I just gave you a theater."

She rolled her eyes as she sat, feeling the stage boards with her fingertips. "You know very well I would love you even without a theater."

"But it helps, right?"

Helena patted the stage beside her, and Oscar sat. "It does."

She kissed him, and Oscar's body tingled. Helena shivered as the pleasure they had forsaken during their carriage journey demanded to be explored.

"We can't," Helena said, breaking the kiss and looking around. "Someone will hear."

Oscar shook his head as he raised his hand to cup her face. "Everyone has strict orders not to be here for the next...oh, six hours?"

"Six hours!"

"Yes," said Oscar, his heart soaring and his loins desperate for relief. "Now, let's christen this stage."

EPILOGUE

December 15, 1814

HELENA LEANED FORWARD so quickly she almost hit her head on the glass. "I think it's them!"

Her husband sighed. He was lounging on a sofa near the fire, the flames crackling and spreading heat through the Blue Drawing Room. Helena smiled. It was heat that had brought them together, of course. The heat of the summer. The heat of the first spark of attraction between them.

"You have said that for the last hour," Oscar said lazily.

"I really do think it's them."

Excitement was flooding through her body. She was certain this time. The other few times—well, they had been accidents. This time, she knew.

"It feels an age since we've seen them," Helena said wistfully, turning back to the window. "The family."

The family. Her family.

She was a duchess, and she had a family. No matter how many times a day she heard that, it was still strange.

The carriage rattled by, heading toward the backdoor. Helena's shoulders slumped. *It was not them.* Now the carriage had come closer, it was obviously not theirs. A butcher, maybe, or a greengrocer, come to deliver their wares.

"I told you, just leave the window and come and sit here," came Oscar's voice. "They'll get here when they get here."

Helena sighed and did not leave her position by the window. "Have you received any post today?"

"Helena—"

"Perhaps they wrote to say they're not coming," she said, unable to prevent her fears seeping into her voice.

It would be so unfortunate if they did not. She had been waiting for days.

"They are coming," said Oscar heavily. "I did receive one bit of post, but not for you."

Her curiosity was piqued. *Oscar, receive a letter?* He hardly corresponded with anyone, and anything to do with the estate went through his land agent.

"Who from?" Helena asked, leaving the window for a moment.

Her husband. *Hers.* It was difficult to believe such a thing was even possible, but here they were.

"Timothy Astor," said Oscar with a sigh. "Friend of the family. Not a friend of mine. Well, maybe that's harsh. A bad friend of mine."

Helena giggled. "Charming as ever. What does that mean?"

Her husband pulled out a letter from the pocket of his waistcoat, his eyes perusing it. "He is the epitome of a fair-weather friend. A good man, when you're with him, but utterly useless."

Helena frowned. "I don't—"

"When you're together, Timothy Astor is the height of chivalry and manners and wit and a good time," explained Oscar. "Then he's gone. He'll be in London for a few months, and then you don't see him for a year. No note, no letter, no warning. Just gone."

Helena bit down the remark that gentlemen were wont to do that. It was only a man who had such leisure at his disposal, who did not have to work for an income to keep a roof over his head or bread on the table, who could truly complain about such behavior.

"So why is he writing to you?" she asked instead.

Oscar folded the letter and placed it in his pocket. "Last I heard from him, he was somewhere in Italy, but apparently, he's back in London and wants to see me before he heads off to his family. I suppose we could make a visit."

Helena had stopped listening to him. *A carriage.* "It's them!"

Oscar stood up this time. "I've told you once, and I've told you a thousand times, it isn't—you know, I think it is."

He had meandered to the window during his statement.

Helena glanced suspiciously. "You aren't jesting?"

Excited tension crept into Helena's shoulders. Rising swiftly, she was forced to halt and catch her breath, wincing and holding onto the windowsill before her.

Oscar was by her side in an instant. "You know very well what doctor said about—"

"I know, I know—"

"If you can't take care of yourself then—"

"Then what?" demanded Helena with a raised eyebrow.

She softened as she saw her husband's face. There were gray hairs by his temples now, lines on his forehead etched by worry. Having a baby on the way did that to a man.

"Then I will have to take care of you," Oscar said softly. "You are so precious to me, Helena. Both of you. Please...don't rush about."

Helena smiled and raised her hand to his cheek. "I will. I mean, I won't."

Oscar had to laugh. "Go on. I know you want to."

But Helena did not immediately rush toward the door to the hall to greet their guests. Instead, she lowered her hand to take Oscar's, then placed it on her growing belly.

A movement. A kick. They both smiled.

"It's our son or daughter," Helena breathed. "Saying hello."

Oscar's stroked her belly. "I would rather the first hello be when they arrive, safe and sound, and that includes you!"

"Yes, yes, you don't think I've heard this all before from Dr. Mallard?" said Helena dismissively.

She reached the hall just as Mrs. Morley approached the front door.

This was it. The moment the family arrived—and what an arrival it would be. It was a shame it would not be the entire family, but there was naught they could do about that. Goodness, were they in for a surprise.

It had been her idea.

"I don't want to worry them," she had said, and both of them had known precisely who they had not wished to worry. "We'll tell them about the baby when they arrive."

The first child they had fallen for...it had gone. Helena clenched her fingers as Mrs. Morley slowly unlocked the door and started to turn the creaking handle. Their firstborn. It didn't matter how small that child had been. He had a name. A soul. He would always stay with them.

And now, a second child. An unexpected blessing.

The door opened. "Welcome to our—Amelia!"

"Helena!"

The two women stared at each other, each with a hand on their swollen bellies, eyes wide and mouths open.

Helena's mind could not think quickly enough. *They were both with child!*

Oscar's laughter was joined by that of Hough. "Well, I suppose we should have expected it."

"But what are the chances that—"

"I want to see Auntie Helena!"

"No, I'll go first, I'm the oldest and—"

"What has that got to do with anything?"

Helena could not help but laugh as the three Fernsby children rocketed into the house, shouts and screams echoing around the place, immediately making the old castle feel like a home again.

"You can all talk to me at once," said Helena fondly, stroking the hair of Rowena, which had grown long, and beaming at Sylvia, who finally had her first proper gown on. "How tall you all are!"

"Especially me," said Altan proudly.

Helena nodded, remembering his thirteenth birthday had only been a few weeks ago. *Thirteen. Goodness.*

"And did you leave your father well?" she said over the chatter of voices to the eldest Fernsby. "I hope he feels better…"

Her voice trailed away. It was impossible to speak as a sixth and unexpected figure stepped out of the darkness and into the hall.

Baron Fernsby.

He looked nervous. "I know you weren't planning on having me, but I hope…well, I thought you would not mind if—"

Helena stepped forward to embrace him, but there was a rushing noise, and she saw to her astonishment that Oscar had gotten there first.

"Fernsby," said her husband, showing his unrestrained affection to his brother. "You're here. I'm so pleased."

Amelia came to stand by Helena's side as she wiped her eyes. "I try to blame the baby for making me more emotional, but nothing does my heart good like seeing those two behave for more than five minutes."

Helena laughed. "That is indeed a great excuse, and I will have to use it myself!"

"—so I thought," the baron—Helena was going to have to get accustomed to calling him just Fernsby—was saying. "I thought I could do it if I came to a home I already knew, and—"

"I am so proud of you," Oscar said, speaking over him in his enthusiasm to praise his brother. "So proud…"

Helena was proud of them both. The baron—*Fernsby*—had overcome much to be here; his fears not entirely at bay, but now being ruled rather than ruling. Her husband, a duke, speaking his feelings at once with no shame nor fear.

"Come on in then, all of you," Helena tried to say, but now Altan was attempting to fence Oscar with some walking sticks he had found, and Amelia and the girls were screaming their delight.

"Have at him—go for the chest!"

"Come on, Helena, we need your prodigious skill to meet this blaggard!"

Helena had to laugh. "No, I am not going to help you beat up my husband, no matter how much he deserves it!"

"Some family we've joined, eh?"

Helena looked round to see Brian Hough, fencing tutor and now brother-in-law, grinning. "Some family," she said softly, her eyes taking in the scene. "Some family indeed."

About Emily E K Murdoch

If you love falling in love, then you've come to the right place.

I am a historian and writer and have a varied career to date: from examining medieval manuscripts to designing museum exhibitions, to working as a researcher for the BBC to working for the National Trust.

My books range from England 1050 to Texas 1848, and I can't wait for you to fall in love with my heroes and heroines!

Follow me on twitter and instagram @emilyekmurdoch, find me on facebook at facebook.com/theemilyekmurdoch, and read my blog at www.emilyekmurdoch.com.